THE HILLS OF HEBRON

THE HILLS OF HEBRON

Sylvia Wynter

Ian Randle Publishers

Kingston • Miami

First published in Jamaica, 2010 by
Ian Randle Publishers
11 Cunningham Avenue
Box 686
Kingston 6
www.ianrandlepublishers.com

Originally published in 1962 by Jonathan Cape

National Library of Jamaica Cataloguing in Publication Data

Wynter , Sylvia
The Hills of Hebron / Sylvia Wynter
p. ; cm.

ISBN 978-976-637-257-6 (pbk)

1. Jamaican fiction
I. Title

813 – dc 22

Cover image *The Baptism* by Barrington Watson
Cover and Book Design by Ian Randle Publishers
Printed and Bound in the United States of America

For my Mother and Jan

Contents

Sylvia Wynter was born in Cuba and grew up in Jamaica where she attended St Andrew's High School. She then studied at Kings College, (University of London) and University of Madrid. In London she wrote for the BBC's Caribbean Voices. In 1962 she returned to Jamaica and joined the faculty of the University of the West Indies. She helped to found *Jamaica Journal* writing major essays on Jamaican culture, history and literature. In 1974 she joined the faculty of the University of California, San Diego and in 1977, Stanford University. She retired from Stanford University in 1994 and continues to live in Northern California. Her collected essays on the Caribbean, 'We Must Learn to Sit Together and Talk about a Little Culture: Decolonizing Essays 1967-1984' will be published in 2010.

Anthony Bogues is Harmon Family Professor of Africana Studies at Brown University and Honorary Research Professor at the Center for African Studies , University of Cape Town . He is also an associate director of the Center for Caribbean Thought . His latest book is *Empire of Liberty : Power, Power, Desire and Freedom* (Dartmouth College Press, 2010) He is the editor of the volume , *After Man, Towards the Human: The Human , Critical Essays on the Thought of Sylvia Wynter* (Ian Randle Publishers, 2006).

Demetrius L. Eudell teaches in the department of history and the programme of African American Studies at Wesleyan University. He is the author of *The Political Languages of Emancipation in the British Caribbean and the US South* (University of North Carolina Press , 2002) and co-edited with Carolyn Allen a special issue of the *Journal of West Indian Literature* entitled 'Sylvia Wynter : A Transculturalist Rethinking Modernity.'

Introduction

By Anthony Bogues

Sylvia Wynter and the Black Radical Anti-Colonial Intellectual Tradition: Towards A New Mode of Existence[1]

> To reinterpret this reality is to commit oneself to a constant revolutionary assault against it. For me then, the play, the novel, the poem, the critical essay, are means to this end – not ends in themselves .
>
> Sylvia Wynter
> 'We Must Learn to Sit Sown Together and Talk About a Little Culture'

> For if the history of Caribbean Society is that of a dual relation between plantation and plot, the two poles which originate in a single historical process , the ambivalence between the two has been and is the distinguishing characteristic of the Caribbean response .
>
> Sylvia Wynter
> 'Novel and History, Plot and Plantation'

> But then even history has been partly trapped in the conflict between the official culture of the Caribbean, and the unofficial and excluded culture. To a large extent, history has dealt with the official categories of thought. History has mainly

> been about the European super- structure of civilization. Yet, in the interstices of history, we see, in glimpses, evidences of a powerful and pervasive cultural process which has largely determined the unconscious springs of our being.
>
> Sylvia Wynter
> 'Jonkonnu in Jamaica: Towards the Interpretation of Folk Dance as a Cultural Process'

Sylvia Wynter belongs to the Black radical anti-colonial intellectual tradition. Today she is, perhaps, the most outstanding living figure of a generation of radical thinkers and intellectuals who confronted the various systemic configurations of power in the twentieth and in the early twenty-first centuries. Wynter's entire intellectual life was profoundly shaped by twentieth century Caribbean and African anti-colonial struggles. As she herself recently observed, 'there is nothing that I am that did not come out of that movement; that movement when everything was shaken ,where the order was shaken.'[2] From these origins, Wynter has become preoccupied with some of the central questions facing the current forms of human life on the planet. Taking the radical insights of anti-colonial thinkers Frantz Fanon and Aime Cesaire into new directions, she currently argues that the central struggle today for human life is redefining struggles in "terms of a politics of being: that is one waged over what is to be the descriptive statement of the human, about whose master code of symbolic life and death each human order organizes itself."[3] To put this another way, Wynter presently argues that the power of those who rule the world is so all-pervasive, far-reaching and deep that any radical break from the reach of this power requires ruptures from the *very frames* in which we think about ourselves as human. In her work, Wynter takes this preoccupation of the human and foregrounds it as the *central* problem of the contemporary world. In this sense, she builds upon black radical anti-colonial thinkers and theorists while striving to open up another set of theoretical frontiers through which we can both imagine and think about emancipation in the twenty-first century.

Wynter spells out the implications of this preoccupation with the human when she notes in a remarkable essay published in 2004, 'Unsettling the Coloniality of Being /Power/ Truth/ Freedom:Towards the Human, After Man, Its Overrepresentation- An Argument', that:

> All our present struggles with respect to race, class, gender, sexual orientation, ethnicity, struggles over the environment,...The sharply unequal distribution of the earth resources....These are differing facets of the central enthoclass Man vs. Human struggle.[4]

Basing herself on Fanon's final call in *The Wretched of the Earth* where he proclaimed that, 'we must work out new concepts, and try to set afoot a new man'; Wynter transforms this call into a profound meditation upon the ways in which power through its various historical incarnations has created *man* and failed to create the *human.*

For Wynter, the historical roots of this failure resides in what we may call *colonial modernity.* It is a modernity which included in its most intimate structures, racial slavery, colonial domination, genocide and forms of economic organisation which, while producing great wealth, were inimical to creating sites of human living. In thinking about the centrality of the Caribbean to the inauguration of colonial modernity, Wynter postulates that, 'the Pieza/Negro was the first and total example of the reduction of the creative possibilities of man to one single possibility – man as producer.'[5] She further notes that the:

> Caribbean islands constitute the classic plantation area...the Caribbean islands, were "planted" with peoples not in order to form societies, but in order to carry on plantations....Yet it was to be at the locus of the plantation, and in resistance to

> the dehumanization imposed on him by the market imperative of capitalism, that the black would rehumanize himself as a *native* of the Caribbean .[6]

I suggest that one critical preoccupation of Wynter's work in the Caribbean during the middle of the twentieth century was to grapple with this *rehumanisation,* and that this preoccupation is one of the keys to understanding *The Hills of Hebron.*

From her writings in *Jamaica Journal,*[7] *New World Quarterly,*[8] and *Daily Gleaner,*[9] and her work on the National Advisory Committee which created the Order of National Hero in Jamaica,[10] Wynter's intellectual labour was about placing the cultural forms, religious expressions and ways of life of the Black Jamaican as *the* central element of the newly independent Jamaican nation. The novel *The Hills of Hebron* represented her novelistic foray into what became one of her lifetime preoccupations – the struggle for the emergence of the human; but it did so within an explicit context of the Caribbean anti-colonial struggles.

The Black radical anti-colonial tradition attempts to establish a new set of political, social and knowledge categories which point to alternative ways out of the political, economic and the ideological and philosophical dominance of capital. It does so while conceptualising new grounds for being human. This has been the single most animating impulse of this tradition, its working through the limited humanisms of the West while overturning what Aime Cesaire calls the process of 'thingification'. However in thinking about *The Hills of Hebron* as a literary mode of representation of knowledge production, the following issues emerge in Wynter's thought to which we should pay attention: writing, criticism and literary analysis and then finally, how the 'politics of being' emerges in her early work.

The Hills of Hebron and Wynter's Early Work

We may contextualise Wynter's intellectual praxis and trajectory into four parts. In the first she is engaged as an actress, dancer and playwright in Europe. During this period she is drawn to radical anti-colonial circles and like many other Caribbean figures in the 1950s and early '60s, had a relationship with the British Broadcasting Corporation (BBC). In 1961 she co-authored with Jan Crew the play *The University of Hunger.* At the time, part of her anti-colonial circle was Mrs Amy Ashwood Garvey, who became a personality model for one of the characters in the novel, Miss Gatha. The writing of the novel, *The Hills of Hebron* begins the second phase of her intellectual life. During this period, Wynter returns to Jamaica, teaches at the University of the West Indies and is a co-founder of the publication, *Jamaica Journal.* Her writings in this journal elaborate a series of radical theoretical formulations about Jamaican society, history and culture. In this period, she primarily operates as a literary critic, cultural theorist and playwright. As a playwright, she writes the following plays: *Ballad for a Rebellion:Epic Story of Morant Bay Rebellion; Brother Man; Rockstone Anancy: A Magical Morality* and *Maskrade.* At this time, her provocative theoretical formulations show profound readings of Marx, the dependency school of political economy and a deep preoccupation with the work of the Haitian scholar J. Price Mars alongside the writings of Frantz Fanon and Aime Cesaire. They also illustrate her study of Spanish Literature which eventually leads to a radical and different understanding of Spanish colonial Jamaica in which she examines the influence of the Iberian peninsula's religion, art and philosophical thought on the New World. Her mastery of Spanish history and literature also shapes the writing style of her essays.

This second period ends with Wynter's sojourn to the USA. In America, she works with some of the leading Marxist literary critics of the period as well as with the Institute of the Black World and becomes an important figure in the Black Studies movement. In her current and fourth period Wynter returns to her initial impulses of radical anti-colonialism and begins to develop a theory of human cognition which facilitates a rupture with our present epistemic order. This brief summary of Wynter's extraordinary intellectual life does not do her justice but is adumbrated here so that we may be able to put her work into context while focusing on the second period and the publication of the novel.

The Novel

The Hills of Hebron was published in 1962. It was first written in the late 1950s as a radio play. Living in London at the time, Wynter thought of herself primarily as a playwright and actress. She was moved to start writing seriously because as an actress, she had been given acting parts which belittled not only her talents, but black women in general. She recalls one such instance in an interview, 'there I was made up to be an Australian dancer or something and then I began to feel fed-up and I said look, I'm going to write parts for myself...and then I became gripped by it.'[11] The turn to writing was a profound move and began a journey in which writing became for Wynter a mode of intellectual praxis through which she would challenge the epistemological order of the West. When the novel was completed, she titled it, *The End of Exile.* According to Wynter, it was given this original title because 'there is an exile thematic and therefore the motif is a quest for the promised land in Hebron'.[12] She also notes that the original title was indicative that the quest of the Afro-Jamaican was about 'the bringing to an end...the imaginative exile of the majority population of Jamaica from any overt and official connection to our original homeland –that of the systemically stigmatized (from the colonizer's perspective) "primitive" Africa.'[13] However, I would also suggest that the novel was titled this way because for Wynter, even though the novel is rooted in Jamaica with its characters, setting and themes, it was being written from London.

One other event shaped the writing of the novel at the time and gave Wynter grounds for a lifetime commitment to radical struggles and thinking: the tragic death of Patrice Lumumba. For Wynter, Lumumba was crucified by the 'imperial system of the West'. She says,

> We knew that if Lumumba was destroyed Africa would be finished for generations,...and we knew he was going to be murdered and we could not do anything. It was an excruciating experience....There is something obscene about empires although they have played a very powerful role in human history, and so that is when I decided I am going to try my best to bring an end to empires forever and forever. Amen."[14]

This determination to contribute to the end of empire should be seen alongside the ways in which Wynter was drawn to the powerful forces of what was then called, 'folk–culture.' *The Hills of Hebron* was not only one of the first novels written by a Jamaican woman at a time when many Caribbean major novelists were male figures but it also illustrated Wynter's determination to end empire. With her attention to the *life forms* of the ordinary Jamaican, the novel did not imagine the foundations of a new nation but worked through a different way in which subaltern groups in Jamaica practised freedom. This focus made the novel, in her words, 'an anti-colonial not a nationalist novel.'[15]

An anti-colonial novel

The conventional narrative about the literary history of the Caribbean is that, in the immediate aftermath of the 1935–38 events, there was a flourishing of nationalist literature. In recent Caribbean literary history this narrative has been complicated by feminist critics who argue that since literature, as an imaginative act, was critical for communities to construct their national identities, then many of these literary acts were gendered, making nationalism in many instances a masculine project. These critics correctly argue that the nationalist narrative and the story of this literary history have silenced the female voice and self.[16] Wynter herself, in a publication devoted to Caribbean women and literature, while recognising this fact, produces another way of examining this tradition. Working with the trope of Caliban which emerges from Caribbean anti-colonial criticism and literature, she writes in the afterword of the publication,

> The question is that of the most significant absence of all, that of Caliban's woman [this] absence of Cailban's woman is therefore an ontological absence [one] which[is] functional to the new secularizing schema…[17]

Shirley Toland–Dix in a recent essay on *The Hills of Hebron* points out that, 'Over a period of almost fifty years, Wynter's engagement with feminism has been complex but consistent…she continues to present feminism and women's rights as issues which are a subset with her analysis of Western humanism and the consequences of its racially based definition of "Man".'[18]

For Wynter, this is the overarching frame and her central concern. Standing on this position, she argues that there is a ground outside the present governing orders of our ways of knowing from which we should develop criticism. With regard to literary and film criticism, Wynter calls this mode of criticism a 'deciphering practice [one which] is able to "uncover" the working of these counter –practices and forms part of an ongoing Nietzschean transvaluation of values and, therefore, of aesthetics, an emerging praxis….'[19] This 'deciphering practice,' in Wynter's view, seeks to understand not 'what texts and their signifying practices can be interpreted to *mean* but what they can be deciphered to *do*. Her position also seeks to evaluate the 'illocutionary force' and the procedures with which 'they do what they *do*.'[20] This means that as a writer, Wynter is concerned with the novel as a form of knowledge and *how it functions* in such a mode. In her general reflections on the writing of the novel, Wynter observes that the overemphasis in standard literary criticism on the

> *aesthetic qualities* of the literary text...with emphasis then taken as *an end in itself* has functioned to block recognition of the unique kind of knowledge that is specific to literary texts, knowledge which aesthetic qualities do indeed help to make more illuminating.[21]

Of course, Wynter is moving outside the conventional bounds of literary criticism and suggesting a different way for us to think about the novel as an imaginative artifact. Thus, for her, one of the most important moments in *The Hills of Hebron* is when Obadiah attempts to make a rupture from the normative order.

The Hills of Hebron does not tell a nationalist story. Rather it is preoccupied with the ways that the Jamaican ex-slave engages with the processes of rehumanisation. It is about what life forms are then created through this process. As mentioned before, this key theme of the novel makes it anti-colonial rather than nationalist. For Wynter, the nationalist novel mimics the West. Its frames are those of the West, in part, because such novels do not probe the interiority of the popular classes, those humans that Wynter calls the 'waste products of the system'. At the time, this kind of probing was central to Wynter's thought and intellectual practice as she grappled with an inner human world of Afro–Jamaican history, a world obscured by colonial power and made strange and opaque by the native intellectual. For Wynter, the nationalist novel ignores this inner human world and becomes part of the Western literary canon because it seeks to imagine a nation state on Western grounds. In doing this, the nationalist novel creates the conditions for the new state to be 'redrawn back into the Western system which is a system of nation-states.'[22]

So how does Wynter make her novel, *The Hills of Hebron* anti-colonial rather than nationalist ?

An Afro-Jamaican Symbolic World

The Hills of Hebron is the story of a group of former enslaved persons who attempt to create a new life. The main structure of the narrative is based upon the early twentieth century movement of Bedwardism. Alexander Bedward led 'The Jamaica Native Baptist Free Church [which] was the largest and most important revivalist group in the colony'[23] with branches of the Church in Cuba and Central America. The members of the Church saw Bedwardism as a religion which replaced Christianity. A.A. Brooks, a member of the Church, wrote in 1917 that, 'Bedwardism is a Religious Denomination of very distinguishing features...and was established in 1889 by Shakespeare, (H.E.S. Woods) in Augustown....As Judaisim was succeeded by Christianity, so Christianity is being succeeded by Bedwardism.'[24]

What is noteworthy is how central to Bedwardism was the Psalm, 'Ethiopia shall stretch out her hands to God', and the verse in Revelation, 'The sealing of the last tribe. God is still speaking through his servants and handmaids.' Both these verses were interpreted as integral to Divine Revelation and the foundation for the development of the Jamaica Native Baptist Church.

The emergence of Bedwardism was one stream of numerous Afro-Jamaican religious practices which developed in the late nineteenth century and these practices became the terrain on which many of the ex-slaves attempted to assert their humanness in the face of British colonial power and a white local oligarchy. Bedwardism belongs to a black 'prophetic – redemptive' tradition of thought and praxis in which the counter-symbolic world of the oppressed reconfigures the normative categories of Western political and religious thought. These counter-symbolic practices are redemptive because their philosophies of history and their conceptions of freedom circle around notions of redemption. These philosophies of history and conceptions of freedom are themselves depositories of historical and political knowledges.[25]

In *The Hills of Hebron* the followers of the Prophet Moses are called New Believers. The narrative voice in the novel tells us:

> They survived the loss of gods and devils that were their own, of familiar trees and hills ...of their own land in which to see some image of themselves. And their descendents, the New Believers, survived the exodus from the Cockpit Centre, the passage through the wilderness and up to the hills of Hebron, where the Prophet Moses had promised them those things that had been lost in their trespass across the sea, across the centuries.[26]

In the novel, similar to the life of Bedward, the Prophet Moses is perceived by the colonial authorities as a lunatic: 'In the meantime the Commissioner of Police in Kingston had received a report on Prophet Moses. In the report the Prophet was described as a political agitator and lunatic.'[27] If, as Jean Comaroff and John Comaroff suggest, 'between the conscious and unconscious lies the most critical domain...for the analysis of colonialism and resistance', then the issue of madness becomes central to our understanding of colonial power. Jonathan Sadowsky makes the point that Africans and Europeans in colonial contexts had different cognitive realties[28] and Megan Vaughan has argued that 'the madman and the madwoman emerge in the colonial historical record not as standing for the "other" but more often as being insufficiently "other"'.[29] In Wynter' s view, because human beings weave 'webs of signification', then for the dominated group to assert its humanity required the creation of what she called in the 1970s, 'the counter–world, the counter symbolic order' of the colonised. Wynter suggests that this 'powerful symbolic counterworld…was reinvented in response to the forced exodus of the Middle Passage to the enforced diaspora in the plantation archipelago of the Black America.'[30] For Wynter therefore, the major objective of *The Hills of Hebron* was an attempt to begin to describe this 'counter-world', and in doing so present as allegory a different rendering of Jamaican history.

The novel brings together and illustrates the different ideas of the subaltern social forces that operated in Jamaica in the early twentieth century: the labour movement, the strikes and the Rastafarian movement. These different forces confront each other towards the end of the novel with Obadiah, the successor of Prophet Moses observing all of them. For five pages towards the end of the novel Wynter gives us voices which embody the radical social forces of the period. There is the description of Bellows, the radical who was hounded by the colonial authorities, arrested and released a broken man. Then there was Fernandez, the 'brown man'and then there was Harvey who 'put too much distance between himself and the people'. And then there was Rastafari. Wynter writes :

> One of the men who had sat silent, his mass of black hair and beard like a screen out of which he regarded the others with contempt, suddenly flung a question: "And what about Marcus Garvey? What about the Emperor Haile Selassie, the Conquering Lion of Judah, the Ras, the Negus, the Black Jesus, what about him?"[31]

In the novel, the Rasta voice, after giving a fierce speech on oppression and the centrality of Africa to black liberation to an audience including Obadiah, is carted off to jail by the police. In the moment of this arrest, the police then confront

Obadiah. It is a confrontation which leaves the police officer bewildered because he is not able to understand *what* Obadiah is. This is the scene after Obadiah announces to the police officer that he is from Hebron, 'the place' in the words of the police officer, 'where the madman Moses crucify himself:' 'The corporal started back at him in disbelief. Then he let him go, pushed back his cap and scratched his head. Suddenly he was aware of all the eyes in the market mocking him covertly...he walked back to the van, got in and slammed the door after him. Somehow he felt that he had been made to look ridiculous.' In this scene, Wynter seems to be suggesting that the mode of existence created by the New Believers was so much outside of the understanding of the state that force could not tame it. This then was a mode of existence which would deeply trouble power because it could not easily be captured and reworked. It could not be captured because it operated outside of the epistemological categories of modernity and called into question the very notion of modernity itself.

Wynter pays a great deal of attention to the historical details of Jamaican society and with its ambition to describe the symbolic lives of the ex-slaves of Jamaica in the early twentieth century, *The Hills of Hebron* is a novel of historical fiction in the genre of radical anti-colonialism. And what does one mean here by the phrase historical fiction? Georg Lukacs noted that the historical novel appears as genre at the moment when it is possible for a writer to grasp history as 'the pre-history of the present.' The emergence of the historical novel he argues, produces great writers who operate as writers of realism. For Lukacs, the outstanding historical novel is one in which the writer 'relies upon the riches and profoundity of the total process.'[32] A novel of historical fiction is one in which fiction functions to bring alive erased histories and social processes along with the knowledge embedded within these histories.

As a radical anti-colonial novel, *The Hills of Hebron* points us to the lives and symbolic world of black Jamaicans. This then allows Wynter to leave us wondering about the validity of a certain kind of politics that does not pay attention to these symbolic orders. In making this move, Wynter wants to foreground a 'politics of being'; that is, a politics in which the ontological process of rehumanisation of the Black ex-slaves is given due consideration.

During the 1960s and in her second period, Wynter operates with a notion of culture. In 1977 she says, 'Culture is for me, primarily, the societal machinery with which a particular society or group symbolically codes its sense of self'.[33] By the 1990s, she adds to this understanding a concept of the *imaginary* and argues for a *cultural imaginary,* one which 'enables the phenomenon of aesthetics to be grasped in both its transcultural form...and the form specific to our present order.'[34] By the twenty-first century, she is positing a theoretical conception that human social orders are auto-poetic living systems. There is therefore, a consistent line in Wynter's thought which focuses on the various languages and symbolic systems of human life. Our reading of *The Hills of Hebron* would benefit from understanding this fact.

Some Concluding Notes

After the publication of *The Hills of Hebron,* Wynter's writings continue to be focused on probing the cultural life forms of black Jamaicans as well as working through a theory of Caribbean society and criticism. In her essay 'Jonkonnu in Jamaica', she writes that the history of the Caribbean islands is, in large part, 'the *history of the indigenization* of the black man. And this history is a cultural history – not in 'writing' but of those '*homunculi*' who humanize the landscape by peopling it with gods and spirits, with demons and duppies, with all the rich panoply of man's imagination.'[35] Here, Wynter was engaged in a critique of the idea that Creole theory was an adequate explanation of Caribbean society. Kamau Brathwaite in a seminal essay on the history of Caribbean thought, *Contradictory Omens,* recognises this and notes that 'Sylvia Wynter makes a distinction between creolization, (as imitation) and what she calls indigenization.'Brathwaite then cites Wynter: 'Whilst the "creolization" process represents...a more or less "false assimilation" in which the dominated people adopt elements from the dominant...in order to obtain prestige or status, the "indigenization" process represents the more secretive process by which the dominated culture survives; and resists.'[36] Brathwaite is in sympathy with Wynter's view but feels that she misses the 'acceptance–rejection syndrome; its psycho-cultural plurality.'[37] However, I suggest that Wynter's focus on trying to describe and understand cultural forms of the ex-slaves and colonial subjects who resisted domination in quotidian ways gives her another space to think about Caribbean society, hence her formulation of a theory of indigenization.[38] For her, these cultural forms of subaltern creative invention were constitutive of a drive to find new modes of existence.

In responding to the criticisms of her novel, particularly by Caribbean literary historian Ken Ramchand, who had argued that West Indian novelists saw Afro-Caribbean religious practices as the 'incoherent remains of African religions and magic', Wynter argued that not only was he wrong, but that Ramchand misses an entire swath of creative Caribbean life. She notes that as critic, 'the central distortion of Dr. Ramchand's criticism is a reflection of the ambivalent Creole eye...the searchlight of its gaze is directed by a grid of misconceptions prepackaged in the cornflakes of a colonial education.'[39]

It seems that for Wynter, the major issue facing Caribbean society in its immediate post-colonial period was a form of decolonisation which would take into account the creative *forms of life* of the Afro-Jamaican. In writing *The Hills of Hebron,* Wynter began to formulate a set of critical theoretical formulations about Jamaican and Caribbean society. In the novel, we begin to get glimpses of the preoccupation and directions of this theoretical work. For Wynter, the New Believers and their search was a historic movement and an integral part of what she would call in 1972, *Afro-Jamaicanism.* In her view, while the New Believers in the early twentieth century sought their freedom in an exodus to the rural, Cockpit Centre and the establishment of the community of Hebron, by the 1950s the novels of Roger Mais began to explore the 'exodus into the towns and the creation of the slums which became a way of life of the marginal man.'[40] All of this, she would argue, existed outside the framework of what she calls in 1972 an 'inauthentic nationalism' constructed by the new nationalist elite. At the level of literary production, Wynter feels that the novels of Roger Mais, in particular *Brother Man,* functioned as anti-colonial novels. She also feels that Lamming's *In the Castle of My Skin* belongs to this genre of literary production. She is therefore making another set of claims for the Caribbean literary tradition in which she makes a series of distinctions between the nationalist and the radical anti-colonialist novel.

In discussing the literary production of another figure in the black radical anti-colonial tradition, CLR James, Wynter notes that, 'the fictional characters of *Minty Alley* and of "Triumph" refuse to accept their value of nothingness. Their lives are spent in constant combat to refuse this negation of their being, to affirm by any means...that they have life value and powers that must be realized.'[41] For Wynter, one primary task of the radical anti-colonial intellectual was to grapple with knowledges and practices which emerged from the processes of this affirmation. It was to work through the 'interstices of history.' *The Hills of Hebron* is her effort to show us both how and why this must be done. We may want to read the novel bearing these issues in mind. In this kind of reading another question may be opened up for us: how do we tell the interior human story of the 'wretched of the earth'? How do we give an account of the counter–symbolic orders of the *damnés de la terre* in the Caribbean? In the end, we may have to ask ourselves another question: Forty- odd years after political independence, have we been able to give these accounts ?

Notes

1. Thanks to Sylvia Wynter, whose reading of this introduction continues a dialogue we have had for the past few years and to Geri Augusto, whose critical eye on the final draft was important, especially on the question of Wynter's studies of Columbus and Spanish colonialism in Jamaica. Also, thanks to Kelly Josephs, who proofread the manuscript of the novel.
2. Sylvia Wynter, Interview with Anthony Bogues and Demetrius Eudell , December 2006.
3. Sylvia Wynter, 'Unsettling the Coloniality of Being /Power/ Truth/Freedom: Towards the Human, After Man, Its Overrepresentation – An Argument', p. 319.
4. Ibid., pp. 260–61.
5. Sylvia Wynter, '"We Know Where We Are From": The Politics of Black Culture From Myal to Marley' unpublished paper in my possession, November 1977, p. 22.
6. Sylvia Wynter, *The Native* pp. 1–2. unpublished manuscript in my possession. This citation is taken from a 751 page unpublished manuscript of Sylvia Wynter written in 1971 while she was associated with the Institute of the Black World a radical organisation of Black Diasporic individuals based in Atlanta, Georgia. This organisation included Vincent Harding, William Strickland, Howard Dobson and Robert Hill. Associated with the organisation were George Beckford , CLR James and Walter Rodney amongst others. For a discussion of the politics and organisation of this group see Derrick White's unpublished thesis , 'New Concepts for the New Man: The Institute of the Black World and the Incomplete victory of the Second Reconstruction'(Department of History, Ohio University, 2004). I want to thank Demetrius Eudell for drawing my attention to the existence of *The Native*. In my view, this manuscript represents the most complete elaboration of Wynter's views during the early 1970s and should be published.
7. Wynter played a central role in the formation of *Jamaica Journal.* Her path-breaking essays during her sojourn with this journal include 'Jonkonnu in Jamaica: Towards the Interpretation of Folk Dance as a Cultural Process' (Volume 4, No. 2 June

1970, pp. 34–48) and 'An Introductory Essay to an Adaptation of Federico Garcia Lorca's *The House of Bernarda Alba'* (Volume 2, No. 3 and Volume 4, No. 3, September 1970.) There was as well 'Lady Nugent's Journal' (Volume 1, No. 1, December 1967) and the seminal 'We must Learn to Sit Down Together and Talk about a Little Culture: Reflections on West Indian Writing and Criticism' (Volume 2, December 1968 and Volume 3, March 1969).

8. She was a regular contributor to this journal and a member of the New World Group. See in particular her essay 'Creole Criticism' in *New World Quarterly* Vol 5. No 4, 1972.
9. Wynter wrote regularly for what was at the time, Jamaica's leading newspaper. One of her most remarkable pieces of journalism for this publication is her response to Evon Blake's critical article on Bedwardism and Garvey in which he called Garvey a dreamer and Alexander Bedward a lunatic. In her response, Wynter argues that both Garvey and Bedward followed a basic principle of revolt, 'the basic revolt of men against their being made into merchandise.' See Sylvia Wynter, 'Garvey and Bedward' *The Sunday Gleaner* March 12, 1972.
10. Wynter wrote the pamphlet which established the arguments for Jamaica's National Heroes. The chair of the Jamaica National Trust Commission, the late Frank Hill stated in the preface of the pamphlet, 'At the Committee's request, Ms Wynter prepared the Argument to support this recommendation under three headings…the historic roles of Sir Alexander Bustamante and Norman Washington Manley within the context of Gordon, Bogle and Garvey.' The pamphlet identifies two traditions of revolt in Jamaican society, one represented by Gordon and the other by Bogle, and it paid special attention to the activities of Marcus Garvey. In other words, it constructed a narrative of Jamaican history which did not privilege 1938 but made an attempt to place the events within the context of a longer period of Black Jamaican struggles which began with the Maroons against the Spanish Empire. The pamphlet was published in 1971. Sylvia Wynter, *Jamaica's National Heroes* (Kingston: Stephenson's Litho Press, 1971).
11. Wynter Interview, December 2006.
12. Ibid .

13. Email correspondence between Sylvia Wynter and Anthony Bogues, August 18, 2008.
14. Wynter Interview, December 2006.
15. Ibid.
16. For a recent elaboration of this position and the limits of what has been called the 'Calibanesque tradition of Caribbean Literature', see Patricia Saunders, *Alien-Nation and Repatriation: Translating Identity in Anglophone Caribbean Literature* (Lanham: Lexington Books, 2007).
17. Sylvia Wynter, 'AfterWord: "Beyond Miranda's Meanings: Un/silencing the 'Demonic ground' of Caliban's "Woman"" in Carole Boyce Davis & Elaine Savory Fido, *Out of Kumbla: Caribbean Women and Literature* (New Jersey: Africa World Press, 1990).
18. Shirley Toland-Dix, '*The Hills of Hebron:* Sylvia Wynter's Disruption of the Narrative of the Nation', *Small Axe* Vol. 12. No 1, 2008. pp. 57–76.
19. Sylvia Wynter, 'Rethinking "Aesthetics": Notes Towards a Deciphering Practice'. In Mbye Cham (ed) *Ex-Iles: Essays on Caribbean Cinema* (Trenton, NJ: Africa World Press, 1992) p. 238.
20. Ibid., pp. 266–67.
21. Sylvia Wynter, 'On Reading *The Hills* from Hindsight, After Literary Criticism: Towards the Autopoetic Turn/Overturn', December 2006. (unpublished)
22. Sylvia Wynter, December 2006 Interview.
23. W.F. Elkins, *Street Preachers , Faith Healers and Herb Doctors in Jamaica* (New York: Revisionist Press, 1977) p. 15.
24. A.A. Brooks, *History of Bedwardism* (Kingston: The Gleaner Company Printers, 1917) pp. 12–17.
25. For a discussion of this point see Anthony Bogues, *Black Heretics, Black Prophets: Radical Political Intellectuals* (New York: Routledge, 2003).
26. Sylvia Wynter, *The Hills of Hebron* (Essex: Longman, 1984) p. 51.
27. Ibid., p. 121.
28. Jonathan Sadowsky, *Imperial Bedlam : Institutions of Madness in Colonial Southwest Nigeria* (Berkeley: University of California Press, 1999) p. 70.
29. Megan Vaughan, *Curing their Ills: Colonial Power and African Illness* (Stanford: Stanford University Press, 1991) p. 101.

30. Sylvia Wynter, '"We Know Where We Are From": The Politics of Black Culture from Myal to Marley', November 1977, unpublished mss in author's possession.
31. Sylvia Wynter, *The Hills of Hebron* (London: Longman Drumbeat, 1984) p. 286.
32. Cited in Terry Eagleton, *Marxism and Literary Criticism* (London: Methuen & Co , 1972) p. 30.
33. '"We Know Where We Are From": The Politics of Black Culture from Myal to Marley'.
34. 'Rethinking Aesthetics', p. 248.
35. Sylvia Wynter, 'Jonkonnu in Jamaica: Towards the Interpretation of Folk Dance as a Cultural Process'. Part 1. In 1973, Wynter wrote the play *Maskarade* based upon her understanding of the process of indigenization. It was published as a play for schools and the notes to it in part read: 'It is an excellent play for schools as the cast is large and can take all age groups....Before any attempt is made to produce the play – or even read it in drama class– drama teachers and drama students would do well to read the article.' In *West Indian Plays for Schools.* (Intro) Jeanne Wilson, (Kingston: Jamaica Publishing House , 1979) p. 26.
36. Kamau Brathwaite, *Contradictionary Omens* (Kingston: Savacou Publications , 1974) pp. 15–16.
37. Ibid.
38. This theory was taken from her readings of the writings of the Haitian scholar, Jean Price Mars.
39. Sylvia Wynter, 'Creole Criticism –A Critique', in *New World Quarterly* Vol 5. No 4, p. 2.
40. Sylvia Wynter, 'One Love Rhetoric or Reality? – Aspects of Afro-Jamaicianism' in *Caribbean Studies* Vol 12 No. 3, October 1972, p. 67.
41. Sylvia Wynter, 'The Counterdoctrine of Jamesian Poiesis'. In Paget Henry & Paul Buhle (eds) *C.L.R. James's Caribbean* (Durham: Duke University Press, 1992) p. 76.

Part 1

SATURDAY

At first he is apparently robust, but in process of time he begins to be delicate, not having any real disease...He tells them that he is being carried away by a river. He dreams of many things and his body is muddled and he becomes a house of dreams.

(From an Amazulu account of the initiation of a diviner)

1. The Vow

It was early morning. There were mists over the hills and valleys of Hebron. Down in the square, Aunt Kate sat on the cold earth beside the spring. She rocked to and fro and cradled her arms as she hummed a lullaby. The clear water murmured an accompaniment. She had dressed hurriedly, and her cotton frock was unfastened at the back, her headkerchief askew, like a crumpled hibiscus. A light wind lifted the loose strands of her grey hair. Her face was oval. Pouches of reddish-brown skin framed a beaked nose and black eyes as swift as bees.

The sound of feet squelching on wet grass, of people greeting each other, carried towards her. She remained still and listened. Then she smiled and nodded. Her lips formed words that were propitiatory echoes. The part of her mind which was secret and cunning accepted that she would have to pretend to practise rites which the others used to assure a reality from which she had escaped. For the others were not without power. If they demanded her involvement in their conspiracy, she needed them in hers.

She recognized one of the voices and frowned with a quick antagonism. Ann would see her, would want to take her away. She stretched out her hands and tried to pull the greyish-white mist around her. But another voice spoke, a kindlier one. She cupped a hand to her ear and leaned forward. That was Ann's sister, Sue. She would have to be just as careful with her. Sue always tried to smother her with sly affection, to trap her into forgetting her own child, Maverlyn.

Ann spoke now, grumbling as was her custom. 'I don't know what Elder Obadiah could mean, to hold a church service at four o'clock in the morning, vow or no vow!'

A man answered her. 'True word, Sister Ann! The Elder should know that people's body and spirit too weak to wake them up from sleep, this unconscionable time of morning!'

Zacky's voice hadn't changed much over the years. It was as asthmatic as when he was a small boy down in Cockpit Centre. He used to hover about Ann when he started smelling his sweat, growing up; used to stand at the gate and talk to her, the two of them thin and serious together. Until the day that Sue laughed out in the yard, her breasts shaking like jelly with the laughter. Zacky couldn't take his eyes off her after that. Although, once she had had all those children by him, the breasts didn't matter any longer; his arms embraced the land now, more and more of it. And how many children did they have in all? Nine or ten? And I only had one that lived, Aunt Kate grieved, I only had Maverlyn…

She cradled her arms once more and sang a lullaby. Ann called out her name, bore down on her.

'Aunt Kate, you want worse rheumatism than you have? Up off the cold ground with you this minute!'

'Don't talk so loud, Ann,' she begged. 'Don't frighten Maverlyn!'

Ann, unyielding, pulled her to her feet, and Sue took her other arm. Aunt Kate felt Sue's warm comfortable body bulging against her and appealed to her.

'Sue, you think it's fair for Ann to take her loud mouth and sharp tongue and frighten Maverlyn?'

Ann released Aunt Kate abruptly and rounded on her sister.

'Since it's you she want to complain to, you look after her. It's ten years now since Maverlyn drowned in the spring. It's full time that Aunt Kate get some sense in her head and realize that the child not sleeping, that she is dead!'

She flounced off and Aunt Kate cried out in alarm.

'Look, Sue, look how Maverlyn leaping up in her sleep, how she is dancing on the wings of the wind!'

Sue's eyes followed the steep slope up to where flaming bamboo torches were fixed to posts on either side of the church door. Then she looked down at the reflected light in the spring. The water was as red and restless as flambeaux blossoms in a high wind.

'See, Aunt Kate,' she comforted. 'Maverlyn will sleep sound now. She is tired out after all that dancing. Come, we are late for the service as it is.'

Sue's hand under her arm was as insistent as her compassion. Aunt Kate gave in. She would go with her, would play their make-believe game with them so that Maverlyn could sleep in peace. The two women climbed up the path towards the church. The torches flared in the morning breeze. They reminded Aunt Kate of the first night she had spent in Hebron. Moses had made a bonfire of many of the belongings that they had laboured to bring up with them, of everything that he judged unnecessary for their new beginning. And their past had vanished, like Elijah, riding in his chariot of fire, a conqueror in an empty sky.

****

'Daniel saw a stone rolling down to Babylon,
As Daniel saw that stone, rolling down to Babylon,
Our Elder took a vow
That saved us from destruction.
Glory hallelujah, our Elder took that vow!'

The singing ended with a concerted Amen. The New Believers of Hebron subsided on to stools and benches. From where he stood on the dais, Elder Obadiah Brown moved his hands in a wide arc above the heads of the congregation. His long wiry fingers commanded their silence, like divining rods drew their attention. Then he began his sermon.

'Brethren and Sisters, truly indeed this is a time of great rejoicing, of full thanksgiving for we the people of Hebron!'

'Amen!'

They had all accepted his authority, all except Miss Gatha, who sat to his right on the dais and in her accustomed corner. She knew that the voice, the gestures, the inflections were no more his than the swallow-tailed coat, the black trousers, the Bible on the table in front of him. They had all once belonged to her dead husband, Prophet Moses. She was dressed in black and hunched over on her stool like some ominous bird of prey.

The Elder looked away from her and to Brother Hugh who sat beside him. Hugh was his close friend and together they had planned the sermon. He smiled at him, certain of approval. For an instant Hugh failed to respond. The Elder wondered whether, perhaps, he had made a mistake in the words or in the delivery. His eyes sought out his young wife who sat in the body of the congregation. She was looking through the open door behind him, to where the hills were thrusting through the mists. She seemed untroubled about him. He continued, once more charged with certainty.

'Brethren and Sisters, the storm season is over – and the Angel of Death has flown his bat-wings far away from us!'

'Far far away!'

Brother Hugh led the response with vehemence. He sensed that he had slipped up, that the envy which he felt had betrayed him. He had seen the elder look to his wife, gain confidence, go on. The thought that he might be expendable was like a spur.

The Elder spread his arms wide as his voice rose, instinct with power.

'And the Lord God of Israel and of Hebron has swept away the hurricane to smite the heathen lands, to flood out the infidel lands, to wash away the evil wallowing in the unbelieving lands!'

'Amen!' The congregation were victorious, their eyes bright.

'And He didn't blow wind-wrath at us, and He didn't pour anger-water on us, but in infinite mercy He spared we who at His command did wash away our evil in the rich red blood of the Lamb!'

'The rich blood, the red blood, hallelujah!'

'Amen!' the Elder said, and paused.

With the long memory of the illiterate, he was recapturing every trick of Prophet Moses, with which that supreme actor had created this community in his own image. The Elder looked out through the open sides of the church and at the encircling hills. In the sky, loose scarves of mist drifted together to form a cross against which Razor Edge Peak was the crucified form of the Prophet.

'Brethren and Sisters,' the Elder said, his voice measured and serious, 'today is the first day of October, the beginning of the good time, the bad time all over!'

'Over!'

'But remember back with me, Brothers and Sisters, remember back one year and one month, this same hour, this quiet hour, this cool time, this dark time, before the sun burst bright on us. Remember September!'

'September!'

'And recollect with me, Brothers and Sisters, recollect the face of the Lord turned from us, recollect the hand of the Lord heavy upon us, recollect us as chaff in the path of the hurricane winds, as leaves in the wind of the hurricane water!'

'Chaff in the wind, leaves in the water!' they mourned. Their voices were like the wind soughing through the tall grass.

'Then recollect the hungriness, the sore distress, recollect the nothing that remained to us!'

'The nothing!'

****

Elder Obadiah looked at the Senior Brothers and Sisters of the church who were seated in a semicircle on the dais. To his left sat Brother Hugh. Beside him was Brother Zacky and his wife Sue, and beside her was Aunt Kate. Aunt Kate, as the widow of the second Elder of Hebron, had a permanent place of honour. When Obadiah smiled at her she smiled back, sweetly and uncomprehendingly. On his right hand was Brother Lazarus, a round, smooth-faced man; the rolls of fat on his belly showed through a missing button. Beside him Sister Ann twisted her work-worn fingers in her lap, her expression doleful. And beside Sister Ann was Miss Gatha.

She did not return Obadiah's look, but stared ahead of her, her eyes hooded under a projecting forehead. Tight black hairs, tinged with grey, clustered inside her widespread nostrils. Her mouth and chin were hidden behind the large rapacious hands that she kept clasped over the knob of her stick. The dull black of her skin merged into that of her long-sleeved dress, boots, and cotton stockings. She was like a gnarled and knotted tree-trunk in a forest of saplings.

The Elder forced himself to keep his look casual. Now was the moment, as he and Hugh had arranged, to attack and rout any threat to his eldership which Miss Gatha's silent presence might imply. He made his voice conversational.

'And also you will remember with me, Brothers and Sisters, how on that sad occasion, our dearly beloved Sister, Miss Gatha, once wife, now widow, to Prophet Moses, who heard the call, Prophet Moses who led us all up out of Sodom, up out of Gomorrah, and did find us a goodly land, a new Canaan in which to enter!'

'A new Canaan, hallelujah!'

'All honour to Prophet Moses who washed away our sins in the healing stream of his sacrifice, and gave up his life, crucified, so that Hebron might live for ever!'

'A…a …men!'

The Elder bowed deeply to Miss Gatha.

'And all honour to his spouse, Miss Gatha, who last year, when the land of Hebron flowed a black river, charged me as Elder with bringing down God's wrath upon us by indulging myself too much in the pleasures of the flesh!'

He smiled hugely and the congregation laughed. They relaxed, the men lounging back on the benches whilst the women sprawled open their legs, their skirts forming an apron between them, the way they would sit gossiping on their doorsteps or by the spring. The Elder waited for their laughter to die down. He stood just over six feet, and his powerful shoulder-muscles strained against the black broadcloth of his jacket. When he was not preaching his movements were clumsy. But when he spoke and was caught up in the rhythm of words, his body flowed like water. His face, with its high sloping forehead, fleshy nose, drooping lips, and heavy jowls, was like some rough-hewn and unfinished carving. A perpetual self-doubt lurked in his eyes.

He leaned forward now, his palms flat on the table.

'Ah, but I did not laugh, Brothers and Sisters. I said to myself that if it was true and I, as Elder of Hebron, brought down God's wrath on us as Miss Gatha accused me of, then it was up to me to do something about it. And what did I do then, Brother Hugh? What did I say to you?'

Brother Hugh stood up and stepped forward. Obadiah made a sweeping gesture, ceding him the platform, and sat down.

Brother Hugh was in his late thirties, a year or two younger than the Elder. He was a short man with a paunch and great self-importance. He wore a white drill suit, black bow-tie, and patent-leather shoes. He placed his hand on his heart and spoke with emphasis.

'Brethren and Sisters, New Believers, it is a great honour for me today to testify to what the Elder Obadiah said and did last year when great trials and grievous tribulations were upon us. Elder Obadiah came to me and said – his exact words – "Brother Hugh," he said, "I am the man chosen by Prophet Moses and anointed by his hand to rule well over Hebron and save it from disaster as he himself would have done!"

'Amen!'

Brother Hugh, as a speaker, did not have the impact of Obadiah. He tried too hard, and his gestures were fussy and distracting. But he sensed the changing moods of the congregation and was quick to adapt himself. He glanced at Miss Gatha to emphasize that his preamble had been aimed at her, before he continued.

'And furthermore the Elder said to me, "Hugh, the people of Hebron are my people and I love my people. So, although I am a man new-married to a young wife…"'

The congregation looked at Obadiah's wife, Sister Rose, who sat in the second row of benches. Her eyes were fixed on the grey sky which spread out over Hebron waiting to be despoiled by the sun.

Brother Hugh, undeterred, swept to his climax.

'And after saying this, the Elder, acting on my humble advice and suggestion, made a covenant with God, took a singular vow!'

'Singular!'

'He took a vow that as Elder of the Church of the New Believers of Hebron he would continue to lie beside his wife Sister Rose as he is usual to do, but…'

'But…?'

'He wouldn't touch her, he wouldn't know her, or any woman else, for the space of one month and one year, until the next hurricane had passed its bitter cup far away from us!'

'Amen!'

'So praised be King David, praised be King Saul, but praised above all be our Elder who for one year and one month kept his singular vow. Kept his covenant with God, saved Hebron from the wrath to come, Amen!'

'Amen, praise the Lord, praise Elder Obadiah!' they thundered. They clapped their hands and stamped their feet. The tambourines clamoured agreement.

Miss Gatha waited her moment well. As the shouting died away, she asked drily:

'You are sure of that, Brother Hugh? You are sure of that, all of you?'

Their startled eyes looked at her as she appraised them steadily, her face like granite.

****

Aunt Kate's eyes darted from one face to the other. She nodded and smiled, taking part in a charade which had stopped. The silence persisted, and she worried whether she had missed a cue. Then she noticed that everyone was looking at Miss Gatha, and decided that the silence had nothing to do with her. Her mind slipped down the steep path towards the spring; it was cold down there, quiet, the verging grass wet with dew. She felt a twinge of pain in her leg. And yet it was as though it belonged to someone else. She accepted her rheumatism as a penance she paid for having Maverlyn.

Sister Sue's shoes were too tight, and the strap across her instep cut into the flesh. She was anxious to return home to the children. If Miss Gatha were to start something now, she might be late. Her narrow slanted eyes, embedded like chips of black quartz in her full cheeks, stared at Miss Gatha with malevolence. The old woman was the only person for whom Sue felt an active dislike. Miss Gatha always tried to reduce her femaleness, had always held a grudge against her since that time long ago – with Prophet Moses down in Cockpit Centre...

The shed at the back of the shop had been close and hot. The midday sun crackled against the zinc roofing, and her young bare legs stung with the heat that rose up from the earthen floor. One minute she had been helping Prophet Moses to sort out the gifts which his followers had brought, the next she was lying on her back with the Prophet's bushy beard looming above her. He pulled at her skirt, urgently fumbling with the safety pin, and explained that the sacrifice of her virginity was necessary to their successful exodus into the promised land of Hebron. She helped him with the pin. She felt lapped in the warm still air and casually acquiescent. But she was too much in awe of the Prophet to look at him. She kept her eyes fixed on the roof, on the pencils of light which pierced through holes in the zinc sheets and played hide-and-seek in his matted hair. From the yard came the sharp smell of fish being fried. Miss Gatha knocked on the door and shook it violently. But Prophet Moses had locked the door when they entered, had snapped the padlock shut. Miss Gatha knocked again. The Prophet did not cease the rhythmic rise and fall of his body against hers, but called out that he was praying for the soul of a young Sister and could not be interrupted. Later on, when they came out, he compelled his wife to ask forgiveness of himself and Sue for unworthy suspicions and evil thoughts…

Brother Zacky smothered a yawn and wished that Miss Gatha would hurry up and say what she had to say. He longed to get back to the plot of land which he was ploughing with the new wooden plough he had made. He liked, more than anything else, to turn over the dark red earth, to feel it in his hand during the cool of the morning when it was still moist and firm. Under the heat of sun the earth crumbled away, dry and brittle through his fingers.

Brother Hugh waited for Miss Gatha to explain herself. He gestured to the Elder to leave the matter to him. Fencing with Miss Gatha was his preserve, and he was adept at it. When she remained silent he decided to make the first move.

'What fault you have to find now, Miss Gatha?' he asked with elaborate tolerance.

'You have eyes to see with, Brother Hugh. Why you don't open them and see?'

'See what?'

'Yes, what?' the congregation echoed.

Miss Gatha looked from one to the other of them and shook her head.

'You are foolish, the whole of you. Like sheep!' she said.

'And the sheep,' Hugh answered glibly, 'will ask their shepherd to protect them against those of us who are so ambitious for their children that they can find no peace, they can have no rest!'

'I know well whom that stone was thrown for, but the Lord can see for Himself that…'

'The Lord's tabernacle is not a market stall, Miss Gatha,' Hugh interrupted, 'and we want no stone-throwers, no word-exchangers inside it!'

'And the Lord's tabernacle is not a housetop either, but I am going to shout secrets from inside it!'

The congregation had listened with enjoyment to the familiar exchanges between the two.

'Shout out the secret, Miss Gatha, shout it!' they urged her now.

For the Elder, Obadiah, the ritual of existence was as immutable as Prophet Moses had left it when he had sealed his handiwork with the stamp of his crucifixion. Until now, the service that morning had followed a singing cadence, well known to him, running in his blood. But underneath the verbal commonplaces of Miss Gatha and Brother Hugh he sensed that a new and different element had been brought in. Something ugly and harsh, like the mood of the sun at midday when the sky is without clouds, and the hills lie green and defenceless, and the land is dotted with stunted shadows.

Obadiah stood up and bowed formally to Miss Gatha.

'Miss Gatha, we are in the house of the Lord. If you have anything to say, please to say it!'

He sat down and beckoned Brother Hugh to his seat. Miss Gatha rose and stood erect, her hands still grimly holding on to the stick in front of her.

During the past few months she had felt her hatred beginning to slip like a warm but weighty shawl from her shoulders. From time to time she was assailed not so much by compassion or understanding, as by an indifference towards the others. But whenever she summoned up the image of her son Isaac, her mind recoiled from the final obscenity of his club-foot and she felt herself rearmed. As now, when, her manner quiet but impassioned, she began:

'Elder Obadiah, Brethren and Sisters, hear my testament before the Lord!'

A shiver ran through the congregation. From amused spectators, they had become the accused. Miss Gatha was the prosecutor, and behind her the awful visage of God the Judge menaced their confidence. Brother Hugh's wife, Gloria, a young girl whom everyone called Sister Gee, shifted her eyes away from Miss Gatha. But when she looked outside at the sky, a remnant of mist shot through with the first splinter of light was like the hair of God; and the blue of His eye was cold and hard like ice. Sister Gee covered her face with her hands. Hugh noticed the gesture. He inclined his head and said gravely:

'We are hearing, Miss Gatha!'

The congregation were now the Judge and not the accused. Sister Gee took her hands away from her face. Outside, God's hair floated away on the wind and His eyes were benign.

In the corner of the church behind Miss Gatha, a spider had built its web. The grey diaphanous threads almost touched her black headkerchief. She was a tall woman when she drew herself to her full height. No one in the congregation quite remembered when she started carrying a stick, crouching over it as if to concentrate the integrity of her purpose. All they knew was that this stern, spare woman who hovered behind Prophet Moses, had, at some time after his death, emerged from her anonymity, stamped herself upon their consciousness. Whilst her husband was alive she had been something of a spectre at a feast, someone whose inability to laugh made them uneasy. But they had taken no more positive notice of her than a man takes of his shadow. Then all at once she was there, enforcing respect. They were afraid of her; she reminded them of something lacking in themselves. They listened with reserve as she testified, her eyes closed.

'Thou knowest, O Lord, that it was not envy or

vainglorious ambition that caused me to work hard and sweat much, sleep little and eat less, so that I could send my son Isaac to school in Cockpit Centre, from whence he won scholarship to the teacher's training college up in Kingston and from there will return in December, able to read and write and figure as his father Moses could do before him, and as nobody else in the whole of Hebron is able to do…'

Hugh clasped his hands, lowered his eyes, and intoned:

'And if a people know Thy Word, O Lord, the Word of Thy Holy Book, and treasure Thy Word in the chest of their hearts, what more they should want to know?'

'What more, Brother Hugh?' the congregation agreed. They resented Miss Gatha's criticism of a handicap that seemed to them irrelevant.

Under the froth of her words and theirs, the reality of Isaac mocked Miss Gatha, making faces and gibbering like the obeahman long ago, who, cotched in a dilapidated hut next door to her hard in Cockpit Centre, haunted her respectability with red drugged eyes. She remembered a day when Isaac was about four. He played on the floor of the lean-to kitchen whilst she sweated over the wood fire, cooking. Every now and then she looked down to see if he was out of harm's way. When he gazed back at her, she saw mirrored in his eyes her own once-trusting expectation of love. As she stirred a pot of cornmeal porridge she felt Isaac's club-foot brush against her. And before she could stop herself she drew away her skirt. After that he avoided coming close to her; whenever she bathed him he fought against her touching him.

When he was ten she sent him away to school in Cockpit Centre, boarding him out, during the week, with the head teacher and his wife. At weekends and during his holidays she drove him relentlessly. Day after day, when the sun burned over Hebron and the other boys scrambled over the hills, flying kites and hunting birds with their catapults, she saw to it that he studied; and at nights he sat with his books under the light of the kerosene lamp. Across from him, Rose, Miss Gatha's adopted daughter, worked at her sewing. On those evenings when Obadiah came to visit them, he would sit at the table opposite Miss Gatha and link the communing silence between them with the odd remark. And outside, in the moonlight, the other children played and sang and bragged of the birds shot and runs scored and laughed at Isaac. But she would see to it that he had the last laugh, Miss Gatha vowed to herself…

'Lord,' she testified, 'it is written in Thy Book that an ignorant and lazy people shall perish from the face of the earth, and Solomon prayed for wisdom, yet people talk whose hand don't know enough to feel the tired land sifting away like sand. But my son is studying hard up in Kingston, studying books that will tell him how to care for the land of Hebron over which he will be Elder when he come back in December, as his father Moses was before him!'

'And Lord,' Hugh interposed, 'Thou knowest that the eldership of Hebron is not from father to son as Thy Prophet, Moses, decreed it, but from the man most worthy to the man most worthy…'

'And for a man to be a worthy Elder to Thee, O Lord, he must be pure in heart and spirit. And my son never once looked at a woman to lust after her unseemly, like the Elder Obadiah, who is now so wrapped up with his wife that after he preach Thy Word a few hours of the day, he lay down the tools of his trade, whilst the whole of Hebron fall into rack and ruin, the very church roof above us leaking, and all because the Elder can't lift up a hand to drive in a nail…'

Miss Gatha's direct attack took the Elder by surprise. He knew that Isaac was due to return in December, and Hugh had warned him that she would make her bid for the eldership soon. And he had always known how much she wanted this ultimate gift for her son. For himself alone, Obadiah would have stood down. Since his marriage, he had become content tilling his land, making additions and improvements to his house. But Hugh expected Obadiah to appoint him as his successor; and since they were small boys he and Hugh had been inseparable. Obadiah had once suggested to Miss Gatha that Isaac could be designated Elder after Hugh. But Miss Gatha had objected. She wanted to see her son fulfilled as she had never been, and now, whilst he was young.

Obadiah felt a special love towards the son of Prophet Moses. He had stood as godfather at his christening, and, as he held the child in his arms, wished that the deformed limb were of wood so that he could have reshaped it with his knife. Instead he made a small wooden horse that helped Isaac to walk; and when the child started to ask questions, it was he who first answered them. After Isaac went away to school, he became a stranger to him.

In the evenings when he visited Miss Gatha, Obadiah had tried to make contact with the boy who sat remote and absorbed in his books. He searched for questions to ask Isaac about school, about an experience which he himself had never known. The boy watched him coldly and the questions stumbled on his lips. When Miss Gatha prodded her son to answer, he spoke with cold formality that embarrassed Obadiah. His own outsized limbs seemed to him suddenly a desecration aimed at the frailty of his godson; the boy's hard intelligence made him conscious of being imprisoned in the mass of his flesh. But Isaac's rejection of others did not include Rose. When she looked up from her sewing and smiled shyly, the antagonism engendered by stumbling questions and reluctant answers would dissolve, and soon, through the window, they watched the moon slipping up from behind the trees. Then Miss Gatha ordered Rose and Isaac to bed, and she and the Elder talked about Hebron…

****

Brother Hugh was angry at Obadiah for the complacency with which he sat, not making a move to defend his eldership. He noticed also that several members of the congregation nodded their heads as they looked up at large water-stains on the roof of the church. Hugh knew how easy it was for many of the New Believers to build up a sense of grievance, to feel that they were being cheated and had cause for complaint.

'Miss Gatha,' he called out brusquely, 'it's getting late!'

She hesitated, then spoke with a new gravity.

'Lord, we all know about the singular vow of our Elder Obadiah and we all respect him for it. And I am not an unbelieving Thomas, but…'

She opened her eyes and looked out into the congregation and directly at Obadiah's wife, Rose.

Rose strained her eyes to see if she could make out the hut. It projected out on a ledge where the last stretch of track sloped steeply to the top of the hill. The light was still uncertain, and now she thought she glimpsed its bulk massed against the spirals of mist, now she wasn't sure. If she saw it, she would take it as a sign that everything would be all right; the hut was her 'guzoo', her good-luck symbol. Last year, the day after the hurricane, she had looked up to see if it was still there. When, miraculously, she had seen it still standing, she adopted it as her 'guzoo'.

As far back as she could remember the hut had been a part of her. It was Gee who, with her curiosity about everything, had first found out that Rose had been born up there. She told Rose, and one day the two children climbed up to explore the hut. Rose had lingered by the door, afraid of the waiting darkness inside. And Gee had called out to her:

'Come on. It's just a broken-down old place. Nothing to frighten anybody!'

Rose entered, and wished that Gee had not come with her. After, whenever she could escape Miss Gatha, she would run all the way up the hill and sit inside the hut, breathless with exhaustion and delight as she peered through the cracks in the side and saw bits of Hebron torn off from the whole, bits of the sky, like pieces of jagged broken glass.

A long time after, it had been raining all day. When the rain stopped, the 'penniwallies', hundreds of them, fluttered transparent wings against the lamp. Rose had felt these rain-flies thick round about her, as oppressive as the brooding presence of Miss Gatha; Isaac was away in Kingston and Obadiah hadn't come that evening to lighten the room with his smile. Rose got up as if going to bed, and instead went up to the hut and lay down on the floor. There was a hole in the roof where the thatch had fallen away. She felt the moonlight slowly filtering in on her face. Coming down later that night she met Obadiah. He walked with her down past the massed grove of mango trees, past Aunt Kate's house and the church. When they came to the square, he stopped, turned to her and said:

'Tomorrow evening I will come and tell Miss Gatha.'

'Yes,' she had said...

The congregation stared with insistence at Rose. She looked around, met Miss Gatha's eyes and felt trapped, at bay.

'I am not a young woman any more,' Miss Gatha said, her tone almost elegiac, 'and my eyesight is a little dim. But I have the instinct of my years with me, and this instinct can see down through the apron, down through the loose frock, down through the chemise to ask...'

She paused, and the curiosity of the congregation blazed up like fire through a heap of cane trash. And a flash of intuition came upon Sister Sue like a black cloud muddying the face of the day.

'To ask what?' she cried out.

'To ask our Elder that if he didn't know his wife Sister Rose, who was it that knew her then? If the child she is bearing now isn't his, whose is it? If he didn't break his vow, whom did his wife commit adultery with?'

The Elder heard the mutterings of the congregation breaking like waves of sound against the anger that started in his belly, pulled him to his feet.

'Quiet!' he shouted.

They were silent. They had never heard him speak like that before. He turned to Miss Gatha and searched her face, trying to fathom the madness that had taken possession of her. For this could only be 'pocomania', the little madness which used to seize his mother when the drums beat their frenzies into her limbs and her eyes became fixed and staring and she was lost to him. Obadiah sought for familiar words that might bring Miss Gatha back to herself, in the same way that as a child he had drawn his mother out of her terrible fits by whimpering with hunger:

'Miss Gatha,' he said, 'this is a serious charge. You are accusing me as Elder of breaking the vow in which the whole of Hebron is involved. Now we all very well know that Hebron was founded on the Word of God, the Word that He gave to Prophet Moses. So if, as you charge, I broke the Word that Hebron, through me, gave to the Lord, how are we to expect the Lord to keep the Word that He gave to us?'

'Let the Lord judge for Himself of that!' Miss Gatha retorted. 'Put the matter to the proof!'

'The proof?'

'Yes. Let Sister Rose come out in front of us and let Sister Ann who birth our sons make a judgment between you and me!'

He would give her another chance, Obadiah decided.

'Miss Gatha,' he warned gravely, 'I have known you a long time now and we have had our differences. But you are widow to Prophet Moses and I have great respect for you. I want to remind you that the punishment for false witnesses is a heavy one. Are you still going to stand by your accusation?'

Miss Gatha nodded. Obadiah turned to Rose and called her gently:

'Sister Rose, please come up here. We all know that you are a modest woman, but please to come!'

Rose got up. Sister Gee, who sat beside her, pressed back on the bench to let her pass. She stepped out into the aisle and walked up to the dais. She climbed up carefully and stood facing the door of the church, from where she could see, outlined between the torches, the dark-green sweep of the hills.

The Elder bowed to Sister Ann and said:

'Sister Ann, will you, too, please to come?'

Ann stood up and edged slowly behind Obadiah and Hugh, keeping her face to the congregation. That morning she had felt the hem of her frock catch on a nail. Now she was sure that it was all ripped out; she felt a heavy dragging weight against the back of her legs. She stepped out in front of Sue. It wouldn't matter if Sue saw the unravelled hem, but not the others, not the men. She felt Sue's whole body shivering as though with ague. Something bad was sure to happen, Ann thought. It was always a sign when Sue shivered like that; their mother used to say that it was because Sue was born with a veil over her face.

'Sister Ann,' the Elder said, 'please to take off Sister Rose's apron!'

Ann's fingers found the knot of the blue chambray apron. She leaned over and started to undo it. She was always happy once she started to do something. Then she became a person, someone definite by reason of doing this act, and not a mass of fears crumbling away in all directions. She loosened the knot and swept the enveloping apron from around Rose and unto her arm. She looked to the Elder for her further instructions. She saw the expression on his face and looked down at Rose. The apron dropped from her arm and she backed away. Now that she had moved, the congregation saw the clear rising of Rose's stomach under her loose blue cotton frock.

In the silence that followed, the bubble of the morning's celebrations was shattered and the fragments went spinning away like the mist in the morning light.

2. *The Curse*

The sun lipped with fire the peaks that fenced in Hebron. Above the church a vulture specked the blue sky. He wheeled and soared, flapping his wings with quick, powerful thrusts. As he flew over the square, clumps of bamboo and tall ferns stirred in a gently rising wind. He dived, and the black shadow of his wings hovered for a moment over them. Then he disappeared. And inside the church, the congregation looked to their Elder for an answer.

What was this all about, Obadiah asked himself. What was he doing up here at all, all these years, far away from the safety of Cockpit Centre, with its stinking narrow streets, the concrete sidewalk burning his feet, the gutters rushing with dirty water, mango seeds, banana skins, orange peel…? At nights the street-lamps cast arcs of murky light on the shops, the houses, the churches, the shacks crowded together in grey slums, the bunched figures sleeping on the pavement, on benches, in the park, but huddled together, secure in their acceptance of the ordinariness of hunger, poverty, and defeat. What were they all doing up there, they who called themselves the New Believers, shut in amidst these arid, thorny, almost inaccessible hills, straining for the embrace of God; cut off like a lost and ownerless kite that trails forlornly through clouds, drifts down and is impaled on thorns, to remain there, torn and ragged, its gay colours fading away, day by day, under the harsh sun?

Obadiah turned to Hugh, wanting as always to gain assurance from his certitude. But Hugh's eyes asked him the same question as the others, imprisoned him more securely in the improbable reality in which they were all enmeshed.

Hugh thought angrily of the day before when he had sat with Obadiah at his house. Together they had planned the order of celebrations. Rose had sat quiet, listening to them. And like a fool he had arranged the celebrations not suspecting a thing. Neither Rose nor Obadiah had even hinted to him that the vow had been broken. They had played right into Miss Gatha's hand. Now she would demand the eldership for her son, and what chance would he, Hugh, have? Not a chance. For he was involved with Obadiah, had saved the eldership for him last year by thinking up the big gesture of the vow. And now the broken vow would rebound to his discredit, unless he showed clearly that he was not a party to the deception, that he was as innocent as the rest of the congregation. He stood up and folded his arms across his chest.

'Elder Obadiah,' he said accusingly, 'we are waiting for an answer. For it is written in the Laws of the Lord, the Book of Proverbs, chapter twenty-five, verse two: "It is the glory of God to conceal a thing: but the honour of kings to search out a matter!"'

'To search out a matter, Amen!' the congregation agreed. Hugh sat down, looked away from Obadiah and waited.

Miss Gatha nodded her head grimly. Hugh's betrayal of his friend was only what she expected. Like a rat, he always left a sinking ship. Once Obadiah was finished it would be easy to deal with Hugh. For Isaac was the son of Moses, and Hugh, unlike Obadiah, had not been named by Moses as in line of succession to the eldership. Yes, Obadiah had named him, but once discredited, his word would carry little weight. But she would have to be on the alert. Hugh was clever. And one thing about him: like Isaac, he would never throw away his chances for a woman's sake.

****

Obadiah felt a separateness from the others. And when he turned to Rose the distances between her life and his were even greater. His shock, bewilderment, and frustration burst out at her. He drew himself up like an Old Testament prophet, and abjured her:

'Sister Rose Brown, as your Elder I charge you to speak out now. From the last day of September last year, did I your husband have carnal knowledge of you? Answer!'

Rose looked away from the hills and the morning. She wanted to reply to Obadiah, to try to explain. But when she saw the hard mouth and violent eyes that demanded answers from her, her mind became a wide and empty space. She had grown up in the midst of long silences, and words came with difficulty to her. Miss Gatha had never told her how to do things, only shown her. When she and Isaac played as children they played in silence. Even when they had fought over the possession of a stone or a flower or a kite, they had bottled up their words in the fury of their blows. After she had married Obadiah his gentleness had broken into her quiet, caused words to be released inside her like a flight of sparrows. But the man who thundered at her now was no longer Obadiah, but a stranger. She stared back at him without recognition.

It came to Obadiah that he was alone, and from a great height was looking down on the others. Below, Hebron was a vast bowl flooded with light, against which the houses, the trees, the church, the animals, the people, were silhouetted shapes, clapping their hands, stamping their feet. In the centre, two giant fighting cocks faced each other. Their blood-red crests were reflected in their fierce eyes. They circled each other, their crops sweeping up flurries of dust. Then they sprang at each other, tearing away tufts of black feathers, gleaming strips of flesh. Drops of blood beaded the ground, changed into grains of corn; and the houses, the trees, the church, the animals, the people, were all fat clucking hens who pecked at the corn, swallowing rapidly, their eyes incurious. In their midst, one of the cocks, his feathers plastered with dust and blood, lay on the ground. Above him hovered the victor. Obadiah peered closely, wanting to see the triumphant expression in his eyes. He saw the victorious outline of the body, the wings half-folded like banners against the sky. But the head kept disappearing in a white light that calcined the valley and knifed into his eyes…

Obadiah walked towards Rose and asked her urgently:

'The man, who was the man that took my place? Answer!' Then he turned and looked from Brother to Brother.

'Or let the man answer for you, let the man answer!' The men smiled sheepishly and looked away from one another.

From where she was still standing on the dais, Sister Ann felt the strangeness that was in Obadiah spread out and widen and catch her up. His insistence pressed against her like the wind. She looked at the blank faces of the Brethren, hated what to her seemed the hint of furtive indecency in their eyes.

'Which one of you did it, Brothers?' she cried out hysterically. 'Which one?'

The women's faces were hard as they scrutinized the men. Then they all turned to look at the back of the church where Obadiah gazed fixedly. The Elder was looking at Brother Ananias. He was a young Brother, about twenty-one; the beginnings of a beard edged his chin. On Saturday evenings when the men gathered to swap stories, or during the week when they stood watching the young girls going to the spring, their upraised arms tightening their breasts, it was always Ananias who was ready with the apt remark. But as the Elder's glance seemed to accuse him now he fidgeted on his seat, then shouted:

'Answer, Sister Rose. Don't let suspicion fall on all of us!'

They took up his cry, men and women alike, the men anxious for themselves, the women for their men, all of them anxious at the thought of this trouble which was threatening Hebron.

'Answer, Sister Rose, answer!' they demanded.

The voices crowding in on her, Obadiah's hot breath on her face, filled Rose with a sense of oppression, reminded her of those times in her childhood when Miss Gatha, punishing her for some task that she had done badly, would lock her up in the small narrow room that backed on to the house. The room used to be Prophet Moses's 'Communing room', the place where he talked with God. There was no window, only the one door. Obadiah's face leaning nearer and nearer towards her now was the door closing, shutting out the last finger of light. And she was alone with him now, alone with this stranger whose spittle stung her cheeks as he spat words at her:

'Answer me. You don't hear me talking to you? Look at me! If you could look at me clear all these months, why you can't look at me now? You see something in my eye? Is murder you see in my eye?'

He had taken her with him last Easter to Cockpit Centre, had parked the cart on a lane and left her there waiting for him. About her the brawling voices were sharp in the sunlight, the cries of street-venders hawking ice and charcoal, yellow-yam, and sweet potatoes. Then came the sudden quiet and the shadow of a man flung across the dirt track as he stalked along, one hand swinging free, the other with his machete held at the ready, sunbeams rippling off the sharpened edge. Drops of sweat blinded his eyes as he searched for someone, anyone, on whom to wreak vengeance for the heat and the foul-smelling latrines, for another job not to be found, another woman nagging at him, another unwanted child born to him, another mouth to feed, another shilling lost gambling, another chance gone; another slight put upon him because he was black and therefore ugly, poor and therefore shiftless, hungry and therefore wanting too much, proud and therefore getting above himself, his station, ignorant and therefore stupid, illiterate and therefore savage. Drunk with hate, his merino vest stained and pitted with ragged holes on back and chest, he grasped his machete and dreamt to shatter the image that had been made of him, to cast the terror of his shadow as far as the furthest point of morning. And a whisper ran through the lane like lightening.

'Look out, that man have murder in his eye!'

Rose had seen people running for cover, had stretched out on the floor of the cart, and through its slatted sides, glimpsed the others peering out from the safety of closed doors at this one of them as he stood alone under the wide, indifferent sky, brandishing his machete at the sun...

Now she saw the fingers of Obadiah's hands like bars in front of her face, and stared at him hypnotized, as she had done at the flourishes of a machete against the sun. She felt his hands close in on her neck, felt herself being forced down into darkness.

Brother Hugh sprang to his feet, knocking over the stool in his haste. The clatter jolted the congregation out of its trance.

'No!' they shouted.

With the help of Brother Lazarus, Hugh pulled Obadiah away, forced him to sit down. Rose slipped, dazed, to the floor. Sister Sue leaned over and fanned her with her apron. Sister Ann sidled back to her place, distraught at the violence which had brushed so close to her. With his hand on Obadiah's shoulder, Lazarus made soothing gestures and murmured:

'Obadiah, man, Obs, man!'

Brother Hugh straightened his jacket, walked to the front of the dais and took control. His voice was reasoned, his manner properly grave:

'Brethren and Sisters, I think that it is plain for even the most unbelieving Thomas amongst us to see that, whatever else took place, our Elder kept his vow!'

'Plain!' they said, with emphasis. And all looked at Miss Gatha.

'And as for what happened just now,' Brother Hugh continued, 'well...Obadiah Brown is our Elder, but he is also a man like us, and we all know how we would feel if a shame like this fell on any one of us. So, I am asking you all to kneel quiet in your places, join with me in silent prayer, and ask the Lord to fortify the spirit of the man Obadiah, so that as Elder he can do the hard duty that it is written in the Book of Books for him to do.'

'Amen!'

They knelt and bowed their heads. Some began to pray in loud, ardent voices. Brother Hugh checked them as he knelt with impressive humility:

'I said *silent* prayer, Brothers and Sisters!'

Miss Gatha did not kneel. She refused to take part in this farce. For her the whole scene that had just been enacted was nothing more nor less than Obadiah's unconscious imitation of her husband Moses; unconscious, because it had paralleled, more closely than any planning could have done, the sweep and urgency with which Moses had told his most barefaced lies. Time after time he had persuaded her to believe him against the evidence of her own eyes, her own instincts. And after he had done it often enough, she became impervious; even the magnitude of the deception implied in his crucifixion had not fooled her. So now she wasn't going to be taken in by Obadiah. She was certain that he had broken his vow. But she would allow Hugh to have his little say. She could wait.

Aunt Kate did not kneel either. She clasped her hands together when she saw the others doing so, but her eyes were wide open, brimming over with the suppressed laughter of a private joke.

As she knelt, Sister Sue could feel Rose's body trembling beside her. She stretched out her hand and patted her shoulder until the trembling ceased.

Sister Gee nudged her friend Eufemia who had moved up into Rose's vacant place and now knelt beside her. With her clasped hands hiding her mouth, Gee whispered rapidly:

'You know, I think I see the whole thing clear. You remember how Elder Obadiah took Rose with him to Cockpit Centre last Easter when he went to buy the watch that we were to give to Isaac as a going-away present when he went back up to Kingston, and you remember that he was to send back Rose to carry up the watch as he had to stay overnight to collect the new axle for the cart, you remember?'

Sister Eufemia nodded.

'Well, I did promise Rose to come and meet her and I went part-way down the road and waited by the plantain patch, and I wait and I wait and downside the hill I could see the road and the rockstone shining on it, but no Sister Rose…'

'No Sister Rose?' Eufemia asked.

'No Sister Rose. All the wait I waited. Then the moon pushed herself behind a black cloud, moonlight jumped off the road and I could hear ghosts breathing out fire and smoke and my heart did catch up in my mouth…'

'So you did run?'

'I did run. Then I stopped. For after, the moon came out and my heart did settle down and I looked down the hill again but still not a sign of her…'

'Not a sign?'

'Not a sign!'

'So then that was when, you think, that…?'

'Yes. And you don't see? The whole things must have happened down in Cockpit Centre…'

'So then it must have been…?'

Sister Gee nodded her head emphatically.

'Yes. A stranger. And not any of the Brethren!'

'I asked you to pray and not to gossip, Sisters,' Hugh said sternly as he rose from his knees.

****

Obadiah sat in his high-backed chair like a god of stone. He would have to wake him up to the urgency of the situation, Hugh thought, force him to perform the rites which would have to be done if he were to remain as Elder.

'Brothers and Sisters,' Hugh addressed the congregation, 'please to sit back on your seats and pay all attention. For what our Elder is about to do now is no ordinary matter. What our Elder is about to do now is a serious thing!'

'Amen!' they confirmed.

He walked back to the Elder's chair, bowed low, and said slowly and with emphasis:

'And the first thing you are going to do, Elder, is to curse the adulterer whomsoever he may be, as the Lord hath commanded it in the Book of Deuteronomy, chapter twenty-seven, verse twenty-four. And it begins...'

'I know, I know,' Obadiah said almost testily. He stood up and walked to the edge of the dais. He looked carefully at the faces before him, men and women indiscriminately, studied them as if he had never seen them before.

'Cursed be he that smiteth his neighbor secretly,' he recited, 'and all the people shall say Amen!'

Their Amen was uncertain, hesitant. The casual cruelty with which he pronounced the curse indicated a new indifference towards them, towards Hebron. And he continued in the same odd manner. He turned to Hugh and spoke with irreverent briskness:

'All right, Brother Hugh, so much for the adulterer. Now for the adulteress, what is the text on her?'

'Two texts on that, Elder,' Hugh said, flustered, 'and the first is in relation to the man who is husband to the adulteress. The Book is Deuteronomy, the chapter is twenty-four, and it says: "When a man hath taken a wife, and married her, and it come to pass that she find no favour in his eyes, because he hath found some uncleanness in her: then let him write her a bill of divorcement, and give *it* in her hand, and send her out of his house." And the second one...'

'No, Hugh, let's finish with the first one,' Obadiah interrupted. 'Pass me the piece of paper that is marking the middle of the Bible!'

Brother Hugh went across to the table with quick, apprehensive steps. He didn't like the way that Obadiah was conducting the business, didn't like the large tolerance with which Obadiah was regarding him, the congregation. Something was wrong. The best thing was to get the service over and done with as soon as possible, before Miss Gatha could interfere. He opened the Bible, a large one with solid black covers. He drew out a sheet of writing paper, fine and white but yellowed at the edges. He placed the paper on top of the Bible and held it out to Obadiah, emphasizing the sense of occasion, of ceremony.

Obadiah took a stub of blue pencil from his right-hand trouser pocket. The point was blunt. It was the pencil which he used for his carpentering. He licked the point and very deliberately drew an X on the paper.

'All right, Hugh,' he ordered, 'put the Bible on the table, pass the paper to the adulteress and give me the second text.'

Brother Hugh held out the paper towards Rose without looking at her. He was angry. Why should Obadiah order him about as if he were a menial? What did Obadiah have to be so lofty about? His wife had deceived him, brought the eldership into jeopardy. And wasn't it he, Hugh, who had had to take command, plan the ritual, as he had done last year when he had thought up the vow? And last year it had been because of Rose, too, that Obadiah's position had been threatened. What Miss Gatha said had some justification. Since he had married a young girl, made a fool of himself over her, Obadiah had come to care less about the eldership, about Hebron. And there was no fool like an old fool. Obadiah couldn't say that he hadn't warned him. He had warned him long ago, year after year when Obadiah had kept himself chaste, claiming that it was only through self-enforced chastity that he would be able to measure up to the vision for which Prophet Moses had crucified himself; and year after year, Hugh had argued that such chastity was not necessary, that it was only a suggestion implanted in him by Miss Gatha who was thus trying to bind him to her, to avenge herself on the memory of Prophet Moses, who had himself been a most lusty stallion. Once, Hugh had instigated Sister Beatrice, who was a widow and well versed in these matters, to visit Obadiah. And when even that failed, he had prophesied to Obadiah that if he kept to his continence, he would be sure, one day, to make a fool of himself, and create a scandal. True enough, this had happened, and Obadiah had caught up Hugh in his folly, made him marry the young and useless Sister Gee who was Rose's playmate, instead of Sister Beatrice, his companion of many years who was ready and willing and regarded him with a due reverence…

Brother Hugh bent over and shook the paper under Rose's bent head. She had drawn herself up and now sat on the floor, her legs crossed under her. Her black hair, coarse and alive, had come loose, and she felt it around her like the tangled wilderness above her hut. It was as though she were shut away there now in the dense undergrowth. There would be 'cirasee' vines with dark-green pointed leaves and golden fruit, which, when dried, exploded small red seeds; pale yellow tendrils of the 'lovebush' wrapping themselves around the prickly arms of the cactus. You could cut open one of the thick leaves of the cactus, she thought, could scrape out the soft flesh and wash your hair with it until it was as smooth as silk…

'Sister Rose Brown!' Hugh called querulously.

Obadiah's voice cut across his.

'Put the paper down beside her, Hugh, and give me the second text!'

Hugh placed the paper on the floor of the dais, straightened up, and said:

'The second text in relation of the Elder to the adulteress is to be found in Psalms, chapter one, and reads: "…the ungodly shall not stand in the judgment, nor sinners in the congregation of the righteous!"'

'Amen!' they said, with diffidence.

'Say *Amen* louder, say it!' Obadiah ordered them.

They obeyed. He nodded, satisfied, then hooked his thumbs under the lapel of his jacket, and looking from one to the other of the congregation, chanted:

'Sister Rose Brown, from henceforth we exclude you from this holy congregation, we cast you out from amongst us!'

'Amen!'

This time their voices were dutifully fervent. They had

already sensed a need to be careful with their Elder as if they were dealing with a madman.

So this was how Hugh was going to resolve it, Miss Gatha thought, put the blame on Rose, say that she had committed adultery. But she knew better than that. She had brought up Rose, since Moses had ordered her to take charge of the child. And she had done her duty by her. Knowing the sin and shame in which the child had come into the world, she had been extra careful to bring her up ringed about with the fear of God. As she had brought up Isaac and even more so. She had never liked Rose. But she knew her inside out. As well as she knew her son. Rose was stubbornly loyal. She would never have gone with another man. But Obadiah was like Moses. Like all men, except her son. Once their eyes caught fire for a woman, they could never restrain themselves. With Obadiah it had taken longer, but once awakened he was the same, in the end. But since that was the way Hugh wanted it, she would play the game his way.

'And the third text, Brother Hugh,' she intervened mildly, 'what about that?'

'Which text, Miss Gatha?' he hedged.

'Brother Hugh, you know your Bible and I know it too. So I ask you now, what of the curse ordained for the adulterous wife as written in the Book of Numbers, chapter five?'

'Which verse?' he asked slyly.

'Brother Hugh, you claim yourself to be the Chief Recorder of Hebron and to carry in your head all the Laws of the Lord that are written down in the Bible, chapter and verse. Now if you can't remember them, then it is time that you give way to someone else who can!'

She struck at the heart of his vanity. From boyhood his memory had been phenomenal. Everyone knew that.

'You mean verse twenty-one?' he asked, belligerent.

'The very same one!' she said.

****

Sister Sue sensed that this curse would be different, would be the presage, the sign, would be the headstone that she always saw clearly in her dreams, a headstone on a grave, in which were buried carnival and careless laughing, eating and drinking and making merry; a headstone that was the mask on the face of a 'junkonoo' dancer, striped black and white with slits for eyes and huge white teeth, foreshadowing terrible days of expiation, of mourning.

'Brother Hugh,' she asked, 'you don't think that we have enough cursing for one day?'

She had expressed what they all felt. The congregation had marked Hugh's hesitation, had understood that this curse was one of those which imprinted with power the thin white pages of the Bible; one of those that were hinted at but never talked out aloud since they were the thunderbolts that God hurled at the Devil, the magic web of words with which He vanquished evil spirits venturing too close to the ramparts of Heaven.

'Enough cursing, enough!' they pleaded.

Miss Gatha ignored the congregation and looked directly at Hugh.

'Brother Hugh, you know, I know, we all know that when a sin commit in the camp of the Lord, we have to do what the Lord command us to. And if not, then we all take part in the sin and the curse instead will fall on the whole of Hebron, on our children, on our children's children!'

Outside, clouds shrouded the morning sky. The fearful congregation saw this as an omen. The rough Cross on the wall, even the big Bible on the table before them, were not enough to secure them from the fear of retribution that lurked in their hearts. Their faces became overcast and apprehensive. Brother Hugh turned to Obadiah:

'Elder,' he said hesitantly, 'there is a third text in relation to the adulteress, and it begins, "The Lord make thee…"'

'Oh that one,' Obadiah said, and continued, 'Rose Brown, the Lord make thee a…'

He broke off as Sister Sue cried out shrilly:

'No, Elder, don't curse that curse. Have mercy!'

That started them off; the women first, and then the men, repeating 'mercy, mercy'. And as they chanted, their eyes half-closed, their bodies swaying, they forgot the church, the occasion, the very reason for their fear. In the back row Sister Beatrice, a middle-aged Sister, heaved to her feet. Her eyelids were puffed and heavy, her face glistened with sweat, and her pendulous breasts shook as she cried out:

'No, Elder, don't curse that curse, don't curse it, you hear me. For if a curse like that against you, even the wind scared to blow on you, grass spring away from you, water curl off your back like oil and fire flare flame away from you. Elder, don't curse that curse!'

'Don't curse that curse!' they begged.

Sister Beatrice had an unerring flair for the limelight and always seized whatever opportunity presented itself. Besides, long ago, down in Cockpit Centre, and before the exodus, she used to be an acolyte priestess in the Pocomania rituals. And somehow she always felt that the services in Hebron lacked a certain exaltation; that it wasn't the same when you didn't 'get the spirit', feel your body light and easy under you, your head whirling with words spoken by 'unknown tongues'; when all eyes were on you and there was fire and ice in your blood and you were as powerful with knowledge as the angels themselves.

'If a curse like that curse against you,' she continued, her voice barely a whisper, 'you walking in the valley of the shadow of death but even death afraid to touch you. No, Elder, don't curse that curse, our ears can't bear to hear it!'

'Can't bear to hear it, Elder!' they moaned.

Miss Gatha's voice jolted them from their ecstasy.

'And our backs, and our children's backs, they can bear it?'

****

Obadiah stood like a sleepwalker staring at Rose as if he had only just remembered her presence. He could see the dark-brown scar on her ankle where she had torn it open on a nail, playing as a child. She looked down at the floor, and from the angle that he looked at her, her face with the slanted Chinese eyes and high cheekbones was all soft lines and indents. He wondered what she was doing, sitting on the floor of the dais. A blankness settled on his mind and he couldn't remember a thing that had gone before.

Miss Gatha rose from her seat, one hand resting on her stick, the other clenched. The congregation now looked to her for a lead. She was standing up to defend them, to defend their children. She had reminded them once more that they had no choice in the matter, that a sin had been committed and the punishment must fall either on the sinners or on themselves. They were at one with her as she called out to the Elder:

'Obadiah Brown, either you are the Elder of the Church of the New Believers of Hebron who live by God's Law and cannot diminish one jot nor one tittle from it, or you are a man who don't have to take a vow, don't have to live by law, a man who can full up yourself in the imagination of your heart with the evil that you are charging up with now!'

He was looking at Rose as he had looked at her that night when he had come early to visit them, and Rose was out in the kitchen. As he entered the door he had said to her gravely:

'Miss Gatha, if you could hear me for a little while I would like to talk to you about a serious matter that I have been meaning to talk to you about for some time now!'

She had steadied herself and feigned an expression of surprise. She knew what he was about to ask her. Everyone in Hebron had begun to expect that one day he would ask her to marry him. They had even made up a snatch of a song to the effect that Elder Obadiah was going to inherit not only Prophet Moses's Hebron, but his widow as well. Instead, he had asked her for Rose's hand. Her pride had fought and won and she had not given herself away. She even managed to consent in firm, measured tones. But then she noticed that Obadiah was gazing beyond her shoulder and there was a foolish look on his face. Rose had come in from the kitchen and he was staring at her as he stared at her now, in full view of the others, his face naked, in the open church. She attacked him, her voice rough with anger:

'So is what you looking at now, Obadiah, down through the loose frock, down through the chemise? At the thigh that going to rot? Is remember you are remembering the feel and the touch of it? Why you don't remember instead how you sat and talked to me about Hebron, how you pledged your life to build it up so that the black man could walk proud on his land and not know hungriness or want? But when you got meshed up in the flesh of a woman, you took a big vow to save us. And now that because of your vow, adultery done commit in the camp of the Lord (or that is what you say), you can't even curse the woman to prevent the curse falling on us, on our children, our black children!'

With the use of the word 'black' Miss Gatha had attached even more securely to herself the emotional allegiance of the New Believers. The men stamped their feet demandingly as the women called out:

'Curse Rose Brown, Elder Obadiah, curse her to save our children, our black children!'

Their voices battered at Obadiah, and when he looked at them their eyes accused him. Sister Beatrice clapped her hands in rhythm and started up a syncopated chant of 'curse her, curse her, curse her, Elder'; the others picked it up, the men drumming on the back of the benches, the women shaking their tambourines. As before, they were carried away by the pulsing rhythms, oblivious to time and place and reason. The Elder, as he listened to them, began to rock his head from side to side and his eyes became glazed. Hugh whispered to him:

'The curse, Obadiah, curse the curse!'

Behind them Sister Sue leaned over and touched Rose. Thc chanting shook the dais and Rose looked up with wide, terrified eyes. She pointed towards the door. For a moment Rose did not understand. The signs Sue made to her were like those of a deaf and dumb man to a blind one. Then Sue pushed away her long skirt and pressed back her body, making an opening between herself and Zacky, who slept with his eyes open, as Sue knew from long habit. Rose saw the open space that led to the back door of the church and understood. On hands and knees she crawled through, and only when she was out of the church did she stand up and stumble up the slope. She could hear Obadiah's voice thundering out the curse:

'Rose Brown, the Lord make thy thigh to rot, thy belly to swell. And the woman shall say Amen!'

There was silence. The congregation opened their eyes, wiped sweat from their faces, inhaled gulps of fresh air.

'And the woman shall say Amen!' Obadiah repeated.

'Amen!' Sister Beatrice called out with fervour.

An irritable note came into Obadiah's voice as he insisted:

'And the *woman* shall say Amen!'

Sunlight pierced into the church, slanting sunbeams in all directions. The spider's web in the corner was shot through with colours, and threads of dust gleamed and danced in the light. Obadiah's hair was bronzed all over, and his eyes, transparent and enormous, were pools of gold. As the congregation watched him, startled, he stretched out his hand and groped in the sudden brightness. Then he shouted in a voice hoarse with anguish:

'Say Amen, Rose, say it. Or else you don't see God going to blind me, to blind me!'

Sister Sue went across to him, put her arm about his shoulder:

'God not going to blind you, Obadiah. It's just His sun he sent to greet you.'

Obadiah saw her standing in front of him, solid, shutting out the light, and was reassured.

Brother Hugh felt tired and discouraged. He was never at his best in this atmosphere of emotional intensity. He had done his best, but somewhere, something had gone wrong. Obadiah's behaviour was more than strange. But he would have to carry on, conclude the service as quickly as possible. As he walked to the centre of the dais he glimpsed a rainbow, its colours still tenuous but clear above the hills. Hugh felt inspired. He would lift up the hearts of the congregation, remove all lingering doubts and send them away exalted. He pointed dramatically and called out:

'Elder Obadiah, Brethren, Sisters, look! Look at the arch and the sweep of it, the blue, the green, the scarlet flame, the lizard's tongue of it. It's the sign, the sign…'

'The sign!' they clamoured, eager, rejoicing.

'The sign as written in Genesis, chapter nine: "I do set my bow in the cloud, and it shall be for a token of a covenant between me and the earth. Amen!"'

'Amen hallelujah!' they exulted.

Obadiah stepped off the dais and walked down the aisle towards the front door. His shoe scuffed on a small pebble and it went flying as if imbued with his own urgency. Hugh called after him:

'Obadiah, Elder, we still have to close the service with a prayer!'

Obadiah stopped at the door and turned round. Behind his head one of the torches had burnt low and was almost extinguished.

'Not yet, Brother Hugh,' he said firmly, 'the service can't close until we hear the woman say Amen and the man, too…'

He looked from Brother to Brother, smiled at them and finished:

'When we find out is who!'

Then he went swiftly down the path leading away from the church.

3. *The Drought*

The Hills of Hebron were bare and parched under the sun. In places where the thickly-wooded slopes had been cleared, the naked earth looked like sores. The houses were stranded, dilapidated arks. Seated on their doorsteps the New Believers looked out over the dead world of Hebron and felt a strange lassitude in their limbs. They could not tame the sun. It was a distant and merciless enemy moving across a cloudless blue sky, day after day. It was the Will of God. In their plots of ground there were stunted growths of cassava and corn. The young banana shoots and the arrowing blossoms of the sugar-cane bowed their crests to the ground.

In the yards around their houses, withered pumpkin vines, flame-coloured 'ackee' pods, black in the heat, and the shriveled blossoms of the breadfruit tree, littered the earth. Only the Jerusalem candlesticks that fenced in one barren acre from the other, the cactus that grew wild all over the hills, the croton plants that lingered in a few front gardens, their shiny leaves ribbed with bright yellow, were unaffected by the drought – they sent their roots down to the secret places of the earth's heart where moisture was hidden. Up on the further reaches of the hills, the great trees allowed their branches to be raped, and hoarded life in their roots, their trunks. Beneath them the exposed coffee plants, the cocoa trees that had once drooped golden pods like rich gifts, perished. The New Believers looked out on a skeletal world, etched in muted browns and beaten down, subdued, under the conqueror sun.

In the square the shadows under the trees were long and

stark. It was nearing ten o'clock and silence held sway. The spring was dry. In the sediment of mud that remained at the bottom, a few tadpoles darted about. On the slope above the spring a dead frog lay on its back, its mottled belly like cured leather. Beside him a banana tree trailed its leaves like defeated banners; and the gashes in the leaves striped the shadow cast by the trunk with slivers of light that gleamed like pools of water.

Sister Eufemia stood near the spring, leaning against a cotton-tree stump. She held an empty petrol can (a kerosene tin, as the Hebronites called it) under her arm. She was of average height, pleasantly rounded, with a coffee-coloured skin and pale hazel eyes, the result of recessive genes left by some anonymous white ancestor. She could relax so completely it was as though the sun had dissolved her bones. She was waiting for Sister Gee. That morning the distance between her house and the spring had seemed to multiply itself and she felt tired. She wiped the sweat from her face with her apron, and shifted her position. Years of malnutrition made her movements indolent, like a sluggish river. As she raised her left foot to prop it behind her, she gave a startled jerk. Her foot had caught in a hollow concealed under the tangle of vines that covered the stump. She eased it out, stuck her finger in her mouth. Then she settled back to wait. She had been in the shade long enough to forget how hot the sun was, and she began to sing:

June and July is a dry, dry hard time,
But drought in November, Lord, Massa
A-sweat out me substance…

Gee rounded the bend. She was balancing the empty tin on her head, swaying as she walked. She had a small face with a pointed chin, a long neck set well back on her shoulders, and high young breasts. But her hips were wide, her legs thick and sturdy. She had not really come for water. She knew there was none. But meeting Eufemia at the spring, talking with her, was a habit. Besides, there was nothing else to do. She lowered her water tin, took up a bamboo pole and stuck it into the spring, stirring up mud and tadpoles.

'Not a drop, eh?' Eufemia called out to her.

'Not a drop!'

Gee flung away the pole, up-ended her tin and sat, resting her elbows on her knees and propping her face in her hands. Eufemia came across to her.

'I dipped the pole down too, but it was the same as yesterday, the same as the day before!'

'Same like the day before that and the day before that, eh?'

'Same way so!' Eufemia affirmed. She seated herself in the same position as her friend.

A gust of wind sent the dry leaves spinning in a vortex. It spent itself and the leaves subsided once more. A trail of fat red ants disappeared into the undergrowth beside the tree-stump, a living caravan taking over an abandoned world; and the two women could have been petrified beings, relics of a people who had carved into face, attitude, posture, their long history of waiting for death, a waiting people, striving for nothing, accepting all.

Sister Gee glanced at the spring and her face was suddenly sombre.

'You know,' she said, 'it seems strange not to find Aunt Kate waiting by the spring, watching whilst we dip up the water, warning us to be careful not to wake up Maverlyn!'

'Yes, it seem strange not to see her!'

Eufemia looked over her shoulder at the spot where Aunt Kate used to sit. The old woman's absence emphasized for them the sharp change that had come upon Hebron. The two girls were the new generation, born and brought up in Hebron and without memories of the town from which their parents had made a triumphant exodus. On occasions they had visited Cockpit Centre with their elders, but had seen only evil lurking at every hand, the evil that they had been told about, and that they, born in the promised land, had been spared. But they had been reared under the shadow of Prophet Moses's sacrifice, his crucifixion. And they were still young enough to reject unconsciously, the constant worship of a wooden Cross and of death.

Aunt Kate's fantasy that her child was still alive, that she was only sleeping, touched a responsive chord in them. Her mad hope had become theirs. Some mornings, standing around her as she sat and cradled her arms, they had almost been persuaded that they could see, glancing on the surface of the water, her child Maverlyn, like some spirit celebrating the eternal life that their youth expected and demanded. And now the spring had dried up. They, as well as Aunt Kate, had been forced into accepting that Maverlyn was drowned and a long time buried, that Maverlyn was dead.

'I went up to see her last night,' Eufemia said. 'But Sister Ann wouldn't let me in. You know how fussy she is. But from the doorway I could hear poor Aunt Kate talking and laughing to herself and burning up with the fever!'

'Till my dying day,' Gee said, 'I am not going to forget Aunt Kate's face that day when the sun dry up the last sheet of water from the bottom of the spring and she was looking and looking and in no part of it she could find Maverlyn. Till my dying day I am not going to forget Aunt Kate's face that day!'

'Me neither,' Eufemia agreed. Then she yawned, hugged herself and said:

'I hope the meeting today is not another prayer-for-rain one. I can't see what purpose they are serving!'

'This is not a prayer-for-rain meeting, I can tell you that!'

'Then what sort of meeting it is then?'

'Hugh say that I am not tell anybody. Only the Senior Brothers and Sisters are to know about it.'

'Well, I will soon know, anyway!'

'Wait until you know, then!'

'Cho, you don't know any more than I know myself,' Eufemia taunted.

Gee bent close to her and whispered:

'Hugh arranged with the others to ask Miss Gatha to take over as Elder.'

'But what about…Elder Obadiah?'

'What about him?' Gee's voice was hard.

'Well…' Eufemia explained hesitantly, 'Brother Hugh… going to throw over his long-time friend like that?

'What you mean throw over? Don't Hugh have the all of us to consider?'

'Yes, I know, but…'

'But what?'

'Nothing, nothing!'

Eufemia's disclaimer had been too hasty, and Gee frowned. Eufemia tried to apologize:

'Gee, I wasn't saying anything against brother Hugh, you know…'

'I didn't say you were saying anything against him!' Gee snapped at her.

With Eufemia, Gee was always very touchy on the subject of Hugh. She never forgot the incredulity with which her friend received her disclosure that brother Hugh, Chief Recorder of the Church of the New Believers of Hebron, had asked her to marry him on the same day that the Elder Obadiah was to marry Rose.

'But Gee, Brother Hugh…is…old!' Eufemia had protested.

'Then what about Obadiah and Rose?' she herself had argued.

'That is different!'

'And why it should be different? Rose is only a little bit older than me! Why it should be different?'

'I don't know, but…'

And Eufemia had left it at that, with the 'but' remaining like a wasp's sting in Gee's memory. At the wedding, too, Eufemia, who was only her bridesmaid, had enjoyed the ceremony more than she, the bride; had laughed and talked with Brother Ananias whom she had not even dared to look at before when Gee was around. Even when, after the months had passed, the two made up their differences and once again met at the spring to gossip, or wandered over Hebron, their bare arms linked and nuzzling against each other as they told their 'secrets', even then Gee had felt cheated. Eufemia had so much more to tell about what took place between herself and Ananias. Instead, she had to embroider details to elaborate the brief ritual which, every Friday, Hugh performed with her in bed, without ever seeming to pause in his endless talk about his plans for the greater glory of himself, of Obadiah, and of Hebron; and leaving her wondering if this was all that there was to it...

Gee got up abruptly and left her water-tin by the tree-stump. Eufemia hesitated, then followed suit. They walked up to the church in silence.

****

Miss Gatha sat in her corner, alone on the dais. It was mid-morning, and outside the sun rampaged over the land. But there was no trace of sweat on her corrugated face and neck, and the palms of her hand felt moist and cool. Her black dress with its long sleeves enfolded her in a perpetual mourning, and even in the hard glare there were few specks of dust to be seen on the thick weave of the linen. Behind her head a spider had left a lattice-work of fine threads that sagged, broke loose, swayed to and fro, and then tangled again as the tail end of a parching wind blew into the church.

She sat erect, hands clasped over her stick. Before her, the congregation sat hunched on the benches. She knew well what they expected, had guessed it since last night when Hugh came to her house to deliver his formal invitation for her to attend church the next morning. And, on entering the church earlier on, she had confirmed her guess, for Hugh had pulled back the Elder's chair, offering it to her. But she had walked by and sat in her usual place. She noted that the Senior Brothers and Sisters had abandoned their seats on the dais and now occupied the front row of benches. Hugh also joined them. She glimpsed their anxiety, the uncertainty with which they passed their tongues over their lips, the servile expression creeping into their eyes as they prepared to abase themselves before her. She looked away from them.

Brother Hugh had planned his occasion, rehearsed it well. Now, still sitting, his voice restrained, his grief disciplined, he intoned:

'There was a rainbow, Miss Gatha, but there wasn't any cloud. Three months now and the sky still clear, still terrible, still dry! Three months now that the sky still like a bluestone wearing us down, that the sun still like a vampire leeching our blood, that the thirsty wind, blowing away from us, done blow itself to sleep under the bluestone sky, under the vampire wing of the sun! Three months now that this land, our land that was land, the lot of our inheritance, now turning itself into ashes, into dust!'

'Into ashes, into dust!' the congregation mourned.

Sister Sue continued the lamentation. But her voice was harsh rather than supplicating as she looked up at Miss Gatha, addressing her words as if to a blind and merciless God:

'The dust, our feet cover with it, Miss Gatha, our eyes dark with it, our ears blocked up with it so as not to hear our children, hungry, thirsty, crying out for more than dust!'

'More than dust!' they begged.

Brother Hugh stood up, cleared his throat.

'Miss Gatha,' he said with due deference, 'you hear our case, you see our plight. All these years you have looked in trouble's face often and know it well. It's only you can help!'

'Only you, Miss Gatha!'

She wanted to resist making them crawl, for their display of servility demeaned something in herself too. But, although she already knew that there was no limit to their cravenness, she wanted to see how far they would go in their betrayal; life with her husband Moses had introduced her to all the subtle variations of treachery in the human spirit, her own as well as others. Besides, she had been too long shut away in the silences of the defeated not to spread her wings in the rare sunlight of triumph.

'Why you are asking me for help?' she asked them. 'Why you don't ask your Elder?'

'Miss Gatha, you know as well as we do that the Elder is sick!' Sister Sue answered with impatience.

Hugh was anxious for Miss Gatha to know that they were not in any way defending Obadiah. He added quickly:

'Yes, Miss Gatha. He now reach to a stage where he believes that it's only when we catch the adulterer that the rains will come, and the earth once more give up a sweet savour. But in the meantime, we the people of Hebron are the sufferer!'

'The sufferer!' they complained, glad to blame their misery on one particular person.

****

Sister Ann sat dazed and exhausted. She had come directly to the church from Aunt Kate's house. Her eyelids felt gritty from lack of sleep. She rubbed at them, fighting to keep awake. As a Senior Sister she must not fail to do her duty by Hebron. But she could not remember the careful phrases that Brother Hugh had worked out for her to say, nor even when she was supposed to say them. She heard Brother Hugh and the others accusing Obadiah. Then there was a pause. Could it be her turn now? She stood up and continued the accusation against the Elder with acrimony.

'And the Elder don't do one thing for us, not concerned with what happening to us, but instead spend all his time sitting up the hill on top of a big rock that overlook the old hut where Rose is hiding out now...'

She sensed that she should stop there, that she had said enough. But another train of thought started up inside her head and she could not stop herself:

'That old hut, the very same one where Rose's mother gave birth to her, and where I did see the travail with which children come forth into the light, children who born from sin…'

Sister Ann stared ahead intently. All these nights that she had sat up with Aunt Kate bathing her hot face with warm water and listening to her ravings about the past, Ann had felt her own unhappy memories stir up like dust within her. The old woman talked and talked whilst the fever burnt her up and her eyes were points of light illuminating a ravaged shrunken face. Ann's mind went back twenty years; she saw herself running down the hill, knocking on Aunt Kate's door and calling to her to come quickly. As she waited by the door she closed her eyes to shut out the darkness and the scene that she had just witnessed.

Her mother had been the midwife of Hebron then. Sue, as the elder of the two daughters, had already assisted her when she had practised down in Cockpit Centre. But this birth up in the hut on the heights of Hebron was the first one in which Ann took part. And the girl writhing on the bed, her face oily with sweat, her lips clenched and bleeding, her black hair standing away from her head, was only fourteen, the same age as Ann herself. Ann had understood her trapped look, had started to whimper as she stood at the foot of the bed. Her mother looked at her impatiently, told her that if she couldn't be of any use she had better run and fetch Aunt Kate. When she returned with her, Ann remained outside the door. So she hadn't been in the hut when Rose was born, when Rose's mother died. But she had heard the screams…

Brother Hugh looked at Sister Ann with annoyance. What was the woman rambling on about? Why didn't she say what he had told her to. Sue thought that, living alone as Ann did, she was bound to end up talking to herself as she was doing now.

'…And where Rose's mother paid her wages and died,'

Ann continued, 'and where Rose is waiting to pay hers now, and it's on top of a big rock that overlook that old hut that the Elder is sitting now, watching for the adulterer, whilst the sun sucking through his skull and at night the moonlight turn his hair into ashes and his eyes jutting out wild...'

Ann broke off as suddenly as she had begun. She sat down feeling foolish, agonized at the thought that she had made a spectacle of herself. She could feel the eyes of the congregation on her with a drowsed speculation. A drop of sweat detached itself from the close, plaited cap of her hair and trickled down her back.

'And the fact of the matter is, Miss Gatha,' Hugh summed up, 'that the Elder put his woman-nonsense above the whole of us, above Hebron!'

'Above Hebron!'

Once the initial treason had been voiced aloud, the dam of complaint was opened. Brother Lazarus was feeling irritable. He was hungry. He had unbuttoned his shirt, seeking relief from the heat, and sweat coursed through the matted hair on his chest, dripped from the disconsolately drooping folds of his belly on to his trousers.

'And searching for the adulterer he isn't doing a single thing to help feed us or our children. And nothing we say can make him believe that Rose sinned with a stranger from Cockpit Centre and not with any of us...'

For weeks now, Brother Ananias had been the butt of jeering remarks, the implications of which were, in these circumstances, highly dangerous.

'And the Elder keep looking at us, Miss Gatha, from the one Brother to the other, until we all begin to look at each other and to wonder!'

Brother Zacky folded his arms across his narrow chest. They had not been long enough to hold his land together, to prevent his many acres from being reclaimed by the dust.

'And for all the Elder prayed for rain, Miss Gatha, he prayed in vain, for while his lips were asking the Lord to help us, his eyes were opened wide asking each one of the Brethren: "Is it you, or you, or you?" And all the while our land dying little by little and our life with it!'

'Our life!'

Hugh spread his arms wide in dramatic appeal.

'Help us to live, Miss Gatha, and our children! Until Isaac come back in December to be teacher, leader, and Elder over us, will you take over as Elder and tell us what to do?'

'Tell us, Miss Gatha!'

She searched the rows of submissive faces in front of her, then asked, her voice neutral:

'Why me, Brother Hugh? Why not you? You had your heart set on the eldership and schemed long enough for it. Well, here's your chance at last, why not take it?'

Hugh was too startled by her directness to answer.

'Or why not you, Brother Zacky?' she continued. 'You own more land than all of us put together...Or you, Brother Lazarus? You are a man and well favoured, and I am just an ugly old woman who is always making trouble.'

'Don't say that, Miss Gatha...' Lazarus protested.

'It's true and you say it often yourself. So why not any of you as Elder? Why me?' she snapped.

'Well, you see, Miss Gatha,' Hugh stammered, 'we are not worthy enough, and besides...'

Sister Sue cut across his fumbling:

'Miss Gatha, you know our position. We have neither food nor water. The people in Cockpit Centre say that if we want either we will have to pay cash. And the little money that we had is now all gone. You are the only one of us who have money saved up, and besides, we all know that Isaac have money that Prophet Moses left for him, money that you are keeping safe until he comes back. Without your money there won't be any Hebron for anybody to be Elder over!'

Hugh tried to plaster the sore of Sue's raw explanation:

'And besides, Miss Gatha, you are the most deserving of us, and with you as Elder, God will return to be well well pleased with us!'

The congregation were grateful for the touch of ritual.

'Well well pleased with us!'

For an instant as they chanted the well-known words to the familiar rhythms, they almost forgot their plight. They were aware of being seated on stools and benches that had been sculpted to their shapes during many years, and felt themselves safe inside a church that had for so long protected them. Last year the testament of their disaster had been plain for all to see – in the fields of ruined crops, the houses that had disappeared, the land sodden and cheerless under the sun. This year the drought crept up on them like a thief. During August and September whilst they had watched, fearful, for the threat of storms, the drought settled on Hebron, remained with them, invisible, and like a eunuch, burgeoned no tender new shoot, no blossoms, no fruit. And even now, they could yet be lulled into believing, by the gradualness with which it besieged them, that the ultimate would not be demanded of them, that God would return to be well well pleased…

Miss Gatha stood up. She gripped the knob of her stick, and the knuckles of her fingers shone like polished ebony. She spoke, and her voice was unemotional, precise:

'The fig tree refused for its sweetness, the vine for its wine, and when at last the trees couldn't find anyone else to be king over them, they went and asked the bramble!'

Brother Hugh confidently assumed his position in the new order:

'The Book of Judges, chapter nine, verse…' he began.

'Chapter and verse don't matter now!' she silenced him. And waited until he had taken his seat before she went on:

'I am going to help you, not because I want to, but because I have to. I am going to help you so that Hebron can continue and my son Isaac can have the lot of his inheritance, can have his father's vision to carry on!'

'Amen!'

She looked at them with contempt. She was not prepared to allow them any illusions.

'And what you all can know or care about vision?' she said. 'I am going to use the money that I worked hard for to buy food and water for you and your children. But I want you to know that the eldership that you are selling me now is dust and ashes, and the taste is bitter in my mouth!'

They bowed their heads. The instinct for survival was as strong in them as in their slave ancestors. Some weight of memory in their blood carried the ghosts of dark millions who had perished, coffined in the holds of ships, so that some could live to breed more slaves; and they, after their freedom had been won, survived the rootless years. They survived the loss of gods and devils that were their own, of familiar trees and hills and huts and spears and cooking pots, of their own land in which to see some image of themselves. And their descendants, the New Believers, survived the exodus from Cockpit Centre, the passage through the wilderness and up to the hills of Hebron, where Prophet Moses had promised them those things that had been lost in their trespass across the seas, across the centuries.

Miss Gatha walked across to the Elder's chair, which had been placed in front of the table and in the centre of the dais. She placed her stick on the table, then stood with her hands resting lightly on the arms of the chair. It was an ornate, high-backed one, a symbol of authority. Moses had designed it, Aloysius shaped it out of mahogany, and Obadiah decorated it with carvings. Standing with her skirt brushing the seat, Miss Gatha sensed something of the mad grandeur that must have possessed her husband when he had stood there with the waiting congregation below him.

'I am your Elder now,' she said.

'Our Elder!'

There was an almost lascivious note in their submission to her, and Miss Gatha recoiled. Her way would never be like that of Moses. She would never drug them with dreams of glory. She would spur them to work. She spoke to them with a harsh clarity:

'I am the bramble in the parable and I have no shade to offer you, no soft words to give you. All that is happening to you now is happening because you are a lazy and slothful people. When Isaac once suggested that you should dig wells, you turned your back on him. "What we want with wells?" you said. "Prophet Moses didn't dig any, why should we break our backs to dig wells? And who is this club-foot boy Isaac that we should have to listen to him? What he can learn from books that we don't know already?"'

They could not meet her eyes. That was what they had said, over and over again to themselves. And whatever was said in Hebron always seemed to reach Miss Gatha in the end.

'But Isaac will come back in December, and he will teach you how to dig wells, and he will teach your children how to read books, and you will have to do what he says, for club-foot or not, he will be your Elder then! Brother Hugh!'

'Yes, Miss Gatha!' Hugh replied, taken off guard by her abrupt summons.

'Harness your mules to the cart!'

'My mules…but my mules are half-dead, Miss Gatha,' he protested.

Brother Hugh was proud of his mules. All the others owned land, but he and Miss Gatha alone owned a pair of mules. The rest of the New Believers paid him in kind for taking their produce down to the market in Cockpit Centre, his mules pulling the communal cart. But Miss Gatha had always marketed her own produce, used her own mules to take her ground provisions to the town. Since food and water had become scarce Hugh had deprived himself and his wife in order to feed and water his mules, but even so, it was very little that he had to give them. Hugh was secretly planning to leave early one morning for the town to try and sell them before they got any weaker. If they were now to draw a cart down to Cockpit Centre, that might be the last of them:

'No, Miss Gatha, the cart is too big a burden for my mules in their condition!' he said, shaking his head.

'The drought is a burden on all of us, Brother Hugh. Harness the mules to the cart. Brother Lazarus and Brother Ananias, after Brother Hugh harness the mules, help him to load the drum-barrel and the food hampers on to the cart. Sister Sue, take your big Spanish jar…'

'My Spanish jar, Miss Gatha?' Sister Sue asked, surprised.

'Yes, Sister Sue, your Spanish jar!' Miss Gatha said.

The way in which she said it alerted the congregation. For they all knew the story behind the jar. Sister Sue had found it buried under a thick undergrowth when she was clearing the land behind her house to plant vegetables. It was large and pear-shaped and made of clay. After Sister Sue had scraped away the dirt and washed it thoroughly, it turned out to be a coveted prize. But apart from Miss Gatha, none of them thought of how or when the jar had come to be abandoned, whether it had not been the booty of an escaping slave who had fled to the forests and hills, and had perished there from sword or gunfire, from the sharp teeth of pursuing dogs trained to hunt him down; or perhaps the fugitive had lived to found a land for himself as other slaves had done, multiplied and increased, fought off invaders, and his descendants, when it was safe for them to do so, had drifted back to the plains, leaving the jar behind them. Perhaps his descendants had even made the jar themselves according to a pattern which had been preserved and handed down.

For the New Believers the jar belonged to a precise past of facts and dates and figures of which they were totally ignorant. And even if they had been able to read, in the history books they would have found themselves only in the blank spaces between the lines, in the dashes, the pauses between commas, semicolons, colons, in the microcosmic shadow world between full stops. Between the interstices of every date on which a deed was done, they haunted the pages, imprisoned in mute anonymity, the done-tos who had made possible the deed.

On such and such a date, Hawkins founded the slave trade, laid the corner-stone of the Empire on which the sun will never set as long as Britannia rules the waves and the Englishman is the foremost of all men. One or two of the New Believers who had had a brief schooling in Cockpit Centre before their exodus, had once recited a borrowed welter of charms, stood in the hot sun waving flags, gleaming new pennies clutched in their hands as they rejoiced for the birthday or coronation of some heir to Queen Elizabeth, during whose reign they had first been enslaved, made to till the soil, breed and die to manure the earth that sprouted forth a glittering excrescence of sugar. And when the sugar-coated Empire was crumbling away, Queen Victoria bestowed upon them a freedom that was more shadow than substance. They cried out to her that hunger was darkening their eyes so that they could not see this freedom, and she told them to make bread from their sweat. And black Deacon Bogle led them in a rebellion, but the Lord was not on their side, and Governor Eyre hanged them in their hundreds, so that along the seashore the coconut palms were as innumerable crucifixions against the sky.

****

But Miss Gatha had speculated about the jar. She had stroked the smooth glazed surface inside, the rough exterior, felt how coolly the clay breathed under her hand. And because the jar had seemed to her to have extensions linking Hebron to a people who had lived there before, she argued that it should be placed on the dais as a symbol for their community. But Sister Sue claimed the right of finders-keepers, and Prophet Moses, wrapped up in planning the future the way he wanted it, had impatiently allowed her claim, and the next Sunday preached a warning sermon on covetousness.

The congregation remembered the argument between Miss Gatha and Sister Sue, the Prophet's decision and his sermon. They were all attention now as Sister Sue asked patiently:

'So what is it that you want me to do with the jar then, Miss Gatha?'

'Your jar holds a lot of water, Sister Sue. As Brother Hugh said, we won't burden the mules too much. Cockpit Centre is eleven miles down, but you have plenty of strength stored up. And plenty children to drink of the water that you will bring up!'

'Look here, Miss Gatha, Elder or not…' Sister Sue began, then checked herself. She could not afford to be angry, for the children's sake. She rose, walked down the aisle, and when she reached the door threw back at the congregation, challenging their too obvious relief at her surrender:

'Don't take too long to catch up with me!'

As she stepped massively from the doorway, Sister Gee's protest welled up:

'But Miss Gatha, it's a far reach to Cockpit Centre and it's a big jar and…'

She faltered, then stopped. Miss Gatha allowed the silence to settle, then said drily:

'Since you have a big mouth, Sister Gee, and like to talk, you can go with Sister Sue, keep her company and bring back an extra tin of water with you!'

Gee got up to leave, then hesitated.

'Hugh!' she called.

He looked away from her, his eyes sullen-cold, like the spring after a morning of heavy rain.

'Don't you hear what Miss Gatha tell you to do?' he said savagely.

She turned and ran out of the church.

Miss Gatha gave peremptory orders to the men, assigning each one of them to special tasks; some should cut away the dead plants, others should burn them, should mend the church roof, fix the benches, should put their own houses, their own plots of land, in order, so that when the rains came they would be able to begin their lives again, tidy and in good condition.

She paused and looked at the women with distaste. Now

that the land was dying they were careless of themselves. They sprawled on the benches, their dresses crumpled and soiled, their bare toes indolent on the earthen floor, the nails invisible under layers of dirt. The reddish dust of Hebron had powdered their faces and necks, settled into seams and wrinkles, gathered in secret whorls of unkempt hair.

'Sisters, go home to your houses and sweep the floors. Since you don't have water, take little spit and wipe the dust from off you. Then comb your children's hair and comb your own and when you are a little less frowzy than you are now and can appear in the presence of the Lord, lock your doors and kneel down and pray for rain as you never prayed before!'

They nodded their heads, accepting their tasks, resigned and complaisant; all would be well now that they had someone to tell them what to do. She wanted to warn them, to leave some anxiety lingering in their minds, to let them share some of her own fears.

'And I may as well tell you now that the time that is coming isn't going to be one of milk and honey. Nobody can tell how long the drought is going to continue, so the little money that I have will have to last until Isaac comes back and dig up the money-box that his father left buried for him. And even after Isaac come back, the drought may still go on and the money-box have a bottom...'

If the drought continued it would be a bad beginning for Isaac, a bad omen, she thought. She felt the weight of the congregation burdening her, saw herself as an immense crutch supporting Hebron. She looked out at the sky, a crystalline arc, the pale blue of goat's milk. She picked up her stick from the table, rested her hands on it, and asked, like a teacher making her pupils repeat a lesson:

'You all remember what I tell you to do?'

'Yes, Miss Gatha!' they chorused.

'Well, do it!' she said, and listened for the scraping of benches on the floor, the rustle of skirts, the hum of conversation, but it was strangely silent. They sat like enormous black fungi in a petrified forest, their eyes fixed on something behind her. She looked around in time to hear Obadiah say:

'Do it? Who do it? Who?'

He stood in the doorway, a silhouette against the hard white light of noon. His eyes blazed like small mirrors that had caught the sun. He hesitated as though he could not make up his mind what to do next. His long arms hung down like wild-mango branches after a high wind had broken them. Finally he entered, stepped on to the dais and walked across, his widespread toes curling upwards as if they were still feeling their way over stones and thorns, still flinching away from the burning earth. Carefully he walked down the steps at the side of the dais and stopped in front of the senior members.

Obadiah comes back.

4. *The Search*

He looked like a stranger, and yet they knew him as their Elder, for they had been seeing him daily. They had watched him come and go, a moon-struck prophet shut away from them in the troubled forests of his flesh, in a private world of jealous fantasies. They had seen his hair sprinkling gradually with grey, a white patch like an arrow pointing at the top of his forehead; his mahogany skin darken to a charcoal-black, tighten like cured leather around his skull, his left knee-cap showing through a hole in his trousers whose seat had been rubbed shiny and threadbare; the piece of vine he used for a belt, holding up the spare folds of cloth around his waist, his shirt torn and caked with dust, stained by the sap of leaves, the juice of berries.

He closed his eyes and flicked out his tongue to moisten his cracked lips. Sister Eufemia thought that he looked like an enormous iguana lizard towering back on its tail. She saw him stretch out his hands and touch Brother Zacky's face with his finger-tips, and shuddered; it was as though she could feel the iguana crawling across the fine hairs of her bare legs, his touch dry and rough and old like stone.

His fingers traced every curve and indent of Zacky's face. That's what he had come for, to use the eyes his finger-tips sprouted to find out the adulterer. If he opened his eyes the faces would be the same, all of them – black outlines washed with the patina of the sun, everything flattened out and smoothed away. So he followed the shape of Zacky's skull, the narrow forehead, the line of the jaw projecting out to the mouth, the skin stretched taut over the cheekbones, sunken where he could feel the teeth. He confirmed what he felt, talking to himself:

'This face is a tough face, it beat against plenty years…'

The congregation leaned forward. Miss Gatha, gripping her stick even tighter, stood motionless. For the moment they had forgotten her, were caught up in Obadiah's new madness. Yesterday he had been like Aunt Kate used to be, slyly mad, with a pretence of being sane, going through the motions of praying for rain, thinking that he was fooling them. But today his madness blazoned an authority that was involving them in his blind search, making it seem important to them too. And this desperate quest of his had nothing to do with water, or rain, or food, with the things that a man could hold in his hands, could see with his eyes.

The face that Obadiah traced with his fingers was as familiar to him as a Bible text. He knew that the eyes, like the face, would be set hard against him. But they would hold no fear. He was glad that this was not the face, this one that was so resolute in its ordinariness. He turned away and cradled Lazarus's face in his hands. Brother Lazarus offered his face, obliging, placatory. Obadiah's fingers moved along the line of the balding forehead, the broad cheeks, then he drew his hands away:

'No, this is not the face, this one that is quiet against my hand. These eyes wouldn't covet. These eyes would be warm with me,' he said, and smiled.

The congregation was mesmerized. They had a respect for madness. It was a private nirvana a man could reach when he was pushed beyond the limits of human endurance, when his spirit was so troubled that his body became a temple of dreams. It was the refuge of those who could not bear the betrayal implied by death; and yet was the absolute triumph of a man over the exigencies of life. In the hearts of the congregation there lurked memories of a time before their exodus, when they too had been pushed near their limits, when they, the poor, the shirtless and the unremembered, had walked trails that bordered on heartless rivers of night, had striven to shut out from their ears the shrieks that echoed around them, lest, blinded with fear, they too should drown. As the congregation watched Obadiah, they saw some buried part of themselves, disinterred, laid bare before their eyes. They sat still, but the church was filled with their uneasiness.

Hugh saw Obadiah's hand reaching out towards him and squirmed in his seat. He didn't want to be touched. In Hebron one touched a friend when talking to him, prodded him in the ribs, rested one's hand on his arm, reinforced one's words with a physical token of friendship. But when a man was no longer one's friend, when one had denied him…Hugh felt Obadiah's hand on his face and pulled away. Obadiah opened his eyes, all the veins on his face swelling as he asked gently:

'It's you do it? You…?'

Sister Beatrice's heart leapt as she looked at the Elder. At this moment his face was the face of his mother, years ago, down in Cockpit Centre, when the big drums had pierced into the night, beating against the temples of the worshippers, pulling them down into the darkness, then tossing them on a wave of stars. Of all the Pocomania dancers, Obadiah's mother became the most completely possessed. Perhaps because she fought hardest against this exaltation, this wild release that sent her spinning, leaping, whirling, her body held stiffly, breasts erect and pointed, her nostrils flaring, her lips slightly parted and pressed against white teeth that glinted in the light of the torches; and the men silently circling her would be infected by her passion, for it went to their heads like strong rum, embraced them all in a feeling that was sullen, violent, and cold at the centre. Beatrice recalled how in the aftermath of this wild, explosive delight, Obadiah's mother would sulk and sleepwalk for days, how at nights she would cry out with anguish in her sleep, and if anyone tried to comfort her she would open her eyes and stare as Obadiah stared at Brother Hugh now. With eyes that saw so clearly, they were not seeing at all…

Obadiah bunched Hugh's shirt in his fist, lifted him off the bench, drew him close:

'You...you do it?' he asked, incredulous.

For Hugh, this was the final humiliation. An hysterical rage seized him and he pummeled at Obadiah's chest with his fist, hating the hand that held him so remorselessly, the eyes looking at him like Christ at Judas. Why should Christ think that he was any greater than Judas, Obadiah any better than he? He had power, like Judas. He wrenched at the hand that gripped him, held him fast no matter how he struggled. Unable to break loose, he shouted, the pent-up words tumbling out:

'Do what? What I do to you? I must put you before everyone else, before even myself?...Take your black hand off me! Why should I walk in your black shadow? Obadiah Brown the Elder of the Church of the New Believers of Hebron who wanted to measure his might up to Prophet Moses and took a singular vow, a vow that I thought up for him! Well, you are Elder no longer and you know who decided against you? You want to know?'

Hugh found himself sobbing and was angry. For the congregation had sensed his weakness, sensed that he was only an idolator rebelling against a fallen idol. And because he was as helpless as themselves they withdrew their involvement, looked towards Miss Gatha, and assumed her attitude of waiting. Hugh was left alone with Obadiah and his madness and he wanted to escape, to be just another one of the congregation. He screamed at Obadiah now, claiming his place with them:

'It's me, me who decided against you, took away the eldership from you. And you know why? You want to know? Because you let down Hebron, let down the whole of us, bring down God's wrath and the drought on us and all because of a woman whom you weren't man enough to keep in order!'

Hugh pulled at Obadiah's hand once more and this time the hand released him. He dropped down on the bench and smoothed the front of his shirt as he said, almost whimpering:

'So what is it you want of me now? Leave me be, you hear me! Just leave me be!'

Obadiah stared at Hugh, bewildered. This was his friend with whom he had once sailed paper boats, foraged for food in the market, run away to Kingston; his friend who long ago, when Prophet Moses was gathering the chosen ones around him for his exodus to Hebron, had spoken up for him; his friend who afterwards had ruled with him over Hebron, given him advice, suggested the vow. So why was Hugh looking at him like that? Why had he just grabbed Hugh like that?

'But this is you, Hugh? What is wrong? I troubled you, vexed you. If I did that I must have been mad. For you are my friend, my long-time friend...'

He smiled and patted Hugh's shoulder, then wiped the sweat that was falling into his eyes with his shirt-sleeves.

'Hugh, from we were small boys together, you always had common sense. So tell me, as friend to friend, who you think it is eh? For up on top of Hebron, Hugh, sun hot and bright and at nights the moon is full, hiding away the adulterer, wrapping him in the shadows...'

He broke off and remained still, grieved and disconsolate.

Hugh looked at him with a mute indifference. He wondered how he had allowed this madman to upset him. He noticed that Miss Gatha was frowning and webbed his own face with a strong disapproval.

Miss Gatha frowned because she was trying to shut out a suspicion that perhaps Obadiah's madness was not a pretence; that perhaps he had not broken his vow after all.

She searched the faces of the men who turned their heads to her glance like sunflowers to the sun – they were all placid, undifferentiated in their lusts. She should have felt reassured, but instead an obscure worry nagged at her.

Brother Zacky folded his arms the more sternly as Obadiah spoke to him, his words falling like leaves on the dry earth.

'Zacky, you know Hebron well, for you own plenty land in it, from the top to the bottom part of it. So tell me...'

He leaned close to Zacky. His breath came in short gasps as if he were encompassing the whole of Hebron and it tired him. His bottom lip was dark-red and moist with spittle. He whispered:

'Where you think it took place in, Zacky, which part of Hebron?'

His voice stirred memories of concupiscence that disturbed Zacky.

'Look here, Obadiah,' he said harshly, 'we have enough of this!'

Obadiah straightened up, turned, and prepared to mount the steps leading up to the dais. His eyes fell on Miss Gatha who stood in front of the Elder's chair, then drifted away incuriously to the dead landscape outside. He turned around quickly and spoke to Zacky once more as if they were continuing an amiable disquisition.

'You mean to say it didn't occur to you to think is where, Zacky? To wonder whether perhaps it could have been above the spring where young bamboo shoots close you off from Hebron and long green ferns and dead man's beard trail to the ground...'

He walked to where Sister Ann sat, stood in front of her. He gestured with his hands and she felt herself ringed in with his arms.

'Sister Ann, you think it could have been up on the hill-top? But that would have been to take sin too near to God?' He frowned and shook his head.

'Or you think it is right there in the hut where she is hiding now?...No, that couldn't be. For I would be sure to feel it all around me, taste it, smell it...'

Through the holes in his torn shirt Sister Ann saw the iron lines of his ribs, the line of black and grey hairs that led down to his navel. His smell, pungent and sour and male, mixed in her nostrils with that of the savage uncleanness of birth, the unwashed sheets, the blood, the slime. She sprang up violently, forcing him to step back.

'Obadiah, mad or not, please keep your private nastiness to yourself!' she cried out.

The congregation nodded with approval, and Zacky called out:

'Obadiah, Miss Gatha is waiting on us. Please to go about your business and leave us to go about ours in peace!'

'Yes, yes,' they muttered, 'you go about your business, leave us to go about ours.'

Their faces to Obadiah became the distant sullen peaks of the hills, and he himself was the sky, lowering with bile, pressing demonic clouds against them. So his business was not theirs, they said. He would show them, would hurl down hail and thunder and lightening, and a black rain to flatten trees, sweep away the soil, cut deep wounds and crevasses in their slopes as a reminder of his fury. So his business was not theirs? And yet, days after his initial rage had subsided, his rain still cursed through secret channels of the hills to feed the roots of living things, to send the sap pulsing through branches which sprouted green leaves that sparkled as they caught the sun and breathed in moisture that would one day renew his anger, would one day force open the bowels of his wrath, his business always theirs, theirs, his...

He walked down the aisle, his head made dizzy by visions. The congregation sat passive, withdrawn, not looking at him. He would have to explain to them that he was searching for a truth not only for himself, but to save them all.

'My business is your business,' he said. 'Prophet Moses called me to come up to Hebron because I had skill to hew timber and the land where we were going to was a wood. And I hewed down the trees. And I built up Hebron. And I left my trade and the working of wood that my hand understood so well to become Elder to you. And I did only what you wanted me to...'

He saw that they were not listening to him. Their impatience for him to be gone pricked him like thorns, and their indifferent thoughts stung him like angry bees flying in widening circles around a hive. What was this madman bothering them for? So his wife was having a baby and it was not his? So that was a thing that had happened over and over when they lived in Cockpit Centre, and men fathered children as casually as they drank water when they were thirsty; then drifted away, chasing a mirage – the promise of work and green pastures. So if Obadiah felt strongly about this ordinary happening, let him take a machete and chop up his woman, as others had done before him. Let him do that and leave them alone. After all, they had played their part. They had helped him to curse Rose.

And cursing was the most that a people could do, a people for whom Fate was a blind beggar blinking at the sun. For as far back as they could remember they had never been their own masters. Always behind them there had been a 'boss' and behind the 'boss' a Government, and behind the Government, the white Governor, and behind him, the King of England with the power of ships and guns and myths and distances of wide seas; and behind the King of England, there was, white like him, God. For a brief while Prophet Moses had changed the hierarchy, had led them up to Hebron, set himself above them, made them believe that behind him there was a God, black and made in their image and partial to them, His Chosen People. Then Prophet Moses had crucified himself to redeem them for ever and ever, but after his death, the hurricane had come just the same, and the drought. Above them now was Miss Gatha, and behind her the face of God was anonymous and not to be depended upon. For he might turn out to be white after all, and harsh. So in order to placate the unknown, they would deny their neighbours, betray, even when such treachery was not asked of them.

Obadiah felt rage mounting inside him, spreading up like a bright flame from the soles of his bare feet. Then it burst out of him and the congregation looked up in alarm at this man, possessed and thundering at them.

'I took the vow for all of you. So as your Elder I charge you now, search out the adulterer from amongst you, find him out, drive him out! I charge you! I took the vow for all of you!'

Lazarus walked quickly down the aisle towards Obadiah. He was at home with this sort of madness, this uncomplicated one that exploded, spent itself, so that afterwards you could soothe the man, crack a joke or two, get him to laugh with you and forget. He put his hand on Obadiah's shoulder, said comfortingly:

'Easy now, Obadiah man, easy. You can't really think that any of us would have done this to you? It's somebody different from us, man, a stranger…'

Obadiah shook his head, but answered quietly now:

'No, Laz, man, it's not a stranger. A stranger don't have to prove himself on you, don't have to magnify himself against you. It's never a stranger who hate you but someone who is tied up and involved with you. A stranger don't kill you, slate always clean between you, can't traitor you, don't covet your house, your cattle or your wife, you not neighbour to a stranger, he not neighbour to you…'

He went down the aisle, looking fiercely from right to left.

'So tell me, neighbours, which one of you was small enough to have to magnify himself against me? Which one of you was dead enough to have to prove himself alive on me? Which one of you did cast eyes on my wife and catch fire to covet her?'

He paused in the doorway, then added, his voice intimate:

'You don't want to tell me now? You don't want to tell me here? All right then. I will go and wait for you on top of the big rock that overlook the old hut where our hen is hatching out your egg. And you don't think it now, but you will come, you will come. I'll see you then, eh?'

He turned around the corner of the church. In a few seconds they could see him, behind Miss Gatha's head, scrambling rapidly up the hill.

Miss Gatha felt drained and exhausted. Her red eyes burned like charcoal in the pouches of skin, and there was a look of foreboding in them. Lazarus stood where he was in the aisle, not knowing what to do next. The congregation waited. The minutes passed. Finally, Zacky coughed and said loudly:

'Miss Gatha, we are waiting, please!'

Miss Gatha's fingers tapped nervously on her stick.

'What you are waiting for? Didn't I tell you already what to do? Told all of you?'

'Yes, Miss Gatha.'

Their apathy discouraged her, weighed her down, and she shouted at them:

'Well, what you are sitting there staring at me for? Go, go and do it!'

She watched them scurry away like chickens after corn. Then she seated herself, rested her head against the carved wooden back of the chair and tried to grasp the elusive fear that had started to edge into her mind. She wondered if amongst the men of Hebron there might be one who lived a secret life. As she tried to speculate further the oppressive noonday heat made her sleepy. She dozed off. The stick slipped from her hand and fell. Even as she slept her hands gripped the carved arms of the Elder's chair.

A confusion of voices echoing from the square as the New Believers went about the tasks assigned to them, awoke her. She picked up her stick, stood up, shook her head to banish the lingering stupor of sleep, and walked out. Her hunched shadow followed her, lying dark and flat against the rutted path.

5. *The Adulterer*

Long shadows stretched across the valleys, across the parched hills, and brought a brief coolness to soften the harsh memory of the sun. Sister Sue and Gee were returning from Cockpit Centre. The water in the jar that Sue carried, in the tin that Gee balanced on her head, sloshed from side to side as they walked. They came to a large tamarind tree which marked the bend in the track where two paths branched off to Hebron. One snaked circuitously round to the square and to their houses, whilst the other sloped straight up into the hills. Sister Sue turned up the steep path.

'But why you are turning up that way?' Gee called out.

Sue stopped. She was so tired that standing still took a great effort of will. Her feet wanted to carry her on and on. She gripped the rim of the jar, easing her weight.

'I have to take some water up the hill,' she said.

'Up the hill?'

'Yes.'

'For Aunt Kate?'

'No. You go on home. I will see you in the morning!'

'But Sister Sue…' Gee cried out. There was a tremor in her voice. She looked fearfully around her at the trees and bushes that massed solid black patterns against the sleeping hills. Everyone in Hebron believed that this twilight time was when ghosts walked, when substance and shadow merged.

'If you are afraid to go by yourself you can come with me, as long as you keep what you see to yourself!' Sue called back, turned and continued uphill.

Gee staggered along after her. But she would have walked all the way back to Cockpit Centre rather than go home alone past the predatory darkness that lurked under trees in the silent square, past the mounds and stones of the graveyard where Prophet Moses's ghost wandered, dragging his cross behind him. She huddled close to the other woman and asked:

'How you mean I must keep what I see to myself, Sister Sue?'

Sue groped along, she knew that she must not stop, that if she did she would be giving in to Miss Gatha. She had obeyed her, walking to the town and returning with the jar of water. She would defy her now by taking some water for Rose, water that Miss Gatha's money had paid for.

'I am taking up some water for Rose. How else you think she's been living?'

'I was wondering...'

'Yes, but it never occurred to you to do anything about it? After all, you and she were playmates together, adultery or not!'

'I know. But Hugh warned me not to have anything to do with her.'

'Well, make sure you don't say anything to him or to anyone. Or it will be sure to get back to Miss Gatha and it would be war between you and me!'

'I won't say a thing to anyone, and especially not to Hugh, especially not to him!'

They went on in silence.

She felt her thighs rubbing together, the soreness exploding in sparks of pain that made her dizzy. The chafing had started half-way down and when they finally reached the market, with sweat spreading out in dark circles under their armpits, dripping into their eyes, she had sprawled out on the pavement, opening her legs wide, closing her ears to the gibes of the loungers, who pointed Gee and herself out as 'two of Prophet Moses's righteous chickens who had run away, lost their way and come to sell themselves in the market...'

Some time later, the cart came rattling along with Zacky driving and Miss Gatha seated beside him. Sue stood up painfully and she and Gee walked behind the cart, through streets that were subtly besieged by the drought. They entered a lane that led into a blind alley. From the ramshackle shop that blocked off the alley, a man came out with hands as furtive as his eyes. After a sharp exchange with Miss Gatha he brought out tins of water with which he filled the small barrel on the cart, Sue's jar, and Gee's tin. Miss Gatha told the two women to start back immediately. Later on, when the cart overtook and passed them, Zacky raised his whip to Sue in a grave salute. She would show Zacky, Sue vowed to herself she would show him…

Twilight merged into night. In the distance an owl hooted. From the dark hollows rain-frogs cracked sharp sad notes, and crickets chirped listlessly in the still air. Gee felt the emptiness, the silences pressing in on her, more threatening than ghosts. She strained her eyes up the hill to where a light in the window of Aunt Kate's house glimmered an uncertain hope.

Sue saw the light too, and wondered how Aunt Kate was. She would have liked to have helped with her nursing, but Ann was jealous of her duties. Sue remembered how wrapped up in her own concerns she had been on the day when the old woman came weeping to tell her that Maverlyn was not sleeping, Maverlyn was dead. That night, whilst all of Hebron slept, Aunt Kate had gone down to the spring to hold a wake for the child that had been dead more than ten years. Ann had found her there the next morning, singing 'Abide with me' and burning up with the fever…

'Sister Sue, what's that?' Gee whispered.

She looked to where Gee pointed high above them. Outlined against the gathering night, a figure darkened the sky. As they watched it seemed to spread out wings, to swoop down, to pounce on its prey. Gee clutched at Sue's shoulder and hid her face.

'Lord have mercy, mercy!' Sue prayed. Then she made a decision. 'We are not going a step farther in this darkness. We will sit right here and wait for the moonlight!'

They helped each other down with their vessels and squatted on the ground close together, their backs resting against a pimento tree. After a while Sue started singing and Gee joined in. They sang a hymn as if it were a charm to keep phantoms at bay. Their voices raised echoes that rang like tolling bells.

****

Obadiah waited for the adulterer, certain that he would come. A grey and dusty twilight settled over the hills and valleys, defining trees and rocks and bushes, revealing familiar curves and shapes and angles that had been flattened under the sun. He traced all the subtle changes in the vast amphitheatre below him, the arena in which, every day for weeks, he had been re-enacting the drama with the deceiver. He could feel his body sharp and taut under him, every separate part of it imbued with a sense of touch as omnipotent as that of his fingers.

There was a snapping of twigs farther down the hill. He stood upright on the rock and pivoted, listening. He could make out the divi-divi tree a few yards away from the old hut in which Rose had taken refuge. For days he had imagined that the shape of the tree-trunk was that of a girl dancing, one arm raised above her head, or of a man, his shoulders bent forward as he raised a machete to strike. But now something had been added to the tree-trunk, something which moved, detached itself. The tree became once more a man with his machete raised threateningly, a girl dancing, her arm reaching to pull down the heavens…

He crouched, leaped ten feet down in a shower of dust and stones, and pounced on the adulterer. A remnant of light patched the tree and the petrified intruder with clearer shadows. The face remained in the darkness. Obadiah forced the adulterer to his knees, glad that he did not struggle, that he allowed this thing to be done with the dignity one needed for a trial and an execution. And the submissiveness of the kneeling figure strengthened Obadiah's identification with God the Judge. His monologue was kindlier than he had intended:

'I told you would come, neighbour, this thing too strong, too close between us for you to stay away for long. I knew you would come. But don't talk. For if I find out who you are I might find it hard to have to kill you...'

He wrenched away the weak hands that tugged at his. As the adulterer tried to struggle to his feet, he pressed him down with one hand, and with the other covered his mouth. In the tussle, his foot kicked against a small water-can. It clattered against the stones. He waited until his breathing steadied itself, until he was calm once more.

'And don't fight me, man! Stay down there on your knees. I don't want to see your face. For I might lose my temper. I don't want that to happen. Everything must be done right and proper according to the fourth text in the Bible, the one that Hugh forgot and Miss Gatha was afraid to remember...But wait...you're crying? It's eye-water this I'm feeling? Don't waste your eye-water, man. The ground is too dry to use it... You can't stop crying, eh? You must be young then...and restless for living. As I used to be...before Prophet Moses caught me up in his vision, put fire in my belly to come up to Hebron and build a black heaven on earth...But once we built up heaven and shut ourselves inside it what did we leave for you, what dreams, what visions, for you who young enough to have skin smooth like this...?'

For a moment he wondered which one of the young Brethren it was after all? Then he shook his head and frowned. He must not find out until after the execution. He had decided upon this the afternoon he left the church. He would show the congregation what it meant to be an Elder. They all thought that he was mad, that he had not noticed Miss Gatha usurping his place, standing in front of the Elder's chair. He would show them, although there was now a great gulf between him and them. Not one of them could understand him. Except this one man, this Brother, this neighbour, who had come skulking in the darkness, drawn close to him through his guilt. This guilt was the bond between them. As the woman Rose was. Her brown body linked them. And would soon, according to the curse, rot on the ground. Now they were close, all three of them, and would show Hebron how an Elder could act according to the Words of the Lord and not diminish one jot nor one tittle. But this man, the adulterer, did he really understand this necessity, could he understand it? It was important that he should understand the Law, should acquiesce in his sentence.

'You understand why I have to kill you, don't you, man?' The adulterer lay inert against his knee. He explained slowly, as to a child:

'You see, man, what you did, isn't so much that it's right or wrong as that it just can't be done. Man, what you did was to take away from me the one thing that was private to me... private from my neighbour, private like what was between the wood and me when I was shaping it with my hand. You must and bound to understand that, man. I know you understand. Stay same way, stay quiet to hear your sentence.'

He cleared his throat, made his voice formal:

' "The man that committeth adultery with another man's wife, even he that committeth adultery with his neighbour's wife, the adulterer and the adulteress shall surely be put to death," Leviticus, chapter twenty, verse ten, Amen!'

He waited a few seconds. Above them, a light wind rippled through the leaves of the tree. In the distance there were faint echoes of voices singing, voices that had a familiar ring. But he would not be fooled. Not ever again. The voices, he was sure, were those of Prophet Moses and all the dead Hebronites singing to pass the time as they waited, to claim amongst them the adulterer, whom they too had judged, must surely die.

He fitted his hands around the slender neck, felt for the pulse. The indent where the pulse beat was smooth, like satinwood. Wonderingly he drew his hands away. His fingers brushed against the rising of a breast. The moon rose from behind the hills and brightened the dark sky. He looked down and called out:

'Rose! Sister Rose!'

He felt his heart pounding, his voice strangled inside him. He knelt down beside her. The moonlight turned Hebron into a magic world with silver branches, glittering leaves, and live crouching shadows under the trees.

****

Farther down the hill the two women helped each other up with their vessels. Gee went in front this time and sang gaily, intoxicated by the moonlight. Behind her Sister Sue walked weary and disgruntled. The rest had made things worse. Her legs felt as stiff as planks. She wished that Gee would shut up, her head was splitting; wished that she had waited until the next day to take up the water for Rose, hoped that Rose would remember to leave the water-can in the usual place, since she didn't want to tangle with that mad Obadiah. Moonlight always seemed to inspire madness. Listen to how Gee was carrying on! And yet she could understand why Gee sang. She herself had forgotten that Hebron could be so beautiful. The moon had never been the same in Cockpit Centre, clear and untarnished.

Rose heard the singing. She picked up the water-can from where it had fallen and placed it in a clump of bushes behind the tree. Then she went into the hut and Obadiah followed her. The earthen floor was swept bare, and in the corner there was a pile of banana leaves. Obadiah helped her to sit down. The leaves rustled under her. The moonlight slanted in through holes in the thatch. He saw that her face had grown thin, had become that of a woman. But she was no longer a stranger. He sat down on the floor.

They heard the singing draw nearer, then stop, the sound

of water being poured. He waited for the footsteps to die away down the hill before he asked:

'What happened, Rose? Who worked this evil, brought distance between us?'

Speaking quietly, she told him how she had been raped. He heard her voice echoing inside his head, until it became the rushing of a hurricane wind. He felt himself possessed by furies, wanted to sweep away Hebron and the hills that had witnessed this defilement of his love, this betrayal of his friendship. He wanted to get hold of the man, to shout abuse at him, stamp his face in the dust, erase all memories of talk and kindliness between them. At that moment, if they were face to face, he would have killed him. Then his anger ebbed away. He grasped at the its remnants, trying to hold this anger to him. Without it he would be left naked to the compassion that edged in upon him, to the understanding that overwhelmed him. For he knew, better than any other, how this man, whom he had loved, had been forced to do this thing, and why.

And although the thought of the other imprinting his own image on his wife's body still burnt like a dagger in his brain, he turned to her, held her, and comforted her. And he knew that he would have her back. For, in searching for the adulterer, he had stumbled upon himself.

6. *The Star-Apple Tree*

The New Believers submitted to the new order. As their reward they ate and drank enough to keep the life in their bodies, to continue with the ritual of living. In the meantime Hebron became a corpse, embalmed and well tended. The fences had been strengthened, the church and the houses repaired, the dead plants and the fallen leaves all cleared away. In the square not even the ghost of a wind stirred the naked trees. Aware of the creeping death around them, the children no longer played by the spring. They remained at home, lingering by their mothers or sitting on the doorstep beside their fathers. And they wondered at the silences which had sprung up between their parents, between neighbour and neighbour.

Through the long days Eufemia no longer wandered with Gee all over Hebron. There was nothing to gossip about and she had no new secrets to tell. Instead, she leaned on her gate and looked across at Ananias, who sat in his yard and flicked at lizards with his machete. He pretended not to see her, but every now and then demonstrated his prowess by slicing away a tail, a claw, a tongue, of bright flame. Above them the sun was a molten disk in a steel-blue sky.

To pass the time, Gee slept late. She got up, dressed, swept the floor of her house, and walked gravely beside her husband to the church, where Miss Gatha, aided by Brother Zacky and Sister Ann, doled out the rations for the day. After they returned home and ate, Gee sat quietly on the floor, braiding and unbraiding her hair whilst her husband brooded over his loss of status. Soon, Gee knew, he would turn to her. She was the only person left to whom he could affirm his importance, the only person whom he could compel to recognize him still as Brother Hugh, Chief Recorder of the Church of the New Believers of Hebron.

First he would pace up and down the room, then stop as if seeing her for the first time, and she would lower her eyes, challenging him with her silent contempt. When he deliberately closed the door and the window she half-smiled to herself, and stared at him unblinkingly as he came across to her, forced her to the floor and demanded of her:

'Who am I, tell me that, who am I?'

'Hugh, only Hugh, nothing more!' she answered, shrugging.

He wrestled with her savagely, trying to subdue her, to bend her body to his will. And she laughed at him as he wore himself out ploughing into her again and again. When he was near breaking point she pretended to be conquered, admitted:

'You are Brother Hugh, Chief Recorder of the Church of the New Believers of Hebron!'

Then he would release her, throw himself on the bed and fall into a dreamless sleep. Gee smiled to herself. Tomorrow it would begin all over again.

Up on the hill, Aunt Kate recovered from her illness. Now that she was forced to accept that Maverlyn was dead, her mind, too, began to heal. Day after day she prodded Ann, asking her questions about things that had happened in the twilight years during which she had shut herself away with a dream. As she explored the past she grew more and more lively and assertive and once again resented Ann's continual fussing over her.

Ann was happy. She felt at ease in a Hebron that was tidy and well ordered, with trees whose withered blossoms no longer sprang a riot of colour to disturb her spinster's tranquility. She liked looking after Aunt Kate, liked the touch of her soft wrinkled skin, her grey hair, the cleanliness of nursing the aged instead of the new-born. She enjoyed telling Aunt Kate about the past and talked unimaginatively of all the happenings, the hurricane, the vow, the curse, the drought. Her tale of disasters filled her with a ghoulish satisfaction.

In the church a subtle alliance was formed between Brother Zacky and herself now that they had become Miss Gatha's assistants. And Ann had her revenge on her sister for the time in Cockpit Centre when Sue had snatched Zacky away from her. With his new authority Zacky resisted his wife's dominance, and he and Ann, as if the intervening years had never been, returned to the bloodless contact of their Cockpit Centre days.

Sue felt herself well rid of them and their resentments. Her only concern was with her children. The drought had turned them into wizened creatures. Instead of filling Hebron with their laughter and shouting as they had once done, they sat rooted to the house like stunted plants. Looking at them, Sue felt that life itself had died, and she would go out into her yard and shade her eyes against the sun, trying to see up the hill-side. If she was lucky she caught glimpses of Rose, heavy with child, moving about in front of the hut. Sue calculated how many more weeks it would be before Rose would give birth. Unconsciously Rose had become a symbol to her that one day life would return to Hebron.

Often she had felt tempted to slip away from her house and make her way up to Rose, if only to sit and talk for an hour or so, to share vicariously in an experience that had once been so familiar. And perhaps in telling Rose the details of many a childbirth, she would be able to recapture the sense of triumph, of power, which had welled up in her on each occasion. But she knew better than to visit Rose. For when the New Believers realized that Obadiah had gone back to live with his wife, their silence was ominous.

To the entire congregation, Obadiah's going back to Rose was clear proof that, despite his denials, his attempt to strangle her in the church, his divorcing and cursing of her, his subsequent madness and search for the adulterer, he had broken his vow after all. They hesitated to speak openly, because any comment might have led to the conclusion that the death of the land was a punishment for their former Elder's broken vow, that the drought continued because he now flaunted his sin in the face of God. And they all felt violence stirring inside them. But their violence was held in check by their fear of offending Miss Gatha. They looked to her to give the command that would send them up the hill to burn down the hut, to unleash their anger against the offender. But Miss Gatha was silent.

And because their violence had to be hidden it was all the more dangerous. They watched Obadiah grimly whenever he passed by the church and through the square on his way to Cockpit Centre. One evening when he returned, weighted down with a hamper of food and water, hatred and envy burned their eyes, and they were like wolves waiting to spring. But they had kept quiet, and the quality of their silence warned Sue that for Rose's sake it was best not to visit her and excite their anger by breaking a ban which was the more binding because it was tacit and implied.

****

Miss Gatha opened the door of the lean-to shed at the back of the house. Moses had had the shed built on as his 'place of communion'. This was where he had retired night after night when he had been seized of the obsession that had sculpted his face with hollows, drained his body of blood and sap, and driven him to die on a cross for the greater glory of God, of Hebron, and of himself. The warm stale air enveloped Miss Gatha as she entered. For a moment her confidence deserted her. She hesitated. Always she had been defeated by Moses, always in the end he had made her bow to his will. Once she had even kneeled before him, pleading with him not to crucify himself, for then what would become of their son with no father to look out for him, protect his interests? But her pleas were futile. For how could she have persuaded a man like Moses to think of his son instead of Hebron? How could she have persuaded him not to sacrifice himself for the greater glory of God, and above all, of himself?

A pitcheri bird hurled its shrill melody at the sky. She smiled to herself, shrugging off the ghost of Moses, then went and propped the door of the shed open with a large stone. As she stooped over she felt the sun through her dress, felt it on her back. It simmered in her blood like the boiling cane-liquor her grandfather used to stir with an outsized ladle, until slowly, sullenly, the liquor disappeared, and left a residue of brown crystals of sugar. She re-entered the shed and the sun rushed in with her, flirting with the cobwebs, teasing the solemn darkness in the corners before peeling it away to wrap spirals of light around the posts that supported the thatched roof. The sun and Miss Gatha had taken over. Prophet Moses was gone.

She walked across to the farthest corner, where, under a bench, was the wooden chest in which Moses had kept his 'vestments of office'. She pulled out the chest and raised the heavy lid. The smell of cured wood and the musty fragrance of dried herbs stung her nostrils; and for a moment she thought she saw the dead body of Moses, his beard and hair combed, his face washed and shining. He was wearing the purple robe of silk which he had her make a few days before his crucifixion. Only the lacerations on his wrists and ankles bore witness to his last agony. The figure dissolved before her eyes and instead she saw Obadiah in church, in the grip of madness, his black trousers torn, his white linen shirt in tatters. Bitterness swept over her. She had exchanged her shop and plot of land in Cockpit Centre for that very shirt and trousers, for the swallow-tailed coat of fine broadcloth, the expensive boots. A quarter of the money that she received from the sale of her property had gone to purchase these 'vestments of the office' for her husband Moses. After his death they had passed on to Aloysius and after him to Obadiah.

She had made a bargain, Miss Gatha thought – her land

and property for a few pieces of clothing, for marriage to Moses and twenty bitter years; the name of Randall for that of Barton when her maiden name had been a legitimate name, a respectable one bestowed on her by her great-grandfather, Cato Randall. Old Cato, a former slave, had called himself after his English master, fused his being with the name so that it could symbolize the freedom which he had newly acquired, the land which was his, the shop and the sugar mill and the boiler room and the girl-child that his wife had borne him. And not having had an identity of his own, a line of ancestors that he could trace, Cato was determined to found a dynasty. He married off his daughter to another ex-slave, a young man who had been given his freedom by a master who had also taught him to read and write. Cato left all his possessions to his son-in-law on condition that he adopted the name of Randall and passed it on to his children. But after the old man's death, the son-in-law took to drinking too much of the rum he fermented. There had been no money or ambition left over to send his son, Miss Gatha's father, to school. She in turn had grown up illiterate. One of the things that she had most admired about Moses was his ability to lift the magic of words from the printed pages of the Bible. And she had always felt that it was this lack in herself that excluded her from everything that she most desired.

Miss Gatha seated herself on the bench. The sun streamed into the shed, into the opened chest before her. She remembered the star-apple tree in her yard in Cockpit Centre, the one her great-grandfather had planted. One day, when she was about eight years old, she had tried to pelt down a star apple that dangled on its tough stem high above her. It was important to her to get this tantalizing fruit, and she set about it with a determination which fascinated her grandmother. The old woman, looking out from the kitchen window, watched her throwing stones at this elusive prize with a concentration which would not admit defeat. After she had been stoning the fruit for what seemed like hours, Gatha heard her grandmother calling:

'Gatha, come on out of that hot sun, child. I make some

lemonade for you!'

'Coming, Grannie,' she called back.

Whilst she drank the lemonade, the old lady shuffled about the kitchen attending to chores which she forgot about as soon as she started them, and explained to Gatha:

'It's no more use your throwing stones at that star-apple tree, child, for the star apple is a mean fruit, the meanest one of all. When it's ripe and ready for eating it would rather stay on the tree-branch and wither away than drop down like any other fruit. If you want to knock it down, then you have to find a sharp stick and throw it so that it can cut across the stem. Even then you can't be sure that it will fall down.'

Gatha put down her empty mug, went to the window and looked outside at the offending tree. The leaves were reddish purple on the upper surface and a shiny green underneath. They stirred in the wind whilst the purple fruit swung languidly. Her grandmother came up behind her.

'Yes, child, it's a mean fruit all right. And that was why that star-apple tree was the first tree my dead father, Old Cato Randall, planted. For I am telling you, child, old Cato was as mean and evil as a night of strife, God rest his soul, and that star-apple tree that his hand planted bears all the black fruit of his sins!'

'But the star apples are sweet, Grannie,' Gatha said.

'All things of the devil are sweet, mi' child!'

That was true, Gatha thought to herself, for when you broke open the star-apple fruit, the white flesh streaked with pink and purple opened out in your hand like a bruise, stained your tongue as your teeth bit into it. And the sweet white milk flushed down your throat, some of it dribbling down the side of your mouth, and remained there, dried by the sun and itching all day long.

Her grandmother called Gatha away from the window and seated her on the floor between her knees. Whilst she combed and plaited the little girl's hair, she told her the story of Cato Randall, her great-grandfather.

****

When he was born, his English master, Randall, named him Cato. Even as a small boy he was handsome and full of low cunning, but his master was fond of him and made his mother a house-slave so that Cato could grow up in the big house. At the age of six he became Mr. Randall's personal houseboy. He grew up to be mean and treacherous, but his master thought him loyal, especially when he revealed the details of a rebellious plot that, unknown to Randall, Cato himself had fomented amongst the field-slaves. He sold the secrets of this conspiracy to his master in exchange for a signed document granting him his freedom. On the same day he lured Randall into an ambush, and as the other slaves slashed red ribbons from Randall's curling white flesh, Cato looked on impassively. When the deed was done he ran five miles to the estate of a neighbouring white planter, told of the rebellion and of his vain efforts to defend his generous master who had only that day granted him his freedom.

When the captured leaders of the revolt were being burnt to death by slow fires, they cursed Cato with their last breath. But the slave-owners rewarded his loyalty with a gift of money and endorsed his freedom. And Cato bought land, built a shop, and planted a star-apple tree behind it. Like the tree, he put out green branches and prospered, trading ruthlessly with his fellow black men, circumspectly with the white gentry who held him up as an example of the heights to which even a black could rise if he served God, was faithful to his master, and profited by the lessons he was taught.

Only in one way did the curse of the dying slaves affect Cato. He never had a son. His wife, a strong, healthy house-slave of his former master whom Cato bought at the sale of the Randall property, bore him a girl-child. And the midwife who attended at her birth put it about that even this one child had been wrung from Cato's seed like milk from grated cassava.

And try as he might with numerous other women, Cato never had another child born to him. He seemed to carry a contagion of barrenness with him. But in every other way he thrived, and died quietly in his bed, and had a splendid funeral at which even white men paid their last respects. At the grave, an old slave-mother cursed Cato Randall, his children and his children's children...

When Gatha's grandmother came to this part of her story she noticed the little girl's eyes wide with fear. She hastened to comfort her, telling her that she should not be frightened by a curse, for good Christians like themselves should be free from heathen superstitions. And, anyway, look how Cato Randall had succeeded in spite of the curse. And as for his not having a son, well, many people had hinted that that was because of Cato's closeness with his master, which had started when he was very young and the white man had first observed the smooth black of Cato's skin, the big, gentle, liquid eyes of a wild beast, the tiny pointed ears, the rows of perfect teeth, the delicate limbs moulded by some ancient civilization that had refined itself out of existence. Cato Randall didn't have a son, many people said, not because of any curse, but because he had tried to be a man when it was already too late.

Gatha nodded her head solemnly, but she did not understand her grandmother's veiled explanation. For weeks after that the curse lingered about her like the mists that rose up from the earth after the long rains. The face of the 'obeahman' began to haunt her dreams. He lived in a ramshackle hut next door to her yard. People said that he smoked marijuana and worked black magic. And, after hearing her grandmother's story, whenever Gatha set out for Sunday school, dressed in her neat white frock, and lifted up her eyes to meet the obeahman's, she began to feel a complicity with him; as if he, too, knew of the curse, sensed that she carried the seed of it inside her, and that the white man's church and all the words in his Bible could not destroy that seed any more than the stones she had thrown had dislodged the purple fruit, which when it was cut open vertically, had its portions arranged like a star.

****

Miss Gatha looked up and saw the sky blue-bright and clear as water. Despite the curse, in spite of everything, she had won. Tomorrow her son Isaac was due back from Kingston able to read and write like her grandfather, old Cato's son-in-law, like Moses, but without the weakness for drink of the former, without the womanizing tendency of the latter. Moses was dead, and could not witness Isaac's return, his triumph. But she, Gatha, whom Moses had ignored and trampled on, before whom he had flaunted his paramours, she was still alive with the sun leaping somersaults in her blood. Tomorrow her son Isaac was returning, the son from whom Moses had turned away in horror, seeing his club-foot as one more sign that he should die upon a cross, redeem them all from sin and capture Hebron in the thrall of his memory for ever and ever, Amen. 'Amen!' Miss Gatha repeated to herself. Moses's crucifixion had been a final betrayal. The cross had strangled him in its embrace, left him a crumpled corpse as ordinary as any other, with the same empty eyes and rigid limbs. Moses was as dead as dirt and she and Isaac were alive!

She slid her hand under a tattered sheet of newspaper that lined the bottom of the chest. Then she pulled out a folded oblong of white cloth and shook it loose. It was yellow with age and smelt of camphor. She spread it out on her lap. It was an apron of fine linen, and she looked ruefully at the streaks of black where the dust had accumulated in the creases. She tried to straighten out the limp frilled edging, then she looked at the sun, gauging of she would have time to wash and starch the apron in time for the next morning. But an indolence invaded and subdued her spirit. She shook her head and sat drowsing in the sunlight, stroking the apron with her gnarled hands.

The apron had belonged to her grandmother. Miss Gatha had taken it up to Hebron with her as the one symbol to mark her difference from the others. On their first night in Hebron, when Prophet Moses ordered them to bring to him all their belongings, the unnecessary reminders of their past, Miss Gatha had hidden the apron. A secret stubbornness made her hold on to it, almost against her will. And this action marked her first impulse to withdraw a part of herself from Moses, the first beginning of an unconscious retreat if she were not to be annihilated.

For looking back now, she could see that when Moses made the bonfire that night, claiming that he wanted to destroy the symbols of their past sufferings, what he had really planned to do was to leave them all like the naked clay to be shaped into an image of his making. He had burnt none of those things which would be useful to him, only the little fripperies that might speak to them of a life more ordinary, more chaotic, but more easeful in spite of hunger and lack of dignity. Miss Gatha remembered how they had clapped their hands, cheered, wept for joy and shouted 'hallelujah' as their few possessions, their pathetic, shop-soiled memories blazed up in a brief monument of fire to the vision of Moses which was now theirs as well.

Before Obadiah had made the wooden chest and presented it to Moses and herself, she had kept the apron hidden inside her black Sunday dress. Whenever the urge for rebellion against Moses and his empty striving for glory with which she was, willy-nilly, identified, came upon her, she would sit quietly on the bed, hold the apron in her hand, and reaffirm her private betrayal. At first she had done this fearfully, half-ashamed, half-wishing that she could be caught, so that, reassured that God and Moses were all-seeing and omnipotent, she could be without need for rebellion. But she was not found out, and her suspicions as to Moses's infallibility were confirmed. Gradually she changed from a shadow flitting to and fro in the house, tending her husband's wants, cushioning his occasional spells of self-doubt with her idolatry, to become an unknown presence, silently challenging his dominance, wearing it away like water chafing against a stone.

Miss Gatha got up and, taking the apron with her, walked out of the shed into the sunshine. She went round the side of her house, up the steps of the veranda, and into the cool 'bottom parlour' with its drawn blinds. She stepped on to two pieces of felt which she kept by the door so that she could always be polishing the bark-stained wooden floor as she walked up and down. She crossed the room and her indistinct shadow loomed up at her from the mirror-like floor. She stretched the apron out on the table, placed the heavy Bible on top, then sat in the rocking chair and relaxed. The triangle of sunlight that peered in through the half-opened door touched her like quicksilver as she rocked to and fro.

Every afternoon during the past few weeks she had sat at the table and counted her money, calculating how long she could make it last, willing each coin to double its value so that she and Hebron could hold out until Isaac returned. For the savings in the money-box that Moses had left, and that she had added to from time to time, were Isaac's; the money was his. Once he became Elder he could use it to buy food and water for his congregation. But in the morning she would have to dig it up from where it was buried and take it down to the station, so that he could purchase provisions for the little banquet with which they would celebrate his return. She had spent the last of her own money on Christmas Eve. She smiled grimly to herself as she thought of how panic-stricken the congregation would be if they suspected how little money she really had. An idle, lazy lot, they were convinced that for her, money somehow grew on trees.

When she had not issued extra food on Christmas Day there had been murmurs of discontent. Sister Beatrice had complained loud enough for her to hear that 'certain people were holding on tight to their money in spite of other people starving'. But Miss Gatha ignored the remark. It was only when their muffled derision changed to angry murmurs that she threatened to give up the eldership and stop helping them if she heard another word. Having cowed them, she promised that things would be better, would be different, when Isaac returned. With his knowledge of books he would know ways of fighting the drought, would tell them how to dig wells deep into the earth, would know the particular spot to dig, as Moses in the Bible had known which rock to strike in order to get water for the children of Israel. Things would be better, for Isaac would share with them not only the contents of the money-box, but the knowledge that he had obtained from books and from the big world outside. The congregation had listened sullenly, but there had been no more grumbling.

When Isaac left Hebron after his holiday that Easter, she had told him to stay in Kingston over Christmas and return on the first day of the new year. For that would be the twenty-first anniversary of their arrival up in Hebron, an auspicious day on which to return and lay claim to the eldership. She wondered now what he would say tomorrow when he came back to find that the eldership was already his. Perhaps he would not say anything at all, only nod his head and leave her wondering whether he had any will or any desires of his own. There were times, too, when she was frightened at how completely he could shut himself away from her by agreeing with everything she said.

The last night of his holiday, trying to reach through to him, she had talked about Hebron, its beginning and its future. She had told him of the money that his father had left for him, of the amounts that she had added to it, of the place where she kept it safely buried waiting for him to return, to become Elder, waiting to be spent on books and clothes and little luxuries which befitted his new status as an educated man. She had looked to him for some sign of approval, but he only nodded, his face as expressionless as ever. After a while he got up and told her that he would go for a walk. Waiting for him, she fell asleep with the lamp still burning beside her. He must have come back and stolen past her, because it was the sputtering of the lamp and the smell of smoke and kerosene oil that woke her up the next morning. She said nothing to him and he offered no explanations. She saw him off at the railway station that afternoon and when he said goodbye, he did so with the politeness of a stranger. She waved to him as the train pulled out, but he was already seated and opening a book. As he turned the pages she caught a quick glimpse of the wrist-watch that the congregation had given him that morning at the farewell service in the church. Obadiah had returned in time from Cockpit Centre and had presided. Miss Gatha had been forced to admit that he was ungrudging in his eulogy of Isaac. She even felt a slight shame for her son at the way he had sat on the dais, his eyes averted from the Elder's friendly gaze.

An inexplicable fear flashed across Miss Gatha's mind. She stopped rocking. It was the same fear that had descended upon her that day in the church when she had taken over the eldership, and Obadiah intruded with his madness. She stared out through the half-open door at the hills that were like knife-blades, flat and silhouetted against the sky. Then, across her line of vision, blocking it, the dumpy figure of Sister Beatrice knelt, rooting and rummaging amongst the dead vines on the hill-side. Miss Gatha smiled. It had taken the drought to stop Beatrice from chasing young men, to search for food instead.

She watched Sister Beatrice in her vain search and, after a few minutes, lulled by the waves of heat that fanned out over Hebron, she fell asleep. She dreamt of the great procession of the New Believers that would welcome Isaac home, would acclaim him as their Elder, make up to him for his deformity, his father's contempt and rejection, her own instinctive revulsion, make up to him for everything. She smiled in her sleep.

Sister Beatrice passed by the house on her way home. Habit made her look up hopefully at the guinep tree that overhung Miss Gatha's veranda. She saw a carrion crow perched on the topmost limb. He was lean and fierce, his folded black wings as stark as the limb on which he sat. His red crest gleamed hungrily in the sun.

7. The Money-Box

The sun reared up over Hebron like a wild horse. It streamed across the sky, tangled with the naked branches of the trees, brightened the hills, illuminated winding paths, glittered like incandescent dust on the heads and shoulders, the marching feet of the congregation; rimmed their flags and banners with light, and settled in the gleaming river of morning that flooded the land.

Eufemia stood by her gate and watched her parents. They walked heavily down the track, and their feet, clumsy in the unaccustomed shoes, trampled down the parched grass, flattened the dew-drops that still quickened the earth. When they disappeared round the bend she crossed the path and went up the steps into Ananias's room. He sat on his bed flexing his muscles and shaking his head to clear the sleep away. As she entered, he stretched and yawned. She could see the sweat glistening on the cluster of hairs under his arm-pits. And, in the shadowed secrecy of the room, his eyes appraised her body. She turned abruptly and went out, calling after her:

'Hurry, man, hurry!'

He dressed quickly, smoothed his moustache, took up a triangular blue banner and followed her down the hill.

Brother Hugh waited on his small veranda. He was fully dressed except for his shoes. Behind him, in the room, Gee sat polishing the shiny black leather. Her body strained against her dress and her straw hat bobbed up and down. Sweat beaded her face, dripped from her forehead, as the dress became an elastic band tightening round her, and the hat on her head was like the weight of the sky. The uneven floor boards whirled like a top beneath her. She dropped the shoe, lurched over to the bed and pulled out an enamel chamber-pot. Her eyes focused on a black spot where the enamel was chipped, and she retched violently. Hugh heard the noise and came in. He frowned as he saw his shoes still unfinished. But when she looked up at him and he saw the fear in her eyes, he helped her up on to the bed. Then he flicked the polishing cloth over his shoes and put them on.

Flies buzzed round the chamber-pot as he carried it outside, emptied it, and buried the vomit. When he returned, Gee was sitting up. The customary dark glow of her face had replaced the ashen pallor of a few minutes before. Her black eyes were as brilliant as fireflies' wings.

'So now like you give me baby?' she said.

Hugh looked at her quickly then shrugged.

'So what? What else God make woman for?'

He took a banner from the table and went out. She followed him, closing the door. They walked on in silence. But Gee noticed that he carried himself with a new authority.

The long, drawn-out echo of a cowhorn sounded from the tamarind tree below the spring, and the New Believers hurried to answer its summons. The thought of Isaac's imminent return played upon their already heightened fantasies. The money-box he was due to resurrect became a source of magic. Once it was opened, water would gush from springs, the land would bloom again with yam and corn and cassava, sugar-cane and sweet potatoes; giant pumpkins would appear on lush vines, coffee and orange blossoms would once more scent the air. Even a clear promise of rain would not have seemed as exciting. The money-box that Moses had bequeathed to his son expanded in their reckoning until it contained the whole run and course of their great expectations.

****

Aunt Kate awoke to the stir and bustle of Hebron. She imagined that she was back again in the time of Moses when each day brought fresh excitement. She looked at the pillow beside her, expecting to see her husband Aloysius meet her gaze with his serious weighty look. A cowhorn sounded plaintively in the distance. She got out of bed thinking that her memory had tricked her again. For anyway, on a weekday such as this, Aloysius would have been up before her, and if she didn't stop him, would have lit the fire and put on the pot for the strong black coffee. But she never liked him to do so, was shocked at a man encroaching on what was a woman's domain. Aloysius, too, would have been shocked before the change came over him.

She drew on her long brown stockings with their patchwork of darns, and tried to remember when it was that her husband had started to change, to become almost humble, to lose his stiff pride of place? Was it after Maverlyn was born? No, it was much later than that. After Moses crucified himself, Aloysius had been afraid to take on the eldership. That was why he had died soon after. But what did he die of? She couldn't remember his being sick. How was it that she could recall some things so clearly and others not at all?

She opened the door and stepped down. The pain stabbed through her leg. But as she hobbled along, the fresh morning breeze blowing in her face eased the pain. The cowhorn sounded loudly now and she could hear voices calling to one another. She was a child again and a 'junkonoo' procession was jigging by with drums and whistles and fantastic costumes. She hurried down past the church and round and into the square. Ann waited for her there, her arms akimbo, her joyless presence shutting her in. Aunt Kate tried to get past her, to reach the others whose laughter carried so clearly.

'Move out of my way, Ann. Let me go and see off the others!'

Ann took her arm and led her over to the spring where she had spread a hessian sack on the ground. She helped Aunt

Kate to sit down, then placed a can of water and a small piece of unleavened bread beside her. Then she took a comb from her pocket and arranged the old woman's hair. Aunt Kate submitted. But she willed Ann to leave soon. For weeks now she had been imprisoned in her sick room with Ann's unquiet presence, her unceasing mechanical activity. This one day, at least, Aunt Kate wanted to herself.

'Oh no, Aunt Kate,' Ann was saying fussily, 'you weren't going down that steep stretch of hill to see anybody off, not even the Lord himself. For tonight it's me who would have to sit up with you listening to you groaning and moaning with pain. What you are going to do is to sit right here where you can catch the sun. Then later on when it's fire-hot you are to go across to my house and rest yourself on the bed there. Now you must promise me that you will do that. For if not I shall have to stay up here with you today, for you are not quite better as yet...'

'No, Ann, I will do anything you say,' Aunt Kate vowed hastily. 'You go off with the others and leave me in peace!'

Ann took up her small basket and turned away, her face grim. Now that she was going Aunt Kate thought that she could afford to be conciliatory. She caught at Ann's skirt:

'Don't leave in vexation, Ann. You know I don't mean half what I say in the heat of the moment. If it were not for you, how I would manage in my old age and sickness, answer me that? To tell the truth you are as good a neighbour to me as your mother Liza was and it's only a pity that when she died I didn't have my head about me to sing wakesong and cry my heart out at her funeral...'

'You don't have to worry about that,' Ann said, mollified, 'for when Mama died you cried louder than anyone else and we couldn't get you to leave from beside her dead body. And at the funeral...'

Aunt Kate interrupted her, frowning with concentration:

'Ann, Ann, don't we held the wake out in the yard and the coffin was on a bench and we had Liza all dressed and ready and her face was glinting in the moonlight and we were all singing…?'

'Yes, Aunt Kate,' Ann said, 'we held the wake out in the yard, same place, same way!'

Aunt Kate remembered her old friend. Liza lay dying, an enormous, inert mass of flesh, only her face quivering from time to time as she tried to inhale. The heavy jowls hung loosely and her greedy lips, dry and creased, sucked in the air. Aunt Kate herself sat at the foot of the bed. Death should not have come to Liza like that, she thought. It should have crept up on her like sleep had come to Maverlyn, quiet and mysterious. And as if she had willed Death to do her bidding, Liza died when the first shaft of sunlight slanted across the room; and remained, coffined in her flesh, ageless and indestructible.

Aunt Kate kept vigil all day, seeing them wash and dress the dead body. Afterwards the women thronged into the room, weeping and wailing as they commented on how the body had become swollen, the legs and ankles distended, and, under the skin, a yellow fluid, like bile. The men trooped in dutifully, glanced quickly at the corpse, and left, avoiding the women talking about death and disease, afraid of being infected by the miasma their whispers cast over the room.

At the wake that night Aunt Kate saw the dead face through her tears. It looked like a drowned moon in the spring, submerged in a thicket of stars. The singing was mournful, harsh, insistent, a requiem of fear and terror. She could hear herself singing with the others:

Before Jehovah's awful throne,
The nations bow with sacred joy,
Know that the Lord is God alone,
He can create, He can destroy!

There were showers early the next morning, and puddles formed on the track along which four of the Brethren carried Liza's coffin to the graveyard. Aunt Kate walked immediately behind the coffin, flanked by Sue and Ann. The others came behind them. There was no singing. Aunt Kate carried a bunch of wild flowers in her hands. The stems trembled as the rain drummed down on them. The feet of the mourners as they walked along were heavy with mud. But all round them the trees were wet and sparkling; raindrops chased each other off the surface of leaves, torrents of water eddied about their roots. Here and there clumps of fern had been beaten down by the rain, their beaded intricacy stamped against the earth to moulder and bring forth new life.

The grave gaped forlornly under a grey and sodden sky. The rain striped the piled-up mounds of earth on either side with runnels. The coffin was lowered and muddy water splashed against the sides of the grave. Obadiah was preaching and raindrops tangled in his hair:

'Man that is born of woman, born unto trouble…as the sparks fly upwards…'

She had heard it all before and her attention wandered. Across from her she could see Moses's tomb with its marble headstone and huge, rotting wooden cross. Beside this was a mound marked by a small tablet. That was Aloysius's grave…

****

Miss Gatha's voice, harsh and strong, cut across the quiet of the morning. She was marshalling the congregation for their departure.

'Everybody ready now?' she called out.

'Ready, Miss Gatha!' they shouted.

There was the sound of tramping feet and singing. Aunt Kate nodded her head in time to the rhythm. She heard Miss Gatha reminding them to keep together in one group at the station and to wait until she arrived in the cart before going on the platform. There was a note of fulfillment in Gatha's voice, Aunt Kate thought, as if she were now suckling the whole of Hebron. When Isaac had been born Gatha's breasts had been dry. It was she, Kate, with her milk abundant as a river, who had suckled Isaac. Gatha had never quite forgiven her for that.

The voices of the congregation died away in the distance. Suddenly, from an overhanging branch above the empty spring, a bird called. Aunt Kate shivered and Ann asked quickly:

'It's the fever coming on again, Aunt Kate?'

Aunt Kate looked up, surprised that Ann was still there.

'No,' she said slowly. 'A ghost just walked over my grave!'

The two women listened as the tap-tapping of Miss Gatha's stick resounded in the hollow brightness of the square.

She swept up the track and into the square, her triumph like a robe about her. She nodded to Aunt Kate, swung round to Ann, and, seeing her standing alone, asked sharply:

'Where's Zacky? Where's Zacky with the money-box?'

Ann looked blank and she explained:

'Yes, yes, the money-box. I showed Zacky where to dig it up over an hour ago, and told him to wait for me here. I wonder what…'

She broke off. Ann's slowness and lack of understanding filled her with added urgency. What did these creatures with mud in their veins know about the dream that she had nursed for twenty years? She motioned to Ann:

'You wait here. I will go and see what's keeping him so long!'

She hurried up the narrow track to the church, her boots raising clouds of dust. The sun spread out over Hebron and tinted the hills and the tree-tops with pale gold.

The morning lengthened. Under the trees, the dancing shadows grew still. Miss Gatha re-entered the square. She walked, hunched over on her stick, as if warding off a blow. Her face was once more set in its grim lines. Brother Zacky followed behind her. He carried a spade and a fork on his shoulders. The prongs of the fork were encrusted with a dry, reddish earth. As his eyes met Ann's he shrugged his shoulders in a despairing gesture. But Miss Gatha took no notice of Ann.

She went straight across to Aunt Kate and asked her:

'Kate, it was you that Isaac used to talk to, so see if you can help me now. Try and remember back to last Easter when he was here on holiday…last Easter, you remember?'

'Last Easter?' Aunt Kate repeated, slowly.

'Yes, yes,' Miss Gatha said, controlling herself with a great effort. 'Did he ever talk to you then, tell you anything about the money-box?'

'The money-box?'

'Yes, you see, it's gone. It's not anywhere where I buried it. And Isaac was the only one who knew where it was…I told him that last night…and he didn't come home until late…I fell asleep at the table...and when I woke the lamp was smoking…outside the sky was clearing…so perhaps that night he might have come to you as he used to…talked his secret story…tell you about the money-box…where he was going to hide it…'

But there was no recognition in Aunt Kate's eyes. Miss Gatha stooped and searched the other woman's face, pleading for reassurance. For an instant she wanted to panic, to give reign to a suspicion that lurked in her mind, tightened her belly, made her throat dry. But she mastered herself and continued speaking rapidly, her voice shrill.

'And don't you remember, Kate, what a secretive sort of child he was? Always hiding away things? I am sure that that night he must have gone and dug up that money-box from where it was, then hid it away somewhere else…That's what he did, I am sure of it…For don't you remember, Kate, that time when he was a small boy, and I bought the boots for him to wear to school, and after the first week, he hid away the one that I had made specially for his club-foot, and for all I flogged him he wouldn't tell me where he hid it, you remember, and there was that other time when…'

Miss Gatha put her hand to her mouth and stood up. Her eyes stared through Zacky and Ann as if she were unaware of their presence.

Miss Gatha's insistence had unbalanced Aunt Kate, made her mind a blank. Now, in the ensuing hush, she saw Isaac as a young boy, returning from school, his shirt and short trousers stained with sweat, his eyes red with weariness, his club-foot dragging like a cross behind him.

'I remember now, Gatha, I remember the time with the boots,' she called out eagerly, 'but he wouldn't tell me where he hid them, and there was another time when he hid a ball for…'

She hesitated before she continued:

'…for Maverlyn…but he made me close my eyes…so that I wouldn't see where he was hiding it…'

Aunt Kate nodded to herself and retreated into her memories.

Miss Gatha was glad that Kate had stopped talking, now that she had given her the confirmation that was needed. Now she could believe what she wanted to believe – that Isaac had dug up the box, hidden it in another place. That was the explanation, she was sure of it. She would banish doubts and would listen to nothing else now, nothing that could destroy her new surety.

'Zacky,' she called briskly, 'unload the drum barrels and the hampers from the cart, but leave the kerosene tin and the basket. Then pick me up here. Hurry!'

Zacky went off. Ann stared at Miss Gatha with an expression of doubt on her face. Miss Gatha snapped at her:

'What are you standing there staring at me for? Go and help Zacky. And hurry! I don't want to be late for Isaac!'

Ann hustled away. Miss Gatha pulled off her wedding ring, a broad gold band. She would pawn it in Cockpit Centre, she decided, buy enough food and water for the day. When Isaac returned and dug up his box, then he could start off as Elder, could buy food for his flock. She tied the ring into her handkerchief and hung it round her neck. Her finger where she had worn the ring was the color of ashes. As she rubbed at it, she spoke aloud, almost with defiance:

'For I made Isaac go to school barefoot, since he had hidden the boots, and that is why today he reach to the top. That is why today he can come back as teacher and leader to his people. For he will come back. I know that. I know that!'

Aunt Kate heard her voice like a distant echo. Soon the cart rumbled into the square. Its sides had been newly painted and glistened in the sun. The mules looked well fed and spruce. Miss Gatha climbed up beside Zacky. Ann sat in the back of the cart, and, as they drove off, she waved to Aunt Kate. The old woman did not wave back. The past had taken over in her mind once more.

8. The Ball

It was mid-afternoon. Kate sat under a tree on the ledge above the square. She was sewing, and kept an eye on Maverlyn and Isaac as they played. When the other children were around, the two hardly took notice of each other. Some instinct warned them that their closeness, revealed to the others, would only aggravate the teasing with which Isaac was already burdened. But whenever the other children were away, shooting birds or flying kites high up in the hills, Isaac would whistle and Maverlyn would run down to the square. Kate, too, had been silently drawn into the conspiracy. She would sit and do her chores and keep watch. As soon as she saw any of the others returning she would call Maverlyn, and Isaac would creep back to his own yard.

Maverlyn was wearing her white frock with the red dots. Kate noted in her mind that she had to let out the hem. The child was already several inches taller than Isaac. He was dressed in the greyish-white shirt and trousers which his mother made from bleached flour bags. They were playing a game, using a lime for a ball, throwing and catching it. Maverlyn moved like the wind. Isaac kept up with her, hopping around, achieving his speed and agility by an act of will. Soon Kate heard them quarrelling. As always, Maverlyn was the aggressor.

'Now you see how you throw the ball crooked and let it slip out of my hand, Isaac. And now I can't find it anywhere!'

'The ball is only a lime, Maverlyn. I can pick another one.'

'I must find this ball. This ball isn't a lime. How you can stand there and say that this ball is a lime?'

'A lime is only a lime. It's not any ball,' Isaac persisted.

Kate heard a noisy chorus of children racing down the hill. She gathered up her sewing, called Maverlyn, and the two retreated to their yard. It was sundown by this time, and the sky was bright with the afterglow. Later that night, about eleven, Kate woke up, sure that in her sleep she had heard someone whistle outside the house. She listened, straining her ears. Only the rise and fall of her own breathing filled the room. She felt for Maverlyn beside her. The bed was still warm where she had been lying. Kate got out of bed sluggishly, groped her way across the room and opened the heavy board window. When she looked out the moon was hard and crystalline in the sky, and the hills cast enormous shadows. She hurried to the door, pulled it open and stepped out. As her bare feet touched the cold stone step a chill invaded her whole body. Her eyes scanned the surrounding landscape, the crouching shadows, the moonlit islands between them.

'Maverlyn! Maver...lyn!' she called.

An owl answered her, and a night bird screeched. And the church was a grim and silent monument, a dark tomb where the sleeping Hebronites had buried their secrets for the night.

She reached the square to find Isaac stooping beside the spring. He had a bamboo pole in his hand and was stretching across the spring to fish something out. She could hear the water bubbling up, then lapping against the sides. Isaac wore his red flannelette nightshirt. The tight whorls of his hair caught the moonbeams. He was frightened when he saw Kate, but she made no move towards him. He smiled at her, tentative at first, then with assurance. She walked over to the spring and, as she climbed the little mound of earth, felt her knees giving way. She steadied herself, then looked down.

The skirt of Maverlyn's nightgown had floated up above her waist and ballooned behind her head. Her black hair looked like seaweed. Her legs doubled themselves up in the curve of the spring. Kate remained rooted, still as a tree-stump petrified by fire and decay. Seeing her so quiet, Isaac explained:

'The moonlight was so bright that I called her to come down and let us look for the ball. We saw it floating over there under the banking, and I turn my back to get the pole. She call out to me that the ball change into two and that the one underneath was a star. By the time I turn round she fall right into the water. And she must have been well tired for she just lay there and go to sleep. And don't you see for yourself, Aunt Kate? Don't you see that she is only sleeping?'

'Yes,' Kate said and stood waiting for him to tell her what to do next.

He took up the bamboo pole which he had laid down beside him.

'I am going to try and reach the ball so that I can hide it away for her, and she can have it safe and sound when she wake up. You sit down beside me and sing to her, so that, in case I trouble up the water a little bit, she won't wake up sudden and startle and get drowned.'

Kate sat down, crossing her legs under her. She cradled her arms. 'What I must sing?' she asked him.

'Anything, sing anything!' he said, reaching down for the lime with the bamboo pole.

Kate sang the tune of the game that she had heard them singing earlier on, for it was the only tune she could think of.

'Pass the ball and the ball gone round...' she sang.

Isaac fished out the lime and squeezed it dry. He told her to shut her eyes whilst he hid it. She obeyed and went on singing. She was surprised when the others came, crowding around her, calling out in alarm, stretching out a forest of hands to help her up. They led her across a landscape of stone – the faces were stony, the eyes of granite, and when they made her lie down, the bed was as hard as rock. Only Isaac's eyes made four with hers, only his eyes were human. The next day there was singing and much weeping, and some of the women urged her to kiss an inert thing that lay inside a box. She refused.

Isaac winked at her and she started to giggle, and the more serious the faces around her became the more she laughed. The sky became populated with dancing suns and her head whirled around with them. She woke up months later. The world was bright outside her window and Isaac sat like a shadow at the foot of her bed. He smiled at her and patted her hand. His eyes told her that everything was all right, that they had buried the nameless inert thing and left Maverlyn, untouched, in the spring.

Three years later Isaac went away to school in Cockpit Centre. During the week he was boarded out with the head teacher and his wife, and came up to Hebron for the weekends. The first Friday evening of his absence, Aunt Kate sat by the spring and waited anxiously for his return. All that week she had missed him. Without him, there was no one else in Hebron to share her fantasy, to reinforce her mistrust of reality. When he finally appeared, late in the evening, she chided him:

'Isaac, Maverlyn and me waited and waited. Why you took so long to come back to us?'

He did not answer. She beckoned to him to come close, but he made no move to obey. He was wearing a khaki shirt and trousers, and his new boots were covered with dust. He stood looking at her for a few moments, then abruptly accused her:

'Aunt Kate, why you told me all that story about how my father was a big prophet who had visions from God and crucified himself like Jesus? Why you told me what wasn't so at all? Why you told me what wasn't true?'

'But it was true, Isaac, it was true,' she cried, surprised at the condemnation in his glance.

'Yes, it was true, but not the way you told it. Not that way at all. And I hate school. I hate it!'

'They teased you about the foot?'

'Yes, but that didn't so much matter. I long accustomed to that. But they have a song that they sing, everywhere in

Cockpit Centre when they see me and hear my name they sing it…'

'A song…?'

'Yes, a song that say that my father was a… madman…and that he tried to fly to heaven, and after crucify himself to fool people that he was Jesus. And it say in the song that it wasn't God who gave Hebron to…my father, but a white man who gave a baby to a young Sister, and wanted her out of the way because he was afraid of the scandal. Those are the exact words of the song. And don't it's true?'

He searched her face anxiously, and she hedged:

'Well, you see, that was only part of the story…'

'Then why you never me told that part of the story then, Aunt Kate?' he cried out to her.

She wanted to explain to him that the Cockpit Centre people were a bad-minded lot, a slave people with tongues as sharp as swords and bitter like aloes; that they lived fenced in by vacant, hopeless days, and out of their own misery and wretchedness divined only what was mean and petty in the lives of others; but that for all the songs they might sing, his father Moses Barton was a great man, and with men like him there were a lot of things, good and bad, that could be said. But as the years passed, people had a way of forgetting the good and holding on to the bad memories. She wanted to explain all this to Isaac, to give him back his faith in her. But he had raised his voice as he spoke to her and she was afraid that he might wake Maverlyn.

'Isaac, don't startle Maverlyn, boy. Sit here with me until she fall into sound sleep and then I will tell you the whole story about your father and about how we all…'

He didn't wait for her to finish. He turned his back on her and walked away.

Part 2

FRIDAY

Shall we, then, live thus vile – the race of Heaven,
Thus trampled, thus expelled, to suffer here
Chains and these torments?

-Milton: Paradise Lost

The god who created the sun which gives us light,
Who rouses the waves and rules the storms
Though hidden in the clouds he watches us…
Our god calls upon us to do good works…
Throw away the god of the whites
Who has so often caused us to weep.
Listen to the voice of liberty which speaks
In the heart of us all!

(From the incantation of Boukman, the Haitian prophet, on the eve of the Haitian Revolution)

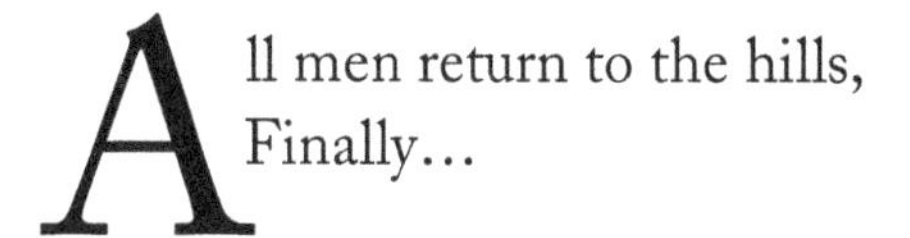

All men return to the hills,
Finally…

-Roger Mais

9. The Kingdom of Heaven

Moses Barton came to Cockpit Centre as a prophet of the castaways, a cavalier of the impossible, seeing visions, dreaming dreams, and the town was never the same after his coming. He came to Cockpit Centre when it was a cruel town, a place where stinking hovels crowded close together, where multitudes were packed into shacks to live and die like grass. He walked into Cockpit Centre one day when the sun curved over the land like a machete blade, and the range of hills that towered in the distance were the edge of the blade, made jagged with constant filing.

Moses Barton wore a blue turban, a long white robe, and leather sandals, and he carried a shepherd's staff. He walked up the main street, past the row of wretched houses, keeping his eyes on the hills, wanting no truck with the poverty and defeat that had vanquished the town. For he had come with a message from God to stir His people out of their apathy, out of their waiting on faith, hope and charity under the sun. He had come to break the neck of cowardice and slavery, to lead the people of Cockpit Centre out of bondage and into the Promised Land.

He entered the market-place, his feet seeming to glide over the litter of leaves, mango skins, squashed guavas, slippery jackfruit, scraps of paper, and flattened matchboxes. Miss Gatha Randall was the first to see him. His beard and robe reminded her of Jesus walking on the waters. She pretended to ignore him and went on selecting fish for her shop. Moses stopped in the centre of the market and stood still under the blazing sun.

One by one the brawling, raucous voices fell silent. The men stared at him, wanting to laugh at his strange clothes, but subdued by his fierce, red-rimmed eyes. The women fidgeted like mares sensing the approach of a stallion.

Kate Lansing arranged her mangoes, laying them out in heaps of four on the ground. She felt his eyes on her and looked up. A curious power seemed to emanate from this stranger, and to draw her towards him. Her breasts rounded themselves under her frock. But he looked away from her as he noticed Gatha Randall, the strikingly ugly young woman who alone wore a uniform of respectability – boots and stockings and a long-sleeved dress with a high neckline. She had already wound up her business, and swept out of the market, her head held high. Moses concentrated instead on his first convert, a middle-aged woman, Liza Edwards, who sold home-made candy in the market, sat next to Kate, and was her friend.

****

Liza Edwards the candy-seller owned half an acre of land in Cockpit Centre. Two of her children were alive, the other five having died of hunger. The men who fathered her children had all left her and gone off in search of work, chasing a mirage of greener pastures. Prophet Moses sat in her ramshackle two-roomed house and listened patiently to her outpouring of troubles. No one had ever bothered to listen to her before. She had become a staunch 'Sister Believer in the Kingdom of Heaven Now'. The Prophet baptized her and her two little daughters, Sue and Ann.

Prophet Moses was reticent about his past. Perhaps he wanted to forget the events that led to his coming to Cockpit Centre, the brutal life he had known in his youth. For the majority of his followers, his silence surrounded him with an aura of mystery that encouraged their devotion. But since Liza Edwards was his first convert and a chosen star in his firmament of dreams and prophecy, he confided in her, gave her a doctored but suitable version of his origins. He told her that his parents died when he was a baby, that a princess who was the reincarnated daughter of the Pharaohs adopted him after being instructed to do so in a dream. His foster-mother had gone under the name of Sister Barton to hide her true identity. When her brother in Kingston became a widower, he sent for her to care for his four children and keep house. The brother, an ignorant and irreligious man, drove Moses out when he was still a small boy to serve an apprenticeship in the school of hard knocks and toil. After the Lord had tested the young Moses for many years, He finally guided him to the house of a white man, an American Baptist preacher. Moses worked with this man for three years, going to church with him, where he instructed himself in the faith, versed himself in the teachings of the Holy Book.

The preacher lived in a cool suburb in the St Andrew foothills. One day, working in the garden, Moses had seen his first vision. Now swearing Liza Edwards to secrecy, he told her in hushed tones how the Lord had appeared to him:

'It was just a day like any other, Sister Edwards. No sign to mark it as different. I was watering the flowers. I came to a rhododendron bush that stood alone by itself. As I poured out water at the root, I see the whole bush light up with fire before my eyes. I step back, I stand still, I watch. The bush flamed orange and green fire. The Presence of God was all round about me. I fall on my knees, I bow my head to the earth. I make to take off my shoes but as it wasn't Sunday, I wasn't wearing any. And the ground on which I was standing, Sister Edwards, was holy, holy, ground.'

The Prophet rose from his chair, his eyes turned inwards, his face ablaze with revelation. Liza Edwards looked at him with awe. Her heavy breasts, pendulous from suckling seven children, rose and fell with emotion. The Prophet made quick dramatic gestures acting out his vision. He had a curiously sibilant tenor voice which he used like a musical instrument. He spoke softly now, his tone almost plaintive:

'I remain there, on my knees. I wait and I watch. The sun peeled itself from the sky, sink into the sea. I remain there. The fire flame away from the bush. I remain there. The moon creep up into the sky and the stars after her in procession. I remain there, I wait and I watch. The moon start to fall quickly towards the north. The Voice of the Lord was loud in my heart.

'"Moses, run and catch the moon," He said. "Moses, run and catch Me!"'

'I run and I run. Up and up into the hills. I come at last to a place where the waters tumble down in a waterfall. The bamboo trees rubbed against the wind, the fireflies hummed and sang and sported their wings. The moon drop into the water. I see it glimmer and dance. I stretch out my hands to reach it. The wind and the water, the bamboo trees and the fireflies were silent. The moon turn... into God Himself. And I see His hair float out in a stream of gold, His eyes shine forth blue sparks like chips of His sky. I fall on my face. He speak to me stern, but He called me...Son! He told me to shake the dust of Kingston off my feet, to cross the high mountains to the north side of the island, to a town where the sea dashed itself against the white sand. Then I was to turn my back on the sea, mount several miles up to a place surrounded by hills which were His arms. And there, in the market-place, I would find a woman who was my true mother, as Mary was the mother of Jesus. This woman would help me to prepare for the ascension of His children to heaven. For He was wearied of waiting for our coming. He hungered for our coming...'

Moses placed his hands on Liza's shoulders and called her 'mother'. Her joy was boundless. She knelt before him, touched the floor with her forehead, and called him her Saviour whom she would not dare to call son. For that the finger of the Lord had touched her, was too much for her to bear. Moses lifted her to her feet, with some effort, for she was a big woman. He was her child, he assured her, the child of her spirit and her will, to forge that which would be acceptable to her Lord. Then he asked her for space on her land to build his temple, as much money as she could spare to help in his proselytizing mission. All of which she gladly promised and, in addition, prepared a bed in her house for him, and fed him well, going hungry sometimes and depriving her daughters; keeping them quiet in the mornings whilst Moses meditated, lying in bed. And she washed his robe and turban, starched and ironed them with a fervor that could only have been equalled if he had been God Himself.

****

Prophet Moses came to Cockpit Centre in October. By the end of November his following had increased to several hundreds. As his fame spread, disciples came to him from the neighboring mountain villages, from the seaport town of Paradise Bay, and even from as far away as the capital, Kingston. He ordered them all to sell their possessions and put the money in his hands. He fed them and clothed them in white robes and turbans, even those (and they were in the majority) who brought nothing with them. And he preached to them night after night, invested their raggedness with dignity, and set a time and limit to the travail which had been theirs and their ancestors' for three hundred years. On December 31st of that same year, he promised, he would fly to heaven. Once there, he would send back golden chariots to take them up so that they could lay claim to the Kingdom. And in heaven, he promised them, the masters would be slaves, and the slaves masters. Stars and new continents would be theirs to rule over, and their subjects would be angels, white angels. The date, December 31st, became the magic word which insulated the Brethren Believers in Heaven Now from the mockery of unbelievers.

Someone who scorned Moses and his flock with the dull, impotent anger of the respectable was Aloysius Matthews, the master carpenter. He was a member of the Wesleyan church in Cockpit Centre and proud of the fact. The gentry of the town, white planters and brown mulattoes, attended this church because the minister was an Englishman. Little by little, the shirtless ones for whom the church had been originally established were excluded. Only a few worthy black citizens like Aloysius Matthews dared to mingle with the pale-skinned gentry, and to listen to the exhortations to repentance of the white parson. The parson, an elderly bachelor, was, at the time of Moses's coming, staying at a friend's plantation in a neighbouring parish, resting from the heat and spiritual aridity of his own diocese. In his absence the church was left in charge of the deacon, who, in his turn, delegated all the work and responsibility to Aloysius. The latter enjoyed his importance. Besides, he obtained work from the wealthier church-members and made a substantial living from his carpentry. He was an excellent craftsman. In November of the same year of Moses's arrival he married Kate Lansing.

Kate was twenty-three years old at the time of her marriage. Her mother had died and left her, at sixteen, with three young brothers to care for. She managed this, scraping a living from odd jobs, and with little help from neighbours all as poor as herself. At times she had almost given up in despair at the near hopelessness of her task. On such occasions she swore to herself to have nothing to do with men. The only legacy they left one with were children. She kept to her pledge partly because her body was always exhausted from the work she was forced to do – weeding grass, cutting cane, breaking stones; partly because all her love was poured out on her brothers; and, most important, none of the men she met offered the material security which had now become indispensable to her. When he was sixteen, her eldest brother left for Kingston. He was bright and intelligent and managed to get a job as an apprentice printer; by the time he was nineteen he was well enough established to send for his two younger brothers. There would be better opportunities for them in Kingston, he said. He asked Kate to come too, but as he had recently married a well-off widow some twelve years his senior, Kate thought it wiser not to go. Besides, at that time she could not envisage a home for herself outside this town which she had made her own.

After her brothers left she began to trade in the market. She bought fruit and ground provisions wholesale from small farmers and sold her purchases retail in the market. Her profit and turnover were small, but enough for her needs. And she liked the bustle, the noise, the explosive gaiety of the bazaar life which made it impossible for her to feel lonely. One day, after closing time, finding that she had a basket of mangoes still unsold, Kate went from door to door trying to sell them. They were ripe, and if kept overnight would spoil in the heat. As she was passing by Aloysius Matthew's shop she heard the sound of hammering and went in. He was working late that evening, and he bought a dozen mangoes and asked Kate to drop by again. He lived alone and seldom had time to go to the market. Kate returned again and again. She sensed that he was attracted to her and, at the same time, afraid of her. She encouraged his attentions. His obvious success as a carpenter, his shop and the room behind, equipped with some solid pieces of furniture, made him a good catch. For his part, Aloysius had been courting, for some years, a Sunday-school teacher and fellow church-member, a Miss Emma Withers. She was from a 'good' family, the daughter of an elementary schoolteacher, and was studying to be a postmistress. She was like a fallen fruit, dried up by the sun, while Kate was ripe and luscious and unplucked. He married Kate. Her vitality and warmth left him with little inclination for the chaste embraces of the teacher's daughter.

The deacon of Aloysius's church presided at the marriage service, and afterwards was master of ceremonies at the reception in the shop. The deacon was the mulatto son and heir of a wealthy absentee Scots planter, and was famous in the town for his drinking bouts and his way with the women. His small eyes, inflamed with drink, cast lascivious glances at Aloysius's bride. He rubbed himself surreptitiously against her whenever she passed by him, and, when she went into the back, followed and threw her down on the bed. Aloysius stood outside the door, listening and undecided. After all, the deacon was a brown-skinned 'busha', a 'squire' who owed much land and many houses and gave him plenty of work.

But Kate struck out at the brutish face leering down at her. She was strong and vigorous, and the drunken deacon was no match for her. She left him sprawled out on the floor, breathing noisily as he slept off his drunkenness. When he recovered, late that night, she told him that he had struck his head against the low ceiling and passed out. The deacon left, swearing to himself at the presumption of this black woman. Didn't she know that on his estate he could use any of the labourers' women the way he wanted to? That the labourers and their women considered it an honour and a privilege? As Aloysius was useful to him, the deacon held his tongue. But whenever Kate went to church with her husband he deliberately ignored her.

Prophet Moses's temple was near enough to the shop for the newly-married couple to hear the frenzied singing and drumming that lasted far into the night. Sometimes the wind brought Moses's preaching right into the shop. Aloysius would comment bitterly on the 'false prophet and his hooligans', shut the window and retire early. Kate, lying in bed beside him, listened to Moses and often felt an urge to take part in the festivities. But marriage and respectability were still a novelty to her, and she did not want to endanger her new position. She was particularly proud that she had won Aloysius away from a Sunday-school teacher. Aloysius had a great respect for education. He himself was illiterate and had often told Kate that it was only this drawback which kept him from moving to the capital and starting a business there. In Kingston, he said, a man had to be sharp in order not to be tricked, had to be able to read and write. He despised Moses, mainly because, like himself, the Prophet was a stranger to the written word, an outcast striving to belong.

So, in spite of constant urging from her friend, Liza Edwards, Kate avoided Moses's temple. And, when she passed him on the street, she refused to meet his demanding gaze, nor would she listen to the other women's gossip about his sexual prowess. Instead, she worked hard at being a good and proper wife to Aloysius. She helped him in the shop, cooked his dinner and served him at a table set with a knife and fork and white tablecloth and paper flowers in a cheap vase; and washed and ironed his white shirt and high collar for Sundays. She wore a hat and shoes and stockings and a long-sleeved white dress to church, and looked at her husband with great pride when he passed the plate round for the collection.

****

From her fried-fish shop farther along the lane, Miss Gatha Randall, too, heard the sound of drums, night after night. But when her aged mother suggested that they go to the temple to 'see what it was like', Miss Gatha sternly forbade her to 'mix and wrap up with those hooligans'. One evening, Sister Beatrice, one the young Believers, came to buy fried fish and loaves. Prophet Moses, she said, had run out of food to feed his flock. The next day the Prophet himself came to the shop. It was during the afternoon when the whole town seemed deserted. Miss Gatha's mother dozed in the room at the back of the shop, while she sat sewing on a high stool behind the counter. The shadow of the Prophet fell on her, and without looking up she knew who it was. They exchanged greetings, then the Prophet spoke to her about trivial things, never once mentioning his temple, his followers, or his plans. Instead he asked her about her shop, business in general, her family, the town. In spite of her ingrained reticence and suspicion, Miss Gatha found herself not only answering his questions but enjoying his interest. He made her feel important, that he was impressed by her acumen, by the history of her family, and especially by the story of her great-grandfather Cato Randall.

She asked him to sit, and offered him a glass of lemonade. She never touched anything strong, she said, and he declared that wine was a mocker, strong drink an abomination. Flattered and excited, Miss Gatha went into the kitchen, and, moving about, woke her mother. The old woman came out and sat down beside Moses, asked him about his mission, and expressed a fervent desire to join his Believers. She would like to go to heaven with them in a golden chariot, she said, and avoid the harsh and mortal passage of death. Moreover, she was bored with the dull life in the shop, had had enough of the smell of fish. Miss Gatha, entering, overheard her. Her mother's free and easy ways with the Prophet made her stiffen with outraged pride. Moses saw at once that he would not succeed in converting her, would not get a penny out of her to help feed his followers. He drank his lemonade and left. Miss Gatha said goodbye coldly, and afterwards ordered her mother not to have anything to do with 'these criminals – you don't know where they come from!' Having made her mother promise, she was also bound by this promise. Miss Gatha despised her mother, who had worked as a servant before her marriage into the Randall family, and had never lost her servant's habits. But for a moment she was sure that she saw a malicious gleam in the old woman's eyes.

****

The Pocomania worshippers in Cockpit Centre were even more opposed to Moses and his Believers than the respectable citizens. These voodoo followers of the 'obeahman', Ambrose, believed in the malevolent, cruel spirits opposed to man. Theirs was a lost god of Africa, who, for their sins, had abandoned them. And the only contact they could have with him was realized during the passing ecstasy of being possessed by the 'spirit'. Then they could feel the closeness of his presence, even divine his name.

Once a week, the big drums summoned the worshippers

to the ‘spiritual dancing’, so that the faithful could labour together in search of their god. But three weeks after Prophet Moses’s arrival in the town, the group of forty or so Pocomanians dwindled to ten. Sister Beatrice’s defection was a serious blow to Ambrose. She was a medium and the most promising of his younger followers. Beatrice had already begun to play a key role in his ritual ceremonies. He had been training her to succeed Sister May-May, his chief medium.

So, day after day, Ambrose sat before his backyard altar and concentrated on Prophet Moses, willing this intruder to fail, so that his wayward followers would return to him. A few of Ambrose’s disciples urged him to try his most powerful ‘obeah’ against Moses; and he was tempted to go down to the river, drink of the water, spit it out, and then wish that every drop of water Moses drank, every crumb he ate, should be poison to him. But Ambrose was scrupulous in the use of his black magic and decided against this final step. For, in his heart, Ambrose was certain that the white man’s God whom Moses worshipped would be sure to let him down in the end.

Besides, Ambrose was pleased that Sister May-May showed no signs of wanting to desert him. As long as she remained faithful, his prodigal flock was bound to return. In all his long years as an incarnation of the dark spirits he had never known so genuine a mystic, so plastic a medium as Sister May-May. She had a mass of coarse black hair, skin like black satin, a long wiry body, and an evil face. In the hiatus between the frenzies of being possessed and the aftermath of emptiness, she worked as a washerwoman.

May-May had an eleven year-old son at the time of Moses’s first coming to Cockpit Centre. She had named him Obadiah.

The boy often stood outside Prophet Moses’s temple. Children were not allowed inside unless their parents were members. So Obadiah stood on the pavement, a spectator to the drama of singing, hand-clapping, exhortation, and the feast that followed, when the Believers would gorge themselves with bread and fried fish and lemonade. Amongst those who, night after night, joined the young Obadiah to gaze at the happenings in Moses's kingdom was Hugh Pryor, a small-boned, agile boy with an impish, copper-coloured face. Hugh was an orphan. His old and ailing great-aunt, with whom he lived, looked on helplessly whilst he ran wild. The other boys envied him his cunning and toughness. He and Obadiah, keeping their nightly vigil on the pavement outside the temple, struck up a friendship, and were soon inseparable.

****

The time approached for Prophet Moses's flight to heaven. The faithful became restive. They had wound up their affairs on earth – sold their lands, their livestock, furniture, most of their belongings to shrewd unbelievers who did well out of the sales. And for days now 'the chosen ones' paraded about the town in white robes and gold paper crowns. The robes were getting soiled, the crowns losing their glitter. The unbelievers, inured to watching their neighbours try to escape from the circus of destitution into which they had all been born, to search for gods and devils and prophets to set them free, knew that it was best to 'laugh and let live'.

The Brethren Believers celebrated Christmas Day as the birthday of Prophet Moses. Some of the town's idlers joined in the 'freeness', and when they were discovered, fighting broke out. Prophet Moses quelled the riot, reminded his followers sternly that they were men of peace, and decreed that there should be fasting and prayer until December 30th. The Brethren Believers, many of them with blood-stained robes, obeyed their leader and slunk away to wait. And when the period of penance had passed there was another banquet. No uninvited guests turned up this time. No advance notice was given and the doors were bolted.

Early next morning when the town was asleep and the grass drenched with dew, Prophet Moses led his followers out to the foothills, and to a place where a giant breadfruit tree spread out its broad leaves like an offering to the rising sun. The Prophet climbed up to the top of the tree. As soon as the sun came up, he promised, he would take off for the Kingdom. Three hours later he would return with a fleet of golden chariots driven by white angels, dressed in tunics with gold buttons.

The faithful clustered beneath the tree, faces upturned, their eyes bright with hope. From where they stood they could see their Prophet through the dark green leaves, the silver-grey branches writhing like limbs in agony. He looked to them like some strange and magical fruit about to be plucked by a hand from heaven. They sang joyously and tears rolled down their cheeks. They clapped their rough hands together and banished silence from the hills and valleys. They held themselves erect for the first time in their lives. Were they not the dispossessed on earth about to inherit all the vast spaces of heaven? Were they not outcasts, prodigal sons, trekking back home after epochs of homelessness? Their hymns of praise were a benediction over dark hills hunched against the sky:

Behold the wretch who lust and wine
Had wasted his estate,
He begged a place among the swine,
To taste the husks they ate.

I die with hunger here, he cries,
I starve in foreign lands,
My father's house have large supplies,
And bounteous are his lands...

And as the sun rose above the hills, they fell on their knees. Their singing shook the land and their tears mingled with the dew. The sunrise was the presage of the long-delayed fulfillment of their hopes:

On Jordan's stormy banks I stand
And cast a wistful eye,

On Canaan's fair and promised land
Where my possessions lie.
We will rest on that fair and happy land
Very soon.
Just across on the evergreen shore
Sing a song with Moses and the Lamb
Very soon,
And dwell with the Father evermore.

****

There are garbled accounts of what actually happened to the Prophet that morning. Some said that his fall was an accident, that his foot caught in a branch and he stumbled. Others maintained that he literally spread out his arms and flew off, and when he was half-way up was cast down again by the forces of Satan. Whatever the truth was, Moses became a fallen idol, abandoned by the great majority of his followers. Liza and a few of the faithful carried him home, called in a doctor to set his broken leg, taking turns to nurse him. In the town itself there were empty lamentations amongst 'the chosen ones'. Some, blinded by the rage of losing everything, stood outside Liza's house and abused the Prophet. Liza, bursting out of her house, cowed them with a passionate rebuke. Grumbling, they departed with nothing but their robes and crowns to call their own. They had to start the business of earning a living in a cruel town all over again.

The laughter of the unbelievers echoed through the valleys and over the hills, rolled down to Paradise Bay and reached as far as Kingston. The anger of the Believers passed swiftly and they, too, joined in the laughter.

Aloysius Matthews laughed but little. He was not a man with much time for mirth. He worked hard and liked his work. And Kate's heart was heavy. Many of those who had lost everything were market women. She had seen their lives touched by the magic of new hope. Now she saw them return defeated, heard them quarrelling, fighting, screaming, saw them like scorpions stinging themselves to death, impelled by self-hatred and the bitterness of a broken dream. She was better off than they were, but she was still one of them.

Ambrose chuckled and rubbed his hands. His flock had returned, and ten new members with them. Sister May-May, reaching deeper into the abysses of her own spirit, became more possessed than ever. This was the true way, the only way for the lost ones, the disinherited in search of God, of themselves, of the Kingdom. And young Sister Beatrice looked on entranced, felt herself drowning in the strange fury Sister May-May scattered around her as her limbs fused with the drumming and she leaped and whirled and reached for the sky, as her body trembled and she wept and spoke in unknown tongues. Ambrose, presiding, would pass by and strike Beatrice with his rod. And she remained still, shivering like a sapling in a high wind until he led her off to his room; and the earth would shake with stamping feet, the drums thunder in her ears as he towered over her, masterful, demanding.

One morning after a Pocomania ritual, Obadiah came to fetch his mother. He found her as always stretched out on the ground in Ambrose's yard, rigid and unconscious. With the help of his friend, Hugh, Obadiah hauled her across the lane to her room and pushed and pulled her up on to the bed. Then they left her and wandered about the town, searching for scraps of food, begging. In the evening they ended up outside Moses's silent and abandoned temple. They missed the excitement of the singing and the shouting. When he returned home that night, Obadiah found his mother still in bed, her face contorted, her body writhing with pain. Her eyes stared beyond him towards the private horizons which only her tortured spirit could encompass. He drew close to her, called her name. She clutched at him, and her long nails raked his face savagely. He broke free and ran away, hounded down by a terror which did not ease its grip on his young heart until he reached Paradise Bay and the sea.

When he returned to Cockpit Centre the next day, he found that his mother was dead. After the funeral, a neighbour took him in. Another neighbour introduced him to Aloysius who employed him in his shop as an apprentice. Obadiah proved to be a good worker with a gift for carpentry. He and his employer got on well – they both had a habit of silence. He slept on a bench in the shop and had his meals with Kate and Aloysius. For the first time in his life he ate regularly. He began to fill out, and the lassitude in his limbs, the result of malnutrition, fell away from him. The only complaint that Aloysius had against him was that his friend Hugh was always hanging round the shop. And for Aloysius, Hugh was a bold-faced delinquent with respect for neither God nor man.

****

In the meanwhile the Commissioner of Police in Kingston had received a report on Prophet Moses. In the report the Prophet was described as a political agitator and a lunatic. The Commissioner was a conscientious administrator of justice. But he had been long conditioned to follow the book of rules rather than to think for himself, and had come to use words like 'duty', 'law and order' to cover up a lack of imagination. He had Moses arrested, bundled into a truck, and transported to Kingston. There the Prophet was tried on a charge of lunacy, convicted, and sent to the Mental Hospital which sprawled its assortment of shacks, green lawns, and trees between the hills and the sea – a fortress for lunatics erected by a society which regarded madness as a contagious disease, which equated stupidity with sanity, social injustice with law and order.

The Commissioner was also a member of the Church Synod in Kingston. He suggested to the other members that the success of the Prophet's mad mission may have been partly due to the fact that the parson of Cockpit Centre Church had been abandoning his parish for months on end. The Synod reprimanded the erring minister and sent him back to England.

His successor, a younger man, not long out of England, arrived, as always, burning with zeal to gather in a harvest of souls amongst the poor, the black, and the damned.

And in the meanwhile, in the town itself, both those for Moses and those against him made a legend of his name.

10. The Legend

Two days after the Prophet's arrest and his departure from Cockpit Centre, the Reverend Richard Brooke and his wife arrived. During their three month's stay in the capital they had both been disturbed by the casualness with which the better-off Jamaicans took their religion, and shocked at the pagan beliefs that still flourished amongst the poor. But in Kingston, the Reverend Brooke had been unable to do battle for the faith as strongly as he would have liked. There, he was constantly under the eyes of superiors who shared one idea in common – they disliked change. However, in Cockpit Centre, thanks to Prophet Moses's challenge to orthodox religion, the Reverend Brooke had been voted a free hand by the Synod. With the help of his wife, he plunged at once into his campaign, started his struggle against the mountains of frustration, indifference, and poverty which now sat even more heavily on the shoulders of the shirtless ones of the town.

He did not find it difficult to win over the bulk of Moses's followers. They were now a flock without a shepherd, destitute and despised by everyone, even by themselves. They filled the church pews, Sunday after Sunday, dozed their way through or listened to his sermons uncomprehendingly, and sang the hymns with a passion that disturbed the parson. There was something atavistic about their singing, as though they were shouting to recall lost gods from the primeval forests of Africa. And at times their singing stirred up secret urges in the Reverend's own heart which had been slumbering through centuries of civilization. He did not tell his wife about this; he could not.

Cecilia Brooke had not gone to university like her husband, but she was well read. She was the only child of a wealthy widower, a scholar, who led a retired life in the English countryside and from time to time put out slight, exquisitely bound volumes on some hitherto neglected aspect of European civilization. He had not entirely approved of his Nonconformist son-in-law. He himself was aggressively High Church, and was Chairman of a small select committee that met in secret to devise ways and means of returning the Church of England to the bosom of Rome. This was his only passion. But he was shrewd enough to understand his daughter's attraction to the parson. Without life-force herself, or even desires, she needed someone who had a positive, clearly-marked 'mission' with which she could be identified. He did not really miss his daughter when she left England with her husband. Busy with his writing and his conspiracy, he found himself well rid of her silent demand for attention. But he answered her letters scrupulously, recounting to her anecdotes of his small literary world, enclosing the occasional but always favourable review of his books.

Mrs Brooke attached herself to her husband with the same passionate devotion which her father had drily repelled. She adopted her husband's likes, dislikes, attitudes, parroted his beliefs whenever she was given the least opportunity. England, she maintained, owed a great duty towards her subject races. As the Mother Country she could have no justification for Empire unless all the heathens under her rule were led out of darkness into the light, were converted into true Christians. On her arrival in Kingston she was horrified at the contempt with which the white rulers regarded the coloured peoples. She was determined, genuinely, to do her best to erase the effect of this attitude. For it was one of her husband's most strongly held convictions that one could not convert other peoples unless one first made friends with them.

And when her husband started on his Cockpit Centre ministry, Mrs Brooke made eager overtures to the black and more ragged members of the congregation. The gentry, angered by her familiarity with racial and social untouchables, dismayed by what it might lead to, withdrew one by one; and each Sunday ordered their carriages and drove fifteen miles down to Paradise Bay to attend service at the Anglican church there. For the minister in charge, a white Jamaican, made no bones about armouring his stone church with the taboos of race, shade, caste, social position; in the Anglican church of Paradise Bay, God and the Christian religion remained exclusive. The only rich member of the Cockpit Centre church who remained steadfast was the mulatto deacon, James Macleod.

The Reverend Brooke did not like his deacon. He disapproved of his rum-drinking, his bawdy stories about women, his slighting references to the 'stupid black people', his coarse anecdotes about the 'madman' Moses. Most of all the parson resented this 'black' fellow Macleod having the impertinence to treat with him as an equal, even, at times, to patronize him. The Reverend Brooke was ignorant of the autocratic feudal upbringing of the sons of the Jamaican planters, white, brown, and even, rarely, black. A secret feud was sparked off between the two men. And the languishing glances that the deacon cast at his minister's wife did nothing to diminish their mutual dislike.

Mrs Brooke was tall, slim, with blue eyes, golden hair, and a soft pink complexion; and was therefore extremely beautiful in the deacon's eyes. But she did not attract him as a woman. Only as a symbol. Conquest of her would prove that his father's white blood had cancelled out the black blood of his mother. And as he had been brought up in a society where for a man to be a man, he must know his crops, his horses, and his women, the deacon despised the Reverend Brooke who evidently knew nothing about these things. And assumed that it would be easy to triumph over him.

Mrs Brooke liked the deacon. This was the only point on which she differed with her husband. Rebuffed in her efforts to be friendly by the poor black members of the congregation – they shook her hand gingerly at the church door, averted their eyes, regarded her excessive warmth with suspicion - she could at least feel, as she wrote to her father, that with the deacon she had succeeded in breaking down one racial barrier. The deacon, on his part, took her smiles as a tribute to his virility. Whenever he was invited to tea at the manse he plastered the springy curls of his hair with oil to make them lie straight, put on his best suit and tie, and drove in the buggy instead of riding horseback. He sat politely taking tea, smiled at Mrs Brooke and outfaced the minister's hostile glances.

One afternoon, when he saw the minister leave for Paradise Bay, the deacon decided to bring matters to a head. He dressed carefully, ordered the buggy, and drove to the manse. The maid ushered him into the drawing-room. Mrs Brooke was taking her afternoon nap. When the maid woke her she dressed hastily and went into the drawing-room, wondering at the deacon's coming at that hour, alarmed that some mishap might have befallen her husband. She entered the room. The deacon strode across to her and pulled her to him. The smell of the coconut oil on his hair was sharply acrid in her nostrils. She was overcome by a sudden nausea and pushed him away. He swung out of the house, hurt to the quick. She was a white bitch like all the others, he told himself, and thought herself too good for him only because he was part black. But he would show her if he cared a damn! The deacon never set foot in the church again, nor in any other church for that matter. He was too busy breeding children from all the peasant women for miles around. Until today the numerous Macleod tribe of descendants in Cockpit Centre are outstanding for their strange combination of dark skins, hazel eyes, and crinkly reddish hair.

Mrs Brooke thought it wiser not to tell her husband of the incident. She accepted her defeat and gradually fitted into the mould of a minister's wife and white lady, smiling only with the brief politeness that was expected of her. And she got on excellently with Aloysius Matthews, whom her husband appointed as the new deacon. Aloysius reminded Mrs Brooke of her father's secretary, so well did he know his place, so tactfully did he keep her to hers. And Aloysius's wife Kate was friendly and outgoing, and even, Mrs Brooke noted, seemed to have a protective attitude towards her. But Mrs Brooke, try as she might, could not like the woman. Kate was big with child and her protruding stomach and large vitality overwhelmed Mrs Brooke. She struggled at first against this feeling of repulsion. When Kate's labour pains started up in church one Sunday she took her home and did what she could to help. But she was soon forced to hurry out of the poky room at the back of the shop, with its strong smell of femaleness. She went home to the manse. It had been originally a rich planter's house and had spacious rooms. She had had furniture sent out from her father's home in England and had furnished the house to as near an English pattern as she could manage. When she closed the shuttered blinds against the sun, the loud voices, and the black faces, she could occasionally fool herself that she was no longer in exile.

And, lying in the four-poster bed in the high-ceilinged bedroom, she and her husband talked long into the nights about their mission.

'We are carrying out the Father's work, Cecilia, but on very stony ground, I fear.'

'But think how happy it makes us, dear Richard, how happy!'

Their repeated failure at coition left them convinced that they were of the spirit; and at nights when the moon cast big blue shadows in the room they were glad that it left them unmoved, that they had been able to give up the desperate fumbling with each other's bodies which left them miserable, degraded, and unsatisfied.

And never once did the Reverend Brooke mention to his wife that her beautiful complexion had faded, that she was no longer slim but thin, that her golden hair had become dry and lifeless. Mrs Brooke did not remark to her husband on how much older he looked, on the fact that Sunday after Sunday his congregation drifted away, not from the call of another faith, but from boredom. The new deacon, the master carpenter Aloysius Matthews, still came every Sunday, as punctual as ever. His wife Kate was frequently absent, and Mrs Brooke enjoyed the peaceful hush of the near-empty church on the Sundays when Kate's splendid animal walk did not disturb her husband's sermon.

****

Kate's first child was stillborn, and after they buried it in the churchyard nothing was ever the same again. The house, the shop, became oppressive. She began to miss the free life of her unmarried days. She drifted back to the market to find that things had changed there too. Now that she had joined the ranks of the 'respectable', the others were suspicious of her. And Liza Edwards no longer sold in the market. Defending Moses, Liza had become involved in too many brawls and was refused admittance. She now traded her home-made confectionery on the pavement outside the Chinese grocery, paying the proprietor a few pence a week for the 'concession'. When Kate went shopping she would sit beside Liza on the pavement and dally a few hours away.

Liza remained faithful to Prophet Moses and talked of nothing else. She still saw herself as the virgin mother and nothing could disillusion her. Before he was taken to Kingston, Moses had warned her that she might have to endure much persecution for his name's sake, but that some day he would return. She was prepared to wait for ever, the guardian of his dreams of glory. Even when several babies were born in the town bearing a marked resemblance to the Prophet, she remained steadfast. She discounted all the rumours about her 'son'. To have her belief in him shattered would have robbed her of all reason for living.

She was glad to have Kate to talk to, and soon their

sessions on the pavement became a daily routine. Liza infected with her enthusiasm for the fallen Prophet, making him loom larger than life, a harbinger of hope on a desolate horizon. And on those few days when rain kept Kate away from her rendezvous with Liza and the memory of Moses, she felt a growing discontent with Aloysius. As she paced up and down the house, an innocuous remark from her husband would spark off an outburst which bewildered and frightened him.

One evening Liza went into Miss Gatha's shop to buy fried fish. Miss Gatha's mother had died some months before and she was alone. To Liza's surprise, the usually prim and stand-offish young woman struck up a guarded, desultory conversation with her. Given this lead, Liza soon began talking about the Prophet. Before she left Miss Gatha offered her a job helping her in the shop three days a week. The pay was good and Liza accepted at once. And after, Liza and Miss Gatha would sit in the backyard, cleaning and gutting the fish, then they would go into the kitchen with its strong smell of wood-smoke, hot oil, and fish; and Liza would talk on and on about Moses, and Miss Gatha would listen.

Two more children were born to Kate. Both died a few hours after birth. And feeling the need for company even stronger, she started to spend most of her time away from home; for the ordinariness of her husband's life was suffocating her. As an unconscious act of defiance she dressed carelessly, left her hair uncombed, her shoes dusty and misshapen. She spent long hours with Miss Gatha and Liza. She and Miss Gatha never had much to say to each other, but they both listened to Liza's legends of the Prophet. When Kate left, Miss Gatha spoke acidly about her, telling Liza that she was behaving like a mad woman. Aloysius, too, grumbled when Kate reached home. She was threatening his good name, he said. She had even stopped going to church, saying that she didn't believe in any God who could kill children before they had a chance to live. But the more Aloysius berated his wife, the less she had to say to him. She did her chores in silence and when she served their meager dinners, only Obadiah noticed that his employer ate little or nothing. Things were not easy for Aloysius either. His trade was falling away. Now that the gentry had abandoned the church to the barefoot rabble they no longer ordered furniture from Aloysius or sent for him to do odd jobs. He worried and grew thin as he struggled to hold on to his shop and to keep his apprentice.

With her husband going to pieces before her eyes, Kate's single obsession was the dream of Moses's return. Liza had assured her that Prophet Moses would intercede personally with God for her, would see to it that a live child was born to her. Sometimes, when she sat outside the grocery with Liza – who still sold her home-made candy there on the days when she was not working for Miss Gatha – Kate would look longingly at a little girl of nine who sang to herself as she played hop-scotch on the pavement. The child was the daughter of the Chinese grocer and his negro common-law wife; she had copper-coloured skin, curly black hair, and clear eyes. Although her father did not allow her to play with the 'nigger' children, she too, knew and would sing in a high clear treble the song that all the children and adults had sung so often that it was now part of the folklore:

Moses told all his righteous flock
He was flying to heaven for a chariot,
Climbed right up on a breadfruit tree-top,
Oh Moses!
Moses called out, "Here Lord I come,
Please be ready to receive Thy Son!"
Jump up, fall down right to the ground.
Oh Moses!

11. The Kingdom of Hebron

After his fall from the ramparts of heaven, Moses felt as though sharp splinters of bone were being jabbed into his leg, and the pain caused everything that happened after that to seem remote. Even Liza's solicitude only hovered on the fringes of his agony, and he did not hear the angry voices outside her house. But when they took him away in the police van, every jolt registered like daggers in his brain. The van drove round hairpin bends, passing through Paradise Bay and then up along the tortuous mountain roads to Kingston. They took him first to the hospital, and out-patients thronged the entrance to see the man who was already a legend, who had tried to fly to heaven.

In the hospital they laid him on a narrow bed, put his foot in a plaster cast and suspended it above him. And as he lay there breathing in the smell of disinfectant and the nauseous stink of sickness and ailing bodies, the faces around him were like devil-shaped masks; and the nursing sister was a she-devil in her crisp white uniform, her voice dry and inhuman as she ordered him to be quiet when he cried out at nights: 'Why, why, why O Lord?' forbidding him to call the Lord's name in vain, reminding him that he, a poor black illiterate, had no right equating himself with the Almighty.

At the trial, Moses faced a white bewigged Judge and a bevy of brown and black barristers with snowy wigs. The senior Counsel for the Prosecution and the Counsel for the Defence asked Moses questions loaded with an oblique contempt. When he refused to answer, they smiled first at each other, and after, wittily, at the Judge. With their smiles they were pleading their own case, absolving themselves:

'Look, we are different. Don't associate us with this savage, this lunatic. All we have in common with him is the colour of our skins. We are civilized!'

The Judge's eyes of Arctic ice looked with equal indifference at the barristers and the prisoner. They were all black clowns striking postures in a circus of civilization. And both barristers worked out their frustrations on the prisoner, attacking him for being black and stupid and not knowing the white man's ways, not talking like him, not hiding his black madness under a wig and gown, as they had done.

'I am sure, Your Honour, that you will agree that there is a strong case to be made out here for the exercise of some leniency. And, if the Reverend gentlemen will forgive my saying so, they are somewhat to blame for freely entrusting the violent teachings of the Old Testament scriptures to ignorant illiterates such as my client, Moses Barton...'

'Your Honour, may I remind my learned friend that we are not here discussing the wisdom of the Church. May I submit, that in the whole length and breadth of English Common Law and legal history, there has never been recorded a clearer case of arrant madness than that displayed by the prisoner, Moses Barton. And I am sure you will agree with me that the only leniency that can be safely shown to a man who attempted to take the Kingdom of Heaven by storm and by force, is to send him where he justly belongs. To the lunatic asylum!'

Moses hardly knew when the sentence was passed. All he could feel was the pain stabbing into his leg, all he heard was his own voice calling out, 'Why, Lord? Why, Why?' As they took him away, the well-dressed people in the court-room smiled with amused satisfaction. But outside the court-house, the ragged crowds cheered and laughed, for he was their clown, their 'junkonoo', their Carnival King, larger than life, magnificent.

His leg healed quickly and he began to take note of his surroundings in the mental hospital. At nights he heard the sea rushing up and down the long beach, the sound of coconut palms rustling in the wind, the howls of the insane crying out in their own wilderness. Moses felt that he had been hurled into a dark pit and that he alone was sane; the others, his accusers, the warders, the staff, and his fellow-inmates were all insane.

The superintendent of the mental hospital was an Irish doctor in his mid-forties, named O'Malley. He had black hair, greying prematurely, and a face made red as flame by too much drink and the sun. He was the second son of a landed family, and the product of Wellington and Trinity College, Cambridge. Appointed to a senior post in a London hospital soon after finishing his medical studies, he had a brilliant career as a diagnostician before him. He married an English girl from the minor aristocracy. But his love-hate relationship with her and all that she stood for, and her sterling qualities of patience, consideration, and self-discipline which aggravated his own lack of character, drove him to drink. He became daily more fluent in his passionate abuse of her, of her background, of everything she believed in. After three years she had a nervous breakdown and was taken away by her outraged parents. O'Malley's craving for drink increased and brought him to the brink of ruin. A further career as a doctor in England became impossible. He hated Ireland too much to return there. A friend in the Colonial Office wangled him a job in the colonies – that of Superintendent of the Mental Hospital in Kingston, Jamaica. On the day of his appointment, he bought a map and traced with an unsteady finger, until he located the small red dot – the island on which he was to be exiled.

When Moses was admitted to the asylum, O'Malley was in the midst of one of his drunken spells. And the doctor had a hangover on the day that he was looking over the Prophet's case-history. His secretary, serving him black coffee and waiting for him to sign and proceed to the next case in the file, was surprised when he dismissed her and sat back to read about a man whom she considered just another nuisance in an already overcrowded hospital. But the case fascinated O'Malley. It was a novel example of paranoia; a man offering transportation on golden chariots to heaven, involving a whole community in this imaginative scheme, a black Icarus taking off from the top of a breadfruit tree!

He sent for Moses and began questioning him. The Prophet saw at once that this strange white man, who, unlike the white Judge and the black barristers, did not 'act white', was genuinely interested in hearing about his mission. He answered his searching questions, and the two men struck up a friendship. For drunkenness and madness were, at that time, the most effective social levellers in Jamaica – under the influence of one or the other all men became equal.

As part of the Prophet's treatment, the doctor prescribed that he should be taught to read and write. He assigned his chief assistant, a dourly respectable negro who had once taught in an elementary school, to the job of drilling the patient in the three Rs. It was as though the doctor wanted to bridge the impossible distances between his drunken fantasies about helping the 'black man' and Moses's delusions of grandeur; as though he sensed that in Moses, for lack of opportunity, some strange new genius had been lost to the world.

The Prophet, still seeking the reason for his downfall, took advantage of his belated education. On the printed pages of the Bible he might find some clue. He insisted that his instructor should take him through the mazes of the Holy Book. By the end of his first year he could read it through from cover to cover. His intelligence was like tinder, and the sparks of learning set off by his tutor made it burst into flame. But the better part of his education he obtained from O'Malley himself. The Irishman looked on Moses as a kind of dancing dog who could amuse him during his spells of drunkenness – although, scarcely admitted to himself, there was also the intention of making Moses his political disciple, of introducing the Prophet to the earthly facts of their common condition. For they were both 'colonials', Moses the mad Prophet and he, a drunken Irishman; only Moses, through madness, had begun to liberate himself from the spiritual shackles which held the Irishman in their grip, however much he ranted against them. For in him was the secret desire not to defeat his colonial master, but to join him. To help Moses to rebel was to erase a deep-rooted shame.

One day the doctor and Moses sat in his office. It was mid-morning, and from where he sat the Prophet could see some of the other inmates working in the grounds whilst the warders lounged in the shade. But because of the white doctor's special interest in Moses, the hospital staff treated him with deference, some of the warders even getting the Prophet to take up their grievances with O'Malley. And Moses, whose cunning was never to be underestimated, used his position to get better food, clothing, and accommodation, as well as to be let off the more menial tasks assigned to the inmates.

The doctor was drinking white rum that morning. For the sake of appearances he drank out of a teacup. The Prophet sat in a canvas chair opposite him. Moses did not drink. He invariably refused the doctor's offer of a 'cup of tea'. He wanted to keep alert, to learn all he could from this white man whose mind seemed to encompass the world. Moses was always astonished at the number of words the doctor had stored away inside his head. With half those words, the Prophet thought, he could hypnotize the whole island into doing his bidding. So, whilst the doctor talked, Moses noted words that seemed weighty and valuable, and later, in bed, repeated them over and over to himself.

The doctor leaned back in his swivel chair and sipped his white rum thoughtfully:

'Have you ever heard of Shakespeare?' he asked Moses.

Moses shook his head. He was sure that he had not seen that name anywhere in the Bible. But he knew that the doctor would not be deterred by his ignorance. Whenever O'Malley asked a question like that, it only meant that he had a spate of words bottled up inside him to which he would give vent one way or the other.

'You and Shakespeare have a lot in common, Moses,' he continued .

'Shakespeare was a black prophet, then, doctor?' Moses asked with great interest.

'He was a prophet all right, Moses, but he was not black, he was English.'

The Prophet looked puzzled. But he had become accustomed to the unbelievable twists and turns of the doctor's dialogue.

White rum always heightened O'Malley's feelings of persecution, incited him to rant against Jamaica, the claustrophobic provincialism of the island's white minority, the cravenness of the few educated black and brown 'natives' whom the whites patronized, the monotony of the sun and the seasons. The rum would also inspire a new hatred for Ireland and all things Irish – 'its macabre humour, vampire women, and degutted men, its centuries of servitude and suffering, its ancient treachery, its love-hate relationship with England'. But the English were his special target, one to which he invariably came when the rum had mellowed him:

'Yes, Moses, Shakespeare was English, the only extraordinary Englishman, for the English are the most ordinary creatures God ever made!'

The doctor filled up his cup, and Moses settled back in his chair. He could sense that this would be a long session, that the doctor would throw a multitude of words at him. And sitting there in the cool office was better than cutting grass in the hot sun. Besides, the doctor always told him secrets about the 'white man' that he had never dreamt of. There were many things he did not understand in O'Malley's monologues. And yet he got the message just the same. The words set off vibrations which he could feel. He watched the doctor's face as he spoke, saw the deep unhappiness of his febrile spirit in the red-rimmed eyes. The Prophet felt no pity, only exultation that the 'white man' was not as superhuman as he made himself out to be, was not as invincible as he, Moses, had been made to believe.

But the doctor looked at Moses with maudlin affection. This madman was his 'black brother', his Man Friday. Together, one day, in this very island, they would raise a flag of revolt that would tumble the English on their supercilious backsides. But he would have to educate Moses, instruct him in all the subtleties of rebellion. First they would have to tear down the symbols of power that the English had used to dominate others. He wanted to discuss these points with Moses, compose a political manifesto, but once he started talking, his thoughts darted hither and thither. But one day, when he was sober, he would write a book, a manifesto against colonialism, that's what he would do. And he wouldn't be a drunk for the rest of his life, as his wife expected, as she wanted him to be, the bitch!

The Prophet saw that the doctor was becoming morose. He knew how ugly and brutal O'Malley could be once he reached this stage. He would have to keep him talking; as long as he was talking he was happy.

'You were going to tell me about this English prophet, doctor, Shakespeare you said his name was…' he reminded him tactfully.

The doctor's face brightened; he poured himself some more rum.

'Yes, Shakespeare, he used to write books, Moses, plays and poetry. He made the English language reach up to the heavens, touch the stars. He spanned the entire length and breadth of human emotions. Like Columbus, he discovered new continents, populated them with living creatures of flesh and blood and poetry. At a time when the rest of his countrymen waited like jackals to rob the Spaniards who returned with their blood-stained plunder from the New World, he created men of grandeur, big villains, towering heroes, new-world men…'

The doctor chuckled as he went on:

'But you know, Moses, even old Shakespeare never succeeded in making epic heroes out of his shop-keeping countrymen. He tried with Henry the Fifth, but he turned out to be a half-baked paper hero, spouting blood and thunder... Macbeth, now, was a Scot, Lear, an Ancient Briton and the archetypal figure of madness...The big tragic heroes were people like Hamlet, a Dane, and Othello, a Moor – there's a black man for you, Moses – come to think of it, given half a chance you might have been an actor, might have played Othello...the English actors have forgotten the secret of how to play him, have forgotten the secret of life...Just watch an English actor walk on to a stage and you will see what I mean...he doesn't know how to use his body, apologizes for its very existence...and listen to him talk...all the rhythms have been ironed out...We Irish intoxicate ourselves with words, drown what little sense we have in words...The Irish actor could play Othello if he would only stop wanting to be English or being as Irish as the English want him to be...and Othello is above all, himself, the embodiment of the choleric man, giving full rein to his passions, love, hate, anger, jealousy, even tenderness...The English actors are good at make-up, they paint their faces black, roar in well-bred accents, and strike postures, whilst the real Othello escapes them. But they are excellent as Iago. Note that, Moses. They are excellent when they act the part of Iago...'

The doctor's face had grown sombre. He gently stirred the rum with a teaspoon, then swallowed the contents of the cup, and wiped the back of his hand across his mouth. He had become oblivious of Moses's presence. Moses thought it time he asked another question to show his interest.

'This Iago, was he a prophet too, doctor?'

'No, Moses, he was not a prophet, but a merchant, a merchant of lies. And Iago is the patron saint of the British Empire, Moses, a parasite, using guile to defeat the innocent and the noble. How else do you think it was that these insignificant islanders who were barbarians when we Irish were civilized, managed to steal half the world? How else but by trickery? But now like Iago, their spirits have been eroded by an excess of cunning, by their centuries of trickery. My God, look what they did to your people, Moses. Sent their missionaries to trade in African souls, to promise them the Kingdom of Heaven in exchange for a few strings of beads and a paper with a big red seal. Your African chiefs signed away a continent for a Christian conscience, bartered their land, their souls, for a slice of the Kingdom of Heaven. And when the Kingdom of Heaven did not materialize, the missionaries, those traders in blood, conjured up a God in the image of an Englishman, a wise and holy father-figure who never existed. They sold this God to the natives as a new kind of fetish. Take my word for it, Moses, Christianity was the greatest fraud ever perpetrated on any peoples. That's why they put you away, my friend. You were dangerous. You challenged this God of theirs, went in search of this heaven that you had been offered in exchange for your malnutrition, disease, ignorance, and poverty. You wanted to feel this Heaven in your hand, see it with your eyes, not later in the by and by, but right here, right now!'

The doctor stood up, crossed the room, and took out another bottle of rum from the wall safe. When he returned to his desk it was to find Moses on his feet, leaning across to him, his eyes ablaze with excitement:

'Doctor, you said that this Englishman make God in his own image, not so?' he asked.

The doctor was flattered by his reaction, and surprised.

'Yes, Moses, old chap, that's what he did, made God in his own image, made God a hypocritical bastard just like himself!'

The Prophet sank back into his chair. A revelation as to his first failure had come upon him like a lightening flash. His imagination was on fire with this new concept that he had just learnt – the concept of man creating God in his own image.

When the doctor sat down and continued with his diatribe he only heard snatches of it.

'These people held down a quarter of the globe, sold all kinds of races their myths, and the myths they sold were in no way as imaginative as that of the Catholics...the English were conquerors without imagination...that's why their Empire lasted so long...no matter where they went, they remained parochial... they went towards the wealth of the Indies and carried with them the mentality of shopkeepers...and from the wealth of the Indies got Industrial England and power, grey ugly cities, castrated men and unfeminine women...and two separate breeds of people...one clean and elegant and dead...the other festering a murky life in savage slums...and these slums they created wherever they went...Take this island, for example...'

The doctor noticed that Moses was not really listening and he pounded his fist on the table as he repeated:

'Take this island, Moses, your island!'

'Yes, doctor, yes sir!' Moses said hastily.

'In this island, the lunatic asylum and the prison provide the highest standard of living for the native masses...your people, Moses!'

'Yes sir, yes!'

'And it was the same thing with my people, after they had ruled Ireland for six hundred years...they sacked and plundered and raped us, and left us only our religion, since they knew it would keep us in greater bondage than even they had managed to...And yet they were the least savage of the colonial powers...but the deadliest...You see, the French had culture, a few of them, a greed for land and a taste for black women, black art...The Spanish had their religion, a greed for gold, and, one or two of them, a sense of honour...all the English ever had was the satisfaction of being prigs and horse-traders...they make a religion out of...snobbishness...'

The doctor paused and leaned his elbows on the desk, put his head in his hands. He was fighting against the drunken stupor that crept up on him. But he continued:

'The English were only able to sustain the greatest Empire on earth because they themselves were happy to be slaves... but now the lesser breeds who have been carrying these...slaves...on their backs are beginning to get restive...One day the British Empire will tumble down, Moses, like a pack of cards, and I will live to see that day, I will live to see it...In the meanwhile, take my advice, Moses...and don't let them sell you their God and their heaven, second-hand. Take my advice and straighten up things here on earth before you plan your next trip to heaven!'

The doctor gave a triumphant smile and flopped over on his desk. Moses put him to bed. He had become used to this job. Then he seated himself in the doctor's chair.

The idea of man being able to conceive of a God of his own provided Moses with the answer to his defeat. He had been stupid enough to accept the white man's God, had worshipped Him and had been betrayed. The doctor who scattered words like spray above his head, and whom he did not trust, had given him the key to a new kingdom, a kingdom here on earth. And he, Moses, had failed, had been punished, cast down into the lower depths so that he could achieve true wisdom.

From then on, the Prophet worked with concentrated zeal. He learnt all the trades he could – carpentry, shoemaking, cabinet-making and stone-masonry. After a while he was sent to do jobs outside the asylum. He made money, and it was easy to save with the Government providing him with free board and lodging. The doctor continued to send for Moses, but he noticed that his patient was becoming more and more preoccupied with his own thoughts. And sometimes O'Malley would see the Prophet's eyes flash with a savage hostility, but he was always too drunk to care. The negro was amusing and he liked having him around. Besides, he could tell him things that he would never dare to do if he were sane, and white. When he was exhausted he would encourage the Prophet to repeat the story of his attempt to fly to heaven. He never tired of listening to this tale. He wondered how old Moses really was. It was hard to tell. There was something almost decadent about his beautiful black face, with its sloe eyes and its suggestion of an ancient ebony carving. There was a disciplined vitality in his sturdy athletic body, for how else could he have survived a fifty-foot fall from the top of the breadfruit tree? And during his years in the asylum, strenuous exercise, regular meals, and plenty of sleep had toned up his muscles until he moved like a panther, the indolence and tension in his limbs striking such a perfect balance that even when he was standing still one was aware of his limitless reserves of strength.

****

The order for Moses's discharge came through during his fifth year at the mental hospital. The Director of Medical Services had issued a memo stating that all marginal cases should be released, since there were hundreds of certified cases waiting to be admitted.

The night before he left, the Prophet performed his usual duties. Because of the shortage of staff and his own good record he was often assigned to duties which a warder usually carried out, and sometimes even left in charge of his ward. A high wind was blowing from the south-west, and as he served cocoa and bread to the others he could hear the dull roar of the sea. In the silence between an onrush of breakers pounding on the beach, he heard a voice calling him:

'Come down, Moses! Come down to the sea!'

As he walked out into the darkness the wind swept the rain-clouds away from the face of the moon and he could see the glittering palm-fronds ringing the shore. The ebb-tide chafed against the pebbles and the jewelled sands, leaving garlands of foam strewn along the beach. There was a cluster of mangrove to his right, and long twisting fingers, reaching down from their trunks, grasped at the elusive sands. Their broad leaves smelt of musk. Moses fell on his knees. Something moved in the shadows behind him, and he waited. He felt a hand on his shoulder, and knew that it was the hand of the true God made in his own image, the God of black men. The hand felt like fire at one moment, and at another, like ice. When he turned his eyes to the hills, the hand was still there. It raised him to his feet. There were lights like fallen stars glimmering on the dark hill-sides. All night long the sea spoke to him in soft whispers and with many tongues, telling him what he should do. And the words crystallized into prophecy. When morning came his head and shoulders were wet with dew. The hills were like mounds of sediment under the grey bowl of the sky. The moon had vanished and there were no fallen stars.

****

Moses left the asylum later on that morning, a man with a mission, absolutely sure of himself. With part of his savings added to O'Malley's gift of five pounds, he bought a black serge suit, tie, shirt, and leather boots, an umbrella and a top-hat, and the biggest Bible he could find. He traveled by train to Cockpit Centre, and, getting off at the station, hired a buggy to Miss Gatha's shop. The man who knocked at her door was a new Moses, a man who could read and write, a prophet chosen by the God of black men, of the oppressed, a man with all the craftiness and the cunning of the deity he was to serve. He arrived like a thunderbolt on her doorstep and swept her away in the steam of his newly discovered certainty.

After he had contacted Liza, he and Miss Gatha set out for Paradise Bay. They returned a few days later as man and wife. Moses then outlined his plans to Liza and his wife: he would found a kingdom on earth in the name of the God of black men. At first Miss Gatha was uneasy at his juggling with the established image of God, but he wore down her resistance until she begged his forgiveness for having doubted.

Using the money Miss Gatha had hoarded, Prophet Moses built a new and imposing temple in her yard. Hunger was his chief ally in reassembling his flock, and the fried-fish shop was a magnet which so attracted those who hesitated, that no amount of derision over his initial fall from grace could stand in his way. Miss Gatha, with her habit of thrift and her reticence, was reputed to be very wealthy; and Moses's marriage to her gave his new venture stability. Moreover, the Prophet no longer preached about a kingdom in Heaven, but of one on earth where they would all be landowners, eat suckling pigs roasted with yams. Moses called his new sect 'The New Believers', because they were worshippers of a new God, followers of His Chosen Prophet. And because their God was black He would be on their side for ever.

Then the Prophet of the New Believers took a journey into the hills in search of the new Canaan. The night after his return, he lay beside his wife on their hard wooden bed, too tired to sleep. He had been looking for a land which he could call Hebron. He had wandered around for days, hungry and thirsty, accepting the hardship as part of the travail Jesus had known in the wilderness. And he had finally come to a sheltered valley which curved around a breast of hills. In the centre was a spring gushing clear water. With his clothes torn, his body scratched and bleeding, his throat parched, he fell down to the ground and cried out:

'A land called Hebron, a land of hills and valleys that drinketh water of the rain of heaven! A land that the Lord Thy God careth for!'

The rain fell and the wind cooled his burning body. This was indeed a sign!

The Prophet marked out the ground with stones and set out for home like a man possessed. He had found the kingdom of the black God imprisoned in its own fastness of hills and forests. After his return he held a service of rejoicing. The temple was crowded and Moses was able to pick and choose his disciples. And not only was he able to tell them that he had seen and surveyed the land of Hebron, but he was able to display to them a Government document which, he said, assigned to the New Believers the right to settle on the land. And although they could not read, the big red seal was plain for all to see. Ever since Dr O'Malley had told Moses about how the missionaries had bargained with the African chiefs for their land, he had been obsessed with the question of the legality of his new kingdom. Several days before his journey of exploration and discovery, the Lord had shown to Moses a way in which he could obtain from the Government the legal right to the land which he would call Hebron; and like the missionaries that Dr O'Malley had told him of, Moses had schemed for the greater glory of His Lord.

Lying in bed, sleepless after the excitement of the service and his successful expedition, Moses laid his further plans for the kingdom. He would need more young men like the two he had 'called' that night, the big strapping apprentice Obadiah Brown and his sharp-witted friend, Hugh. He would need strong young men to clear the land, fell the trees, cut away the underbrush, lay the foundations of the kingdom in what was now a wilderness. He would find them tomorrow, and at their head he would put Obadiah Brown. He would bind this young man to him with special ties. In him, Moses had divined something that he had once had; the same innocence of heart that had made him believe that with wings of faith, a black man could fly to heaven to be welcomed as Son by a white God. But he, Moses, had woken up to the fact that God was black, to the truth of himself. The day when Obadiah Brown did the same, he would be powerful in the land of Hebron, a worthy heir and true successor.

Through the curtains the Prophet could see the first glow of dawn tinting the sky, banishing the darkness. Over and above all, he thought to himself, he would need the services of a master carpenter and cabinetmaker such as Aloysius Matthews, for they had to build and furnish houses in Hebron. If Liza did not succeed in spurring on Kate Matthews to persuade her husband to join his flock, he himself would have to take a hand. Aloysius would be invaluable, and once converted, would make a good follower. The best bribe he could offer a man like that would be the offer of status and authority. He would make Aloysius Matthews his second-in-command, Moses decided as he fell asleep. Beside him Miss Gatha lay wide awake, and listened to the dogs barking at the fading moon.

12. *The Rootless Years*

The clock-tower in the market square of Cockpit Centre struck three. A dog howled, then it was silent in the town again. In the shed behind the temple of the New Believers, Obadiah Brown lay sleepless. Through a crack in the side of the shed he could see the cold moon veiled with clouds, the sky still sown thick with stars. Beside him, stretched out on the floor, Hugh snored heavily. But Obadiah's mind raced with excitement. Earlier on that evening Prophet Moses had 'called' the two young men to follow him up to Hebron; and, after the service, had himself led them across to the shed where they were to sleep for the night. He had even stayed on talking to them a while. And Obadiah gave his allegiance to this stranger whose eyes were blinded by visions and whose fiery tongue could enmesh other men in his own magnificence.

After he left them, the two young men talked far into the night. At first they spun out fantasies round the promised kingdom into which they were soon to enter like men, new-born to positions created for them, their feet firm on a land of their own, that, up till then, restless like the wind, they had searched for. After, and for the first time, Hugh told Obadiah about his early childhood:

'Mother!' Hugh began, propping himself up on his elbow. 'Man, that was just a dirty word to me. She spewed me out when she was sixteen, then ran away and left me right here in this rubbish-jungle of a town. After she left, my grand-aunt Sarah just make me up into a bundle and send me down to my Grannie in Paradise bay…Grannie wasn't all that old, but you never see anybody's face wrinkle up like her own. She used to say that it was hard brute work that cause old age to ambush her, sudden like night...She was good to me...After she die, like a dog, water never come into my eye for nothing and nobody else ever again!'

Hugh's grandmother had worked as a cook in a guest house in Paradise Bay that backed on to the sea. Her room was a broken-down one adjoining the kitchen, and she was allowed to keep her grandson there as long as he did not in any way disturb the guests. She disciplined Hugh harshly in order to keep him with her – even as a baby he sensed that it was wrong to cry, and knew how to crawl out of the way when he was not wanted.

At nights he was mostly alone – his grandmother worked until midnight serving the guests with drinks, waiting up when they went out in case they should require a late supper on their return – and he would whimper as the sea dashed itself upon the shore and receded mournfully, peopling the dark corners of the room with ghosts and demons.

He was soon earning his keep, helping in the garden, cleaning shoes, running errands for the guests. To amuse them he shuffled a minstrel dance with his wiry legs, stirring up the red dust under the high veranda; and caught the pennies that they flung him between his teeth. On Sundays his grandmother dressed him in the cast-off clothing of her mistress's son and sent him off to the near-by Baptist church. He attended the morning service as well as Sunday school and, on the rare Sunday evening when she was off duty, accompanied his grandmother to the evening service. He had a quick and extraordinarily retentive memory which won him all the prizes (brightly coloured pictures of Jesus surrounded by children with blue eyes and golden curls) at Sunday school. On week-days he astonished the guests with his parroting of Bible texts which he had memorized, chapter and verse.

One morning his grandmother complained of a nagging pain in her right side. She dragged herself out of bed and carried on with her work. But towards midday she fainted over the open wood-fire in the kitchen, grazed her elbows and burnt her hands. Her mistress was upset; a boatload of English tourists had come straight off a cruise ship and were waiting for lunch, seated on the veranda. She ordered the gardener to help Hugh take his grandmother to her room. She took over the cooking herself and all available hands were summoned to help. Hugh was left alone with the sick woman in the small dark room.

He tried to smear Vaseline on her burnt hands, but she dragged them away and clutched at her side, moaning and crying out. Hugh watched helplessly, as her face became ashen and her body doubled up like knotted rope.

'Let me run for the doctor, Grannie,' he begged, 'let me run and get Doctor Robertson!'

She shook her head. Doctor Robertson was the only doctor in the town; he charged a guinea for each visit, and insisted on being paid in advance by his poorer patients. And she had been saving up her wages and hoped soon to return to Cockpit Centre, pay down on a half-acre of land, plant ground provisions, and earn enough to give her grandson a proper schooling; give him the kind of opportunity that none of her family had ever had. She was adamant. When Hugh turned to run for the doctor she gripped his hand and would not let him go. He only knew that she was dead when her fingers fell away, leaving dark red marks where she had bruised him. He was seven years old and had never seen anyone die before.

In the hot, sweltering room, with the sound of laughter coming from the tourists, the ring of cutlery, clinking of glasses, and hastily-shouted orders from the mistress, Hugh stood and thought about what to do next. He took off his grandmother's apron and trampled it on the floor without knowing why he did so. Then he folded her hands on her breast and placed her hymn book between them. With memories of her dressed for church, he straightened her frock, pulled on her cotton stockings and canvas shoes, brushed back her disheveled hair, and placed her straw hat on her head. He thought of reciting some Bible verses over her, but could not remember a single one.

When he had finished he could hear the scraping of chairs as the tourists, having eaten, prepared to leave. Hastily he wrapped his clothes in a bundle, lifted up a loose and rotting floorboard, and took out the old stocking in which his grandmother had hoarded her money. Then he slipped out through the back gate and started to run. When he found himself sufficiently far up on the steep road leading to Cockpit Centre, he sat down and wept.

****

Hugh finished, and the two remained silent. In the street, close by, a group of stragglers laughed loudly. As their footsteps and voices were swallowed up in the darkness of the side streets, Obadiah turned to Hugh, wanting to explain to him the one thing that he had never told him before, the one thing that had almost come between them, almost broken up their friendship. He had been working for Aloysius Matthews at the time. One evening, he sat with Hugh on the pavement outside the shop. As they chatted together he whittled idly with his knife at a piece of wood. He was unaware of what he was doing until he realized that Hugh was nudging him and grinning slyly. He looked down at what he had made and saw a roughly-hewn miniature of his mother as she danced at a Pocomania meeting, her eyes wide and lost in a cold ecstasy, her breasts taut like thorns, her legs strong and powerful, the muscles raised and trembling as if with a fever Obadiah had recaptured and imprisoned all this in the wood for ever.

Hugh snatched the carving from his hands and ran shouting to the other boys who idled along the lane to come and see the naked woman with the naked breasts, to come and see the 'freeness'. Obadiah leapt on Hugh in a rage, shoved him to the ground, pinioned his arms behind his back, took away the carved figure and broke it into pieces. And with Hugh avoiding him for days after that he found himself unable to apologize, to explain why he had behaved that way. Until now.

'Hugh,' he began, 'that time with the carving that I made of my mother, that time when I broke it up and you didn't understand…'

He stopped talking. Hugh was fast asleep.

The carving had reminded him too much of his mother, of those times when she had been remote, her spirit ugly and set against him – like the spells during and after the frenzies of her dancing, like the nights when men came to visit her one after the other and she pushed him out of the room and slapped him when he started to ask why; like that particular night when he had been alone in the room and a thunderstorm burst over the town and lightning flashed like arrows of light tearing open the black sky. He had crawled under the table to hide. After a while his mother came in, a man behind her. Fearful that she might turn him out, that he might be left alone to face up to the wrath of the heavens, Obadiah kept quiet and huddled farther under the table. He heard the bed creak sharply and his mother cry out as if in terror. In a panic he scrambled out, rushed to the bed and thumped at the man with his fists, trying to pull him away from his mother. A blow from her hand sent him sprawling across the room. She sprang out of the bed, her face contorted with rage and shame. It was the man who had to stop her as she punched and kicked her son. The man went away, leaving a shilling on the table. His mother took the money and went out to a shop that remained open late. She returned with rice and salted cod and cooked Obadiah's favourite meal. Although it was the first time he had eaten that day, he did not feel hungry. But he forced himself to swallow, seeing that this would please her. After, she wiped him down with hot water, rubbed coconut oil on his bruises and put him to bed. But he never felt that the room was a safe place again.

After his mother's death he went to work for Aloysius Matthews and lived at the shop. The master carpenter and his wife, between them, made the world seem secure for the first time in his life. Aloysius taught him how to hammer in a nail sure and straight, taught him that this was the measure of right or wrong; and took him along each Sunday to the church where he was deacon. Kate saw to it that he ate as much as they could spare him, kept himself clean, and took time off to play with the other boys. And when Aloysius voiced his strong disapproval of Hugh, Kate argued and insisted that the shop was Obadiah's home and that he had a right to the friends he had chosen.

When Obadiah first met Hugh, Hugh was living with his grandmother's sister, Miss Sarah, a feeble old woman. Her older children had all drifted away from the town and the younger ones ran wild on the streets. When Hugh had first come back from Paradise Bay he had given her the money left by his grandmother. But this was soon squandered on food and clothes for the entire tribe. He learnt, after that, to keep what he earned to himself. He made it a habit to attend Sunday school at Aloysius's church. There, the Sunday school teacher, Miss Emma Withers, gave pencils as prizes in the Junior Bible competitions. Hugh won all the pencils and later sold them. At the time of Prophet Moses's first venture he tried to be admitted as a Brother Believer in Heaven Now. There, too, he hoped to win prizes. But he was too young and would have had to be accompanied by an adult. His grand-aunt and her brood were amongst those who scoffed at Moses, having long since ceased to believe in a benevolent God. Hugh had to content himself with looking on from the pavement, with Obadiah. The two boys had learnt of the secret plans for the Prophet's ascension and had planned to witness it. But Hugh overslept and, as he should have called for Obadiah, they both missed this legendary event.

After Aloysius Matthews was forced to give up his shop and to let his apprentice go, the two boys ganged together, looking for jobs, the odd meal. They slept on the sidewalks when it was fine, and, when it rained, cotched with Miss Sarah and her children in their one-room shanty. The two complemented each other – Hugh liked to have someone to whom he could display his cunning, someone to protect. Obadiah was glad to be told what to do, was a good listener, and greatly admired his friend's acumen.

Several months before Prophet Moses's second coming, the two, now young men in their late adolescence, ran away to Kingston. They were accompanied by two of Hugh's cousins, girls of fifteen and sixteen who had taken to casual prostitution. Hugh was already expert at getting them their few clients from amongst the sailors whose ships occasionally docked at Paradise Bay. He and the girls would make the trip down and linger by the docks, waiting for the 'new' deck-hands who were new to the red-light section of the town.

On the way to Kingston both girls made advances to Obadiah. But he was frightened of them, of their hot breasts as they rubbed themselves against him, their loud laughter and bawdy jokes. When they started teasing him, calling him a 'woman-man' and challenging him 'prove himself', Hugh warned them off. His possessiveness would not tolerate either of them attracting his follower away from him.

It was raining on the night that the four walked along the long winding road that led into the capital. The squalid houses and shops that loomed up out of the rain-shrouded darkness did not seem at all different from Cockpit Centre; and the lowering sky seemed to close them in as the hills had closed them in at home. They felt discouraged. For once the girls even ceased their chatter and joking. But Hugh tried to keep their spirits up. The next day, he was sure, the sun would be shining and ships would be tied up at the wharf, and there would be hundreds of sailors loose on the town, just hungry for black flesh, and they would make money like fire and set up in a house and rake in the pound notes and eat and drink and live easy for the rest of their lives. Tomorrow, the sun would be shining, just wait and see!

When they arrived at the big park in the centre of

Kingston, the rain poured down even more heavily. They entered the park and hurried to take shelter under a growth of mangrove trees. Some twenty others, many of them from country parts and new to the city, were also crowded together there. The four waited under the trees for several hours until the rain ceased, and, through the leaves, they could see clusters of stars. It was nearing midnight, but hunger drove them to leave the park. Hugh had a sixpence and they wanted to find a cold-supper shop. As they came out through the big iron gates they looked left and right trying to decide in which direction they should go. A watery moon, which gleamed out from banks of dark grey clouds, outlined them against the railings. The driver of a buggy who had been trotting his horse slowly up the street, saw them and stopped. He could tell at once that they were from the country. He turned to the two sailors who sat sprawled in the covered back of the buggy. Their caps and uniforms shone white in the gloom.

'I think I see what you want,' the driver told them briefly. 'But you keep quiet. I can get it for you cheap!'

'To hell with the price, just get it!' one of the sailors muttered.

The driver eased up to the kerb, stopped the buggy, turned up his coat collar against the raindrops that still dripped from the trees, and stepped down. His face in the light of the headlamp was as grave and serious as that of a high priest. He crossed the street, looking at the girls impersonally. Their cotton dresses were still damp and pasted against their bodies. Their full breasts showed clearly. This was the main requirement that the sailors had insisted on. And they were country girls and stupid, which was what he wanted to ensure that his cut would be profitable.

Hugh noticed the way the driver looked at the girls. He glanced at the buggy and saw a glimmer of white at the window as a face peered across at them. He stepped forward, ready to bargain. But the driver's narrow black eyes, half-hidden in a forest of wrinkles, were like flint as they looked through him.

After a second's pause the driver spoke to the girls, his tone off-hand.

'I have two sailors in the back. They want country girls because they think you less risky. I will arrange the price, pay you sufficient after. If you want to, come on. Plenty women around and I don't have time to lose!'

He turned on his heel and walked away. The girls hurried after him, calling back to Hugh that they would return to the park. The buggy trotted off quickly. Hugh and Obadiah could hear the shrill laughter of the girls. By the time they found a cold-supper shop it was closed. They went back to the park, drank some water at the fountain, settled themselves on a dry spot under the mangrove trees and fell asleep.

They woke to an explosion of sound – hooters blaring, the rumbling of carts drawn by bullocks, piled high with grass and cow manure, the clamorous bells on pushcarts, the shrill cries of venders as they hawked their wares; the traffic policeman in a glory of white and scarlet shouting commands above the confusion; a street preacher with a turban plaited from multicoloured rags, bare feet and lips whitened from hunger, mouthing mad warnings of the end of the world, 'as it was with Sodom and Gomorrah, so it will be with us now and for ever, Amen–' whilst above them all, the sun burnt like an immense and red-hot coal in the sky.

They waited all day, hanging about the environs of the park, but the girls did not return. That night they went in search of them, combing the narrow streets. Hugh entered the dark, ill-smelling rooms, Obadiah kept watch on the pavement to see if he could spot them amongst the prostitutes who sauntered by. After several fruitless hours they left the alleys with their lurking darkness, strange disembodied noises and brawling presences of unkempt women fighting over clients, and headed towards the sea. They walked along the sea-front, kicking at the stunted plants and scattering the sand. The sea crept up and then receded with a dull roar. Across from them the rock quarries of the Wareika hills cut strange and formidable shapes against the dark sky. At last they arrived at a cluster of houses beside the sea. Hugh had been advised to search there by a 'madam'. New girls, she had said, usually began there, and served a more exclusive clientele.

A lamp burnt low in the window of the first house. There was a loose board on the veranda. The loud creaking noise that it made as they went to the door immediately called forth a response. There was a rustling sound from inside and the door opened. The woman who peered out at them was in her early thirties. Her face was garishly painted, her hair piled high on top of her head. The orange rouge formed hollows on her brown skin. She had evidently been asleep. She looked at them with surprise. She was evidently accustomed only to regulars, and of a certain class. She hesitated, then shrugged, and opened the door wide:

'Come in. I wasn't expecting anybody tonight. But since you come all this way...'

She crossed the room and turned up the lamp. They could see that there was a little girl about ten asleep on the bed. The woman shook the child, who sat up and rubbed her eyes. Short pigtails stuck out all over her head.

'Miriam,' the woman said, 'just go out to the kitchen. Lie down on the bench. I will come for you later on!'

The girl blundered through the back door that her mother held open for her. She was still half-asleep and had not noticed the two visitors. Hugh looked on, and rapidly calculated whether there might not be any other possible advantages now that it was obvious that the two girls were not to be found. The woman was well-made, thin and wiry but young-looking and strong. He stepped into the room as the woman beckoned to him, only to find that Obadiah had vanished. He hurried out after him. After that, Obadiah refused to continue the search for the girls any longer.

The next day they wandered about the city seeking work. Hugh stole mangoes from the market women to still their hunger. The second day they left Kingston and walked out to the suburbs. They came to a large house surrounded by acres of terraced gardens. The owner, a rich Syrian merchant, hired them on the spot. He offered four shillings a week between the two of them, frugal meals, and the garden shed to sleep in. His other gardeners, he said, had left the day before, and all because the people of today didn't like to work hard, and only spent their time envying people like himself who had come to the island peddling with a pack on his back, and now look where he had reached!

They stuck it out for several months, labouring all day in the garden under the fierce sun. In the evenings they helped in the kitchen and served at table; and at nights, after the rest of the household was asleep, the polished the wooden flooring of the vast verandas that encircled the house. But one Saturday, when they carried down several baskets of vegetables to the central market in Kingston, they met a wagon-driver from Cockpit Centre. He told them about the return of Prophet Moses, of how he was now promising land to all his followers in a place called Hebron. The wagon-driver was returning to Cockpit Centre that night and they asked him for a lift. After collecting their pay that evening, they left the dirty dishes piled up in the kitchen and sneaked out. They rode on the back of the wagon, sleeping most of the way, and arrived back in the town on the very evening that Moses returned from his expedition to Hebron. That night they attended the service of rejoicing to celebrate the discovery of the Promised Land.

They arrived early and managed to gain places at the back of the temple. The building could not contain the multitudes, and people spilled out into the street. It seemed as if Prophet Moses's weariness of body exalted his spirit. As he described Hebron, the promise of triumph in his glittering eyes, the power that vibrated outwards from him caught up the congregation in an ecstasy of belief. Obadiah felt himself swept and shaken by an anxiety to make his presence known to those hypnotic eyes that drew him with pincers of fire, to declare his submission, to be admitted as a disciple. He reached out towards the Prophet, but his gesture was blocked by the mass of Believers who stood before him. He let his hands fall back helplessly to his side.

Hugh, too, gazed at the Prophet with an admiration which he rarely accorded anyone. But at the same time his mind was alert as he planned how best to insinuate himself amongst the chosen ones. For now that the Prophet had land to offer, now that the Government had confirmed this offer with a big, shiny, red seal, plain for all to see, it was obvious that Moses could select disciples at will.

The Prophet's sermon reached a crescendo:

'And I saw, laid claim to, made fast to the New Believers for ever and ever...the land of Hebron that the Lord gave to me in a vision, the land of Hebron like a wild ass's nest amidst the stars!'

'Amen hallelujah!'

'A land of hills and valleys that drinketh water of the rain of heaven, a land that the Lord Thy God careth for!'

In the pause that preceded their Amen, Hugh's voice rang out, fervent and clear:

'The Book of Deuteronomy, chapter eleven, verse eleven, Amen!'

The congregation repeated his Amen and Moses called on the man who had proved himself worthy of Hebron to come out in front of them all, declare his name, testify to his faith, and be a witness for the Lord. Hugh stepped out, motioning to Obadiah to follow him. The two walked up the aisle. Moses asked which one of them it was that had given chapter and verse. Hugh bowed his head in acknowledgment, bowed once again to the approving Amen of the congregation. Obadiah stood beside Hugh, unable to withdraw his eyes from the face of the Prophet. Impressed by his adoration, Moses asked him who he was and what was his name. But he was covered with confusion and could not answer. Hugh answered for him and extolled his capabilities as a carpenter. The Prophet then formally appointed them his young disciples, laid his hand on

Hugh's head and called him James, on Obadiah's and called him John. And for the first time, Hugh felt a flicker of envy and resentment against his friend. For it was he who had spoken up, but it was on Obadiah that Moses's hand had lingered as he blessed them.

****

Obadiah heard a cock crowing in the distance. It was almost morning and he had not slept. Beside him Hugh had stopped snoring, but lay in a heavy drugged sleep, unusual for him. Obadiah touched with his forefinger the spot on his forehead where the Prophet's hand had touched him. He felt that he had been labelled with a great seal. After the rootless years in the hedges and by-ways he had found the father he had never known, the God he had never seen, a man who was now leading him to a great banquet of the spirit, leading him home. From tomorrow, he vowed, he would devote himself body and soul to the service of the Prophet; and there would be nothing too difficult that he would not undertake, too lowly or menial that he would not perform in the building up of Hebron. He was glad that he had learnt a trade, that his body had grown strong and powerful. For, after the service, Moses had told him that he would need his strong arms to hew down cedars out of Lebanon, he would need all men who had 'skill to hew timber', since the land that they were going to 'was a wood'.

Obadiah remembered Aloysius Matthews, the master carpenter who had been his mentor and employer. Now that he had lost his shop, perhaps he too would go up to Hebron, so that together they could perform miracles for the greater glory of Hebron and of the Prophet. Tomorrow, Obadiah decided, he would go to Aloysius and persuade him to join the New Believers, tomorrow he would do that first thing. He smiled to himself as he saw how he could render his first service to Moses. Another cock crowed, nearer this time, and the day was already clear in the sky when, at last, Obadiah fell asleep.

13. The Convert

Kate dreamt that she was in strange land, a land of drought. In her dream she moistened her lips and closed her eyes against the sun. The blue bowl of the sky floated upside down and the bare branches of the trees framed a coffin in which she was struggling with Prophet Moses; and her breasts thrust against him like angry birds. Then she was alone, an old woman sitting in an empty square, encircled by hills. As their sombre peaks moved towards her, shutting her in, she cried out with fear.

Aloysius turned over in his sleep and nudged his wife's elbow. Kate woke up to feel the child kicking inside her. She placed her hands on her belly and stared round the room, trying to make out familiar landmarks, to shake off the terror of her dream. She made out the door, then the windows, and began to calm down. It was the two green mangoes she had eaten earlier that had lain on her stomach, she thought, had caused her nightmare. She listened for a stirring in the next room, wondered if Liza had heard her cry out, through the flimsy walls.

It was over a year now that she and Aloysius had been renting a room in Liza Edward's house. Their bed was the one Moses had slept on during his first mission. Now he was back after five long years. But this time he had married Gatha Randall and slept with her in her concrete nog house behind the shop.

Kate lay awake in the darkness, puzzling over her dream. Why had she wrestled with Moses like Jacob with the angel?

She summoned up the image of the Prophet as he strode about the narrow streets, filling them with his presence. Whenever he passed by he would fix her with his piercing glance. Kate shivered as she remembered how she had seen herself as an old woman, her skin withered and hanging in folds. She drew her hands away from her belly, reached up to touch her face. It was round and firm, the flesh smooth on her arms and shoulders, on her breasts that were heavy with milk. But she was not reassured. Her dream showed plainly that all that the future held for her was old age and death. With Prophet Moses she would not just sit waiting, but would be caught up, like all the other New Believers, in a prodigal outpouring of life.

She sat up abruptly and shook her husband. He grunted, turned over on his back, opened one eye, shut it again, and asked wearily:

'What you want now?'

'I want you to listen to me!'

'You do enough talking in the daytime, you don't have to talk at night...' he muttered, and fell asleep again.

Kate looked at him with hostility. He lay with his mouth open, clusters of pimples breaking out at the ashen corners of his lips. She would have to plan her attack, she decided. Aloysius was very stubborn. Particularly now that he had lost everything – his shop, his apprentice, his black suit, his position as deacon. After he sold the suit to buy food, he stopped going to church. When the odd jobs that he used to do became even more infrequent, he had given up the shop and they moved in with Liza. Kate took in washing to help pay the rent and to buy food, and she abandoned the meal-time ritual which had meant more to Aloysius than the food itself.

He was a man for whom order was a necessity; everything had to be done in the right way. He came from a peasant family who took pride in their land, in earning bread by their sweat. After his father's death, the three acres of land went to Aloysius's elder brother; and he himself was taught a trade and given a lump sum to buy tools and to set himself up in a shop. Without his shop he was as uprooted and lost as his brother would have been without his few acres of dry and infertile land. And as he came to depend on Kate for the little that they had to eat and a place to sleep, the feel of Kate's flesh became his substitute for the shop, for his lost pride. Times grew more difficult, and the orders for Kate's washing dwindled until they ceased altogether. In their common defeat she and Aloysius drew closer. Kate became pregnant once again. Aloysius lowered his pride enough to beg his brother for help, but the odd dozen mangoes, the few heads of yams, the bunch of green bananas, stretched out over months of hunger, did not help much.

She shook him, pulled away the sheet and, pretending to be angrier than she really was, burst out at him:

'Aloysius Matthews, wake up and listen to me! Whether you like it or not, we are joining Moses Barton's church, we are going with him up to Hebron!'

Even half asleep his reaction was violent. He swung away from her.

'Hebron! What sort of a damn fool do you take me for at all? What sort of a fool...?' His words trailed off in an incoherent muttering, but sleep had left him this time for good and Kate knew it. She sat and waited.

Beside him, Aloysius felt her body, heavy with child, generating a heat that threatened to suffocate him in the airless room. He reached up and grasped the metal bed-rail, pulling himself up into a sitting position. The coolness of the metal against his palm made him feel better, cleared his head. He knew what Kate was leading up to. They had had it out many times before. And always when Kate talked about going up to Hebron or about Moses, there was something in her voice that made him vaguely jealous. Hunger and humiliation had sharpened his wits, had destroyed some of the clichés by which he had lived. Only one of these he still clung to – that as a man with a trade he was 'respectable', could have nothing in common with Moses Barton and his ragged mob. Yet, day after day, as he walked up and down, fooling himself that he was looking for work, he had not failed to notice the purposefulness of those who called themselves the New Believers, who had braved derision to believe again. At the street-corners, on the pavements, in the market, their talk of the Promised Land, the positions they were going to hold in Hebron, reached Aloysius's ears; and part of him wanted to be one of them, to share their hope.

That very night, on his way home, he had stood in the shadows outside the temple and listened as Prophet Moses told his followers about Hebron, told them how he had measured out the land, apportioned to each of them as much as their eyes could encompass. Aloysius's hunger for new roots had battled with his pride. At one moment he had even walked towards the entrance of the temple, where the torches flamed, beckoning him to their light. But as he drew near he saw Obadiah, his former apprentice, step out from the back of the temple and walk up the aisle; and in front of him marched Hugh, whose impertinence Aloysius had had to check many a time when he was himself a master carpenter, with a shop of his own. He couldn't demean himself before these two. They would recognize his defeat, would force him to admit it. He turned and walked away rapidly. Because he had been tempted, his denunciation, now, was the fiercer:

'Moses Barton and Hebron, hell! I hear about that damn foolishness on all sides when I walk out of this yard. I don't want to hear about it at home, in my sleep!'

'It's not any foolishness and you know it. And the proof is that he was able to climb right up through the wilderness to find Hebron right near the hill-top and no one ever did it before him!'

'Nobody ever tried!'

'Nobody ever tried anything yet and that's why, this time, we are going to try!'

Aloysius took this as a reproach for his own failure. He countered by attacking the Prophet.

'You can try. Not me. Everybody know that Moses Barton is a madman and the five years that he spend in the asylum prove it. And anyway, who you think is going to profit a damn on that barren land on the hill-top? Just sweat out your guts for nothing at all...'

'And what else you think you have been doing all these years? What you have to show for them, all these years that you slaving like a donkey tied to your bench? And anyway how you know that the land barren? You ever been up there?'

'No. And what's more I am never going up there!'

'Other people going though, and they will find out. Other people who not cowards!'

'Other people! Don't tell me about those other people! People who so damned stupid that five years back they sold out all they had and give it to Moses in exchange for a golden chariot to ride to heaven in, and a golden star to rule over. At least Moses was mad. They were just plain ignorant. Golden star, my foot! Golden chariot, hell! And the same story it was with heaven, the same story it bound to be with Hebron, you just wait and see!'

'Aloysius,' Kate asked quietly, 'answer me one thing. You got a work today?'

It was a question she had never asked him outright before. To do this would have been to exacerbate the hopelessness that he carried on his face like an open sore when he returned home in the evenings. Besides, she would have known as well as he what the ritual of the day had been: in the morning, washing his face at the stand-pipe in the yard, drinking a mug of water, fastening his belt so that the buckle reached far past the last notch, then turning out of the gate into the lane, right or left, it didn't matter, standing about with the other workless men, watching as the sun burnt away the last vestige of cloud from the sky; for a while, the aimless clinging to the back streets, the hot earth sizzling under his naked feet, piercing the calloused skin like the thorns of a crucifixion; at last, the forcing of resolution to turn out into the few broad, well-tended streets where bougainvillaea blossoms ran riot over dazzling whitewashed fences, behind which bungalows like fat well-fed faces lurked in their fastnesses; the timorous entrance through the back gates, careful not to walk on the grass, smiling hesitantly at the dogs, patting their heads as they snapped at his ankles, then the humility with, the bowing and scraping to, the insolent servants, in their turn harangued from a window by a loud-mouthed mistress, indolent in dressing-gown, her face white or black or brown, making no difference, only shouting at him through her servant the words that he had heard so often, that they remained with him like a song: 'No, no work for you – you know that already – so is why you come to bother me? You are all a worthless pack of idlers – get back to the street where you belong before I call the police – I don't want any old criminal hanging about my yard saying that they looking for work…' the dogs and the servants shooing him out, and he in his heart agreeing with them that for a man to be out of work was his crime and his shame; he, in their position, would have done the same. And all the way home he carried his secret agreement like a cross.

'No, I didn't get a work today, I didn't get any!' he said, exploding against the malice of his wife's question.

Kate brooded over what he had just said, her fingers drawing together the ragged strands of the bed-spread. She had bought it the day before her wedding. It was of imitation silk embroidered all over with green and gold dragons. Now they used it as a blanket in December and January when the nights were chilly. Its brightness had faded, the outlines of the dragons blurred. Beside her, Aloysius twisted and turned, trying to avoid the final honesty which her silence suspended between them.

'And anyway,' he argued, 'this land that Moses talking so much about, how he can have it to give? It's Crown land and belong to the Government up in Kingston and through them to the King of England. How the Lord can give it to Moses in any vision?'

For a moment she was tempted to tell him the truth behind Moses's claim to the land up in Hebron. 'Caesar's facts', as Liza had explained it to her. But she suspected that Aloysius might find more excuses not to go up to Hebron after all, and might insist that he was too law-abiding to be mixed up in any 'shady business'.

'Crown land or not,' she said instead, 'it's lying there going to waste and nobody not using it. So if Moses want to claim it for himself and he offer you work to do, clearing away the trees, and cutting down the bush...and...'

'My work is carpentering. I don't want to clear any bush or cut down any tree,' he grumbled.

Kate wanted to be reasonable. She knew that his resistance was only a token gesture before surrender. But the pain pricked in the hollow of her back like needles, then crept up on her with gentle furred tongues. It was three months early, and this child, like the others, would die. She wanted it to die. With its death she would be set free from the years of waiting in a closed room, in a closed town, with only Liza's talk of Moses's second coming holding out some promise. Now he was here at last.

Lately she had taken to sitting on her doorstep in the early morning, looking up at the distant blue-green hills. She looked towards the hills, for pressing in upon her was the fantastic reality of squalor. The dwarfed houses, the shrunken streets, the trees gnarled and blackened with grime, the pit latrines with their evil smells and lowering multitude of flies, the dripping stand-pipe over the concrete cistern whose sides gave birth to a moss-like growth, dark green, and oozing disease and death, the yard with its litter of trash, scavenging dogs, dead rats and dead people crowding in on her, forcing her back into her cluttered room with its bed, chair, table, bugs, and cockroaches.

And her child would be the child of this room with its leaking roof, its rickety walls, plastered with newspaper pictures of the Governor in his white plumes, his lady in her finery, and ragged crowds waving and smiling; and here and there, hiding the pictures, framed Bible texts that read: 'Behold I stand at the door and knock', 'The meek shall inherit the earth', 'Come unto Me, all ye that labour, and I will give you rest'. It would be the child of Aloysius's disillusionment, the child of hunger, growing up to see its parents scrounging around for rent, begging for time to pay; whilst out in the lane children chased sunbeams bright as new pennies, or played, grave and silent, their emaciated legs coated with dust or spattered with mud, their protruding bellies casting distorted shadows; and at nights the quiet air made violent with the sounds of people copulating, their act loveless, compelled by a blind animal quest for existence.

Kate raged against her husband as the pain assaulted her.

'Work that you know to do! Carpentering, the big master carpenter. And whilst we are waiting on work that you know to do, all the children that kick inside me must be born and die like grass!'

The pain reached it peak, forcing her to expel her breath in low rhythmic gasps, and to hold on to her belly with both hands. Aloysius reached out his hands as if to help her, but she shook her head violently at him, and, under her breath, muttered all the obscene words that she knew. Aloysius crouched away from her, her curses falling upon him like stones. When at last she lay still, sweat washing over her, he sprang up, pulled on his shirt and trousers, and rapped hard on the wall. He knew that Liza was awake, that she had been lying there, listening, glad that they were quarrelling again. And he knew that she was only pretending to be half-asleep as she called out:

'What...? Who...?'

'It's Kate. She start up with the pains,' he called back.

He could hear the heavy thump as she lowered herself from the bed, could hear the rustling of the mattress as she ordered:

'Sue, wake up and light the lamp. Ann, catch the fire and boil the big pan full of water, and pass me that candle over there on the shelf…and the matches too, child, the matches!'

She loomed in the doorway, the lighted candle in her hand, her cotton nightgown ballooning about her. Tiny scattered plaits were like a moth-eaten bird's nest on her head and her alert eyes dismissed Aloysius as she leaned over the bed and crooned to Kate:

'Everything going to be all right now, Kate, don't fret yourself, everything going to be all right, you just wait and see.'

****

Aloysius stepped out into the yard. The cool morning breeze was like a benediction. Somewhere a cock crowed, and looking up, he could make out the dark outlines of the hills. Then Kate screamed, and his bitterness poisoned the morning. In their five years of marriage this would be the fourth time that she had given birth to a doomed child. And although neither Kate nor any one of the neighbors had ever blamed him to his face, he knew that they all indicted him secretly. The time before, when Kate's labour pains had started, Liza sent him to the shop for some castor oil. Returning, he could hear her talking volubly to Kate, could hear his own name being mentioned. When he came into the room the talking ceased abruptly. For days after that he could sense Kate looking at him, assessing him.

And after all, Kate had been lucky to get him, he thought with resentment. He could have married Emma, the teacher's daughter. She was the postmistress of Cockpit Centre now, and people had to call her Miss Withers when they went to collect their letters. Aloysius had glimpsed her only yesterday. She hadn't seen him. He had hidden behind the guinep tree. It was in the afternoon when, after the usual round of rebuffs from servants, dogs, and mistresses, he had gone down to the railway station to watch the train from Kingston arrive.

For this had become with him a habit, a daily ritual; as if the train might bring something as magical as the smoke in its wake, the belching grey smoke that sifted new horizons in the sky.

****

He had stood in the sparse shadow of a guinep tree between the railway station and the post office, and had watched as the train chugged up the steep incline into the station, as one of the loungers detached himself from the wall of the building, entered the train, and emerged with two leather suitcases. Behind the man walked Mrs Brooke, the minister's wife. Aloysius flattened himself behind the tree-trunk, not wanting her to see him. He had cut all connection with his church over a year and a half ago. Often, since then, the Reverend Brooke, meeting him on the street, had urged him to return to his position, but he refused. For how could he explain that his black serge suit was the mark of caste, a status symbol which elevated a black man, made him fit to be a deacon; and that without the suit he felt unworthy in the presence of the white man and therefore of God? The Reverend Brooke had sighed, patted him on the shoulder, and gone off to the church to pray for guidance.

Aloysius much preferred Mrs Brooke's attitude. She only smiled faintly when she saw him and never spoke. But for some time now he hadn't seen her, and Kate told him that the doctor had sent her away for a holiday to the cool hill-resort of Mandeville.

She stepped briskly out of the station now, waved to the man with her luggage, gesturing to him that he should wait for her, then walked towards the post office. She passed close to Aloysius and he could see that her eyes were bright, that she was humming a little tune to herself. But as she stepped out into the full glare of the sun, her face set in a quick frown. He remembered Kate saying that the minister's wife fought against the sun as if it were a living enemy. He felt a suddenly hostility towards this white woman for her hatred of the sun.

Mrs Brooke rapped on the fine wire netting of the post office window. Aloysius made out Emma Withers's sharp profile behind the wire netting before she pushed up the barrier, her manner obsequious. She hadn't changed much, he thought. She still wore her hair scraped back in a tight bun. But there was a bald spot, the size of a farthing, to the left of her widow's peak. A pair of gold-rimmed spectacles was perched on her nose. Her projecting front teeth moved up and down as she riffled through a packet of letters, then shook her head. Her high voice, with its persistent singsong in spite of her efforts to iron it out and speak an English as neutral as herself, carried to him clearly:

'Nothing for you, Mrs Brooke, I am sorry to say!'

'Are you quite sure, Miss Withers?'

'Quite sure, Mrs Brooke. I always notice anything for you and the parson, special. One came for him some days ago, I remember, a long envelope from the Government...'

Mrs Brooke pulled at the fingers of her white gloves, turned away from the window, then turned back again:

'I can't quite understand how there could be no letters, Miss Withers...I stayed several days up in Kingston...and she did promise that she would write every day...you know...so that we could keep in touch...'

As she spoke she became more and more agitated. It was the heat, she thought to herself, it always did this to her. She saw Emma looking at her curiously and took hold of herself. She could not afford to let herself go before one of her husband's few remaining church members. She called out to the man with her luggage, told him to take the suitcases to the manse, and send the buggy to fetch her. Then she asked Emma to allow her to wait inside the post office building, where it was cooler. Pleased, the postmistress opened the door and gave a suggestion of a curtsy as Mrs Brooke entered and sat down. Emma seated herself too, and searched for something to say. From where he watched, Aloysius made out their two heads behind the netting. They looked like two birds in a cage.

Mrs Brooke forgot the other woman's presence. She recalled the day of her arrival in Mandeville. It had been raining as she drove from the station to the hotel. She had breathed in the sharp tang of mountain air, felt refreshed by the sight of the gently sloping hills, green and fertile. Mandeville, with its village square, clock-tower and well-tended gardens, reminded her of an English village. That evening, at dinner in the hotel – an old-style 'colonial' building with vast grounds, terraced gardens, a river, and a waterfall – she met the members of the sizeable English colony of 'regulars'.

These expatriates were, for the most part, retired army officers and civil servants, ex-judges and police commissioners, with their wives and families. They had served in different colonial territories for the greater part of their lives, and found themselves out of place whenever they returned to England. By now accustomed to a more spacious well-being, they could no longer conform to the cramped life in the mother country. They chose, instead, to enshrine her memory in their hearts and worship from afar. They were, with a few exceptions, kind and decent men and women with a strong sense of duty and a habit of loyalty. They treated 'their blacks' with a determined benevolence, and were, in many instances, very helpful to ambitious young natives who wanted to further their education.

But they had been brought up to believe that God and the British Empire were in some way synonymous, that their imperial destiny was a Christian and righteous one; and could never admit to themselves that their colonial possessions had been acquired not through the Divine Will, but because of their country's might and cunning. When they found themselves absolute rulers over vast numbers of alien peoples they felt compelled to rationalize their overlordship. The most satisfying assumption was that the natives peoples were an inferior race. To reinforce this belief, they lived their lives shut away from any real contact with the people whom they ruled. They transported a mannered ritual of behaviour from the home country, and wore dinner jackets in the heart of the jungle, like Catholic priests nailing up crucifixes in the temples of heathen gods.

Whenever doubts assailed them, they repeated slogans – the natives were backward, mentally degenerate, naive children, incapable of ruling themselves, savages, primitives, etc. – and these slogans were like charms which they used to ward off an encroaching reality. As the years passed, the roots which they had brought with them from their own country withered away. They put down no new ones. Without spiritual resources, they became caricatures of themselves.

Mrs Brooke was happy to be amongst her own people again, instead of being the 'minister's wife', the 'white lady up at the manse'. Here in Mandeville there were enough white faces to form a charmed circle from which all natives – except the servants – could be excluded. She felt released from long exile. Lady Harrington, even more than the others, helped to bring this about. The old woman was the doyen of the Mandeville group. She was the widow of a former Colonial Governor, and, with great acumen, had helped to further his career. When her husband died of fever in West Africa, she came to Jamaica to keep house for a bachelor brother. He was the Chief Secretary, and lived in Kingston. Lady Harrington had been too long accustomed to being a personage with an official residence and a retinue of servants to pretend that she did not enjoy it. Her brother's house became famous for its social occasions. But, as she was getting on in years – she had been almost fifteen years her husband's senior – she was advised by her doctor to spend several months a year in the cooler hill-climate of Mandeville.

Lady Harrington was the most honoured guest at the hotel where Mrs Brooke stayed. She at once took the younger woman under her wing, for new faces were few and far between. The two women became constant companions. The high spot of their day was when they took tea together under the trees overlooking the lawn. England for them, as for the other expatriates, would never, could never, change; and they talked of the England they had known as if time had stopped. And always they rounded off the afternoon with Lady Harrington's condemnation of the island and its natives. As Mrs Brooke listened to her friend's confident assertions, the feeling of guilt which had haunted her since the day of her arrival in the island was soothed. Lady Harrington was right. The natives were created poor and wretched and damned. God had, for his own purpose, decreed it that way. There was really little that anyone could do to lighten their lot. The failure of her husband's mission in Cockpit Centre was therefore neither his fault nor hers.

For this assurance Mrs Brooke was prepared to give the older woman an absolute devotion. She listened for hours whilst Lady Harrington told and retold her fund of stories about life in India, England, Africa, and Jamaica. The old woman, for her part, was delighted to have fresh and captive audience to whom she could recount the madcap doings of the society friends of her youth – all dead now, but imperishable in her memory – with whom she could recapture her former splendour as a Governor's wife and first lady.

'My dear Cecilia,' she would say, her eyes gleaming as she retreated into the incomparable past, 'you cannot imagine the differences between the blacks in Africa and these Jamaican natives! Of course, there they are still in the primitive stage and quite, quite savage. But once they have been tamed they make wonderful servants. Their capacity for loyalty and devotion, my dear, was quite touching. They worshipped my husband and myself, called us the 'Great white father and mother', were so grateful for the least favours. And these days, with our own working class in England becoming restless, and so my sister tells me in her letters, making all kinds of demands, showing the blackest ingratitude, in these days, my dear, it's more than comforting to know that somewhere in the world, there are still happy and contented subject races.'

The waiter, his enormous body rigid in his white monkey jacket and black trousers, served tea. His face was impassive above the two women, his black hands moved amongst the teacups with a neutral dexterity. Lady Harrington emphasized her expression of disdain. But her eyes, grey-blue and virginal in her withered face, were uncertain. Mrs Brooke, too, felt uneasy. She knew that the waiters all disliked Lady Harrington. The old woman never tipped. As the Governor's wife she had had only to accept services with a gracious condescension; and to tip now would be to admit that her position had changed. So she pretended not to notice that the waiters served her grudgingly. Once, intimidated by a waiter's surly demeanor, Mrs Brooke had fumbled with her purse, but the other woman's imperious look made her pretend that she was only reaching for her handkerchief.

They drank their tea in silence and were both relieved when the waiter, after serving them strawberries and cream, departed. The strawberries were undersized ones which one of the English residents, at great expense, managed to grow in his back garden. The cream, too, was of inferior quality.

'But what else can you expect from these Jamaican cows, my dear! And as for the people! The airs they give themselves, just because they have learnt to wear clothes and use a knife and fork! I am obliged, from time to time, to invite one or two of them to official receptions at my brother's house in Kingston, but, my dear, the relief I feel when I can at last get them out of the place!'

Lady Harrington reached for the jug of cream and helped herself to more strawberries. Mrs Brooke used her handkerchief to drive away the wasps.

'No, my dear, as my husband used to say,' Lady Harrington concluded, 'give me the primitive African any day, but spare me the aspiring blacks!'

She concentrated on her tea. Mrs Brooke seized on the chance to say:

'My husband would be glad to hear you say that, Lady Harrington. He could not endure the middle-class natives who came to his church, not to hear the Word, but to draw nearer to us. He finds it much easier to deal with the poor, and has had his greatest successes amongst them. They look upon him as their earthly father.'

Lady Harrington smiled, as if accepting a tribute. Encouraged, Mrs Brooke talked about her husband's mission in the wild southern region of the island. She had had no one to talk to before. Her husband and herself confined themselves to meaningless phrases which, by precluding dangerous admissions, alone made their life tolerable. Now her eyes shone with emotion as she described to Lady Harrington her trials, her spiritual pilgrimage in the waste land of Cockpit Centre. The rich white planters, she hinted, had wanted to carry her off like so many wild Lochinvars. But she had been steadfast, wrestled with them in the spirit, converted them to the Lord's work.

Lady Harrington murmured an Amen, and thought, with some irritation, that this woman had turned out to be a bore like all the others. They all assumed that, for some reason, she was interested in their drab lives. The next morning, at breakfast, Mrs Brooke told her that her husband had written to say that things were getting worse in Cockpit Centre, that a 'mad' revivalist preacher was seducing his congregation away from the truth.

'My dear Cecilia, if I were you I would not lose a moment. In times of stress men are like reeds without us!'

Lady Harrington saw her off at the station and promised to write.

****

The postmisttress's voice pierced through Mrs Brooke's withdrawal:

'You had a nice holiday up in Mandeville, Mrs Brooke?' she asked, glad to have found the polite phrase.

Her stilted conversational tone made Mrs Brooke sick with longing for the sound of the well-bred English voices she had left behind her in Mandeville. A sudden sharp nostalgia for her own country overwhelmed her. Her father had died some years before, and her few friends in England had become a generation of strangers. Lady Harrington's promised letters had seemed to her to be the one link that would keep her in touch with things English. Mrs Brooke regretted that Englishness was not something integral that she could carry about with her, like her faith, her religion.

A market-woman came to the post office window. The postmistress dealt with her hastily and returned to Mrs Brooke. The minister's wife did not look at all well, she thought, her face had taken on a greenish pallor, and she looked as though she were about to faint.

'You don't look too good to me, Mrs Brooke,' she said anxiously. 'Would you like me to get you a glass of water?'

Mrs Brooke nodded. She wanted to get rid of the woman's importunity, in the same way that Lady Harrington had wanted to get rid of hers, had hustled her off, had never really intended to write. The illusions she had nourished briefly in Mandeville disappeared under the impact of her return home. The familiar desolation filled her once more. She wished that she had told Lady Harrington the true facts of her life in this wretched outpost – told her of the monotony, the spiritual tedium of living amongst an alien people, a people beaten down under the lash of the sun and of hunger, who crawled before you struck them, were grateful before you helped them, and, guilty or not, repentant before you scolded them; a people whose servility exacerbated the instinct for cruelty that lurked in you, whose acceptance of sub-human status made it impossible for you to be human too; a people who regarded your white skin as if it were a talisman against misery and unhappiness, who looked to you as if you were the god that you had made yourself out to be, and were ready to turn against you with a savage indifference if, like a god, you failed to provide them with manna from heaven.

Mrs Brooke was shaken with a terrible anger against herself and Lady Harrington, Empire and missions, Emma Withers, all black faces, the hard-baked earth of the road lined with coconut palms, casting harsh shadows. She ignored the glass of water that the postmistress held out to her, pushed back her chair and stood up abruptly. Pretending not to see Emma's rebuffed expression, she pushed open the swing door and stepped out on to the pavement. She almost collided with her husband, on his way to post a letter which he had in his hand.

She had not written to tell him that she was hurrying back, and the minister had driven the long way round in the buggy and missed the man with his wife's luggage. Mrs Brooke noted her husband's surprise and wondered at its furtive quality. But he recovered his composure at once, explained his pleasure at her return, his gratitude for her 'sacrifice' in cutting her holiday short in order to be at his side. As he said all the expected things, Mrs Brooke allowed herself to be tempted back into her conspiracy with him. She forgot her anger and revolt of a few minutes before. Whilst her husband stamped his letter she said pleasantly to Emma that she was to be sure, now, to let them see her in church that coming Sunday. The postmistress smiled and gave a gratified nod. There were compensations after all, Mrs Brooke concluded, and, as long as she and her husband clung together in their common exile, they might even manage to create a touch of England in the sterile mountain country of Jamaica. And, unlike Lady Harrington and her idle crowd, she and Richard would have the satisfaction of knowing that they were leading useful lives in the service of God...

****

Aloysius had watched the minister and his wife drive away in the buggy, and then had turned left, by the railway station, into Lime Lane. The lane led out into a small square in the centre of which there was a water trough for horses. He perched on the edge of the trough, trailed his fingers through the brackish water, and looked across at the grocery opposite, the 'Chinese shop' as everyone called it. Since the death of the Chinese grocer, his common-law negro wife, who lacked business sense, had let the shop run to seed. It was still open to business but no one was behind the counter. There was little to steal anyway. The goods on the shelves were scanty, and the few loaves of bread in the glass case on the counter were stale and flyblown. The floor of the shop was strewn with litter and dried mud. Its smell of salted fish, washing soap, and decay pervaded the square. The sight of a once-flourishing business, now so neglected, depressed Aloysius. He walked up the lane towards the station. As he hunched his back against the sun he remembered hearing that the woman who owned the shop was planning to sell out and go with Prophet Moses up to Hebron. The fool, Aloysius muttered, to have a good business like that, to let it run down and now to give it all up for a bird in the bush…

Now, the morning after, standing by his gate, he watched daylight spread out over the town like water filtered through a vase of blue glass. In the room behind him he could hear Kate moaning the soft tired moans that are the aftermath of pain. But for him the struggle was just beginning. Soon he would have to climb up into the unknown hills that towered up in the distance, would have to go in search of the security that he had not achieved in all his forty-seven years. He would have to learn to believe again, become a new convert. A cock crowed along the lane, then another. All around him he could sense people stirring in their beds, on the pavement, in the parks. And as he waited to greet the day with them, he cursed this city which had deceived him with bright hopes, then snatched them away when he was past the age of new beginnings, so that he was now compelled to follow a madman up to the distant hills of Hebron.

14. *The Moonshine Doll*

On the eve of their exodus, the New Believers gathered in the temple for a watch-night service; and their rejoicing invaded the dark sleeping places of the town. In the shed behind the church, Aloysius Matthews and Obadiah nailed up boxes, and helped with the final preparations for their departure, while Kate took part in the service. She was seated on the front bench beside Miss Gatha. Prophet Moses had not failed to accord every honour to his master carpenter, appointing him second-in-command and Master of the Household.

The New Believers sang, and Prophet Moses, on his knees in the rough pulpit, prayed for guidance. When he stood up, his expression was that of a man taking part in a mystic communion. The final Amen of the congregation was hushed. They seated themselves quietly on the benches. After a pause the prophet began his sermon, his tenor voice pitched low:

'Brethren and Sisters, New Believers, after divers years of trials and tribulations, the Lord has vouchsafed at last to lead us out of the bondage of our poverty and want! Brethren and Sisters, New Believers, tomorrow morning when the day light up we are going to cross the Red Sea of despair, walk through the wilderness of want, climb up the hills of hope, into the new Canaan!'

'Amen!'

'Yes, the new Canaan, the lot of our inheritance that was showed to me, His Prophet, by the Lord in a vision!'

'Amen!'

'New Believers, if you all could only have visioned my vision with me…'

'If!' they yearned.

'But the gift of vision is not granted to all, only to the One whom, from time to time, the Lord marks out with his terrible mark, the Lord single out with the lightning of His eye, the thunder of His word, the mighty sword of His wisdom!'

'Amen!'

'And through His wisdom, the Lord prepared me for my task, the Lord lead me through devious and untrackable paths, until at last I entered in the tower of the temple of His knowledge, Amen!'

'Amen hallelujah, praise the Lord!' they chanted.

Kate Matthews looked away from Prophet Moses. Beside her, Miss Gatha's face reflected his words and moods like a mirror of polished ebony. All the other faces, too, reflected the same image. Kate had discovered in herself an ability to predict the Prophet's moves as well as his motives. She sensed what his sermon was leading up to. For earlier on that evening she had divined, underneath the triumph of the congregation, an insidious doubt that had sidled into the temple, coiled itself into the hearts of the New Believers, sat like a ghost at table with them during the banquet – a suspicion that what had happened once could happen again, that heaven might be denied them once more; for had it not been snatched away from them? A fear which, because no one had dared to bring it out into the open, was all the more persistent.

Kate felt the Prophet's eyes on her. He could not, she knew, bear even one pair of eyes escaping him. She met his gaze. He threw back his leonine head with its mass of hair, and his lips moved as he selected the words that were to transmute his former failure into a presage of triumph. The moonlight streamed into the church, washed his head and shoulders with a patina of brightness. His eyes stared as if before him he saw the face of God. Amongst the congregation there was awe, reverence, ecstasy. The Prophet spun out his words like a man spending coins whose value was beyond reckoning:

'Brethren and Sisters, New Believers, it was five years ago to this day, five years come and gone, that I, in the false pride of my heart, did exalt myself to lay claim to the kingdom. And when I thought I was on the very pinnacle of power, yea even then…'

'Amen!'

They applauded his choice of resonant words. He clenched his fist above his head.

'Yea, even then, the Lord came to me, white in a blinding light, and smote me hip and thigh as he smote Saul of Tarsus on his way to Damascus!'

'Aa…a…men!'

The approved the parallel. Saul had become Paul, his momentary defeat engulfed in infinite victory. Prophet Moses noted their approval. There was a suggestion of a smile on his lips as he went on:

'And even so, Brothers and Sisters, even so, as the Lord smote Saul of Tarsus, so did He smite me. Only, as Saul was brown, whereas I am black, he smote Saul right down there on the road and smote me from off a breadfruit tree-top!'

'Amen!' they said, laughing. But the seed of resentment which he had planted in them against the Almighty for using him more severely, took firm root. He continued, no longer smiling, his voice grave:

'And, Brothers and Sisters, when my heart was broken as my leg had been, my pride was humbled as my heart had been, then, yea, even then, the Lord came to me soft in the still dark of the night, and the touch of His hand burn me like fire and sting me like ice, but His voice was kind and the hand that He touched me with was…black…like mine!'

For a moment the New Believers hesitated to believe that God could be like them, that, in striving to be like the Father, they would no longer have to deny themselves as sons.

'Black…' they said, wonderingly at first.

'Black,' they repeated, with recognition.

'Black!' they thundered. 'Hallelujah, Amen!'

The Prophet thrust his head forward as if jealous to guard between them what he was now going to reveal. They sat enthralled on the edge of their benches, offering their lives for him to do with as he willed. He felt like God. Their faces were votive offerings gilded by the moon. He thought of Joshua who had stopped the sun, and wished that at this moment he too could be immortal. It was then that the secret longing which was to result in his crucifixion took hold of him.

To break the spell he chuckled, and said:

'And Brothers and Sisters, the Lord said to me, word for word as I tell it to you. The Lord said, "Hard-ears Moses, if I wanted you to fly to heaven, don't I would have given you wings?"'

'Amen!'

They were pleased at God's sagaciousness, His familiarity.

' "But I gave you two big black feet and I gave you the hills!"'

'The hills!'

' "And, as long as you and the New Believers will keep my commandments, and not diminish from them one jot nor one tittle, inside those hills I will give to you as the lot of your inheritance a land called...?"'

'Hebron, hallelujah, Amen!'

Kate felt Miss Gatha's elbow dig into her side as she turned and looked towards the door of the temple. Her face was clouded over like a rain sky. Kate followed her glance and saw, entering the wide door of the temple, the woman Martha, who had lived with the Chinese grocer until his death the year before. Beside the woman was her daughter. She was the same little girl who used to play on the pavement whilst Kate and Liza had sat talking of the Prophet, dreaming of his return; and was now between thirteen and fourteen years old. She was tall and slim, her belly rounded with early pregnancy. The two stood just inside the door, clutching bundles in their hands. The mother stared straight ahead of her and waited with the patience of an ox...The girl gripped the bundle tightly to her breast as if trying to hide herself. Her eyes were downcast. As the New Believers stared, their curiosity aroused to fever pitch, the Prophet stepped from the pulpit and walked with measured steps down the aisle.

He took the young girl by the hand, and, followed by the mother, led them up the length of the church. When he came to the front bench he seated the girl beside Miss Gatha, and gestured to the mother to sit beside her daughter. Amidst the puzzled silence of the congregation he returned to the pulpit. Then, scanning their faces one by one, he said slowly and impressively:

'And if any man be without sin, let him cast the first stone!'

'Amen!' they intoned.

His gesture had its effect. The congregation relaxed. Even Miss Gatha's face seemed to shed some of its dull suspicion. And whilst the Prophet knelt in the pulpit and prayed and kept vigil, the New Believers softly sang chorus after chorus, rejoicing for the Kingdom of Hebron which was at hand.

Behind Miss Gatha, Kate saw the young girl. She sat with her head bowed, but every now and then, during the singing, would glance round quickly. Under the shield of black hair, her eyes gleamed, reflecting an unreasoning fear. Kate felt compassion for her, and saw at once that Moses had arranged this charade in order to silence the gossip in the town; it was being said that he was responsible for the young girl's pregnancy.

Some of the unbelievers of the town had composed new words to the tune of the song with which they had celebrated Moses's downfall five years before, bawdy and suggestive words. Several prominent citizens, outraged, had urged that adults should be fined and children whipped if caught singing it openly in the streets. But in spite of their efforts, everyone knew the song. Even the wind seemed to sing it now.

One day Kate had overheard one of the Brothers, the fat and cheerful young Lazarus, singing it as he pushed his handcart along:

Moses choose out a ripe young chicken
From amidst all his righteous following,

Pick her, cook her just right for eating, Oh Moses!
Then to find out if she was tender,
Tried her right here in Cockpit Centre
The chicken cry out, 'Oh what a rooster, Oh Moses!'

Kate looked at the Brother reprovingly as she passed by, and he stopped at once. But as she went on she thought that the song would help Moses to conceal the real truth of the affair, a truth that was known only to the girl herself, her mother, the Prophet, Liza Edwards, and Kate. Liza had told Kate, swearing her to strict secrecy. For Moses had ordered that not a word should be said to anyone on pain of excommunication. And he himself had divulged it to no one, not even to his wife.

****

It was when the Prophet was away searching for his kingdom in the hills that Liza had first told Kate about what she called, with relish, the 'secret scandal'. The two women sat on the doorstep, talking. A horned moon peered at them from behind a lignum vitae tree. Out in the lane some children lilted the tune of a waltz as they played a ring game,

Jane and Louisa will soon come home,
Oh will soon come home, oh will soon come home.
Jane and Louisa will soon come home,
Into their beautiful garden…

Kate swayed to the tune and listened to Liza's enthusiastic and involved account of the 'scandal'.

'I know that you won't say a word to a soul, Kate. For if the Prophet ever find out! But one thing with you is that you are closemouth and can hold your tongue, not like that stupid Martha who I am sure spreading the story all over the place. Not that I didn't warn Prophet Moses about her. When you see my spirit turn from a person, you must know, and I didn't like a single bone in her body from the first day I clap eyes on her, when Chin-Quee, picked her up in the wilds of the St Elizabeth bush and bring her back here to look after the shop, and I don't have to tell you what else she had to do. Anyway, the whole thing started off after the Chinaman died. You see for yourself how she let the shop run down. Quicktime after, he wasn't even cold in his grave, Martha and the daughter didn't have bread to put to their mouth. So when Martha hear say that the minister's wife wanted a young girl to help in the house, she send her daughter to see Mrs Macey the housekeeper and they employ her straight off. Mind you, the old thieving Chinaman must be turning over in his grave, because to give him his due he used to set plenty store by the daughter, and would never even allow her to mix with any and everybody, you remember?'

Kate nodded. Over the years she had often heard Chin-Quee quarrelling with his woman, Martha, for not keeping the child clean. From business trips to Kingston and Paradise Bay he would return laden with clothes and toys for his daughter. He refused to send her to school, and did not even consider sending her to church. For him, his child was Chinese. So he kept her to himself and did not encourage her to mix with children of an alien race. He had even given her a Chinese name, 'Wild lotus', but her mother stubbornly called her Gloria, until after a while Chin-Quee too had come to call her by that name.

Whilst his daughter was still a young girl he allowed her the freedom of the pavement outside the shop. But as soon as her breasts started to ripen he kept her penned up inside the shop, restricting her to the two back rooms and the yard with its litter of discarded boxes, empty tins, and bottles piled up to shut out the sunlight. And, in the oppressive atmosphere of the grocery with its continual hum of gossip, shouted orders, the clatter of dirty coins flung on the counter, with Chin-Quee seated on a high stool like a Buddha, collecting the money, giving change, and every now and then, arguing violently with the few who owed him money – he gave very little credit – then recomposing his face to its usual impassivity as he moved a feather duster to and fro, brushing away flies and never for one moment losing sight of his paramour as she served the customers; and Martha herself going about, complying with the orders, her movements slow, her limbs heavy, her lips set in a mutinous line against the heavy-lidded eyes that held her in subjection, her body ready to rebel against him with any one of the labourers who lounged in the shop, for whom sex would be casual and sensuous, without the driving mechanical persistence with which, night after night, her 'husband' crushed her flesh, seeking to stir the weight of her spirit – in this atmosphere of tension and dumb hatred, arrogant contempt and slavish resentment, the young girl Gloria thrived like a wild flower blooming on a pile of dung.

'My love, will you allow me to waltz with you, into this beautiful garden,' the children sang as Liza continued her story.

'Well, it turned out that the minister's wife, Mrs Brooke, was quite pleased with the girl Gloria, said that she was neat and quiet about the house. But the trouble started after Mrs Brooke went off for a holiday to Mandeville, although what she want with holiday I don't know, seeing as she never lift her hand to brush fly off her nose – anyway, it seems that the first day after she left, the girl Gloria was alone in the house with the Reverend. Mrs Macey the housekeeper was gone to the market, and although the girl don't full out fourteen years yet, she is big for her age and have ripe breasts. And, according to what she say, she was in the bedroom making the bed and it was dark in the room, the heavy curtains was still drawn right across to shut out the light, the white lady don't like light at all, people say…'

****

It was mid-morning. In the bedroom with its mahogany-panelled walls, the drawn curtains enclosed a silence into which the cackling of hens out in the yard, the braying of a donkey, penetrated like distant echoes. The Reverend Brooke came in to fetch his jacket and closed the door behind him, making sure as always to shut out the light. He noticed the girl smoothing the edges of the sheets, remembered that his wife was away, and went across to the window, to pull back the curtains and let in some fresh air. As he passed by the girl he brushed against her by accident. The skin of her bare arm was cool and soft as silk. He stopped, and found himself unable to move.

The girl leaned over to tuck the sheets under the mattress. Her breasts slipped out from behind the white square in front of her apron and pointed in the wide neckline of her blouse. The Reverend Brooke placed his hands on her shoulders, turned her round to face him. He was hardly conscious of what he was doing.

'I want you,' he said.

He could see the startled incomprehension in her eyes, but was unable to find any other words to explain.

'You want me to do something, sir?' she asked.

It there had been any sign of coquetry in her question, he would have desisted. Even in his extremity, his strong Nonconformist conscience made him ashamed. But her complete innocence erased the sense of guilt which had haunted him since he was an adolescent. And her docility filled him with a sense of power and of mastery that he had never before experienced.

'Take off your clothes,' he said.

She undressed and stood waiting for him to tell her what to do next. His order did not seem strange to her. He had taken the place of her father who had inculcated in her the habit of obedience.

'Lie down,' he told her.

Her body was like a blaze of sunlight in the dark room. Gently, wonderingly, he stroked her breasts, and felt his impotence of years disguised as chastity, his terror of the flesh and fear of his own inadequacy disguised as love of God, felt them tumbling down, like the walls of Jericho, in one overwhelming instant. He flung off his clothes impatiently.

****

The half-moon shone, yellow like ripe corn. The children in the lane were playing another game, one that had been Kate's favourite when she was a child. She could hear them chanting in unison, solemnly:

Moonshine baby, moonshine doll,
Look how the moon a-look on you,
Look how the moon a-shine on you,
Moonshine baby, moonshine doll!

She knew that they would form a ring, and in the centre make the smallest child lie on the ground, then mark out the outline of its body with pieces of broken crockery. When the child got up, there, glinting in the moonlight, would be the 'moonshine doll' round which they now sat in a circle, repeating the chant, the magic words that would make it come alive.

Kate glanced at the heavy clouds that circled the moon. If the clouds veiled the moon, the children would have to dismantle the doll, take up the pieces of china, and then repeat the entire ritual. Liza, who had gone into the kitchen, came out with two mugs of mint tea and handed one to Kate.

'Well, missis,' she went on, between noisy gulps of the hot liquid, 'the first hint that Martha had of the story was when the girl didn't see what she should see every month. So she questioned the daughter, who looked back at her with her two dumb eyes and not a word. She slapped her up hill and down dale to make her talk. Still not a word. So Martha sent a street boy to call Prophet Moses. If you ask me, this was just an excuse, the woman wanted to see him alone. But as I was at the temple with him at the time when he got the summons he asked me to go along with him. For by now he become wise in the ways of the world and didn't want any evil-minded onlookers to see him going into the Sister's shop at night and alone . . .'

The 'evil-minded onlookers', that is, those who did not believe in the Prophet's spiritual destiny, were the very ones who believed most firmly in his extraordinary sexual prowess. They took a vicarious pride in recounting and enlarging his varied and numerous exploits, both real and imaginary. These legends did not fail to reach the ears of the New Believers. Liza, too, had heard the rumour that Moses's conversion of the woman Martha had taken place 'through the flesh rather than the spirit'. There were those who maintained that they had seen the Prophet enter Martha's shop one afternoon, that they themselves, going in to make purchases, had seen no one behind the counter, that the door leading into the back of the shop was locked, and that although they knocked and called repeatedly, no one had answered. It was that very night, they insisted, that Martha first attended the temple, confessed to having lived 'in sin with a heathen man', and, having repented, was taken to the bosom of the New Believers; and after, had seated herself in a corner, glowering contentedly now that she was back again under a dominance similar to that of her late 'husband's'. The next day she put up the sign which the Prophet printed on cardboard for her. It read simply, 'FOR SALE'.

The rumour had not shaken Liza's faith – for too many years now she had entrenched her belief against a host of barbed shafts and malicious stories – but it had added to her strong dislike and jealousy of 'the woman Martha'.

'Repentance or not, I would never trust that woman Martha any further than I can throw her and that is what I tell the Prophet to his face. Anyway, to cut a long story short, when we got there, Moses questioned the girl so gentle that little by little she tell us the whole story. The stupid Martha wanted to rain blows on the girl's back, but Moses stopped her and told her to treat the girl kind and care for her well. For it was a sign, he said, a sign that the Lord had sent to show him a way to make Hebron secure to the New Believers for ever and ever, Amen!'

'Amen!' Kate murmured absent-mindedly. The clouds that covered the moon had vanished and the children were shouting as they refashioned their 'moonshine doll'.

'So the very next day, Prophet Moses got dressed in his new swallow-tailed black suit, his white linen shirt and leather boots that Gatha and me shine until you could see your face in them. Then he put on the red and green turban, took the Bible in his hands, like a sword, he said, and hired a buggy to drive him to the manse. And he and the parson took to each other from the start, the parson treated Moses just as if he was another white man like himself, and they made a bargain that Moses would hush up the scandal, take the young girl, her sin, and her mother up to Hebron, on condition that the parson would get one of his white Government friends up in Kingston to give us a paper signed and sealed to show that we have not only the Lord's rights, but Caesar's right to the land up in Hebron, not only the Lord's facts on our side, but Caesar's facts as well. And the parson kept his promise one week after…'

The gate banged behind a little girl who came running into the yard. One of her tight plaits had come loose and stood up on her head like a devil's horn. Her black eyes flashed with triumph. She tugged at the two women and said, stammering in her excitement:

'Aunt Kate, Miss Liza, come, come and see how they make me into a moonshine doll out in the lane. Come and see how they make me bright and shining!'

15. The Seal

On the afternoon on which Prophet Moses paid his first visit to the manse, the Reverend Brooke was lying face downwards on the sofa in the drawing-room. The windows were unshuttered and sunlight slanted in, stirring up forgotten dust in the corners, picking out worn patches on the brocaded upholstery, glancing off the dark shiny surfaces of the mahogany chairs and tables. The minister felt lapped in a state of quiescence which made it impossible for him to think of anything necessary or urgent. The strange morning in the bedroom had receded in his mind, leaving behind only a vague self-doubt.

He stared at the wooden flooring below him where a knot in the wood had formed a network of lines; and marveled at the variety of patterns they formed. In a crevice between the lines there was a shred of dried wax that had escaped the polishing brush. As he scraped at it with his thumb-nail, the doorbell rang. He wondered who it could be at that hour, listened for the sound of footsteps going to answer the door. The bell shrilled again. He remembered that Mrs Macey, the house-keeper, had asked for the afternoon off, that she had complained at the same time that the girl had not turned out to work that morning.

The bell rang for the third time. There was an imperious note to its summons. He sat up, pulled on his boots, and thought what a subversive effect the tropics had on good intentions. This was the first time since he had been in the island that he had had to answer the doorbell. Yet in England he had taken pride in doing things for himself; and there the servants had humoured his whims without presuming upon their relationship. He had come out to his mission station with a firm decision to continue the touch of the spartan in his daily routine, only to find himself enervated, like the other expatriates, by the forest of black hands only too willing to clean his shoes, fetch him a glass of water, the newspaper, any task that would provide them with food and a sense of purpose. If he tried to perform even the most personal service for himself, they were at once suspicious that they might be robbed of employment, confused by any negation of the great-white-father image. And, amongst the white expatriates, there was an unwritten law that no single one of them could be allowed to 'let the side down', to suggest by any action whatsoever that they, too, might be human and fallible. He had rebelled against this at first, but in spite of himself had been forced to conform. For underneath all the slogans of his faith he was a shrewdly intelligent man, and sensed that once this aura of greatness, this mythology of the Herrenvolk was challenged, the black servants might begin to ask themselves why they did not eat the food he ate, wear clothes like him, have a big house, servants, and carriages, worship God not out of necessity but from gratitude for services rendered. One never knew where questions like this might end. They were the same as those being asked by the rabble-rousing nationalists who were springing up all over the Empire. And concomitant with these queries went the questioning of a God who could so much favour Jacob at the expense of Esau. So one ended up by accepting the way of life in the island as unchanging and unchangeable, since it seemed the lesser evil. For an abyss of change might engulf them all, even reach up to the heavens to threaten God and the Christian religion itself. The parson smiled at his flash of insight, walked to the door, and drew back the bolt.

He recognized the man standing before him with a sense of shock. He had never, until now, met the Prophet face to face. The two had passed each other on the street, but each had avoided acknowledging the other's presence. But the shadow cast by the Prophet had impinged on the parson's consciousness in many ways. Since Moses's coming, the former parishioners of the Reverend Brooke now gazed at him blankly when he spoke to them, or seemed to melt away into the warren of shacks and rooms when he approached them on the streets. When he went to visit them, they closed the door in his face. Some, those whom he remembered as having been the most subservient members of his church, delighted in displaying towards him, now that he was no longer indispensable, an open, and at times violent, hostility. Some of the women spat at him. Only his sick church members still welcomed his visits and thanked him for the packets of rice, flour, cornmeal, and sugar that he brought them. But as soon as they were well again they flocked to the Prophet's temple, and the empty benches in his church were a perpetual reproach.

The Reverend Brooke had never really admitted the existence of the mad Prophet as a challenge to his own ministry. His built-in reflexes would have dismissed the comparison as ludicrous. In his letters to his wife, on holiday in Mandeville, he spoke only about his great fears for the spiritual downfall, the eventual physical misery and disillusionment of those of his members who had given heed to the mad promises of a 'poor crank whose stay in the lunatic asylum had not cured him of his delusions'. In his prayers he implored God's mercy not only for the credulous Believers, but for the 'poor unfortunate' who was leading them astray. Not even to God would he admit the Prophet as a rival.

Now he was confronted with Moses on his very doorstep. And, in spite of the Prophet's farcical attire – the turban, the high white collar and the swallow-tailed coat – the Reverend Brooke could sense the aggressive maleness, the large and violent fantasy of the man, stabbing at him like a machete blade. He gestured to Moses to enter and led the way into the living-room.

They sat opposite each other in straight-backed mahogany chairs, separated only by a round table covered with a fringed cloth. The Prophet placed his Bible on the table. The parson sat waiting for the Prophet to say what he had come for; and adopted the defensive attitude that was peculiar to him – elbows on the armrests of the chair, his fingers loosely interlaced under his chin, his expression judicious. Moses clasped his fingers over his protruding stomach, crossed his feet and pulled them back as if to efface the bright gloss on his boots. His body was hunched in the chair with a subtle suggestion of deference, and he held his head tilted humbly, inquiringly. From the corners of his small, slanted eyes he watched the effect of his attitude on the man opposite.

The minister reacted at once. He felt a tight knot loosen inside him, felt his fear dissolve as the silence lengthened like the afternoon shadows in the room. He did not quite know what he had expected when he found his 'enemy' on the doorstep. But a connection between the Prophet's presence and what now seemed to him a distant and almost forgotten morning in the bedroom, had leaped up in his consciousness. A danger that had only lurked on the fringes of his mind confronted him. Until that morning, life had been for him an exact calculation of cause and effect, a precise measuring of risks and rewards. Then, reckless, and of his own free will, he had stepped outside the stockade of righteousness, and had committed himself to evil. Now, because of that morning, the vast strangeness that should have divided him from this madman, a whoremonger by repute, an ignorant heathen, was absent. The distance between them had contracted to the width of a table. For one moment, as he led the way into the room, the parson had even feared that the Lord had sent the Prophet to him for a reckoning, that he himself was a Samson shorn of the strength of his chastity, and about to be delivered, bound hand and foot, to the might of the Philistines.

But gradually as they faced each other, the Prophet's subservient demeanor had its effect and the parson relaxed. He sensed that the other was waiting to be given a lead, and had come, not with the arrogance of a conqueror, but as a suitor. The Reverend Brooke pressed the tips of his fingers together and asked:

'And what can I do for you, Mr...?'

'Barton, sir, Barton, and your servant!' the Prophet said, smiling.

The Reverend Brooke's relief was mingled with disappointment. The measure of his enemy now seemed so puny that he himself was reduced. This man who sat apologizing for his very existence, like a serf, was the dreaded enemy who had robbed him of the souls of his parishioners, who had disturbed him to such an extent that his very manhood had been called in question, forced to prove itself on a morning bright with sun in a shuttered room. Now that he no longer feared the Prophet the parson's mind was clear: the girl must have told her mother – Mrs Macey, the housekeeper, had mentioned that the mother was 'ignorant enough' to have become a New Believer – and the mother must have told the Prophet, who had obviously come for money, to keep his mouth shut. Rumour had it that the Prophet had almost exhausted his wife's fortune and was now hard-pressed to feed his increasing flock. The parson calculated how much money from his small private income remained to him. Yes . . . he should have more than enough. The Prophet was, after all, a peasant, and would not ask for too much. The thing to do was to wait and see how much he wanted, not to give him a lead at all, keep him on the defensive. He would deal with Moses as his teachers at school had dealt with him – the stony silence, the air of grim judgment, the firm righteousness which intimidated the most innocent into admitting an offence. The Reverend Brooke was suddenly grateful for his training. He pursed his lips and looked at the Prophet with a hint of impatience.

The Prophet uncrossed his legs and leaned forward in his chair. But not too far forward. From his dealings with the Irishman, Doctor O'Malley, he had learnt never to bargain with the white man as 'man to man'. He would have to open the matter delicately, convince the other of his simplicity.

'Reverend Mr Brooke, sir,' he began, 'I hope that you will excuse my humble intrusion within your gates into which I have come, a stranger and humble suppliant. From what I have heard of you, sir, I know you to be a man of excellent wisdom and large understanding. Finding myself, peradventure, in a position of dire difficulty, I ventured to draw near, and request of you, sir, if you could spare me some of your valuable time to grant me some meaningful advice…'

The Reverend Brooke smiled indulgently, as at a child. The Prophet, with his eyes averted, as if ashamed of bringing up so sordid a story, explained that a certain young person whom the parson had honoured and aided by taking into his household as a maidservant, finding herself scarlet with sin and shame in the…family way…through her evil association with some nameless unbeliever of the town, and being given to lies and fantasy, had tried to cast the blame on an honourable name, to be frank, on none other than the Reverend Brooke himself. When her mother, a member of his flock, came to him with this vile suggestion, he had sternly enjoined her to silence. For he himself was not unaware of the great harm that such calumnies could do to the Lord's work…

'You may have heard of my feeble efforts in this cause, Reverend, not that I am in your street at all, but each one of us when touched by His hand, must do what we can, what we can…'

'Of course, of course,' the parson agreed. He was anxious that the matter should be concluded before the return of Mrs Macey. The housekeeper had a nose for secrets and an instinct for gossip. He inclined his head and gestured to Moses that he should continue. Moses bowed, and continued.

'And wherewithal, sir, I took the great liberty to come and lay before you a little plan, whose merit if any is only that, perhaps, the Lord has seen fit to employ me as a humble and ignorant instrument in His hands. For, as you may have heard, sir, it is my professed intention to lead the New Believers up on an exodus into a New Canaan, which land the Lord hath granted to His unworthy servant in a vision. And because it is also His will that the mother of the erring Magdalene should be of my persuasion, it is therefore my behoven duty to lead this young girl and her mother up with me to live within the confines of the hills and be kept separate from the evil-minded people of this town. The which being done, no tongue of scandal will fall upon the high name of one who serves the Father.'

Was this not indeed the hand of the Lord, the Reverend Brooke wondered. Had the inexplicable origin and coming of this mad Prophet been indeed ordained by the Father in His divine omniscience, in order that his own single deviation from the Way and the Truth could be obliterated as if it had never been? Had the Lord, then, divined the numerous doubts that he had never even admitted to himself, but which had nevertheless sorely beset him these past few weeks, when his wife's absence had left him without the spiritual armour to resist the forces of Satan, his guile, his temptations? Could the girl too have been sent as a scourge to his pride that had dared to question the Lord's purpose? And had the Father now sent His Spirit to summon him back to the green pastures of righteousness, His Spirit speaking through the mouths of babes or sucklings or, in this case, through the mouth of an ignorant madman? At the mere possibility the minister felt his soul refreshed and vigorous after his tired years in the wilderness.

'The Lord moves in mysterious ways, Mr Barton,' he said.

'Praise His name, sir, praise the name of the Lord!' the Prophet said with fervour. And he sensed that now was the moment to strike, to ask as a favour that which would really be concluded as a bargain.

'And if I may make bold enough to tell you of my one worry, sir, it is this – that what the Lord granted to me, Caesar may deny. As you know, Reverend, the land of Hebron is Crown land, and it occurred to me that as you are a man well known and esteemed by those set in authority over us, you might intercede with the powers and principalities to confirm the gift of God, to grant to my humble self and the New Believers the right to the lands up in Hebron, signed with the Government's hand and sealed with a red seal. That is, sir, for...'

'But my dear good man,' the Reverend Brooke protested, tapping nervously with his fingers on the arm of his chair, 'Crown land belongs to the Government and I have no such influence at all. Besides, it is impossible for the Government here to grant you Crown land. Such an act would be within the jurisdiction of the British Parliament, and to be quite frank, I hardly think that...'

'Oh, I am not asking for the land itself, Reverend,' the Prophet interposed blandly. 'How could I ask for that? All I ask, sir, is that if, in your gracious beneficence, you could obtain for me a paper giving me the right to squat, a paper with a big seal which I could show the New Believers and strengthen their belief. For you know, Reverend, that many of the faithful, like Thomas, ask for signs and portents. But all I ask, Reverend, is the right to squat, and a paper to show my flock. After all, in this life itself it is only the right to squat that the Lord hath granted unto us, the right to dwell upon the face of the earth for three-score years and ten which is the life of a man, so why should I ask for more?'

The parson glanced with incredulity at the Prophet's smiling countenance, then looked away. He would go up to Kingston tomorrow, he planned, go to the Arawak Golf Club where he would be sure to find an official of the Land Department. He would tell him of this mad Prophet who wanted the right to squat, signed and sealed, would hint that although a madman, ignorant and illiterate, the man had a big following, that if balked in his whim he might turn his energies to political agitation. Better to give him a few barren acres on a hill-top than to have him ask for the whole island, he would suggest jokingly; and they would laugh together, draw up the mock document, and sign it with the biggest seal available...The Reverend Brooke looked at Moses with affection. They were like children, these natives, he thought, like children playing at life. Was a superior intelligence then, he wondered, some sort of evolutionary compensation for the loss of unlimited sexual virility?

The Prophet kept his eyes lowered. It had been easy to fool the Reverend Brooke. It was always easy to fool the white man. They carried their sense of superiority about with them like a thick hide which prevented them from seeing the truth. They were like those extinct animals that Doctor O'Malley had told him about, animals who, through their overweening confidence in their strength, had refused to bow to circumstance, to evolve with the times. And had perished. But still, the Prophet thought, he must be careful. The parson must not see his triumph, must not suspect that the piece of paper that he asked for was intended to lay the foundation of a new Empire, a new religion. And black men would be no longer strangers to their God. His image would now reflect theirs, and they would see themselves without self-doubt, self-hatred, self-mockery. No, the Reverend Brooke must not imagine what was being asked of him – as the African chiefs had not suspected when they had signed away their souls to the missionaries in exchange for beads, mirrors, and a mess of pottage.

****

The parson's trip to Kingston was successful. His story about the mad Prophet alarmed the head of the Land Department, an elderly man, long past retirement age but kept at his job, because the younger men who should have replaced him were fighting and dying in the First World War. Anxious to avoid any trouble in the colony at a time when the mother country was fighting for its survival, he agreed to the Reverend's suggestion that the mad agitator should be placated. He went to great trouble to produce an imposing document; the paper was of thick vellum, the red seal enormous. The script was in his own beautiful long-hand and consisted of the words: 'To

Prophet Moses Barton, the right to squat on the land of Hebron, given under my hand, this day of grace, etc...' He signed it with the Latin version of his own name and sent it off by post to the Reverend Brooke.

The parson summoned Moses to the manse and give him the document. He handed the envelope to the Prophet with some ceremony, and his attitude was firm and paternal. He warned that no word of this transaction should be revealed to any one. If the matter was bruited abroad, the Government might be forced to reconsider their decision, etc. etc. The Prophet vowed eternal secrecy and went his way, triumphant. He now held in his grasp the paper which was to root Hebron firmly in reality. The Lord had sent the white parson as an instrument to ensure the success of his, Moses's, mission. This time there would be no possibility of failure. This time innocence had been replaced by guile, the Lord's gift endorsed by Caesar. The Prophet had never forgotten the harsh lessons learnt from his fall. As he drove home in the hired buggy, he recalled the exact words of the Irish doctor, that had shown him the way to lay the foundations of a black kingdom on earth:

'Mark well, Moses, the wisdom of these Christian merchants,' the doctor had said, 'and if you want to succeed when God calls upon you again, emulate them, my boy, emulate them! These missionaries carried the Cross before them, but behind them came ships and soldiers and guns. They could have taken what they wanted by force. But they knew that all empires won by force are wrested away again, in the fullness of time, by others stronger than themselves. So they dreamed instead of an empire of land and souls that was legal, annexed by consent, governed by consent. And the piece of paper with the marks of the chiefs and the red seal was the tangible ratification of their dream of empire, the bridge between the shadow of their faith and the substance of wealth and power to come!

****

On the first day of the new year the Prophet led the New Believers on their great journey up to the land of Hebron. As had been agreed, the young girl Gloria departed with them, and the Reverend Brooke, although he had already pushed the unhappy incident to the back of his mind, was relieved. His wife's presence once more about the house brought home to him even more forcibly the danger of his momentary folly. And, in order to banish what had happened from his memory, he suggested to the Synod in Kingston that they close down their branch in Cockpit Centre and start up instead in Paradise Bay. There the scope was wider, and already, he hinted, several other denominations were boasting of marked successes in the capturing of souls.

The Synod agreed, and, heartened by his new-found ability to deal with them, to find their weak spot, the Reverend Brooke insisted that the members of the Synod should vote him the necessary funds to start a school as an adjunct to the church. There was no point, he argued, in explaining the Scriptures and its higher mysteries to a people so illiterate and ignorant that they could be seduced at any moment by imposters. Besides, one day, the religious agitators would give way to political ones. It was the duty of the Church to train an educated élite whose influence could be invaluable in maintaining law and order amongst the less fortunate.

The Synod voted him even more than he asked for, and he was written up in the daily newspaper as a man of vision. The Reverend Brooke discovered in himself a rare and genuine gift for teaching, and his school prospered. His church membership was swollen with the vast numbers who saw a chance of winning a free education for their children. With his new flock the Reverend Brooke was a benevolent despot. He did not embarrass or confuse them by trying to accept them as friends and equals. But he was showing their children how to realize a better life on earth, in the here and now. In return for this they were ready to sit through his sermons, however long or tedious they might be. But his sermons also improved. He saw himself as a teacher with children, and preached to them as such, and he could see through their small deceptions, their cunning ruses. They came to accept him as the earthly symbol of God, respected and even loved him.

The minister's wife was caught up in her husband's new enthusiasm and sense of purpose. She taught in the kindergarten, and although not as good a teacher as her husband, was fond of the small children with their shy smiles, solemn black eyes, and downy hair. Now that she and her husband had become involved in the lives of the people around them, they rarely missed England. Several years later, the Reverend Brooke was appointed headmaster to a new secondary boys' school in Africa, the first in that part of the continent. The school became famous, and many of the future leaders of black Africa were educated there. The Reverend Brooke had only one regret: that he and his wife never had a child. He knew nothing of the daughter born to him in Hebron.

Part 3

THE NIGHT

She was an old woman of a family with a long genealogy. Leza, the 'Besetting One', stretched out his hand against the family: he slew her mother and father whilst she was yet a child, and in the course of years all connected with her perished...Even the children of her children were taken from her. She became withered with age, and it seemed to her that she herself was at last to be taken...

Then came into her heart a desperate resolution to find God and ask the meaning of it all. Somewhere up in the sky must be His dwelling. She began to cut down trees, joining them together and so planting a structure that would reach to Heaven. Finally she gave up in despair...Somewhere on earth there must be another way to Heaven. So she began to travel, going through country after country, always with the thought in her mind:

'I shall come to where the earth ends and there I shall find a road to God and I shall ask Him, "What have I done to Thee that Thou afflictest me in this manner?..."'

As she passed through different countries, they asked her:

'What have you come for, old woman?'

'I am seeking Leza!'

'Seeking Leza? For what?'

'My brothers, you ask me? Here in the nations is there one who suffers as I have suffered?'

'How have you suffered?'

'In this way: I am alone. As you see me, a solitary old woman; that is how I am!'

'Yes, we see. That is how you are! Bereaved of friends and husband! In what way do you differ from others? The Besetting One sits on the back of all of us and we cannot shake him off!'

She never obtained her desire: she died of a broken heart.

(A legend of the Ba-ila people of Northern Rhodesia)

16. *The Crucifixion*

In Hebron, Kate insisted that Aloysius should build their house high on a hill. The others had all chosen to cluster together below the church. Only the woman Martha and her pregnant daughter lived near to Kate. Their hut was even farther up the hill. Miss Gatha had urged that they should not live too close to the 'camp of the Lord'. But Kate was glad to have a neighbour. Without Martha to talk to, she would have been lonely. Aloysius was away, working, from sunrise to sunset.

Early one morning Kate awoke and lay listening to the wind. It prowled about the house, probing at door and window; and was as familiar to her as the insistent clamour of the town had once been. Beside her, her husband slept with the measured breathing of a contented man, now that he had an abundance of work and a full pride of place. But Kate was still on guard with expectation. Only a child would make real to her her arrival in the Promised Land. But there was no sign of one.

A gust of wind swooped down and battered at the door. A voice called out to her:

'Aunt Kate, Aunt Kate, the girl take in bad with the pain! Mama say you must hurry!'

It was Liza's daughter Ann. Kate was out of bed in an instant. She threw a frock on over her nightgown and opened the door. The wind caught at her as she stepped outside. She tugged the door shut behind her, groped for Ann's hand and forced her way up the hill. The mists billowed and swirled about them. They kept with difficulty to the steep path.

At last they plunged into the hut, left the rawness of early morning and the wind, hissing and coiling behind them. A small tin lamp on a rough bench beside the bed flickered, and shadows danced about the room. In the corner, Martha sat on the floor. She rocked to and fro, already keening for the dead. Her daughter Gloria – 'the girl', as everyone called her – lay on the bed, her eyes closed. Over her was the midwife, Liza Edwards, sweat dripping from her face as she gripped the girl by her shoulders, ordered again and again:

'Wake up and try, and try, child, wake up and push… push, and try!'

Liza's elder daughter, Sue, was seated at the foot of the bed. She helped her mother, echoing her cry. But the girl did not move.

Kate kneeled at the side of the bed and took her hand.

'Gloria,' she called, 'it will soon be over, soon. You will see how quick it will be over. Just try and see!'

The girl knew Kate's voice and tried to open her eyes. But the 'thing' inside her weighted her down. She slid even farther into the waiting darkness. The minutes passed. Soon, Kate found herself caught up in Liza's frenzy. The two women laboured with the girl, matching their will against hers, determined that she should give birth. They slapped her on both cheeks, pulled her to her feet, made her walk up and down. From the foot of the bed Sue watched with interest, but Ann cowered outside the door of the hut, hiding her face in her hands. In the corner, Martha still rocked to and fro. But her eyes were blank, as if she had forgotten for whom she was mourning and why.

The urgent appeals of the women at last reached through to the girl. She thrashed about on the bed, leapt up and banged her head against the side of the hut several times before they could subdue her. She felt their hands holding her down, wanted to be rid of them, and of the 'thing' that gripped her with cold clammy fingers, held her back from the brightness that beckoned to her. She fought to expel the encumbrance and heard the women's voices pounding their approval. She was leaving them all behind now, now she was out of reach, now she had won…

Kate pulled out the child by its shoulders and Liza severed the navel-string. The girl opened her eyes and saw the sunlight flooding the room. When they turned to tend her she was dead.

The child was the first one born in Hebron, and her birth, Prophet Moses declaimed, marked the beginning of new generations in a new land. The christening was held a week after. They called the child Rose and there was great rejoicing. Only Miss Gatha refused to attend, pleading illness. But several of the New Believers, passing by their Prophet's house that morning, had overheard him raging against his wife's obduracy; and they had pursed their lips and shaken their heads. It was now all over Hebron that the newly-born child was the daughter of the Reverend Brooke, the white parson in Cockpit Centre. No one could tell how Miss Gatha had got hold of the rumour. She had spoken to none of the others, nor had she, like the other women, gone to visit the child on its day of birth, bearing gifts. She was conspicuously absent at the funeral of the child's mother. But she had come to know the truth as she always did and had at once divined what had not occurred to the others – that the paper with the red seal giving the New Believers title to the land of Hebron was payment of some sort, for what, she was sure, had been her husband's condoning of sin in high places, his complicity in the wickedness of Sodom and Gomorrah.

During the first few months of their sojourn in the new land, Miss Gatha had come to believe that her husband was the father of the girl's child, and had accepted this with a bitter joy. His proven weakness would have increased her power against him. That the truth of the matter had been different, and that Moses had excluded her from this truth, started an anger inside her that fanned into a resentment against the child. Rose's light-brown skin became for her a symbol of evil, marking her recognition that she was as nothing in the eyes of the man who was a Prophet, and was her husband. She refused to stand as godmother for the child and Kate took her place. Moses himself was the godfather.

****

The death of her daughter left Martha vague and listless. Moses, consumed with the fulfilment of his vision, had no time for women. Without a man Martha was without purpose. Kate took over the tending of Martha's grandchild and spent the greater part of her time in the hut up on the hill-top. When the child was three months old, Martha sickened. A nail ran into her foot and she paid no attention to the wound. For two days and nights Kate sat at the bedside of the dying woman and applied poultices in an attempt to draw out the poison. As the still-powerful black body sweated away its last hours, Kate looked at the stoical face and wondered if it were only for this meaningless end that the woman had been born to some domestic servant or land-slave in the St Elizabeth bush country, had sprung up like a dandelion to be plucked by an ageing Chinese shopkeeper whose body had need of young limbs to comfort him; and whose fear of death, overcoming all racial sophistry, had impelled him to root himself in a strange land. Was it only to this end that Martha had cooked his meals and washed his clothes, sold goods over a shop-counter, borne a child and cared for it, kept to her silence? Was it for this purposeless death that she had come up to Hebron, to the Promised Land?

Martha died, as she had lived, without protest. After her funeral Kate asked Prophet Moses to be allowed to bring up Martha's grandchild, Rose. But Moses refused. Rose, he said, was his responsibility; she must be brought up in his own house. Miss Gatha gave in to her husband and became the child's foster-mother. And meanwhile Kate found herself barren, and her days as empty as they had been in the town.

****

It was the eve of the first anniversary of the exodus of the New Believers. Kate sat on her doorstep, waiting for her husband to come home. Early that morning he had left with Moses to bring back supplies for the next day's festivities. Now it was long past midnight and Kate was worried. The heavy fragrance of the wild jasmine that had sprung up near their house oppressed her spirit. Moonlight outlined the hills, made them seem impersonal and cold. Swift-pounding hooves echoed from the path below. Kate stood up, fearful, and walked to meet the moonlit shape that breasted the track and dashed towards her. The mule was pulled to a stop. Kate could see its flanks quivering and silky with sweat. The rider was Moses. He shook his head to the alarmed enquiry in her eyes.

'Nothing to worry about, Sister Kate,' he said, 'not a thing! Brother Aloysius is safe. Just that we had a...little accident with the cart...'

'Accident?' she asked quickly.

'Brother Aloysius wasn't hurt, wasn't hurt at all. Everything all right with him. No call to fret your spirit. Just that the cart got a little damaged, and Brother Aloysius stayed on to get it fixed, and come up in the morning. Everything all right with Brother Aloysius, all right with him...'

He spoke jerkily and his words tailed off as if he had forgotten what he was talking about. Kate saw that his face was ashen with weariness. His body was slumped in the saddle and his eyes did not meet hers; they wandered about as if in search of something that eluded him. Yet, she sensed, his distress had nothing to do with Aloysius. She was sure that her husband was safe and well, as Moses had said. She rested her hand on his arm, looked up at him:

'Prophet Moses,' she said gently, 'you look tired unto death. Come, sit and rest yourself, let me give you a drink of water...'

He dismounted awkwardly, walked across to the step and seated himself. Kate fetched some water in a tin mug from the barrel at the side of the house. And whilst he drank, she watered the mule. When she turned to him he was staring intently at the hills, like a man awaiting a sign. The empty mug was on the step beside him.

'You want me to dip up some more water for you, Prophet Moses?' she asked him.

He looked at her, and, as if she were still questioning her husband's absence, he answered:

'There wasn't any help for it, Sister Kate...Brother Aloysius had to stay with the cart...and I couldn't stay to help him...'

He half-rose from the step, stretched his hand before him as if to avoid a blow, spoke hoarsely:

'For evil was on every hand...in the land of Sodom and Gomorrah...storms and tempests...my soul was battered and sore distressed. On every hand, darkness! And I called out, "Lord, Lord! Where are you, Lord?"' He sank back on to the step, his eyes turned inwards:

'But...He...didn't answer at all. So I said to myself: "Moses, hardears Moses, go up to the land of Hebron that He gave unto you in a vision...that's where He sent you...that's where you'll find Him...to the hills, Moses, to the hills!"'

The moon wearied of its harsh brightness, shrouded itself in a light mist. Moses felt Kate's presence beside him. She stood with her arms folded across her breasts, passive, like the sea. He unburdened his spirit, told her about what had happened that day, about the overwhelming moment in the market-place when his faith had been shaken, he had felt the earth give way beneath his feet, felt the heavens, hitherto fixed and immutable as the mansions of the Father, dissolve in flux and chaos. And he had come flying back to Hebron, in search of refuge, of the God whose existence had been denied him.

****

That morning he had felt the hand of God strong in his affairs, and had traded his ground provisions – yams, sweet potatoes, pumpkins – at a profit. With the money he bought bags of rice, flour, sugar, and even a few bottles of white rum. For did not the Chosen People of the Bible drink wine and dance before the altar to rejoice in the blessings that their God had heaped upon them?

As he returned with Aloysius to the market-place where they had left the cart, he outlined his plans for Hebron. Now that they had survived the first year, they would build more and better houses, a proper carpenter's workshop, a bakery, a foundry, storehouses, a sugar mill; and, at the end of five years, a new and more imposing church as a testament to the goodness of God. Aloysius nodded approval. The Prophet's plans were sane and practical, he felt.

At first they tried to ignore the great crowd thronging the market-place. For the shadows were already lengthening and they did not want to travel at night. And, almost unconsciously, the mood of the crowd, the mounting acclamations spurred them on to hurry away from Cockpit Centre. They loaded their purchases hurriedly. Then Aloysius remembered that he had to collect an order of nails from a shop behind the railway station, and went off. Moses finished loading the cart, covered the goods with tarpaulin, and then climbed up to the driver's seat. The mules champed at their bits and he soothed them, calling out softly:

'All right, all right, whoa! whoa!'

From his vantage point Moses could look over the heads of the crowd, could see the man who dominated them. Who was this intruder? Was he some new Prophet? The man stood on a packing case, was short and bearded and wore a khaki shirt and trousers stained with sweat. At first, Moses dismissed him; he did not look very impressive. But as he spoke, he seemed to grow in stature. His large eyes flashed out of a narrow ebony face, his voice sounded like the roll of drums. As Moses listened, he found himself caught up like the others:

'Friends and comrades, this is a new time, a new century, a new day. All over the world a new race of men arise to greet the morning. One race, black, brown or white, the race of those who work! Our race! The race of the workers who up till now have been the poor, the hungry, the dispossessed. And in other countries, all over the world, the workers have risen up, are rising up to put an end for ever to their poverty, hunger, their dispossession. Friends and comrades, long live the workers!'

'Long live the workers!' the crowd clamoured. Even when they did not understand the meaning of some of the words that he used, the sense was familiar.

'Comrades, friends, in this island of ours, is not our yoke as grievous as that of those other workers all over the world?'

'Worse!' they shouted.

'Then what those other workers all over the world have the courage and the guts to do, can't we do as well?'

'Any day! Any time! Say the word!'

Their voices were vengeful and they stamped the earth.

The man held up his hand for silence and the crowd responded at once.

'Friends and comrades,' he said, speaking quietly now, 'first let us consider our position. Comrades, after three hundred years of imperialist rule, our island is still a pauper house. The time has come for us to understand the reasons for our misery and to claim our rightful heritage. We are poor, but this island is not poor. And you know why we are poor?'

'Why!'

'I will tell you, why. Because here in this island, it is we who plant the seeds of wealth, but it is others, thousands of miles away, who reap the harvest. The big white gods who rule us from their palaces up in Kingston call themselves empire-builders, but they didn't build the Empire, we did, we built the Empire with our sweat, with the blood of our ancestors whom they bought and sold like cattle. Today we carry this Empire on our backs. Our hunger and malnutrition, the degradation of our children, their rickety limbs, endemic diseases, and swollen bellies are the pillars on which this glorious Empire is upheld. They say it's an empire on which the sun never sets. But for us, the shirtless ones, the black and the forgotten ones, the sun never rose on this Empire that our sweat built. Today, we are the people of the shadows, the children of darkness. The time has come for us to leave the shadows for ever and walk in the morning light!'

There was a great uproar from the crowd, and the market-place shook with their shouting. The man held them in a spell. They were a people innocent of much knowledge of themselves and he was an extension of their secret dreams of pride and dignity, illuminating the dark and lost centuries of their past with his enchanted tongue. He was taking them out of the shadows where they dwelt, robing them in the dignity of men. They were lost in his eloquence, heedless of everything. They did not notice the two plain-clothes policemen who stood quietly on the fringes, one of them taking notes in a small black book. But the man, whose eyes missed nothing, recognized them and pointed them out to the crowd:

'Look over there, friends, look, comrades. You see those two plain-clothes policemen standing over there? They come all the way from Kingston. Now why you think they did that? Why you think they are here? I don't need protection. I am not the Governor. I am not a man making himself rich on the backs of my people. I am a man born poor like you. A man who came out of nothing. I starved, like you, was ignorant, illiterate, couldn't even sign my own name. But I got an education, and I didn't steal it from your sweat. I stowed away on a ship, ran away from the hovels of Paradise Bay where I was born. I went to the United States, and I cleaned lavatories, carried garbage, worked my way through school, learnt the secrets of those who have power over us. And today when I come back to tell my own people these truths that I learnt, the imperialists send policemen to note down what I say. For they are afraid of the truth. They are not afraid of anything else. Only the truth. For, comrades, one day the truth will destroy all men who exploit and rob their fellows. The truth is the greatest weapon of all. So write away in your little black book, comrade Policeman. My friends and I here will give you things to put down that will burn the pages on which you write them down. Write away, comrade Policeman! And make sure you can spell my words before you put them down!'

Waves of laughter swept the crowd. Moses was jolted from a trance. All at once it seemed to him that the man's words, his very coming, held an insidious challenge. Not once had the man quoted the Bible, not once mentioned the name of God. And yet, before his very eyes, this man had captured and held in thrall the same idle unbelievers who had once mocked him, Moses, laughed at him, made up songs to ridicule him. And standing a few yards away from the cart was a woman whom, Moses remembered, he had once tried to convert. She was a black Amazon who loaded bananas on to the ship in Paradise Bay, but occasionally visited her mother in Cockpit Centre. She had laughed in his face when he had attempted to preach to her, Moses thought, but she wasn't laughing now. Her eyes were fixed on the speaker, breathing in his words as he continued:

'Friends and comrades, don't be afraid of those policemen, nor of the imperialists who sent them. We who built empires can destroy them too. There is a way. And that is what I came to tell you about. For, comrades, all over the world the disinherited are rising up, empires are falling, and the poor are inheriting the earth. So don't worry about these arrogant white rulers we have in this island, or about their black stooges who lick their boots to get a few extra crumbs. All of them will go like leaves in a hurricane wind. And we will create the hurricane to drive them out!'

'The hurricane, the hurricane!'

The black Amazon clasped her hands and held them above her head as she shouted with the others. Moses could see her shoulders shaking with the fervour of her belief. A strange feeling took hold of him, one that he could not label since he had never known it before. It was envy. He wished that Aloysius would return so that they could leave. He tried to withdraw into himself, to shut out the voice of his rival. But the man's words, and the deep emotion of the crowd as they listened, forced their way into his consciousness:

'Friends, my comrades, the name of this way that I told you about, the name of this hurricane that I told you about is...'

He paused for effect, clenched his fist, stretched to his full height and shouted:

'The name is Revolution. Long live the Revolution!'

'Long live the Revolution!'

'Comrades, it is a big word, this Revolution, but it means one thing, one big thing, it means...change!'

'Change!'

'It means that our past of poverty and hunger and ignorance is finished and done with. It means that the past is dead!'

'Dead!'

'In the name of the Revolution, comrades, let us bury this past!'

'Bury it! Bury it!'

Slowly he scanned their eager faces, then warned them:

'But comrades, the Revolution is not just a word that can change things overnight. It will take discipline and hard work, your courage and sacrifice. Only you can change things, only you can make the Revolution!'

'Tell us what to do,' some shouted.

'Give us guns!' others demanded.

'Machetes!'

'Sticks...'

'Even stones to throw!'

'Anything! Just say the word, comrade, just say the word!'

A few of the men brandished the cutlasses with which they reaped the sugar-cane crop. Others shook their clenched fists. The women placed hands on hips and looked round with hostile glances for the 'enemy'. The Amazon fixed her eyes on Prophet Moses. He was the only person in the market who remained aloof, who seemed to set himself up above them. But the man was speaking again and she turned to listen; his face was tense now, his manner serious.

'Comrades and friends, hear well what I have to tell you now. This is important. And what I have to tell you is that everything have a time. And this is not the time for guns, for machetes, for sticks nor stones. No. This is not the time for that, this time our weapon will be...the strike!'

'The strike?' they asked, disappointed.

'Yes, the strike. That is our first weapon, the only weapon that we have to hand, a powerful one. The weapon of our labour. Now, answer me this, without your labour what would happen to the fat green bunches of banana?'

There was a silence. The people looked at one another, not quite getting his meaning. Then suddenly a young man, who was perched on the side of a hand-cart, called out:

'They would rot on the trees!'

'Would rot on the trees, would rot on the trees!' they all repeated, delighted at their comprehension.

'Good, very good, comrades. Now another one. Without your labour what would happen to the sugar-cane crop?'

'It would spoil in the cane fields!'

'Women comrades, without your labour who would break the stones to build the road, who would carry the banana to the sea-port, the sugar-cane to the sugar-mill, who would do it if not you?'

'Nobody would do it, nobody!' the Amazon cried out, and the other women echoed her statement.

'And tell me this, women comrades, if you stayed in your houses one day and didn't go to work, who would cook the food for the great ones of this town, who would wash their clothes, their dirty plates, clean their floors, tidy their houses, care for their children? Don't they would have to do it themselves, the great ones, the rich ones, the idle ones who live on our sweat?'

'Let them do it themselves, let them do it!'

'Let them do it. If they can. That is what I came here to talk to you about today, comrades. That is the weapon that I want you to use now. That is what it means to...strike.'

'Strike!' The strange word had now become their own.

'Comrades, what tidings is it that you think I bring you from your comrades in Kingston today? What is the good tidings that you think I bring you?'

'Tell us!" they begged.

'Comrades, the Revolution has begun, long live the Revolution!'

'Long live the Revolution!'

'Comrades, in Kingston today our friends and brothers have started a strike, many of them, the dock-workers, the hotel waiters, the shop clerks, men like you who work for a pittance, men like you who carry burdens and serve others like slaves. Comrades, do you want to help your brothers in Kingston?'

'Yes, yes!'

'Then, comrades, you must strike too. United we stand, divided we fall. Comrades, you must leave the banana to rot on the trees, the sugar-cane to lie unreaped in the fields. Women comrades, withdraw your labour from the proconsuls who are ruling us, from their stooges, make them go into their stinking kitchens and learn what it is like to see their faces in dishwater, let the wood-smoke choke them, the heat burn them, this time let the masters and the mistresses bellow for their slaves…in vain!'

'In vain!' the Amazon cried out, and the crowd roared approval.

But the young man who was seated on the hand-cart had a puzzled expression on his face. He put up his hand and waved towards the speaker. The others stopped shouting.

'But what about those of us who don't have work?' he asked. 'How we going to strike?'

'Yes, how?' others demanded.

'And what about me who plant my little crop and reap it and sell it in the market to feed my children? How I going to strike?' one woman muttered.

'And me, and me. Me too!'

There was, suddenly, an aggrieved feeling amongst them. They felt they were being cheated and could not imagine such an abstract means of battle.

But the man soon had them at a fever-pitch once more. He painted for them the extent of their misery, the hopelessness of their poverty, the lack of any future for their children. He told them that, for a time, the strike might make things worse, some of them would suffer, many of them would starve. The 'employers', he warned them, would play on that, tempt them to take the jobs of their brothers who were on strike. But they would have to hold out, be loyal, one to the other. They would have to starve, perhaps. But they had starved for most of their lives. Now at least they could starve to some purpose. And the sooner they joined their comrades in Kingston and struck, the shorter would be the struggle, the sooner the victory. And each time that they struck and won, they would gain more power, would become more disciplined and prepared to take over the Government when they had driven the 'imperialists' into the sea and overthrown the might of the 'capitalists'. In this way they would initiate the first phase of the Revolution, would shatter the chains of fear and of disunity that had held them in bondage for three hundred years.

When he had them, lost in his passion, submissive to his will, the man gripped his hands together, held them above his head and demanded,

'You will do this then, comrades, begin the Revolution, help your comrades up in Kingston? You will strike?'

'We will strike, we will strike, we will strike!' they chanted.

The Amazon burst out singing a hymn, changing the words in the inspiration of the moment:

We will follow our Comrade,
We will follow our Comrade...

The others picked her up and the singing swelled to a paean of triumph:

We will follow our comrades,
We will follow our redeemer till we die!

Moses was desolate. All that the man said that they would do, he, Moses, had already accomplished. And at one stroke. Up in Hebron they were already free, neither workers nor capitalists, only New Believers owning everything in common, safe from the flood of want on Mount Ararat. And refuged in the arms of God. But why was it, then, that he had failed to convert these unbelievers who now gave their allegiance to this new prophet? What could this man offer them that he had not been able to do? True, the man had a flood of language that rivalled that of Moses's mentor, Doctor O'Malley. And unlike the Irishman, this prophet was not a drunkard. And he was a black man. But what was this strange message that he brought? In this new raceless world that he talked about, what place was there for God, for the black God? What place was there for him, the Prophet and Son of this black God? Had this man come to destroy him?

The man, for some strange reason, appeared to be angry. He waved his arms about trying to stop the crowd's singing. Some, carried away by the song, kept on after the others had stopped. A shushing sound went through the crowd. Then it was quiet. The man leaned forward on the packing case:

'Comrades,' he said, 'no hymns, let us not sing hymns. This is not a church. We want nothing to do with churches. Hear what I tell you. In your churches they will deceive you, will tell you it is wrong to strike, will tell you that God won't like it, that it's a sin. Now, when they tell you that, as them one thing. Ask them to show you this God so that you yourself can ask Him if it's wrong. And if they can't show you Him, tell them that the only religion you believe in is the religion of Man!'

'Of Man, Man!'

'Tell them that for thousands of years you worshipped gods, all kinds of them – stone ones, wooden ones, brass ones, the sun, thunder and lightning, the wind, the Christian God who enslaved you, His Son who brought death and set it up like a graven idol for you to worship. And you worshipped. And hungered. And died. Saw your daughters become whores, your sons sold into slavery, lose the substance of their manhood. All that is finished and done!'

'Done!'

'Tell them that from today there is only Man. And if anyone tell you different, ask them to show you this God so that you can see him for yourself. Ask them!'

The crowd raised their hands, and shook their fists at the sky that darkened with the oncoming night:

'Yes, let we see this God, let we see Him!' they challenged.

'From today there is only Man!' he shouted.

'Only Man!' they affirmed.

But a few were timid and crossed themselves, to be safe.

In the cart, Moses leapt to his feet and searched the sky for a sign. When he saw none he was tempted to keep quiet. What were these people to him, this man even, that he should bother to deny their blasphemy? But why did God delay? Why did He not appear and cast thunderbolts at the blasphemers? Where was He?

Moses felt like one who dreams that he leads a great procession, then wakes up to find that no one is following him, that he carries a banner, whose words are printed in a language he can no longer read, and whose meaning will be lost for ever.

He shut his eyes and groped in the darkness for God. And when he could not find Him, he cried out:

'I have seen Him. I have seen God, a new God, a black God! I am His Son that He sent to save the world. I am His Son!'

All eyes turned to him, even the man's. Moses felt charged with power and pointed an accusing finger at his rival:

'And there is Judas!'

The reaction of the crowd was hostile, but Moses swept on:

'For thirty pieces of silver from the white man, this black Iscariot has come to tell you, to deceive you that there is no God! And you know why the white man paid him to do this? Because now that the white man find out that God is black, he is sending his spies to deny Him!'

The crowd quietened and looked to the man for a reply.

'Speak, comrade,' the man asked Moses, 'this black God of ours, where did He hide Himself all these years of our bondage? Tell us that!'

'Tell us that!' the crowd insisted.

They waited for him to speak. The Prophet saw the mass of their faces below him. He felt words well up inside him, knew how he would capture them:

'Now is His time,' Moses said. And he spoke with a quiet conviction that awed them. 'Now He has come to make the black man powerful on the face of the land. He shall crush the white God underfoot, the One who had imprisoned Him, as the white Son had imprisoned us. Our God has broken free, has come to redress our wrongs. He shall make the masters slaves, the slaves masters. We shall need no strikes, no revolutions. For the black man shall rule, the white man serve under him...'

The woman, who had been eying Moses, suddenly recognized him and called out:

'It's the madman, Moses Barton, it's the madman!'

The crowd picked up her cry:

'The madman Moses, the madman!'

'The Son of the black God, the Son of God!' Moses insisted, flustered.

'Then why you don't crucify yourself, Black Jesus?' the woman shrieked.

'Crucify yourself, Black Jesus, crucify yourself!' the crowd chanted.

'If you deny me, you deny yourself!' Moses thundered at them. But he had lost his assurance and the crowd sensed it.

'Go and crucify yourself, Black Jesus, go and crucify yourself!' they called out, over and over again.

The man waved his arms in the air, tried to make himself heard above the shouting:

'Comrades, enough! We have more serious matters to attend to. Comrades, enough now, enough...!'

But even he had lost his grip on them. Their laughter had changed to muttering that held a deadly intent. The Prophet had become the focus of their easily-charged anger; one man flung the peel of an orange that he had been eating. It struck Moses full in his face. He held up his hands, crossed them before his eyes as the crowd pelted him with matchboxes, potatoes, bits of dried mud, anything that came to hand. They surged against the cart, backed it up to the wall. The mules whinnied with terror.

The man sprang down from the packing-case, tried to cut his way through to the Prophet. But he felt his elbows gripped firmly and turned to find himself between the two plain-clothes policemen. One clapped a hand over his mouth so that he could not call out to the crowd. They hustled him out through the gates and put him in the back of a police van. As they drove off, one of the policemen called out to him:

'All right, Comrade Bellows, we have you now. Let us see you talk your way out of this one. The charge will be...incitement to a riot!'

For safety they drove him down to Paradise Bay to stay overnight in the prison there, and leave the next morning for the capitol.

In the market the news of his arrest ran through the crowd. They forgot Moses and streamed down to the police station. But the doors were shut and no one answered their shouting. As the night grew darker, they became confused and gradually dispersed. But they were never the same again. The words that the man had spoken remained in their hearts, prepared them for the coming of others of whom he was only the forerunner; as Moses had been his.

The press of the throng had broken in the sides of the cart. Its painted slogan – 'In God We Trust' – was cracked and splintered. Moses had been flung against the wall. His head drooped to one side, his arms stretched out in a posture of crucifixion. The market-place had become his Golgotha, his place of skulls; and God had manifested His Presence, not in anger against the unbelievers, but in the sacrifice of His Son. Moses closed his eyes waiting for the moment of death, the last agony. He heard the crowd retreating, felt the silence that they left behind surrounding him. But still he waited. He felt a hand on his shoulder and looked up. Aloysius was standing beside him. And in his eyes was reflected the wariness of someone convinced that he is dealing with a madman. His follower did not believe, Moses saw, had not believed, would never believe. They were alone in the market and the night had fallen. The Prophet left Aloysius repairing the cart and set out for Hebron to find his God.

****

Moses stopped talking and was afraid. Kate had listened without saying a word. The quality of her silence caused him to doubt even his own anguish. He recalled the day that he had first seen her. She had been stooping over a basket of mangoes and he had noticed her breasts. But his instinct had warned him against her – she would not be like other women he had known, shadows in his sun. He had avoided her then, he would avoid her now. He stood up to go.

'Prophet Moses,' Kate said unhurriedly, 'you couldn't change your mind and give me the child Rose to bring up? Gatha isn't really happy with her. And my house is empty!'

Moses handed back the tin mug. Kate took it from him but remained where she was, waiting for an answer. The Prophet looked away. Hebron offered no secret hiding-place in which he could find his God. Even here God was absent too. The moon was going down. He could see his shadow dissolving on the ground. He told himself that he should not risk antagonizing his valuable master carpenter. And yet he was compelled to turn to the woman, compelled to take her.

Some time later Moses walked his mule down the steep path. The moon was pale, her light extinguished by the morning. The taste in the Prophet's mouth was bitter. When he came to where the track widened, he mounted his mule and sat still, held in the grip of superstition. Had this woman, like Delilah, come forward from amongst the numberless others, to rob him of the secret of his strength, to draw out of him the substance that had made him inviolable, the Son of God? He rode down past the church, through the square, and came to his own house. In the trees, the morning birds fluttered and sang and day-clean brightened the sky behind the hills. Their peaks seemed forbidding and immeasurably high. He went to his room, woke up his wife and took her brutally, striving to erase the image of the other woman who had diminished him.

****

Nine months later, on the same day, a boy, Isaac, was born to Miss Gatha, and a girl, Maverlyn, to Kate Matthews. When the Prophet saw his son's club-foot he took it as a sign. That his seed had been despoiled was a token that he should not live through the descendants of his flesh. His true heirs would be those of his spirit, sealed to him by the blood he would shed on the Cross to confirm eternally that God was black, in the image of His Son.

At the joint christening he announced his intentions to an awe-struck congregation. And he anointed Aloysius as his successor. The master carpenter, he knew, flattered by his new position, would work even harder to build up Hebron. But after Aloysius, he decreed, the eldership should pass to

Obadiah. And he anointed the young man and laid his hands on him and blessed him. For Obadiah's clear faith fortified the Prophet's spirit, gave him strength.

Miss Gatha introduced a note of discord. She wanted her son's succession to the eldership proclaimed. It was rightful that he should be Elder over Hebron as soon as he was of age, she insisted. The Prophet rejected his son in front of the whole congregation, intoning solemnly:

' "And if there be any blemish therein, as if it be lame or blind or have any ill-blemish, thou shalt not sacrifice it unto the Lord Thy God!" '

Brother Hugh gave chapter and verse. Miss Gatha's further protests were drowned in the general exaltation. The New Believers saw now, beyond all doubt, that the Son of God would die to save them. The blackness which was their secret shame would be atoned for, would become their pride, their joy. They sang now with a foretaste of triumph:

In the Cross, in the Cross,
Be my glory ever,
Till my enraptured soul shall find,
Peace beyond the river!

17. *The Betrayal*

On the night after the Prophet's announcement, Aloysius and Obadiah were together in the carpenter's shed. They had worked late, putting the finishing touches to the wooden cradles for Isaac and Maverlyn. The master carpenter worked on Madelyn's with particular care. At first it was difficult for him to believe that his wife had at last given birth to a child that lived. As the days passed and he overheard the frequent and favourable comparisons drawn between Maverlyn and the puny, lame, ill-favoured son of Moses, he felt his manhood fully restored. In the house Kate found his new arrogance almost unbearable. But she was glad of it. This way he would have no inkling of the truth. The child looked like her. All that it had of Moses was his grace and vivacity. No one suspected. Even the Prophet himself had pushed the memory of the night on the hill-top into a limbo of oblivion. And Kate was content. For Maverlyn was hers, the gift of God, the dream which had drawn her to Hebron. And the others, Aloysius, the Prophet, the host of New Believers were irrelevant.

But when she saw the lame Isaac she felt a spasm of fear gripping her heart. Would some penance be demanded for her sin? She could not rid herself of the thought that the perfection of her own child might have been achieved at the expense of Gatha's son, that his club-foot was a reminder of a debt she owed. When Liza brought the boy to her and asked her to suckle him since Gatha's breasts were dry, Kate took this as a confirmation. And she squandered love upon Isaac, happy that in this way she could atone.

In the shed, Aloysius heard Obadiah whistling under his breath and frowned. He felt like ordering his apprentice to stop whistling, but he feared that such an order might make him seem ridiculous. Besides, Obadiah would be sure to obey with the unfailing good-nature that irritated Aloysius. Of late Obadiah had often been puzzled at the sharp tone of the master carpenter when he spoke to him, but he thought it best to take no notice. It was precisely this failure to acknowledge a change in their relationship that annoyed Aloysius. With the birth of his child Maverlyn, he wanted his manhood to be recognized and marked by a greater deference from the others. Unwittingly, Obadiah refused him this.

Aloysius was thinking of the day in the church when Moses had anointed him to succeed as Elder. His pride had been mixed with resentment. This was after all only his due. Why should it be offered as gift? He had looked away so as not to see the adoration with which Obadiah accepted his own investiture. The latter had never looked at him like that. Yet it was he, not Moses, who had made Obadiah, who had taken him from amongst the nameless legions of the unskilled, taught him the secrets of his craft. For without a special skill a man was nothing. Come to think of it, who was Moses? What craft did he follow? What calling? A man with a gift of honeyed words, and nothing more. And a madman besides. He, Aloysius, had seen the madness in his eyes that day in the market-place, when he returned to find Moses with his arms spread-eagled against the wall of the deserted market. But he would keep this to himself, would bide his time…

It was raining, and the window of the shed was closed. Aloysius mopped the sweat from his brow with the polishing rag. Obadiah was intent on his carving, still whistling cheerfully under his breath. The master carpenter was suddenly overwhelmed by the burden of his bitterness against the Prophet. He himself did not know why this rancour should cut so deep, why, in some inexplicable way, it should be tied up with his memories of Kate, the sound of her voice when he had talked about Moses during the waiting years in Cockpit Centre.

****

For Obadiah the first year in Hebron passed quickly. Time fused itself into a regular rhythm of work and sleep. The first event to stand out separate in his memory was the Prophet's proclamation of his forthcoming crucifixion. And after at the anointment ceremony, when the Prophet had called him, Obadiah, 'son', and had blessed him, he was lifted up into a state of bemused exaltation from which he had not yet awoken.

Obadiah felt the rain blowing in on his back, and only then noticed that the door was open. He turned and saw Prophet Moses framed in the doorway. He glanced quickly at the master carpenter, but he had dropped his eyes and was going on with his work, his face expressionless. The Prophet's eyes stared straight ahead of him. He was dressed in his black swallow-tailed coat and best boots. But he wore no shirt, and water trickled down the black V of his chest. Obadiah started to stand up, but the Prophet gestured to him to remain seated. Then he shut the door behind him and stood listening. But only the wind snarled in the tree-tops, whipped through the grass and the bushes in a scurry of violence, and left in its wake the sound of abandoned raindrops dripping from the thatched roof of the shed.

Moses sat on the bench between his two followers. His eyes roved from side to side suspiciously and he kept his voice low as he told them of the plans for his crucifixion. To Aloysius and Obadiah would go the honour of watching with him during his Agony on the Cross, to them alone would he entrust the final revelations that would come to him from the Father as a testament to his sacrifice. The rest of the congregation were to stay down in the church, fasting, praying, and keeping vigil.

The Prophet stood up and pressed his fingers against his temples. Voices were calling to him, beating against his brain like wings, clamorous as birds in startled flight. But soon, very soon, he knew, the turmoil would die down, and a voice, like the first sound of morning, would speak to him sweetly. His eyes lit up with expectation, were enormous in his gaunt face. Obadiah looked at him with awe. Aloysius nodded. What he had suspected was true. Moses was stark, staring mad. And if he were mad, then it would be better that he crucified himself, that he died. If he were to live no one could say what foolish schemes he might think up to destroy them all.

And, after all, this wild dream of Hebron had only succeeded because of the hard work he, Aloysius, had put into it. He had been for many years deacon of the white man's church which, by any reckoning, was far superior in organization to that of the Church of the New Believers. He would lead Hebron better than Moses, would run it as efficiently as the white man whose ways he had learnt, would train Obadiah to be as sober and serious as himself, to follow in his footsteps. And perhaps later on, Kate might bear him a son who would, in his turn, one day be Elder over Hebron. And by the time this son grew up, Hebron would be a mighty kingdom with vast buildings, a palace, Government offices, schools, hospitals, prisons, asylums, as big as those in Kingston. For was he not Aloysius Matthews the master builder? Until now there had been no scope for his dreams. Now there would be. And these dreams, fulfilled, he would pass on to his son. Now that he had a daughter, there was no reason why there should not be many more children. And was not the club-foot of Moses's son a sign that Moses was unfit to lead them? 'And the sins of the fathers shall be visited upon the children even unto the third and fourth generation'. Aloysius glanced furtively at the Prophet. His mouth hung half-open, flecks of spittle had gathered at the corners, and his eyes were vacant.

The voices were still now, and Moses drew his hands away from his head. He felt himself bathed all over in sweat. Then the sweat dried and his body was cool to the touch. The rain drummed on the roof of the shed. A soft clear voice called out to Moses, asking him to come quickly, for the Father was grieved with loneliness, was weary of waiting for His Son. The Prophet wrenched the door open, and was swallowed up in the darkness. Aloysius, his face heavy with disapproval, got up and shut the door firmly.

'Prophet Moses going to spoil that suit, wearing it up and down in the rain like that,' he grumbled.

Obadiah nodded. But he had not heard. His head was ablaze with the imprint of grandeur that the Prophet had left behind him.

****

In the weeks preceding Easter, even Obadiah became aware of the gloom that settled like a fine sifting of dust over Hebron. Moses now withdrew altogether. The services held to anticipate his victory had an air of resigned mourning. This may have been partly due to Aloysius, who presided in place of Moses. The robes of office, the swallow-tailed black coat and the trousers, hung loosely on him. When he raised his arms the sleeves drooped like half-folded black wings. This, added to his lugubrious manner, reminded the congregation of the vulture-like undertaker in Cockpit Centre who used to stand, fully dressed, in the doorway of his shop, as an advertisement for the death that was to introduce him into their lives.

Obadiah planed and smoothed the two pieces of wood that were to form the cross, nailed them together, then planed and smoothed them again. And he made a pledge. During the three nights and two days of the Prophet's agony, he would not sleep, would prove not only that his spirit, but his flesh too, was strong and willing.

His vigil started on the heights of Hebron on the night of Holy Thursday. He and Aloysius sat apart. Isolated from them, and hidden by an outgrowth of rock, the Prophet wrestled with words. The stars were clear, and the moon hung low, almost touching Razor edge Peak. An owl hooted once or twice but otherwise all was quiet. In order to keep awake Obadiah started to count the stars, to identify each one. He woke the next morning to find Aloysius shaking him. Moses stood before them both. He looked like a sleep-walker, a man who had severed himself from any living reality. Stumblingly, Obadiah tried to excuse himself, but neither Aloysius nor Moses paid heed to his words.

Later that morning, the morning of Good Friday, Obadiah returned once more with Aloysius to the farther reaches of the hills. They dug a deep hole, then wrestled with the large rocks with which the cross would be made to stand firm. The two men waited under the sparse shade of a divi-divi tree. They could find nothing to say to each other. At midday a young Brother brought them bread and water. He waited for the mugs whilst they drank, but kept his eyes averted from the signs of preparation. Then he ran off and did not look back.

During the leaden hours of the afternoon they watched as Prophet Moses left the church and, dragging his cross behind him, made his tortuous pilgrimage up the slopes. The sun burnt sullenly behind loose sheaves of clouds. Only the man carrying his cross up the hill seemed alive in Hebron. In the church the congregation prayed, each man immured in his own hopes and fears.

Obadiah and Aloysius, too, were remote from each other, their eyes intent on the figure that crawled up the eroded hill-side. From time to time the glare blinded Obadiah, and Moses looked like an ant tugging at the withered stem of a leaf. But gradually the dragging sound of the cross and the little puffs of dust became magnified and Moses loomed up, his tunic drenched with sweat, his fingers trembling with weariness. He stood still and listened to his breath which came in large surprised gasps. His face was alert, but his eyes were empty.

He was unaware that they had taken the cross from him, and stood with his right hand clutching the air. His head was bowed in an ecstasy of submission. Obadiah glanced at him from time to time as he helped Aloysius to erect the cross. They banked the earth round its base and steadied it with large rocks. The rocks were streaked with the reddish traces of iron ore. The two waited in silence as they had been instructed. When the shadow of the cross fell on Moses he walked to it and climbed up on the highest rock which had been placed in front. He extended his arms, and Obadiah, standing on another rock, bound the Prophet's wrists to the cross with pieces of specially woven rope. Aloysius's bald head gleamed in the sun as he knelt binding Moses's ankles to the cross. He finished first, and felt the spittle filling his mouth like bile. He went across to the divi-divi tree and leaned against the trunk until he felt better. The pool of his spit soaked quickly into the earth.

He returned and helped Obadiah to roll away the rock from under Moses's feet. Obadiah felt the quiver of the Prophet's flesh as it was left to carry its own weight, unsupported. His limbs were taut with the other man's pain, his being confused with his. As he sat with Aloysius, waiting during the long hours, he kept his eyes on Moses, willing him to sense his closeness, willing his own flesh to receive the imprint of the other man's agony. Aloysius sat with his arms folded and his eyes half closed. Obadiah wondered how he could be so calm. He hoped that somehow the Prophet would sense the difference, would accept his anguish and single him out for some special token of his love, as Jesus had singled out John. Or, better still, the crucified thief whom he had chosen to die with him...

The afternoon, departing, striped the Prophet's face with shadows. Twilight came like a lullaby, dried the sweat on his face and body. Night invaded Hebron. A small wind sprang up and carried an occasional echo of singing from below in the church. The moon appeared, flanked by stars. Their light glimmered in Moses's eyes, gilded the wasted flesh of his arms, the hanging folds of his belly, the dry corded legs, the arched feet with their long wiry toes, the purple-black nails curving into the calloused flesh...

The cries of birds filled Obadiah with a dizzy exaltation. They were like heralds trumpeting his victory over the night which was Moses's and the victory of Moses which was his. A fresh breeze blew away the shreds of mist as the first soft flush of the sun wrapped Hebron. The Prophet, hanging on his cross, was framed in the orange wash of morning. Behind his head, grey banks of mist were pierced by spears of sunlight. His eyes were closed. Only the uneven heaving of the matted hairs on his chest disturbed his silence.

Obadiah looked at Aloysius and saw him sleeping, his head cradled on his knees. Suddenly he found himself crying and did not know why. He stood up, walked across, knelt on the ground, bent his head and kissed the cold inert feet of Moses. He remained there until the sun sprang aggressively into the basin of Hebron, capturing the hills and houses in a net of fierce white light. Then he walked over and woke Aloysius.

****

Aloysius stumbled down towards his house. Sleep still clouded his eyes and his limbs were stiff. He yawned, and felt a sharp stab of pain between his ribs. He was too old for all this nonsense, he thought with resentment. He would have to sit out on the hill-side another day and another night, and for what? Just so that Moses Barton could fool himself that he was God. It was all right for Moses, he was mad, for Obadiah, he was young and strong, but what was he, Aloysius Matthews doing in all this nonsense?

The house was cold and quiet, and seemed strange to Aloysius, as if he had been away for years. He called out to Kate twice before he remembered that she would be down at the church keeping vigil with the others, and would have the baby with her. It wouldn't be good for the child either, all this excitement. He went over to the bed and looked at the black suit laid out on it. Kate had altered it so that it fitted him now. And she had pressed the bulging seems so that they lay flat. It would have been better if she had been able to recut it to suit him. But the suit would one day be Obadiah's, would have to be let out again to fit him. Still, it lay there in all its splendour, waiting to be worn by him on Sunday at the ceremony of triumph in the church. And the triumph would be personal to him as well. For with Moses dead he would feel at ease in the robes of office, would be well and truly Elder, would mould them to his body over the years as he would mould Hebron to his hand. He stroked the thick black serge over and over again.

After he had eaten, he went back up the hill and told Obadiah that he had left some food for him. Obadiah nodded but did not move. Aloysius plucked a blade of grass, stripped it and picked his teeth with the stem. A shred of dried codfish had stuck between his back molars and a nerve was throbbing. But even the pain seemed pleasant, there was something sensuous about it.

The day passed sluggishly. At about two in the afternoon Obadiah went down to Aloysius's house. He saw the food laid out on the table but did not eat. To eat would have been a betrayal. He filled a mug with water from the barrel, took a rag and went back up the hill. Aloysius looked on indifferently as Obadiah climbed up beside Moses and bathed his face. The Prophet did not stir or respond to Obadiah's hand. Later on, when the sun flaunted its death to the hills, Aloysius took the empty mug down to his house, ate once more, and returned.

The first vulture appeared at twilight. Soon it was joined by two others which appeared as if from nowhere. Then the three circled ceremoniously above the cross, flapping their wings patiently against the darkening sky.

A sick feeling welled up in Obadiah's stomach. He stretched himself face downwards on the ground and dug his fingers into the earth. Beside him Aloysius moved nervously, changing his position every few minutes, trying to shake off the strangeness which was unsettling him. His restlessness roused Obadiah, who drew himself up on his elbows. He shook his head to clear away the dizzy feeling. The sudden movement made him feel faint, and for a moment the darkness bandaged his eyes. He struggled to his feet, knowing that if he did not eat, he would be unable to fulfil the promise that he had made to Moses, would be unable to watch with him to the end, to hear the revelations of truth that Moses would give them as an inheritance to Hebron, for ever and for ever…Amen…and Amen.

He swayed on his legs. They seemed as insubstantial as the mist. Aloysius looked up at him with alarm as he moved down the hill. He pointed to his mouth and kept on walking. Behind him, in some far distance, he heard Aloysius's urgent demand that he should hurry back and not leave him alone with Moses, should hurry…hurry…Obadiah nodded his head over and over as he groped his way down, zigzagging in his attempt to avoid the rocks and bushes that leapt up threateningly. He held on to the stone step until the house stopped rocking from side to side, then, exhausted, he crawled across the polished floor of Aloysius's house. On hands and knees he pushed himself over to the table, clutched the piece of bread and began chewing it slowly and with great effort. It was covered with fine black ants and one or two escaped and scurried over his face. The window was shuttered and it was dark in the room. He fell asleep.

Towards morning he dreamt that he himself was pinioned to a great cross, that he was heaving and struggling to break free. When he opened his eyes Aloysius was over him, pulling at him, shaking him. He sat up slowly and rubbed his eyes. Aloysius darted over to the corner of the room and took a sharp knife from his tool box. Then he straightened up and turned to Obadiah. His face looked as if it had been struck by lightening. It was grey, shrunken, the flesh on his face seemed like rough bark stretched over a skull. He went through the door and up the hill. Obadiah followed him, burdened by his own sense of defeat which hung round him like a premonition.

Against the dull blue of morning that cleared behind the trees the Prophet's body sagged with the defencelessness of death. The head drooped to one side, the mouth hung open, the eyes stared with a great terror. A globule of spit had dried on his chin. Aloysius hacked at the ropes that bound Moses to the cross. Obadiah held on to the legs, took the full weight of the body when it was loosened, and lowered it to the ground. Obadiah noticed that Aloysius was trembling violently. And yet he himself, as he waited by the dead, unrecognizable body of Moses, felt nothing, nothing whatsoever.

The singing of the approaching congregation was loud and clear. It was the same song that they had sung in the church on the night that Moses had announced his crucifixion:

In the Cross, in the Cross, be my glory ever,
Til my enraptured soul shall find, peace beyond the river.

The New Believers were coming as Moses had commanded them, to celebrate the victory of his death. They waved palm fronds and their white robes billowed gently in the morning breeze. Still singing, they formed a circle round the dead body of Moses, and Aloysius and Obadiah, who sat on either side of him. As each New Believer saw the Prophet's face, the singing faded away. The terror on Moses's face filled them, too, with a dull fear. Miss Gatha stood a little way away from the others, astonished by her grief. Red, orange, and crimson over the green land, and the sun rioted in the sky. It was Easter Sunday.

Aloysius took ill on the following Sunday. The New Believers gathered all kinds of medicinal herbs, and searched through the hills for the different trees whose leaves were said to draw out 'fever' as they drew up moisture from the earth. Kate and Liza brewed these leaves and herbs in hot baths. Day after day Aloysius, propped up in blankets over the steaming brew, sweated out the fever. Day after day his body wasted away and he became weaker. At last he was too weak to withstand the hot baths. Liza shook her head dolefully and muttered that there was nothing else to be done. Of all the cases of 'galloping consumption' that she had nursed, she had never saved one. The others accepted their Elder's death as inevitable. Perhaps, they thought, it was the hand of God. Everything about Aloysius's eldership had augured badly. They thought with relief of Obadiah. He was young and strong. Besides, Moses had liked him far more than he had Aloysius. They found themselves hoping that the end would come quickly for Aloysius, so that Hebron would have a new beginning.

Kate nursed him with devotion, but she too wished him gone. His eyes followed her about the room with tenacity and she could feel his weakness devouring herself and the child as if it was only their life-force that kept him going. The child became fretful. During the days Kate kept her out of doors as much as possible. Obadiah came every day to sit for a few hours with Aloysius, and this was a great relief to Kate. For a few hours, at least, she could be free from the incessant demand in the sick man's eyes.

It did not consciously occur to Obadiah that Aloysius would die. And yet he came every day to sit with him during the long hours of the afternoon, as if by his very presence he could protect the other from death. For him, Aloysius was still the master carpenter and he the apprentice. He did not even want to envisage a time when the other would be gone, when he, Obadiah, would be called upon to lead and not to follow. He avoided this thought as most men avoid the thought of old age and decay.

Even during moments of delirium, Aloysius did not entirely lose his habit of reticence. The most that he did was to hum a snatch of a hymn or recite a Bible text or two. And after these lapses he would open his eyes and glance suspiciously at Obadiah to see if he had given anything away. But on the day before he died, the burden proved too much for him. His right hand gripped Obadiah's wrist, and his fingers burnt the other man's flesh like red-hot coals. At first Obadiah did not realize what he was saying. Then he heard his own name mentioned:

'. . . for Obadiah to come back, to come back. The moon is going away…there is a great darkness…I strain my eye down the hill-side looking for Obadiah to come back. Behind me I hear the cross start to rock and to rock…Don't turn round…don't turn round…I am afraid you see…my mouth as dry as ashes…Who is that? Who? It's him…I hear him…He struggle a little bit…I want to turn round…but I can't…I can't…He's quiet now…quiet…Obadiah, come…make haste…Oh Jesus…he starting to fight again! Why the hell he can't keep quiet? The damned madman…I better go for Obadiah…I better…Ssh…Hush…He hear me…He hear me in the darkness…Moses call out…"Loose me…I don't want to die…Loose me…Loose me!"'

Aloysius struggled up from the pillows, his body shaking. Obadiah put his arms round him, eased him down. Tears streamed down the face of the master carpenter, tears of weakness, almost of petulance:

'I wanted to loose him, it wasn't because I was going to be Elder why I didn't loose him, after all I was once deacon in a big church, had my shop and all, you remember, you remember…?'

His eyes searched Obadiah's face anxiously, and to quieten him, Obadiah nodded.

The master carpenter lay still for a moment, husbanding the little strength that remained to him. For it was important that he should justify his action to Obadiah, make it bearable.

'But he said that he was going to die for Hebron, so why he didn't want to die now? Why at the last minute he had to come and start to fight to live? It wasn't fair. It wasn't fair for him to ask me to loose him. It wasn't fair for him to ask me to loose him. It wasn't fair for him to put all that on me…After all I didn't put him up there on the cross, I didn't tell him to…'

He twisted his head away from Obadiah's gaze.

'He said he wanted to die, so why he didn't want to die now?' he repeated querulously.

Out in the yard, Kate was singing to the child. Aloysius spoke now with his face turned to the wall and in a whisper:

'Then the day start to light up and Moses's voice cry out: "God is white after all...God is white!"'

He turned once again to Obadiah but his eyes were vague, unfocused:

'And he didn't struggle any more after that, you know...He didn't struggle at all!'

He died the following day, and Obadiah's first duty as Elder was to officiate at his funeral. Hugh helped him to compose the funeral oration, and Obadiah extolled Aloysius as the master carpenter who had taught many of them his craft, who had helped to build up Hebron. But of the other Aloysius whom he had glimpsed, he did not say a word, not even to Hugh who was now his assistant and his right hand.

But Obadiah felt the need for a gesture on his part to exorcize the terror that had stamped itself on the Prophet's dead face, and lingered like some evil shadow in his own heart; to exorcize the memory of what Aloysius had told him. He would have to keep this to himself. Obadiah thought of how he had remained chaste all these years, because of his fear of women. They had all seemed to him reincarnated images of his dead mother. And he remembered how Moses had praised him highly for his continence, extolling it as the highest virtue. He would continue that way, Obadiah pledged, until such a time as he met a woman ready to devote her own life, as he would devote his, to the greater glory of Hebron and of their great Prophet who had founded the kingdom, had made the supreme sacrifice to ensure its continuance.

And thus, with his death, Prophet Moses made all the New Believers accomplices in his legend. Their belief became a necessity, was magnified into myth. The wooden cross on the Prophet's grave was the tangible symbol of their faith. There was no room for doubt – to doubt would be to question the validity of the crucifixion, of a God black like themselves, of Hebron. Moses alone had died, but Hebron, its past, present, and future were entombed with him, awaiting his resurrection. The life led by the New Believers after his death was an epilogue, a ritual dance, ossified by repetition now that its original impulse had been forgotten.

18. The Sea

When his mother sent Isaac away to school in Cockpit Centre, he saw Hebron for the first time, through the mocking eyes of unbelievers. On his second day at school, he was gripped by two boys, made to stand in the playground and watch whilst the others re-enacted his father's attempt to fly to heaven, his failure, his trial, his exodus, his crucifixion. They forced him to join in the choruses of the bawdy songs that they sang about the Prophet, and when at first he refused, twisted his lame foot and rubbed his face in the dust.

When he returned to Hebron that weekend, he went to the spring and questioned Aunt Kate. He hoped that she would give back to him the illusions he had been robbed of. But after the first week he could see that Hebron was small, that Aunt Kate was nothing more than a deluded old woman dreaming that her daughter was asleep in the spring. And he knew that Maverlyn was dead. Aunt Kate could not help him. No one in Hebron could. They were all dreamers. Only his mother was different, and nothing would impel him to break the silence between them. He decided not to return to school, and hid the specially made boot for his club-foot in the hollow of the tree-trunk in the square. If he did not go back to Cockpit Centre he would in time forget what he had learnt there. He did not want this new knowledge which, like his club-foot, isolated him on an island of difference.

His mother forced him to go back to school. He hardened his heart and became resigned. He began to regard all the New Believers with a contemptuous indifference. He felt himself a giant amongst pygmies, an adult amongst children. On Sundays in the church it was all he could do to keep himself from laughing aloud at the stupidity of their belief. He looked at the foolish face of his godfather Obadiah, at the ludicrous figure dressed in a swallow-tailed coat and trousers, making inane, puppet-like gestures as he preached, and felt a savage exaltation. This idol, too, had been toppled. In Obadiah, Isaac could see all the farce of his father's mad aspirations. In his mind he trampled on all the memories of tenderness which the big man with his great strength had shown towards him. One evening he smashed the wooden horse which Obadiah had made for him, which had helped him take his first uncertain steps. He did not need it now. He did not need a godfather. He knew that his father was a fool and God a lie.

He did not share his new knowledge with anyone. Secrecy, which had once been a necessity with him, became a habit, heightening his feeling of power. He was most careful that no one should sense a change in him, especially his mother. He had learnt that his safest defence against her was to appear to be exactly what she willed him to be. One weekend, however, he told Rose how he had found out that she was not his sister, as they had both assumed, but the daughter of a white minister and a nameless young girl. And he sang for her the scabrous song which told about her parents and their relationship with his father, Moses. He told Rose all this so that he could rejoice, for a change, in the misery which he was able to inflict on another. But her bewilderment at this new strangeness which had been put upon her drew them close together. They were both conscious of being outcasts.

It was in Cockpit Centre that Isaac first became obsessed with the sea. The boy who sat next to him at school was two years older, not very bright, and had a bad stammer. Isaac sometimes slipped him the answer to sums when the headmaster's cane was raised threateningly. In exchange, when the other boys were not around, he talked to Isaac about Paradise Bay where he had lived for two years with an uncle who was a fisherman. He would tell of getting up in the early mornings and rowing out of the darkness into the rising sun, on and on, for the sea was so big that Cockpit Centre would be lost inside it, so big that...When his tongue got tied up he would open his arms and his eyes as if to embrace the sky, to contain it within the breadth of his arms, the length of his reaching, quivering body. When Isaac saw the sea he was surprised that it was so still.

From the end of Isaac's first year at school, it was a foregone conclusion that he would one day win the teachers' training scholarship and go to Kingston, the capital. From Mondays to Fridays he lived with the headmaster and his wife in the ramshackle bungalow behind the school. The couple had no children of their own. The wife was barren and the headmaster a man of narrow, rigid principles. About fifty years old, his scholarship was rooted in a mechanical knowledge of the structure of the English language, of the arithmetic formulae propounded in the ancient textbooks. For him, English and arithmetic were dead languages, and he taught them as such. He excelled in drilling his pupils in the eccentricities of English spelling, and was often heard to boast that every pupil left his school with a well-tanned bottom and a sound basic education. That this education had no relation to their daily life was irrelevant. The headmaster, as his headmaster before him, was the product of a colonial education which had become ossified over the years. They were like blinkered horses who could see the path before them but could not relate it to wider horizons. But within the limits of the system, the headmaster laboured to impart all that he knew. And when he came upon a pupil of exceptional merit like Isaac, he devoted his whole being to seeing that the pupil should succeed where, he suspected, he himself had failed. These headmasters were like eunuchs, themselves deprived, but guarding carefully the seeds of the future.

Night after night the headmaster coached Isaac. His wife, who trembled before her husband's whims (he wielded the cane as heavily in his home as he did at school), fed Isaac and coddled him as if he were some prize animal due to compete at a fair. In the afternoons, Isaac was allowed to read and re-read the headmaster's complete library. This consisted of the Bible, the complete works of Shakespeare, the *Pilgrim's Progress*, and the complete works of John Milton.

On the weekends at Hebron Isaac would wander over the hills shouting the cadences of *Paradise Lost* at the top of his voice. A rumour started up amongst the New Believers that he was touched in the head. The same mannerisms that had seemed divine inspiration in his father marked him out as a crazy simpleton. When they laughed at him now, they winked hugely at each other. Isaac more and more looked forward to the Mondays when he could return to school. The time spent at Hebron began to be as unreal and as distant as sleep. When he was seventeen, he won the teachers' training scholarship and left, the next year, for Kingston and the sea.

****

The Arawak training college for elementary schoolteachers was hidden away in the Wareika hills, ten miles from Kingston proper. The Church authorities who had endowed the college thought it wiser for the students to be set apart from the squalor and poverty of the capital, from the temptations which it might offer. But from a steep slope behind the college Isaac could see the town spread out beneath him, like a stain against the blue-green mirror of the sea.

The college itself had once been the home of a wealthy planter and was a spacious building, two storeys high, with large rooms and venetian blinds. The forty students slept in upstairs bedrooms which had been converted into dormitories. One wing was reserved for the teachers. The headmaster lived in a house which had been specially built inside the college grounds on a bluff which overlooked the sea. The outhouses, formerly used as servants' quarters, stables, granaries, mills, were now converted into classrooms. The drawing-room of the great house was now the chapel.

The library was a long, high-ceilinged room. Its walls were panelled with mahogany, which lent a cool gloom to the interior. Its collection of books, the pride of its former owner, had been maintained and added to by the college authorities. It had also become a custom for well-off islanders to bequeath their books to the college. Such a bequest was always certain of a eulogy in the daily newspaper and the titles of the books donated were printed in full. Several years before Isaac came to the college, the first black man to be appointed to the college Board of Governors gave the library a gift of two thousand pounds. The headmaster was thereby enabled to purchase books which corresponded more nearly to his own enlightened taste.

The library was the centre of Isaac's new life. He devoured fact and fiction, good and bad, with passion. He attended classes and did the work required of him in order that he might retain his scholarship and so continue to explore the new enchanted worlds that were more vivid and familiar than the narrow ambience of the college.

Once a month the students were allowed a day-excursion into Kingston. On these days Isaac would stay in the college, savouring the silence and the loneliness. All day long he would read, stretched out on the grass under the shade of a mango tree, whilst around him the poui and the poinciana and the lignum vitae trees plastered flames of colour against the blue sky.

It was on one of these days that he started to write. He had just finished reading *Moby Dick*, and under the spell of its power wanted to create an image of himself and of his people that would be epic. For it was through his reading that Isaac first became shamefully conscious of being black. With the exception of Othello and Daggoo, the harpooner in *Moby Dick*, the black characters whom he had come upon in his reading seemed to him a miserable and despicable lot. They were people who scarcely existed in their own right, a muted background against which the good or evil, the tolerance or intolerance, the gentleness or cruelty of real people could be shown. They were always pitied and patronized, the done-tos and never the doers, the slaves and never the masters, the conquered, never the conquerors. And, by the aesthetic norms accepted and established in these books, their 'thick' lips, 'woolly' hair and 'coal-black' skin were equated with everything evil and base, everything that was the negation of light, of beauty. Black was for the night and for darkness, the colour of the devil and of despair. When he read about these people, they were alien to him. But when he looked in a mirror and saw their description reflected, he was filled with self-hatred and turned away, just as he had once refused to touch his club-foot, to acknowledge its existence.

Isaac began to write regularly every afternoon. He used the back of his science exercise book. He wrote carefully, examining each word, paring every sentence. At first he wrote about himself in relation to the literary characters; he became involved in long dialogues with them. Then he started on a novel which was to be set in the college with himself as the hero. For the first time he began to observe the life around him, to scrutinize the students and teachers with whom he lived.

The majority of the students came, like Isaac, from the country; and were, for the most part, sons of teachers or of peasant farmers. Those who came from Kingston were from the new 'middle class'. One was the son of a Baptist parson, another's father was a civil servant, another was the son of a master tailor. One, more cleverly ambitious than the others, was the illegitimate son of a domestic servant. With the exception of the headmaster, the teachers were all from the same background as the students.

The headmaster was a light-brown man whom at first Isaac had thought to be white. But taking his weekly class in English literature, the headmaster had told the new students that he was one of them. One of his great-grandmothers had been coloured and he was proud of it. Isaac noticed that his eyes were watchful even when he laughed. His name was Anthony Holland, and from the Kingston students Isaac learnt that he was the son of an English judge who had married the daughter and sole heiress of a wealthy mulatto planter.

The students venerated their headmaster. His scholastic attainments were legendary. Anthony Holland was a former Rhodes scholar. After gaining a first-class honours degree at Oxford, he studied law at the Inns of Court, then took B.SC. degree at University College, London. It was there that he met and married his wife, Elizabeth. She was the brilliant daughter of a minor civil servant who had come to the University on a scholarship. She was earnest, conscientious, and physically unprepossessing. He was shy, withdrawn, and inhibited by the knowledge that he was partly black. They were at once attracted. Their inadequacies complemented each other. Coming as he did from a feudal background, his social assurance made up for her lack of it. In exchange she offered her 'purity of blood'. They never spoke about this, but it was always present with them, and their relationship consisted of a series of skirmishes in which each side tried to upgrade the value of his or her contribution and to devalue that of the other. Their life together was an emotional stock exchange. They had one child, a girl, who died of meningitis when she was three.

It was the practice of the headmaster and his wife to hold a musical evening once a month and to invite, in turn, ten students and two teachers. Isaac was amongst the last batch to be invited. They went over after dinner and were met at the door by Mrs Holland and a servant, who served lemonade. Then they went into the drawing-room. This was a large, airy room decorated with straw mats and uncomfortable chairs made from local woods. Mrs Holland explained that they were made by local craftsmen who still retained a naivety that was now lost to their English counterparts. Isaac noticed that her eyes behind glasses looked like the sky at midday when the sun had burnt out nearly all its blueness.

Whilst Mr Holland wound up the gramophone and put on the records, his wife gave facts about the different composers, the underlying themes of their works, the meaning of their music. As the record was played, she looked at each student in turn, nodding her head and smiling, insisting that he should share her enjoyment. The students learnt from each other how to respond, how to feign an expression of mystic communion.

A wave of drumming broke in on the recorded sound of the piano, and Mrs Holland frowned. The students looked uncomfortable. Isaac was seated facing the window and he could see out to the road. A group of Pocomania revivalist worshippers were passing in procession. They were robed from head to foot in white and, except for the steady savage beat of their drums, walked in silence. They held up lighted candles and the flames flickered in a light wind. They passed swiftly like ghosts. But the sound of the drumming echoed long after they had vanished. At a signal from his wife the headmaster got up and closed the windows.

Isaac felt suddenly as if he was caged. Mrs Holland was looking at him now, her eyes pinning him down. In the light of the petrol lamp her face seemed to have turned green. As if sensing his resistance, the other students stared at Isaac, their heads moving in time to the tune. Mrs Holland nodded at him. Her smile became brighter and more fixed. Isaac felt strangled by the unreality. The faces had all turned to masks which were pressing in on him, challenging his already precarious identity. Now that the windows were closed, he could not avoid the multitude of eyes. And the room had become stuffy. He could feel sweat breaking out on his forehead, could see apprehension creeping into Mrs Holland's eyes as her fingers plucked at the coral necklace that she wore. The skin in the V of her frock was red and rough. She was almost begging him to respond. Isaac understood that it was only through the students that she could fulfill some human need. Suddenly he stood up and left. His last impression was of the headmaster dozing peacefully behind his pipe. As he fled down the path the record stopped, and Mrs Holland's voice called after him:

'But Mr Barton, you haven't had your cocoa, Mr Barton, really…!'

The night air was cool on his face and the bamboo fronds that lined the road chafed against each other gently. Fireflies darted in and out, and some distance away the Wareika River tumbled over a diminutive waterfall. Isaac walked down the road towards Kingston. Tonight, he decided, he would go to the sea. Only the sea could wipe out the memory of the room he had left behind him and the puppets who sought to imprison him with their importunity. He had no fear now, as once he had had, that the sea would fall below his expectations. For he knew the sea from *Moby Dick*, and there it was even vaster and more powerful than he had imagined it.

The sky was crowded with stars, and it was full moon. Isaac walked several miles before he realized that going into Kingston without permission might possibly get him into trouble. But he brushed the thought aside. The college seemed unimportant. He swung swiftly down the narrow track with tireless, rhythmic strides, unaware of his club-foot. As he passed a small village rum-shop, the swing doors opened and a spear of light flashed across the dark road. Several men lurched out of the shop, clinging to each other and cursing. When they saw Isaac they burst out laughing. He hardly noticed them.

It was after midnight when he finally turned out of the track and into the wider paved streets of the outlying residential districts of Kingston. He walked down the middle of a broad avenue lined with trees. Behind the trees, houses crouched liked sleeping dogs. Then the trees disappeared and there were larger buildings, one of them with lighted windows keeping vigil in the night. Then the wide streets gave way to narrower ones, criss-crossing each other, smelling not of dew and flowers, but of stale urine, rotting fruit, salted fish, spices, and bad drainage. He heard the gentle sound of lisping water and the creak of the boats moored against the sea-wall. He walked along, his shirt billowing behind him. He came to a stretch of sandy beach and sat down. Before him the sea, black and glittering, lay coiled like a snake under the moon.

Several hours later he plunged into the web of lanes and alleys on his way back to the college. He whistled as he walked, head erect, shoulders back and confident. A woman detached herself from the shadows and approached him. He stopped and turned towards her. Her skin was a mottled brown in the darkness, and her breath stank of cheap white rum. Excited by the exaltation which she sensed in him, she rubbed herself against him. Under the thin black frock her body was taut and naked. As she felt him dissolve against her, she jerked away. Her eyes became hard and calculating.

'How much you can pay?' she challenged him.

He turned and walked away rapidly. His desire vanished. Behind him he could hear her shouting abuse. He was glad that he had not taken her. Her spirit would have been too small to encompass the sea inside him.

His club-foot dragged heavily behind him, and he was conscious of his tiredness. He hurried, forcing himself on. It became urgent that he should reach the college before daybreak and slip into bed unnoticed. The ten miles lengthened into an infinity of distance, like that which he had traveled away from Hebron on the first day at school, when the letters on his slate had coalesced to make a meaning, and he had learnt to read.

His return, like his absence, went unnoticed, and the next day he found himself something of a hero with the other students. For the first time they treated Isaac on a man-to-man basis. Holland would be sure to give him hell, they warned him, but he should stick up for himself. After all, if a man didn't like music, he didn't have to pretend. Holland himself only liked music in order to please his wife, to hold her. There was even a story about her running away with a student one week after the death of her child. Holland had secretly threatened the student with expulsion, and the student had walked out on her. She had returned, weeping and hysterical, to her husband. But Holland never quite trusted her after that, and watched her like a hawk.

The whole student body awaited the headmaster's summons with excitement. They were surprised that Isaac could be so calm. At lunch one of the teachers handed him a note. The others crowded round whilst he opened it. It was an invitation from the headmaster and his wife. They asked him to come to tea that afternoon. There was a great uproar. Why was Isaac accorded this special privilege? It couldn't be, one student said, winking lewdly, because Mrs Holland wanted to run away with Isaac? No, Isaac agreed, for one thing, he couldn't run.

Mrs Holland seemed different that afternoon. She wore a high-necked voile dress with long sleeves and was very gracious. She talked to Isaac as if the night before and its awkward incident had never been. Isaac could not relate her to the personage of the students' stories. Tea was brought in by a frightened black girl, fresh from the country and awkward. She was clearly afraid of handling the delicate cups and saucers, afraid of the eyes of her mistress that never stopped checking her actions. Isaac felt himself willing the girl not to make a mistake, not to be as clumsy as her mistress expected her to be. The headmaster came in just then and greeted Isaac heartily. For a second his eyes lingered on the plump calves of the girl as she walked about putting out the tea-things. The girl noticed his look, became more assured, and managed to get through without mishap.

Isaac had difficulty balancing the teacup and plate. The headmaster stood with his back to the imitation fireplace and laughed and joked with his wife to put Isaac at his ease. They asked him questions about his home and about Hebron, and about the books he had read. He answered briefly and waited for them to come to the point.

After tea, the headmaster, to accompanying comments from his wife, told Isaac his life story. He too had been handicapped in his youth, he explained tactfully. In his case it had been severe bouts of malaria fever which had kept him from his books for months on end. But he had gritted his teeth and persevered, and in the end could say, without false modesty, that he had triumphed over all his more fortunate fellow students. And as he had done, so could Isaac. As long as he did not give way to self-pity, did not allow a sense of inferiority to keep him away from social activities such as their little musical evenings. Mrs Holland smiled at Isaac, then at her husband. Isaac sat between them, burdened by the incubus of their pity.

That night in the dormitory he was bombarded with questions, but Isaac's laconic replies soon caused the other students to lose interest and change the subject. Their talk, as always, drifted first to their future careers, then to politics, then to women. Several of the cleverer students planned to make teaching a stepping-stone to the law and then politics. They would teach for a few years, save enough money to go to England, and study at one of the Inns of Court. For the future road to power lay in politics, man, they assured each other. Once they threw out the British a new day would dawn and the world would be theirs. They never discussed how they would grapple with the problems of the future, how they would feed the hungry, provide jobs for the jobless, wipe out the three hundred years of malnutrition and mental atrophy that was the legacy of colonial rule. Instead they argued heatedly over the proper constitutional procedures to be adopted after independence. And always, the high point of their discussion was English constitutional law and practice. They spoke glibly of freedom and democracy, but were incapable of understanding their meaning. They came from the generations of slaves on whose toiling backs the noble slogans of democracy had been conceived. And they were ready to die defending concepts which could have no meaning for them.

One student stood up on the bed and made a violent anti-colonial speech. The night of the long knives would come, he declared, the day of blood. The others applauded, smiling. They had no real feeling of bitterness or of violence. Unlike their illiterate would-be followers, they were spiritually and emotionally emasculated. In exploring the symbols of power that their rulers had trapped in books, they had become enmeshed in their complexities, had fallen victims to a servitude more absolute than the one imposed by guns, whips, chains, and hunger.

Politics for them meant an unending series of meetings, where, standing on raised platforms under street-lamps, they would move the multitude of black faces with the force of their eloquence. And this anonymous black mass would surge like a hurricane through the island, would drive the English rulers into the sea; whilst they, calm and smiling, would don the robes of office abandoned by their former masters, would echo firmly their platitudes and half-truths and compromises and subtle distortions, would make themselves counterparts of the men whom ostensibly they had overthrown. For them politics was a game with a set of rules codified by their adversaries. They would play the game brilliantly without ever questioning the rules.

The talk had gone full circle and come back to women. They discussed the headmaster's wife once again, in subdued tones and with furtive sniggers. They gloated over her alleged adventure with the student, which by telling and retelling had become a legend. Even here, their lasciviousness followed a pattern. For the headmaster's wife was the biggest symbol of all, the token that one day they, too, could have all the apanage of power that surrounded their rulers – their women, their cars, big houses and rituals of behaviour, servants in starched and ironed uniforms...Always they would exchange the substance for the shadow, Isaac thought. They had surrendered even the right to dream their own dreams. Their dreams were second-hand, cut-price, bargain ones. And for the first time

Isaac began dimly to understand the necessity of his father's madness.

****

The next morning Isaac reread all that he had written in his science notebook. As he had suspected, he found it stilted and unreal. He felt a great emptiness inside him, almost a nothingness, a non-being. He read less and less and began to work at his lessons with a savage persistence. His teacher's training course extended over two years and was divided into two parts. The mid-course examination was held at the end of the first year, the finals at the end of the second. On the aggregate results of both parts the student who came first was given a scholarship for an extra year to study at the central training college in England. He would win the scholarship, Isaac vowed, and go in search of new worlds.

He did not return to Hebron for the summer vacation, but remained at the college and studied through the long hot months. In November he received a letter from his mother (written for her by the postmistress in Cockpit Centre), in which she told about the destruction wreaked on Hebron by the hurricane that had swept that part of the island. She advised him to remain at the college over Christmas. He wrote his mid-course examinations in early December and came second. In most of the papers his essays were better than those of the student who had come first. But the Board of Governors, who also served as the examiners, although recognizing Isaac's brilliance, were puzzled and disturbed by his unorthodox views on English literature.

His history papers were even more alarming, the facts dangerously distorted, the opinions suspect. In his essay on "The Rise of the British Empire" Isaac had stated that the true greatness of the English lay in their ability to enslave themselves, consciously, in order to enslave others; on their carefully constructed and chauvinistic vision of the past which enabled them to conceive of a civilization which could flower, like an orchid, on the bent backs of subject races. In another essay, 'The Glorious Reign of Queen Victoria', he had insisted that the most important event of the Victorian age was that, slavery being no longer economically viable, powerful interests backed and obtained the abolition of slavery; that, once the slaves had the freedom to starve they were free to fight; that therefore the Victorian era saw the emergence of the first Jamaican patriots, the mulatto planter, William George Gordon, and the black deacon, Paul Bogle, who led the Morant Bay rebellion of 1865 and were hanged as traitors by Governor Eyre, one of the most efficient butchers of the Empire...

Some members of the Board would have preferred to fail Isaac outright. The headmaster, however, spoke up for him, attributing his bitterness to his deformity and his somewhat eccentric family background. He undoubtedly had a chip on his shoulder, the headmaster argued, but they were all British, their tradition was one of fair play, and although the student's ideas were misguided they could not deny that they were brilliantly expressed. The headmaster's recommendation might have been of little use, so incensed were all the members of the Board, if he had not been supported by the one completely black member.

Theophilius Barker was a solicitor. Working as an office boy in a law firm, he had educated himself and taken his law exams over a period of ten years. By the time he was qualified and taken into the firm, he knew more law than all the partners. By the end of another ten years he was senior partner, the first black man in the island to be the head of a firm of solicitors. He had reached the top by working like a slave, and like a slave concealing his shrewd, thrusting intelligence under a mask of clowning. Once at the top he ruled others with an iron hand. He owned houses all over Kingston. These he had acquired through speedy foreclosure on mortgages which he offered at tempting rates of interest. He was a regular churchgoer. Many of his clients were church members. He got himself appointed to the Board of Governors by subscribing two thousand pounds to the college library. He was about to get himself appointed to the Legislative Council. And these were but the preliminary skirmishes of his campaign to achieve his eventual ambition. He dreamed of being one day Sir Theophilius Barker.

He was even harsher than the others in judging Isaac's history papers. He claimed that the young man's answers showed a base ingratitude, which he for one, as a proud and loyal subject of the British Empire, greatly resented. Legally, he was not even sure if opinions such as these, committed to paper, did not constitute an indictable offence. But they were not in a court of law and must find some other method of dealing with this impertinent and misguided student. And where he agreed with the headmaster was in this: Isaac was known to be studious and intelligent; if they failed him he would be looked upon as a martyr; the political agitators in the island would welcome his case as a ready-made stick with which to beat the Board; but if they were to accept the headmaster's suggestion and place him second, then they would humble his pride. No one could then say they had been unjust and the matter would be quietly disposed of…

Lawyer Barker's proposal was adopted. That evening when he returned home, he made a careful note of Isaac's name in a black notebook which was kept in his safe. Isaac Barton, he decided, could be useful to him. His feelings on reading Isaac's essays were in no way connected with what he had said at the Board meeting. For Lawyer Barker was a secretive man, showing a face of moderation to the white rulers, while in his heart was a blind and inchoate rage against them. On his way home he had exulted in Isaac's opinions. This is it, he had thought, here was a black man for the first time really using the white bastards' language to fling the truth in their faces and kick them in the teeth with it as he would have liked to have done so many times, when they had used him and abused him, insulted and mocked him.

The day after the results were out, the headmaster called Isaac to his study and hinted to him that his papers had been 'erratic', that Isaac had only pulled through because of his, the headmaster's, insistence, his personal faith in his abilities. As a favour to him would Isaac in the next exams hew more closely to the 'correct' line? Not that one wanted to sacrifice one's principles, but after all, a scholarship was in the balance and it could change one's whole future.

That night in the dormitory, Isaac had to endure voluble, but essentially false, declarations of sympathy. Robinson, the student who had come first, was loudest in claiming that he could not understand it, he had not really studied and Isaac deserved it more than he did; besides, Isaac did not waste his time on 'outside' activities! The others laughed and resumed their nightly talk about women, repeating the details of each experience, real or imagined. They were shadow-men, Isaac thought, but their confident virility made them secure. And he had to admit to himself that he envied them.

He left them talking and crept out of the dormitory. He walked the ten miles to Kingston and searched through the alleys and lanes for the woman who had once approached him. This time he made sure to take money with him. But several ships were in port, and only the aged and the worn-out were available. And even they shrank away from the ugly young man with his staring eyes and dragging foot.

The next morning he threw himself into his work and studied as though driven by furies. The groundsman, who often saw him reading under the mango tree when the others had taken their day off, began telling him stories about the students who had gone mad trying to cope with the white man's learning. Early in his second year, he fell ill with pneumonia. The doctors insisted, once he was better, that he return home for a few weeks to convalesce. And he went back to Hebron to find himself even more of a stranger than before.

19. The Rape

The train laboured up the steep gradient to Cockpit Centre. Isaac felt a stir of anticipation. The fifteen months spent away in Kingston, the far journey that he had taken, blurred the outlines of Hebron for him, romanticized its horizons. He convinced himself that, returning home, he would return to the sound of a living language, its rhythms sprung from the earth; he would return to a real people, his people, in whose eyes he could see what he had become, just as they saw themselves mirrored in their land and its seasons: and seeing himself, would see them, and be set free to write without having to share experience vicariously through books written by other peoples, in their language, holding up their images, informed with their rhythms, their words.

But the people of Hebron were disappointed. Isaac was the same. He had not grown any taller than his five feet seven inches; his club-foot had not straightened; his shoulders were still too narrow, his head oversized; his eyes still bulged in his long face. The moustache that he had grown only hardened the lines of his mouth. The learning that they had heard so much about did not show. Perhaps if he had been pompous this would have given them some tangible proof of his wisdom and learning. But his awkward attempts to be one of them only caused them to dismiss him as before.

Miss Gatha and Obadiah met Isaac at the station. They drove up in the cart and went straight to the church. A special service was being held in Isaac's honour. After the hymn of thanksgiving for his safe return, Obadiah, as Elder, welcomed

Isaac and called upon him to tell them about the great world that he had seen outside. Isaac spoke eagerly at first, wanting to reach them. But his eagerness, so out of character, made them suspect that he wanted something of them. What was he coming with now, they thought, and who did he think he was, just because he had gone away to Kingston? They listened to his speech with an amiable lack of interest, and showed their resentment by refusing to admit that he could have changed.

After the service Rose and Obadiah went with Isaac and his mother to the house. Whilst Rose helped Miss Gatha to prepare food, Obadiah asked Isaac questions about Kingston and the college. Isaac knew that he did this partly to make up to him for his failure at the church, and partly because he now had a genuine admiration for his learning. Isaac, like Prophet Moses, had mastered the ability to read and write, to deal with abstract ideas, to treat with the white man in his own language – and for Obadiah this was an achievement, truly to be marvelled at. Although he realized this, Isaac felt a growing irritation, not only with Obadiah's questions but with his very presence. And when they left, Obadiah with Rose, he became more conscious than ever of his own isolation.

They sat on the veranda, his mother in her rocking chair, Isaac in his father's chair with its carved arm-rests. Miss Gatha was always nervous with her son, and this time her nervousness betrayed itself in unusual garrulity. She recounted all that had happened since he left for Kingston some fifteen months before – Obadiah's marriage to Rose and his mad infatuation with her, the hurricane, and the vow he had taken. Not that the vow would be of any use, she was sure: until Isaac came back to guide them with knowledge and wisdom, nothing in Hebron would succeed. But as for Rose and Obadiah, they were well suited. Rose would prove to be Obadiah's downfall, for in her was the bad luck that her mother's sin had left Hebron as a legacy. She had warned Moses about this flaunting of sin in the face of the Lord, and God knew that she had done her best to rear Rose free from her mother's and her grandmother's taint.

But all to no purpose, for what's bred in the bone would come out in the end, and that had already been proved by the sneaking way that Rose had connived with Obadiah under her very roof, right under her nose. She had had no hint that there was anything between them. But they would pay dearly for their treachery, just wait and see!

Isaac felt a touch of pity for this venomous and lonely old woman who was his mother. But her talk about Rose had stirred up his own memories, and he no longer listened. He hadn't liked Rose very much before Maverlyn's death. Rose was older than he was, but he and Maverlyn were born on the same day, and playing with her, she always made him feel that he was stronger than she was. But it was only Rose and Aunt Kate who had believed him that night when he had tried to tell them that Maverlyn was sleeping in the spring. The day after Maverlyn's funeral, he and Rose had planted canna lilies all round her grave. They had flowered prematurely and then died...

Miss Gatha stopped talking and went out to the kitchen to make Isaac some chocolate. He had liked it as a child. She went down the steps and across the yard, her long dress dragging on the moonlit grass. Isaac was alone in the house, and, for the first time since he returned, realized that Rose was no longer what she had been for him, the centre of Hebron. He could hear his mother moving about in the kitchen. Without Rose to interpret as she always did, so unobtrusively, they were like two strangers without a common language. Whenever his mother wanted to scold him or to tell him of her plans for him, she would talk about them to Rose, then Rose would tell him afterwards. If he wanted anything, he would tell Rose, in the presence of his mother. Rose was always the go-between in their indirect relationship. Her presence had eased the friction between his mother and himself. Now that she was gone, they were unsure with each other.

He remembered once when he was about fourteen years old. His mother had not yet returned from a special evening service at the church. He returned from one of his long walks and entered the house. In the stillness he heard Rose breathing in the alcove of the top parlour where she slept. He went up the narrow steps and entered the alcove. Rose lay asleep on a narrow bed in the corner. The moonlight came in through the half-open window and lit up her face and hair. He crouched beside the bed. Strange and frightening thoughts stirred inside him. He stretched out his fingers and touched her lips. She lifted up her hand and brushed his finger away without waking. He felt a sense of utter rejection. He knelt beside the bed, chilled and cold, and watched the moon and the shadows dissolve, as they slipped behind the hills.

****

The days dragged on. The New Believers imprisoned Isaac with the staleness of their jokes and crude witticisms, revolted him with their laughter. In church they laughed behind their hands; their market-day laugh was open to the sun, but the woman-laugh was shrillest of all, annihilating his timorous manhood. And every night he had a nightmare. He was trapped in Hebron, trying desperately to escape; he was running over the hills looking for an opening to the sea; each time he thought that he was free, an opened book, enormous and shaped like iron bars, blocked his way, and printed on the pages was a musical score of the sound of laughter that echoed round him; a voice kept telling him that he would be set free if only he could translate the score of the laughter into exact words before morning; then he would sit writing urgently, his fingers flying over the page, his mind working like lightning. He finished just before the sun pointed over the hills, but when he looked at what he had written it was all gibberish; and in the left-hand corner at the bottom of the page was a drawing of the woman who had approached him in Kingston, her low curved buttocks and high breasts drawn in profile, but her face was the face of Rose.

After his first two weeks in Hebron Isaac had given up trying to write. In the train, with the green stretches of the land spread out before him, he had planned a novel about Hebron: his father's story had returned to him freed from mockery, from the petty interpretation of the unbelievers of Cockpit Centre; freed too, from the ignorant and indiscriminating glorification of the Believers in Hebron. He would write an epic, another *Moby Dick* in which Ahab's search for the white whale would be paralleled by his father's pursuit of a black God. The congregation would be the crew, and Obadiah, Daggoo, the harpooner, 'so broad, baronial and superb a person'; Hugh would be the cook 'who always brought his best ear into play', and he himself, Ishmael, with Rose the symbol of home, the fixed star of his return.

But nothing in Hebron was as he had imagined it. For several days he wrestled with his writing. Then one day he asked himself, 'For whom am I writing? And why?' For a people who could not read, he told himself. And the few who could, so suborned by the false coin of shallow dreams that they would deny Moses and his visions. And to the strangers outside he could only speak across great distances. In order to explain his present he would have to tell them of the submerged past; and in the clamour of their own chauvinistic misconceptions, he himself would be seduced into distortions, and the bare truth that might have spanned the centuries and the differences would vanish, leaving only lost echoes.

Besides, life in Hebron was too loud, too violent, too farcical to trap on paper, except perhaps with the bold outlines of satire. But the people of Hebron were like himself, too spiritually naked; satire would only sweep away the little that they had, replacing it with nothing. He should have come at the end of a tradition and not the beginning, he told himself; his was more a lyric talent than an epic one. And the very bathos inherent in the creation of Hebron would defeat the epic purpose. Under all his excuses, Isaac knew that the failure was his.

Walking past Obadiah's house one afternoon, Isaac dropped in. He sat on the top of the veranda and chatted desultorily. In the lean-to at the side of the house Rose busied herself, preparing a drink of lemonade. Obadiah, naked to the waist, chopped up a tree-trunk into kindling. His dark muscles shone and rippled in the sun. When he was finished he drank the lemonade in deep draughts, then sat with his guest in a companionable silence. Soon Isaac's visits became a daily habit. Some days Rose stood before a wooden tub and scrubbed dirty clothes on a washboard. Her dress rose and fell against the smooth golden skin of her calves. Obadiah and his wife rarely glanced at each other, and yet they were always conscious of each other's presence. Their closeness isolated them from the rest of Hebron, as Isaac himself was isolated. At times he felt non-existent, diffused into these two people, who were his only friends.

Isaac began to tell himself that he only visited the couple to get material for his writing. To bear out his purpose he asked questions about the past in Cockpit Centre. Obadiah answered gladly. But his answers were either bald, bare facts – how many of the New Believers there had been, the date and the hour on which they had set out, the time they had reached Hebron, etc. – or were panegyrics about the greatness of Prophet Moses. If, as sometimes happened, Hugh came over and joined them, he would substitute loud praises for Obadiah and himself.

But one afternoon, when Hugh was absent and Rose sat on the steps with them, shelling corn, she asked her husband questions about his life as a small boy in Cockpit Centre. Isaac found himself absorbed in Obadiah's simple, graphic account of his childhood. The next morning he wrote a short story about Obadiah's running away to Paradise Bay, returning to find his mother dead, and thinking that his whole world had been swept away by the sea. He wrote the story in the first person and his identification with the young boy was complete. The young boy was amalgam, in appearance, of himself and Obadiah. And the young boy's mother looked like Rose. He started off the story by describing her as she looked to the boy. And words came to him new-minted, in their pristine innocence, with all the dross of centuries, the tawdriness and disillusionments, discarded.

He took the story with him to read it aloud to Rose and Obadiah. But on the way it seemed to him that the story would reveal so much of himself that he would never be free of them again. He would be implicated with them in a conspiracy of understanding that, binding him to them, would bind him to Hebron for ever, and to the image that Hebron had made of him. He tore up the story and flung the bits of paper away. He went to see them as he had intended, but all the time his manner was furtive, as if he had committed a crime.

In his last week in Hebron he began staying away from them. He had become afraid. His nights were tormented with dreams. He took long walks, seeking refuge in the thickly wooded hills. His obsession was not only with Rose, but with Rose and Obadiah together. Always, in his dreams, they approached him hand in hand, Obadiah naked to the waist, and Rose dressed like the woman who had accosted him in Kingston, her breasts leaping from the tight dress, her mouth reddened like blood, her breath raw with rum…

This image remained with Isaac, beset him like furies. When in the light of day he felt ashamed and strove to banish it, his life seemed to become absurd and purposeless. He would even find himself standing at the edge of a sheer drop, trying to calculate whether death would be certain, or whether perhaps he might only end up with the inconvenience of a broken leg, as his father had done when he tried to fly to heaven. Then he would start thinking of his father's reputation with women, and this would become justification for his desire. After all, like father like son, and the chip never fell far from the block. Suddenly he felt consumed with an overweening arrogance. All the women of Hebron were his to do with as he willed, as his father had done…

He found himself singing the dirty songs he had learnt as

a boy in Cockpit Centre. He sang and shouted them to the hills and the trees. And the songs dredged up memories of all that he had heard about Rose's birth, about her fourteen-year-old mother and the parson, her grandmother and the Chinese grocer and his father. His knowledge of her past gave him the same sense of dominance that he had felt towards her as a boy, only now it aroused lust instead of pity. As the days passed he expunged from his mind the innocent years when they had been brother and sister, and replaced them with the smell of the sea, of stale urine in a narrow enclosed lane, and a woman's body which had become Rose's, writhing against his.

He drifted through the last days in the grip of an erotic nightmare that drove him to walk miles across the hills, to batter his fists against the rough bark of the tree-trunks. He avoided the New Believers, leaving home early in the mornings and staggering in, late at nights, to sleep. His mother was worried about him. In answer to her anxious inquiry he told her to leave him alone, once and for all, to leave him alone. Confronted with an aspect of her son that she could not understand, she pretended not to see it. He was only a bit overwrought with his studies, she told herself, only a bit overwrought. Still, she was relieved when the day came for his departure. And she would not admit to herself that his manner troubled her, that she had sensed in it a presage of disaster.

****

It was his last night in Hebron, and he sat across the table from his mother. After they had eaten, she had cleared the table, taken the dishes to the kitchen but returned almost at once. She glanced at him from time to time, waiting for him to speak. But she saw that his spirit was as withdrawn from her as it had always been. His face, under the lamplight, seemed strange to her. The lines were harsh, his chin stubbled with spiky black hairs. She had not noticed before how thin he had grown. They sat on in silence. When she could bear it no longer, Miss Gatha told him of the money that his father had left for him, of the large sum that she, by dint of great frugality, had added to it; told him where she kept it buried, six paces to the right of the single hibiscus plant that grew in the churchyard. She had wanted to win some gesture of approval from him. But he only nodded when she had finished, his face unmoved; and in his heart there was a contempt for her sudden weakness in giving away her secret, her only power over him.

He waited until she began to nod, and as she slept, dreaming her dreams for him, he went out to the kitchen, hoisted the spade over his shoulder, and climbed up to the churchyard. As he had expected, she had buried the box deep in the ground. It was some time before the spade rang against it. After he had pulled out the money-box, he shoveled the loose earth back into the hole, and carefully patted it down. Then he cleaned off the spade and replaced it.

At first he was afraid to open the box. He walked with it several miles before he realized that he was on the track leading away from Hebron and down to Cockpit Centre. For a moment he was tempted to continue, not to return. But his habit of caution prompted him to make sure that the money was there, to ensure his escape. He sat down on the verging grass under a mango tree, and felt for the penknife in his back pocket. His glance fell down the track to the rough post which marked three more miles to Hebron. Seated on the ground with her head resting against the post, Rose was fast asleep. The skirt of her dress had shuffled up above her knee; and a healed scar on her leg shone like a bright coin under the moon.

He stood up, forgetting the box, and walked towards her. A mass of clouds drifted across the moon and Isaac stumbled in the sudden darkness. He thought of Obadiah picking him up when, as a child, he had chased his kite, fallen over, and lain helpless. Obadiah was a fool, he exulted. It was his godfather's stupidity that made him kind, made him trustful, had caused him to take such a vow. Now Rose was like a field left to lie fallow under the sun, a ripe fruit to be plucked by him, Isaac. Soon he would be free of Hebron, would be able to leave it for ever. He was powerful with a certainty he had never known since the night that he had first seen the sea.

Rose heard his dragging footsteps and woke up. As he fell upon her she cried out his name with unbelief. Her body writhed under him as she struggled to break free. Savagely, he forced her elbows behind her back, straddled his legs across hers, imprisoned her thighs. She called out to him again and again but her voice was drowned in the sound of the sea that thundered inside his head. He hardly realized it when she stopped struggling and lay still, her breasts taut in the hunger of his hand, her body arched to his.

It was over. He lay face downwards, his fingers clutching at the grass. He heard Rose's footsteps as she ran hurriedly up the slope, heard her weeping. He wanted to stand up and call out his name to her, to reassure himself as to who he was. For, impersonal like the sea, she had taken him, then left him a castaway, without purpose, without being.

He got up and returned to where he had left the box. He did not wait to open it. Now there was urgency in him to abandon this place, to return to Hebron in search of something he had lost.

****

The moonlight spread out on the ground like white starch. There had been showers that afternoon, and all around Aunt Kate could smell the freshness and the fullness of the land. She sat beside the spring humming her lullaby and rocking from side to side. She had woken up that night to hear Maverlyn calling her name. She had waited until it was late and Hebron asleep, then made her way down to the square.

As she watched, the blue shadows cast by the trees drifted together like the movements of a dance. A wind stirred through the leaves. Then she heard the footsteps, hurried and imperative.

Aunt Kate remained still, merging with the night.

The long trousers deceived her for a moment. She saw him put down the box he was carrying, stretch himself on the ground, scoop up water from the spring and drink thirstily. She could see his face clearly now. She leaned towards him from the other side of the spring, and whispered his name. He looked at her without surprise, drew himself up to a kneeling position, and shook his hands to dry them. His quietness assailed Aunt Kate like a rush of wind on a hot and parching day. She made conversation like one scattering the seeds of bright flowers on a waste land:

'Long time now that Maverlyn and me don't bless our eyes with sight of you, Isaac,' she said. 'Not since you go away to Kingston and turn a grown man wearing long trousers...'

He took a penknife from his pocket and prised at the lid of the box. The box was made of tin and painted black. But the paint was smudged with a green mould in some places, and in others was erased. It looked like something evil, like a poisonous plant, Aunt Kate thought. As Isaac worked, trying to break the lock, filings of rust and paint fell on the grass like a stain.

'What's that old box, Isaac?' Aunt Kate asked.

The lock snapped open, he pulled back the lid and drew out a denim bag. When he pulled the string of the bag, and turned it upside down, a stream of coins – sixpenny bits, shillings, and florins – piled up in a heap on the grass. Aunt Kate looked hurriedly in the spring to see if the clatter had disturbed Maverlyn. But Maverlyn slept peacefully, her black hair spread out in the water and tangled with moonlight.

'Where you get all that money, Isaac?' Aunt Kate asked curiously. 'What you going to do with it, boy?'

He picked up a shilling and bit it, testing it between his teeth. Then he arranged the coins in neat piles, counting them as he did so. Aunt Kate found her lips moving with his. Half-way through, he broke off and sat still. She started humming her lullaby once again. Then abruptly he asked her:

'You ever see the sea, Aunt Kate?'

'The sea, Isaac?'

For a moment her mind became confused and Isaac's face was the face of Moses when they had cut him down from the cross on Easter Sunday morning, his eyes surprised by death. She glanced down at Maverlyn asleep in the spring, cradled her arms and rocked from side to side, her lips moving to the words of her lullaby. This was her sign of the Cross to avert the evil eye. Isaac saw that she had gone away from him and was as distant as the hills. It seemed to him that in her very remoteness he might find absolution. Shut away in her fantasy she was like a priest in a cassock, apart from other men, could not judge him in their name. He leaned towards her:

'Aunt Kate,' he called.

'Yes, Isaac, yes me son,' she answered absent-mindedly.

'Tonight, Aunt Kate, the moonlight was peeling off the banana leaf same way as from off the sea. The mango trees downside the hill were like ships waiting to slip away to sea. I could see the road and the rockstone shining on it. And Rose sleeping on the banking, her lips bright like a machete edge. I wanted to touch her lips with the tip of one finger, just to touch them...'

He stretched out his hand, spreading his fingers. In the moonlight they were grey, as if the flesh was melting away from the bone. Aunt Kate moved her head uneasily, avoiding his glance. She did not want to relate his words to the meaning that was struggling to the surface of her mind.

'Then a black cloud tore moonlight from off the road and the dark beneath the mango tree crept quiet with me until her breasts were ripening in the hollow of my hand...She was fighting me for a while, was fighting me...'

Aunt Kate looked away from his eyes. The pupils were like needles of light in drowned spaces of night.

'Then all of a sudden she was like a coconut branch arching up to the sky...And when she got up and ran, I wanted to shout it out to her that it was me, Isaac, me... Isaac...me...'

He pounded his clenched fists on the grass and his voice rose.

'Quiet, Isaac, remember Maverlyn!' Aunt Kate warned him.

'Maverlyn dead, Aunt Kate, Maverlyn drowned dead!' he shouted at her.

Aunt Kate peered at his face, saw it beaded with sweat, distorted and ugly.

'Your face turn stranger-face to me, Isaac. Your face is a dark place,' she said. Then she folded her hands in her lap and rocked to and fro, hushing Maverlyn.

'But I didn't shout out that it was me, Aunt Kate, I didn't shout it out,' Isaac pleaded.

She ignored his words like the passing wind. He pretended to believe once more:

'See, Aunt Kate, Maverlyn is all right, is sleeping sound now.'

Aunt Kate did not stop her rocking as she judged him in the name of Hebron:

'You have a long journey tomorrow, Isaac. You better go and rest yourself.'

As Isaac got up to go she reminded him:

'You are forgetting your money!'

He took a red handkerchief from his pocket and gathered up the coins in it, knotting the four corners. Then he took the empty money-box over to the hollow of the cotton-tree stump. He pulled away the covering of moss and vines and pushed the box far inside with the lime that was a ball and the boot specially built for his club-foot. He turned to Aunt Kate, hesitated, then said:

'I am leaving now, Aunt Kate.'

Still rocking, Aunt Kate answered with the courtesy due to a stranger:

'Walk good,' she said.

Aunt Kate gathered Maverlyn close against her with a fierce exultation. Above all other women the Lord had blessed her, to keep Maverlyn there safe and sleeping in the spring, always the same, always near, whilst other mothers' children grew up or died or went away, like Isaac, on long separate journeys of the soul. She sang her lullaby aloud to the listening hills.

Isaac heard her singing and knew that she had forgotten him already, that in the morning, if she remembered him, it would be with the vagueness of an indistinct dream. And knew that, walking away from her, he was walking away from the land and the people whose reflected image of him had shaped his dreams, fashioned the self that he would now go in search of, to be swept away into the wide indifference of the sea.

Part 4

THE MORNING

With every people, at every period of its existence, the end of the whole national movement is only the search for God, of a God for it, in whom it may believe as the one true God. God is the synthetic personality of a whole people considered from its origins until its end.

-Dostoevsky: The Possessed

20. The Return

Aunt Kate woke up from the past. Night had fallen. The moon sculptured shadows on the barren face of the land. She pulled the hessian sack round her shoulders, felt its coarse weave rustling against her bones. She was afraid. Where were the others? Why had they not returned? Surely they knew by now that Isaac was never coming back? Had they, too, decided not to return, to leave her alone, an old woman sitting in an empty square, dreaming her life away? She looked at the tin mug beside her. It was empty. She took it and upended it. A single drop of water trickled into the dry soil, was quickly absorbed…'like water spilt on the ground and never to be gathered up…!' Where had she heard that? It must have come from the Bible. Everything came from the Bible.

She tried to remember when she had eaten and drunk that day, but couldn't; yet the bread was gone and the water. And she felt neither hunger nor thirst, only a cold chill that made her shiver from time to time. Was she already dead then, and a ghost? She heard a sound of voices calling her name, felt hands reaching towards her, withered hands. Was this the end of her, and of Hebron? She struggled to get up but felt herself pinioned. Then she laughed aloud. The voices and the hands were nothing more than the breeze stirring in the leaves, coming as always to taunt the land with hope in a dry time.

From farther down the hill the dispirited singing of the returning congregation reached Aunt Kate. She put her hands over her ears to shut out this mourning song for Hebron. Then she drew them away and stood up slowly. Perhaps it was right that Hebron should die. Hebron had sinned, had worshipped death and enshrined it, as she had done with Maverlyn. And made it necessary for Isaac to prove himself alive, to prove himself against them.

She walked over to the cotton-tree stump whose hollow lay revealed in the bareness of the drought. She thrust in her hand to draw out the empty money-box. As she groped for it in the dark depths she heard a sharp cry and looked up. On the narrow track, up beside the church, Rose crouched, her body doubled over, her shadow contorted in the moonlight:

'Aunt Kate,' she called, 'the baby...the baby!'

Aunt Kate hurried up the track. She had forgotten the past, left it buried in the hollow of the tree-trunk. For the future now called to her, insisting that her place was with the living; that always there would be Hebrons, all kinds and conditions of them, always there would be men, always there would be visions.

'I am coming, Rose,' she called back. 'Hold on. I am coming.'

****

Their return to Hebron was instinctive, bewildered animals to their lair. Miss Gatha no longer led them, but walked apart, separate not only from them but from their hopes and fears. Isaac was not coming back. Her mind could not reach beyond this. Only Brother Hugh seemed to retain some habit of authority, and the others gradually turned to him for direction.

When the afternoon train had arrived and departed, and the evening train, it was he who suggested that they go to the post office to find out if there was a letter. He woke up the postmistress and persuaded her to read the letter. It had a foreign stamp and had arrived two days ago, she explained. The letter was brief: Isaac wrote saying that he had taken the money and gone away, that he was sorry, that he thanked his mother for all that she had done for him.

The postmistress folded the paper, replaced it in the envelope and gave it to Miss Gatha, who held out her hand for it. She watched as the old woman stared dumbly at the stamp, at her own name printed in block letters which she could not read, as she tested the fineness of the paper between her fingers. And sensing some tragedy, the postmistress became brusque. She was breaking the rules to give them a letter at this time of night, she would be sure to get into trouble; now that she was due for retirement, she didn't want to take risks, so they had better hurry up and leave, she had to get her sleep, unlike them she had to work for a living. Without her false teeth her face was defenceless, her mouth petulant. She hated reading letters for poor people. They always told of bad news.

The eleven miles had never seemed as long. They took it in turns to ride in the cart. But Miss Gatha shook her head whenever her turn came, and trudged steadily on. Once Brother Hugh had stopped them all and shared out sparse portions of water from the single tin which they had brought. Miss Gatha refused to drink. They continued on their way. The moon came up. The sky was encrusted with a jubilation of stars. But no one looked up. The night mocked their hopelessness.

Sister Beatrice started up the singing. They all sang 'Onward Christian soldiers'. Only Miss Gatha was silent. Their voices rose in a passion of grief. Grief was what they knew about. Two generations of life in Hebron, of Moses and hope and a God who regarded them as Chosen and peculiar to Him had not erased three centuries of placelessness. They returned almost with abandon to the familiar despair, more comforting than hope. Their lamentations darkened the sky, menacing, like a swarm of locust.

****

Several miles behind them Obadiah, too, returned. On his back he carried a large hamper loaded with food and water. He walked effortlessly, untiringly, and thought of the journey he had taken away from Hebron and back, the journey that had begun in those first, blind, groping days when his body had been muddled, and had become a house of dreams.

****

Early that morning, after Obadiah, searching for the adulterer, had found himself and returned to Rose, he left her asleep in the hut and went down to the house that they had lived in before. Patches of mist still hovered on the high slopes. The first grey morning light was spreading across the sky. The congregation of Hebron stirred in their beds, and a cock crew. Obadiah walked in through the opening in the bamboo fence that served as a gate. He had built the fence after the hurricane. The long stalks of sunflowers crackled under his feet as he went up the path that Rose had marked out with stones. He crossed the narrow veranda. The boards were dry and warped. In the long room, which he had partitioned into two, the air was sour.

He took up the wooden box in which he kept the carpenter's tools, and stood looking round him. He had built their bed in the corner where it formed a sort of alcove. Behind the bed Rose had plastered the wall with pictures torn from old magazines which he had brought back from Cockpit Centre. Across the bold black type a smudge of oil from Rose's hair had left a stain. Except for the stain there was nothing in the house now that reminded him that they had once lived there. The hut, high on the hill, was now their home. This house held the reminiscences of two people who had vanished.

He went back up the hill and left his tools under the dividivi tree outside his hut. Then, carrying his axe, he climbed high up the slopes as the sun rose behind the hills. After an hour's search he found a bird's nest. It was high up on a silk-cotton tree whose trunk was prickly with thorns. He scratched himself several times. There were four small eggs in the nest. He sucked one, pricking it with a thorn. It was still warm. The bird must have left only a few minutes before. He wrapped the others carefully in leaves and kept them for Rose. He had already selected the tree that he wanted and now he hewed at it, swinging his axe with an easy rhythm. As he worked, he sought for a reason for the grass that lived and died, for hurricanes and droughts that outraged the land, for the briefness of the life of a man, for Hebron, its meaning and purpose; for the long years of his blindness in which he had slept, and eaten, and made gestures of belief, unthinking, unquestioning.

He trimmed away the branches, then stripped the tree-trunk of its bark. He took the eggs for Rose, then returned with his saw. He chose several planks and carried them down to the hut. Rose sat outside sewing clothes for the baby which she had cut out from a white calico sheet. During his absence she, too, had gone down to their former house. She had waited until she had seen the congregation all entering the church, and then had slipped past. Obadiah cut the wood and planed it to make a cradle. But in the early afternoon he put the work aside. He wanted to save his strength. In the cool of the evening he planned to leave for Cockpit Centre. The next morning he would seek work there, bring back food and water for Rose.

But as he sat waiting, he took up a fragment of wood and carved idly, thinking of making a toy for the child. Then as he shaped the rough outlines of a doll, he began to concentrate. For the first time in his life he created consciously, trying to embody in his carving his new awareness of himself and of Hebron. When he had finished he put the doll in his pocket, and left Hebron as twilight settled into the hollow spaces between the hills. He took the short cut down the hill-side that by-passed the church. From time to time he touched the doll as if it were a fetish. For, in carving the doll, Obadiah had stumbled upon God.

21. *The Journey*

Obadiah walked down the main street of Cockpit Centre towards the railway station. It was late at night and his footsteps echoed in the sleeping town. A line of barking dogs rushed out at him, snapped at his heels. His indifference discouraged them, and they crept back to their lairs. He sat on the steps of the station, tried to settle down for the night. Everywhere he looked he was encircled by shuttered buildings and, behind them, the hills. The town was sealed off as it had been when he left it twenty years before. Nothing had changed; if there was no work then, there would be none now. He got up and turned into the road leading down to Paradise Bay.

He arrived just before daybreak and went towards the sea. He crossed a stretch of white sand and came upon an abandoned boat, paint peeling off its warped sides. Then he sat down and watched the sun rise out of the sea. In Hebron, the sky was cooped up between the hills, like the New Believers. When he was there it was hard to remember that there were other places on which the same sun shone. Now he tried to imagine what the other places were like, the other countries, the other men who lived in lands that the sun and the sea encompassed. Three fishing boats had put out to sea. He waited until they were swallowed up by the distance, then returned to the centre of town.

A murmuring of many voices drew him on until he was engulfed in the noise and movement. On the pavement, in front of a tall wooden building, men and women jostled each other impatiently. The sign above the building read LABOUR

OFFICE. The large double doors were closed. And all along the street, on the opposite pavement, people waited, hundreds of them, crowding the streets, parting from time to time to allow a cart or a truck to pass through, then closing ranks once more. They were waiting for relief work on the roads as they waited every day except Sundays. Once or twice a week there might be work. For some fifty of them. But the others stood by hopefully. Some had waited so long that they seemed to have sunk roots into the streets and pavements. They lounged against walls, remnants of straw hats or cloth caps tilted over their eyes, hands folded across their sunken chests, their patched trousers held up at the waist with discoloured rags or fraying neckties; they looked like some strange fungi which crept out to a brief life with the sun, then vanished at nightfall.

Their faces were hostile when Obadiah joined them. He was a stranger. From their own need they divined his own, and resented him for having increased the odds against them. The women in particular eyed him sullenly. They stood about in small groups, arms akimbo, their pent-up anger like balls of unquenchable fire in their bellies. When the doors of the Labour Office were opened they forgot about him.

Two burly policemen came out and stationed themselves on either side of the double doors. They swung their batons casually and wore guns. The crowd eyed them guardedly. Faces became smoothed over with a mask of subservience. They looked through the open doors to where the Labour Officer, an elderly, dark-brown man with greying hair and gold-rimmed glasses, emerged from behind his desk as though from behind a barricade. He took up a sheaf of papers and walked to the door. He looked frail and insubstantial between the two policemen. He glanced nervously at the crowd. Their eyes were fixed on the papers.

Obadiah shared the rising excitement. The words on the paper might mean food and water for himself and Rose. The Officer adjusted his glasses and held up the papers a little away from him. A hush fell on the crowd. The Officer cleared his throat. Obadiah, too, waited as if for the voice of God. But the formal phrases made little sense to him. He looked at the faces of the others and tried to glean a meaning from their reaction. But they too were seeking through the morass of sentences, the confusion of clauses, for a word that could be seized upon. An angry muttering threaded its way through the crowd.

The Officer paused, shuffled the papers, glanced to the right and left of him; and was reassured by the stalwart chests that flanked him, the white tunics, the highly polished silver buttons blazing in the sun; the black hands poised on the holsters of guns, the two black faces, stiff and martial, unreasoning in their defence of law and order. The Officer forgot his fears of the ragged crowd. He deepened his voice to do justice to the formality of the language, the occasion. And felt himself a proconsul, dealing with his subjects.

His Majesty's Government, he read, assured His Majesty's loyal subjects that their just complaints and grievances had not gone unnoticed, etc. etc.…His Majesty's Government had now appointed and sent out to His Majesty's loyal colony and oversea island possession, a Royal Commission which was duly to inquire into the conditions and causes leading to the recent riots and labour disturbances, etc. etc., and make recommendations to ensure the betterment of the aforesaid conditions. His Majesty's Government therefore required that every facility should be extended to his Commissioners for the amassing of information without let or hindrance, and that the appointment of the Commission should be proclaimed throughout the island. Given under His Majesty's hand etc…etc.

Disbelief held the crowd silent. They had come to ask for jobs. The man had given them words. They wanted bread. Once again, they were to be put off with promises. The Officer took their silence for applause, nodded and turned away. Obadiah was swept up the steps. His hands made part of a kaleidoscope that blurred the air, part of a single body propelled by anger. Hands snatched and struck out at the man whose words had tried their impotence too far. The two policemen used their batons freely. The crowd hurled abuse at them. The unintelligible screams coalesced into a war chant:

'What the hell they think it is at all, at all! Work we want, food. To hell with Commission. Lick him, tear him up! Tear up the paper. Mash up the place, break up the whole place…!'

The Officer slipped and fell on the steps. The moving walls of a dark vortex closed in on him. His hands were crossed over his face and he kicked out feebly. Hands tore at his face. His glasses were snatched off. He screamed with all his strength:

'Fire, for God's sake! What you waiting for – fire!'

For a moment the policemen hesitated. They were ringed with faces like their own, faces that they recognized. This one they had arrested some time before for obscene language, that one for being drunk and disorderly, that woman they had slept with, that one was the daughter of a cousin of the policeman's father, many of them they had gone to school with, and it was only by good luck that they were not down there struggling beside them now, only by the grace of God that they had a uniform which redeemed them from the common misery. But the crowd surged against the building like the sea. There was no time for the policemen to take aim. They fired into the belly of the crowd. The guns barked again and again. The crowd was now an obstacle to be removed. The eyes of the policemen were narrow and intent, their lips creased together as they concentrated on their task. The sound of the shots, the yells of fear and anger, the screams of pain became a frenzied orgasm that broke as the multitude started to shift, to back away, to run. The bullets split them into sections, each section disappearing into lanes and alley-ways, behind buildings, anywhere to be out of reach of a swift and eyeless death, to escape the noise, the stench of blood.

Obadiah found himself running with the others, bottled up in a narrow back street. A man stumbled and fell in front of him and he hauled him to his feet. Suddenly he remembered having seen bodies dislodge themselves from the mass and fall like tree-trunks in a high wind. He grabbed at a lamp-post, gripped it with both hands and clung to it whilst the others streamed past him. Stragglers milled about him, then filtered away. Then he ran up the lane. He would go back and help those who had fallen, as he would have done up in Hebron.

He came to where the lane intersected the main street. He slowed down to a walk. The space in front of the Labour Office was as peaceful as a Sunday morning. The Officer sat on the step, his head hanging, dazed. One of the policemen bent over and picked up his glasses, handed them to him. One lens was intact, but the other was broken and the sun shone on the shattered lines of glass. The Officer put on the glasses, blinked, took them off again and peered about him.

Five bodies were lying on the ground. Their shadows were hard and bright in the sun. Three men and two women. They looked like crumpled rag-dolls. The trousers of one of the men, a boy of seventeen, had slipped down. His naked buttocks were like black marble. An old woman, whose sex and race seemed indeterminate, went from body to body, turning the faces, searching for her particular grief. But the faces were all the same. They were all dead faces. She crossed the street, sat on the opposite pavement, rocked to and fro and mourned for them all.

The two policemen stood about nervously, clutching their batons. Then one stooped and started collecting the trampled sheets of paper that lay scattered about. The papers were flecked with blood. The other policeman looked up at the windows where cautious faces gazed from behind shutters. A few flies buzzed over the dark circles of blood that oozed into cracks on the concrete pavement.

There was a screech of tyres and a police car drove past Obadiah, followed by an ambulance. When the car stopped, a policeman jumped out from behind the driver's seat, opened the back door and saluted smartly. The superintendent of police, a man in his early thirties and dressed in khaki shirt and shorts, stepped out. He held his peaked cap under his arm and the sun glinted on his blond hair. He went up to the bodies and stood looking at them, tapping his cane against his long ribbed socks. The stretcher-bearers came up behind and waited. The superintendent narrowed his grey eyes against the glare, then looked round him as if to pinpoint the reason for the dead bodies lying on the pavement. Only respectable faces looked back at him from verandas and balconies and windows. There was no sign of the violence that had demanded this sacrifice. The morning air was innocent. The blood dried in the sun, and its scent rose up like incense.

The superintendent gestured to the stretcher-bearers to carry on, and nodded to the policemen who remained saluting, half relieved, half fearful of his presence. He went over to the Labour Officer and they entered the building. The door closed behind them. The policemen helped the ambulance crew with extra efficiency, rebuilding for themselves their image as public servants. When the bodies were all in the ambulance and the door closed, the two took off their caps in embarrassed homage. From behind the building a gardener came with a hose and washed down the pavement. The water ran off sluggishly, tinted pink. There was nothing that Obadiah could do. Those who had fallen, had died. He spat and looked away.

He turned down the lane and wandered through streets that were almost deserted. The shops were bolted and shuttered in case the mob should avenge the deaths by destroying property. Here and there groups of men stood about, hands in pockets, their mood grim. An undertone of violence had spread through the town, bringing in its wake a muted fear. There would be no work for him today, Obadiah thought, no work for anyone. The five dead bodies had reached out to claim this day for themselves.

A woman with a baby in her arms passed, and for no particular reason Obadiah followed her. Her bare feet slapped against the asphalt. She turned into a narrow unpaved alley. At the end of this alley he found himself in the market-place.

No one bought or sold. The middle-class shoppers had melted away at the first rumours of trouble. The venders had packed their fruits and vegetables and ground provisions into baskets and hampers, and sat beside them waiting for the storm to blow over so that the pattern of their lives could be re-established. The smell of fruit reminded Obadiah of his hunger. He went over to an old woman who sat beside a basket of mangoes. She sat a little away from the others, her eyes half-closed. She reminded Obadiah of Aunt Kate and made it easier for him to approach her. He stooped beside her. As his shadow fell on her she opened her eyes, and looked at him without surprise.

'I am hungry,' Obadiah said.

She looked at his lips, at the cracked corners.

'You want a mango?' she asked.

Obadiah nodded.

'You have money to pay for it?'

He shook his head. She looked at him, measuring him. Carefully she picked out a mango from the bottom of the basket and handed it to him.

He sat down beside her. She watched him tear into the over-ripe fruit, then hesitate. His tongue flicked out to trap the yellow juice that trickled down his chin. Then he picked up a piece of dried banana-leaf from the trash on the ground, and wrapped the remainder of the mango. He answered the inquiry in her eyes.

'I am taking this for my wife. She's going to have a baby.'

She sorted out three more mangoes and gave them to him.

'Take these for her.'

Obadiah felt for the wooden doll in his pocket and held it out to her. She looked at it indifferently, then shook her head:

'What I am to do with a dolly? One son I had to my name, and he didn't bless my old age with a grandchild. Only wander all over the world to where the earth end, searching for what I can't tell, only finding trouble to bring back to me, and his sick and dying self. So what I am to do with a dolly?'

She stood up abruptly, her face clouded with anger, hoisted the basket of mangoes on her head, and walked away.

A group of men who squatted behind Obadiah and who had been arguing fiercely about the morning's massacre, looked after her as she went.

'That's Bellow's mother,' one of them, an elderly one, said. 'If he had been alive today, things wouldn't have gone the way they went this morning, I can tell you that!'

'Who is Bellows?' a young man asked.

The elderly man turned to the others:

'You hear that? Who is Bellows, the man ask. Man, who you think it was that organized that wave of strikes way back in nineteen twenty? Who you think it was but Bellows? And if they hadn't hounded him down, man, by today we would have taken over this island already. But they arrested him in Cockpit Centre, trumped up a charge against him that he was inciting people to riot. Then they locked him away in jail for five years so that they could break up all the trade unions that he started. Without him, the rest of us just went to pieces. When they let him out at last, the police watched him day and night. So we advised him to go away until things got easier. We heard news about him in foreign places, in England, Russia, Africa. Then, at last, three years back, he came home. I went with some others to meet the boat that he came on. The police were right there with us. But he talked to them pleasant, gave them cigarettes, even packets of sweets to take home for their children, called them his brothers. And man, those very police fixed things so that Bellows could go about his business in peace. They told the English superintendent that Bellows had clamed down, wasn't any trouble any more. He and those policemen became the best of friends. You had to convert people, Bellows used to say, not kill them. For when you came right down to it, a man was only as much as his neighbour, as much as his love. We were going to work things different this time, he said, were going to start from the grass roots, form study-groups, teach the people, go slowly, one step at a time, make them ready to demand changes for themselves. And it didn't matter that they couldn't read or write. There wasn't anything that couldn't be put simply enough for them to understand. We would start right away, the next day, Bellows said. But we could all see that death was on him. He had cancer, man, in his throat. Soon he couldn't even talk. And here in the island he couldn't get the proper treatment. He could have gone away, we all scraped up the money for his fare, people used to come and leave food and pennies and halfpennies outside his door. But when he was ready to leave the Passport Office wouldn't renew his passport. Direct order from the Governor, they told us. Bellows died. Since then there hasn't been anyone else like him. He was an…innocent man. He had no hate in his heart. Only love. And besides, he had a plan!'

They were quiet for a while, then started up again on the subject of the 'Governor'. He fancied himself as a 'strong man', and they would have to 'fix him'. The trouble with the black man was that he was too ready to forgive and forget. Look at the white man, how powerful he was, and why do you think that was? Because he wasn't afraid to kill. The black man would have to learn how to kill. Things weren't going to be the same as this morning with the white Governor up in Kingston pulling strings and black people getting killed. One day, they would get guns too, would learn to kill as efficiently as the white man. They would no longer have to kill with a machete, one man at a time and face to face. With guns they would kill from a distance and by the dozen. Look at what happened in Haiti when the black man had guns. They killed all the white people, defeated the French and British armies, became emperors. So let the Governor look out, it could happen here as well. Let the white people look out! And the brown ones and the black ones who joined with the white rulers against their own kind. The day of reckoning would come, the day of blood!

'Killing isn't the answer,' the elderly man insisted. 'What we need is a plan!'

'And besides, colour don't really come into it,' the young man argued. 'When you talk the colour line you play right into their hands. It's what a man believe, not what he is. You have black men in the Legislative Council today who would massacre all the black people in this is island, if the Governor invited them to dinner and gave them a "Sir". And anyway, who is taking up our cause and risking his neck for us today? Fernandez! And Fernandez is a brown man!'

'Fernandez don't have a plan,' the elderly man objected. 'Without a plan he can only go so far and no farther. Besides, he only knows what he is against, but not what he is for!'

'Well, what about Harvey then? Look how educated he is. You can't say that he doesn't have a plan?'

'No. I am not saying that. But Harvey put too much distance between himself and his own people. And Bellows used to say that a leader had to come out of the same earth as his own people, have their fears and their dreams, so that the plans he would make for them, could be the right ones. That's what Bellows used to say. Bellows was never wrong.'

'But Bellows is dead,' the young man said.

One of the men who had sat silent, his mass of black hair and beard like a screen out of which he regarded the others with contempt, suddenly flung a question:

'And what about Marcus Garvey? What about the Emperor Haile Selassie, the Conquering Lion of Judah, the Ras, the Negus, the Black Jesus, what about him?'

'Yes, what about him?' the young man challenged. The others picked up the refrain and flung it at the bearded man with derision. But the elderly man gestured to them to be silent. He sensed that the other was under the influence of marijuana and could be dangerous. And dangling from his waist was a machete. He stood up now and spread his arms wide. The beard reached half-way down his chest. His hair was braided in a multitude of small plaits. The curling hairs on his forehead had been turned a rusty red in the sun. His ears were pointed backwards as though listening to some inner voice.

The pupils of his eyes were filmed with a red haze and did not focus on anyone in particular.

In a high-pitched voice he gave a long diatribe against everyone whom they had praised. You couldn't trust anyone, he insisted. That morning five black people had been killed. Who killed them? The Governor? Who advised the Governor? The white men, the brown men, the big fat rich black men. There was only one answer. They should band together and follow Marcus Garvey, back to Africa, back to Ethiopia, to the Emperor Haile Selassie. Where black men could live in peace and dignity under the shadow of his throne. Until they did that, God would punish them again for their sin of remaining in a heathen foreign land. So down with Fernandez, with Harvey, with Bellows, the thing for all black men to do was to go back to Africa. And nobody was going to tell him anything different, not a thing different, not a thing!

He looked threateningly at them and then started to sing. As he sang he wandered away from them, crossing the market at a zigzag. His voice was an unsteady tenor:

'Ethiopia awaken and hear Thy children's cry,' he sang. He stopped, turned, and flung back at the group:

Some day we'll know thy story
And drink the cup of mirth
Revive thy ancient glory
And bring the gods to earth.

He turned down the road leading towards the sea. His voice was loud now, challenging the entire town, his step defiant, his head flung back:

Oh bright and glorious country
From where the sons of God
Were called to foreign boundaries
To bear the chastening rod,
Torn from thy blessed shelter
We too have suffered long…

The police van came from the direction of the sea. It stopped; two policemen leapt out from the front seat, grabbed hold of the bearded man and struggled to put handcuffs on his wrists. A crowd gathered in the market and watched as they struggled with the fighting, kicking man. Finally they managed to shove him into the van and slam the door. They drove up towards the market square. In a matter of seconds the men who had been sitting together drifted away. Some pushed handcarts busily to and fro, others leaned against the stalls and iron railings as if they had never moved from there all day. The police van entered the market and drove around. The policemen looked suspiciously from face to face. But the men in the market knew that the police were in an 'arresting mood'; none gave cause for complaint. The lips of the women tightened, holding back the abuse they wanted to shout whenever the van knocked a basket out of the way.

Obadiah remained seated quietly. One of the policemen glanced at him on the first time round. The second time the van stopped and one of them came out. He was a middle-aged man with a heavy complacent face, a corporal. He put his hand in the collar of Obadiah's shirt and pulled him to his feet. Standing, Obadiah was several inches taller than the corporal.

'Where you come from?' he asked roughly. 'I never see your face before! Is send they send you down from Kingston to make trouble?'

Obadiah did not understand at first. The corporal tapped him on the shoulder with the baton.

'If I have to ask you one more time you can answer the judge tomorrow. Where the hell you comc from?'

'From Hebron.'

'Hebron? Where in the hell is that?'

'Up in the hills. After you pass Cockpit Centre.'

'Hebron. You don't mean the place where the madman Moses crucify himself?'

'Yes. That is Hebron. Where I come from.'

The corporal stared at him with disbelief. Then he let

him go, pushed back his cap and scratched his head. Suddenly he was aware of all the eyes in the market mocking him covertly. They wanted to see how he would handle this situation. He straightened his cap, drew himself up and spoke sternly:

'Well you better get going back up there. If it's more madness you come to bring here we have enough already. And we know how to deal with it.'

He walked back to the van, got in and slammed the door after him. Somehow he felt that he had been made to look ridiculous. He turned to the policeman who sat in the driver's seat:

'Well, what the hell you waiting for, Forbes? Christmas?'

The van swept out of the market. Through the high barred window in the back, Obadiah saw the bearded man kneeling with his head thrown back, chanting with fervour:

Ethiopia, awaken and hear thy children's cry,
Ethiopia now is free, our cry rings o'er the land,
Ethiopia awaken, the morning is at hand!

The sound of the chanting and of the police van died away. One of the men who sat propped against his hand-cart, his cap over his eyes, lifted his cap for a few seconds, laughed raucously and said:

'The poor fool! He don't even know that Mussolini beat the hell out of the Conquering Lion of Judah and not even there the black man is free!'

Everyone looked at him. They felt that he had committed an indiscretion, rubbed salt in a deep and incurable wound. The man adjusted his cap once more over his eyes and dozed off in the afternoon sun.

One by one the venders, who had been waiting to see if trade would pick up, decided to cut their losses and leave. Some of them muttered that the day had begun badly, anyway, with terrible auguries: this woman swore she had stumbled with her left foot, that one that she had dropped her comb and hadn't stepped on it, another declared that all night, all morning, her right eyelid had been jumping, so she should have known and stayed at home, not wasted all day coming to the market, only to return with her provisions unsold, her yams, her peppers, her bananas, not a penny to take back with her, what a day, what a black black Tuesday!

They streamed out of the market, bundles balanced on their heads, hands gesturing their eloquent anger and disappointment. Obadiah sat under the roof of a stall. He would wait for the twilight to return to Hebron. That way he could hoard his strength. The next evening he would return to try again, in Paradise Bay, in Kingston, even farther. Now distance held no terrors for him. He was prepared to go to the end of all the earth in search of work. He had learnt that morning that the same anguish was common to all men. And the same vision, expressed in different ways. Without vision, a people shall perish, Moses had said; and after he died Hebron declined into ordinariness. Aloysius, frightened of leaving the small enclosures of reality, had willed himself to die. And he, Obadiah, had been like a man struck blind, and was only now beginning to see.

He slept, and waking up, raised his hand to shield his eyes from the glare. For a moment he was gripped with an unreasoning terror. Coming towards him out of the bright afternoon light he thought he saw the white God that Moses had seen in his last desperate moments on the cross, the God that had punished Moses with death for his presumption. Then his fear gave way to anger. He would avenge Moses. He stretched out his hand and felt for the wooden doll he had carved. It lay on the ground beside the three mangoes that the old woman had given him for Rose. His fingers closed round it. He stood up slowly and drew himself to his full height. He held out the doll before him, clenched in his fist, like a weapon. But when God came up to him, the blue eyes were apologetic. The face was that of a stranger and yet it was familiar, was the face of Zacky, Lazarus, of himself, of anyone who had wrestled with the land, and from his very defeat, taken the measure of his strength. The stranger wore a crumpled blue suit, shiny with wear and frayed at the cuffs. He was several inches shorter than Obadiah. The bald patch at the back of his head, fringed by a few grey hairs, had turned a reddish bronze, under the sun.

The stranger was looking with great interest at the doll in Obadiah's hand.

'Can I look at your carving, please?' he asked simply.

Obadiah hesitated. The man used words as if they were foreign to him, and in a way that was difficult to understand. But his eyes were fastened on the doll, and he had put out his hand for it. His face was squat, like the doll's, and creased with many lines. It was a strong face, a good face. Yet Obadiah was reluctant. To put this thing that he had created into the man's hand would be to expose his naked heart to a stranger. For creating the doll, Obadiah knew, he had been saved from despair, from madness. Something that had long been pent up inside him, crying out to be released, had been set free, something outside of his love for Rose, his jealousy, his devotion to Moses and to Hebron, something private to him alone. Carving the doll out of a piece of mahoe, he had felt himself reprieved from a long exile, had left a wilderness and entered a cool watering place. The carving had value to him beyond any price. He had offered it to the old woman, because she was of his people, of his race, because only with a part of himself could he repay the suffering that he had glimpsed in her eyes, her charity that had been as spontaneous as water welling up in a spring.

But whilst he hesitated, the man had gently taken the doll out of his hand. Obadiah watched the stranger as he moved his fingers, with reverence, over the polished surfaces, held the doll up to the light so that shadows could deepen the eyes, define the contours more clearly. And he smiled. For in the same way he had held it up after he had finished it, had examined it; this object which had been dredged out of his anguish, his search for a sense of being, had become an extension, not only of his living body, but of Hebron.

The man looked up at Obadiah and spoke, but more to himself.

'I wonder,' he said in his slow, heavy voice, 'if the soul of man is not to be found in shape, in forms…?'

He broke off and stared at Obadiah, noted his whitened, cracked lips. He put the fingers of his right hand to his mouth.

'I am hungry,' he said. 'Come, we will eat and talk!'

They walked away together. From the other side of the market a solitary coconut-vender watched their departure, the black man and the white, with hostile eyes. He finished drinking the water from a coconut, wiped his hand on the back of his sleeve, pulled out his machete from the side of the cart, and, still looking across at the two, split the shell open with a clean, certain stroke.

They went into an ice-cream parlour round the corner from the market. The proprietress set a table under the lignum vitae tree in her backyard and served them the dinner that she had prepared for her family. She was curious about the connection between the two men, but Paradise Bay had had its share of eccentric tourists. And they always paid her well. So she brought them plates piled high with rice and peas and fried fish, and left them alone. Whilst they ate, the stranger looked at the doll that he had placed on the table between them, and when they had both finished, he asked:

'You made this carving, you yourself?'

Obadiah nodded.

'Who taught you to make this?'

'Nobody,' Obadiah said.

'You…live in this town…?'

'No…I live in the hills…up there,' he turned and pointed, 'up in the hills…of Hebron.'

The stranger nodded slowly.

'The hills…of Hebron…Where I was born there are hills too…many hills. My parents lived on one that was steep and barren...that was in a country far away from here...Tell me, what legend did you carve this doll from?'

Obadiah looked confused.

'You see, this carving looks like ones that I saw in Africa...when I was there...I write books about sculpture...carvings like these...I make too, myself, but in marble, not in wood...like you do...like they do in Africa, where your ancestors came from. And there they carve from father to son, and they carve out of the stories of their tribe, and their beliefs, their gods and devils. I bought a carving once that was made by the Dahomey...they made this out of a belief that each man has four souls, one given to him by an ancestor . . . one, his own, the third, the small bit of the Creator that lives in each man, the last one, that which joins him to the others in his group. The carving was one that I...lost...and yours is like it. That is why I ask, what belief did you carve this doll from? I would like to buy it from you...if you will sell it to me?'

Obadiah nodded. This would mean food and water for Rose and the child. Besides, this man was no longer a stranger, for he had understood at once that there was more to the doll than the wood and the shape he had fashioned. So he told the man the story of Hebron, of their search for God, for it was out of this, the dream and the reality, that he had carved the doll.

After, the man told Obadiah about himself. He came from Germany, and there had worked with others to create a Promised Land. But the attempt had failed, and others who did not believe in the brotherhood of man had taken over. He had been forced to flee. Now he was on a ship bound for another country, for exile. His wife and children had been killed, his sculpture smashed to pieces. But his ship had docked in Paradise Bay and he had found the market-place and the doll. It gave him a new hope, he said, gave him an apprehension of the newer, brighter worlds that could spring from the fusion of men's creative dreams. And in it, he saw that man's attempts to create Hebrons would continue for ever. He gave Obadiah a five-pound note. He was leaving that night, his ship had only docked for a day, but he would carry the doll with him as a symbol that Man, exiled from heaven, would one day return.

****

When Obadiah returned to Hebron that night he put aside the money that he had been given in exchange for the doll. The next day he carved out animals from wood, and dolls, and stained them with dyes that Rose brewed from the bark of trees. He sold them in the market-place of Cockpit Centre and Paradise Bay to the children for a few pence each. He and Rose lived on that whilst they waited for the child to be born. On the day of Isaac's expected return he took money from his store, and bought and brought back food and water for the congregation. For he had long since understood that Isaac would not return, and that the child that was Isaac's he would claim as his own.

He came back to find the new-born child, tended by Aunt Kate and Sister Ann. Rose was asleep. Taking the hamper of food and water with him, he went down the path that led to the church. As he returned to the congregation he sought for words to share with them the long journey that he had taken. He sought for words to tell them of the world that he had entered where there were no far places and no strangers: only men, like themselves, who would one day inhabit together the same new continents of the spirit, the same planets of the imagination.

22. *The Rain*

The congregation of Hebron were assembled in the church. They had come directly from Cockpit Centre. It was nearing midnight. Some of the children were asleep on the benches, while the babies were cradled in their mothers' arms. On the dais, the Elder's chair was vacant. Miss Gatha sat in the far corner. The white moonlight that flooded into the church did not quite reach to her. From time to time the agile flame of the lamp flung shadows across her graven face.

On the opposite side of the dais, Brother Zacky sat alone. Sister Ann had left to search for Aunt Kate as soon as they had returned. The congregation waited, looking to Zacky to tell them what to do. Before, he had played for time, had shared out food and water in small but scrupulous portions. But now they had all eaten, except Miss Gatha, whose bread and water lay untouched on the floor beside her.

Brother Zacky looked meaningfully at Miss Gatha, fidgeted and cleared his throat. But she did not notice. He rose, went across to the table, drew the large Bible towards him and folded his hands on it. This was for him the one sure point of ritual in a desert of uncertainty.

'Brothers and Sisters,' he said, 'whilst we wait for Miss Gatha to give us guidance, we will sing again the hymn "Onward Christian soldiers".'

He sat down. The few minutes of half-hearted singing would give him a much-needed respite. But in the midst of the hymn they started to mutter:

'And from here is onward to where?'

'That's what I want to know!'

'For now that Isaac is gone away with the money-box...'

'And will never come back with one penny of what was inside it...'

'One thing is clear! We can't stay on up here!'

The singing stopped altogether now. People turned to each other on the benches, arguing, gesticulating.

'We must let Miss Gatha know, we must tell her!'

'How? She is sitting up there like Lot's wife after she turn into a pillar of salt.'

'Yes. Just sitting up there, sucking her own sorrow, not caring what happens to us, to our children!'

'It serve her right, putting Isaac above everyone else of us!'

'I never did trust Isaac, book-learning or not!'

'That don't come into it now. The point is, how we going to tell her?'

'Brother Zacky should tell her. He's been her right hand!'

'Yes, Brother Zacky, Zacky, Zacky!'

They were all gesturing to him now. He gave in, leaned across to Hugh who sat in the front bench, his eyes averted:

'You tell her, Brother Hugh. You have long practice!' he begged.

'Yes, Brother Hugh, yes. Tell her!' they all insisted.

Their voices calling to him, needing him, was for Hugh like rain on the parched land. He stood up, even in this extremity, savouring his moment. His instinct for the occasion had not deserted him. When he spoke his tone was quietly solicitous, insistent:

'Miss Gatha, we have eaten, we have drunk. Now we are waiting long. Today we see and know that Isaac, your son, is not coming back. Our hearts grieve for your sorrow. Never, as long as we all shall live, will we ever forget what you did for us these past weeks, how today, you sold the wedding ring from off your finger so that we and our children could have food and water tonight. We will never forget it!'

The congregation took their cue, fervently:

'Never, Miss Gatha!'

'But, Miss Gatha,' he concluded, 'tomorrow soon come!'

He paused and waited. The congregation filled the church with their foreboding. The children moved uneasily in their sleep, the women grumbled:

'And tomorrow what is to happen to us if we are to stay on up here in Hebron, building monument to Prophet Moses's vision?'

'And all these weeks that we spend praying in the sun, fooling ourself that God would return to be well pleased...'

'Is what happening to us, to our life, to our children?'

The men took up the complaint now, impatient to declare their purpose:

'It was good when we had work to do, not to do it now and then...'

'And to curse the having to sweat and to grumble a little bit against it...'

'But now that we don't have our land, is what we are to do with our hands?'

Brother Zacky, encouraged by the solidarity of the others, flung the final challenge:

'The sun dried up the substance of our land, Miss Gatha. Hebron dead done!'

There was silence. Then a woman's voice called out:

'Let we leave it then, before we, too, die with Hebron, we and our children!'

'Let we leave Hebron, let we leave it!' they all cried out, and stamped their feet.

The noise jolted Miss Gatha and she turned towards them. Brother Hugh was quick to seize his opportunity:

'Miss Gatha, we all think that it will be better for us to leave Hebron and return to Cockpit Centre where the Government will have to be a little bit responsible for us, for our children.'

The others listened, and in the stillness heard the sound of footsteps approaching the church. Hugh saw that Miss Gatha was no longer paying attention. She had half-turned towards the door, her face naked with hope. When Obadiah appeared at the door, she looked away from them all and remained hunched over on her stick.

Obadiah slipped the hamper from his shoulders, mounted the steps on to the dais, and said simply:

'Brothers and Sisters, tonight a son was born unto me and my wife, Sister Rose Brown, and before I present him to the congregation I came first to testify and make public witness of the sin that I committed…'

Brother Ananias stood up in the back row and shouted:

'Is he who bring down drought on us. Let we throw him out!' But when he stepped into the aisle, he saw that no one else had moved. Their eyes were fixed on the laden hamper that Obadiah had brought with him. Ananias stopped. In the front bench Brother Hugh sat down. Ananias returned to his seat.

They were ready to listen to him now, Obadiah sensed, ready to respond to his confidence as they would have done to anyone else who offered them some hope. Outside the church, the wind blew stray clouds across the moon, shifted the moonlight which shone on the faces of the congregation. He heard the tree-tops rustling in the wind, their dry leaves sounding like a flock of birds. The eyes of the congregation were like hollows of darkness. He would have to fill them with light. His own moment of vision had been brief, like a rainbow reflected in water. To explain it to them he would need the words and the rhythms, not of a sermon, but a song:

'And after I sinned,' he began, 'I went mad. And after that, day in, day out, sitting out there on top of Hebron, with the sun like fire, and at nights the moon bright-out, little by little I was guided back to the work that I knew to do, where my hand could tell by the feel of it, what wood was true and what was not…'

The wind had died down, and in the church the moonlight was clear. The faces stared back at him like silver masks. He would have to go slowly. What he was asking of them now was for a new response to a new ritual, a new morality, a new right and wrong, a new God. Except they shared his vision, it would be meaningless for him.

'Then I came to myself,' he went on, 'and sat down and began to work a piece of wood and to carve out for the child that was to be born to me tonight, a cloud for a cradle…'

A woman's voice broke in first, with wonder:

'A cloud!' she said.

'A cloud, and at the head I carved out a sun, at the foot a moon, and on the sides all the stars that sprinkle up the sky!'

Their response came after this, tentative like the morning, then gradually widening out, quickening, alive after the dead years:

'All the stars!'

'And after that I put aside the cradle and sat there in front of my hut on a space of ground under the branch of a tree. And I looked down on Hebron spread out before me and remembered back to how it began, to all that it was…'

'How it began, all that it was!'

'And I wanted to put it down in wood for the child that was to be born to me tonight, and I tried and tried, but nothing came forth from my hand, until I started to carve a doll for the child to play with, and then it was as if my hand started to sing songs, and my knife was flying to whittle into the wood all the dreams that a man holds close, in the close places of his heart!'

'All the dreams!'

'And first my hand moulded out a face that was squat and strong, that was the face of the whole of Hebron.'

'The whole of Hebron!'

'And the nose and the mouth and the ears and the eyes came out small enough to lose under the tip of one finger, and still and all it was the nose and the mouth and the eyes and the ears of the whole of Hebron and of their generations before them and before them unto the beginning of them, and the neck of the doll was proud, was long…'

'Was proud, was long!'

'Then my hand marked out two hands and in the middle of them was the sum of all the labour of all the Hebrons, of all their generations before them and before them under the sun!'

'All the Hebrons!'

'And added to that, all the labour and all the visions of all the Hebrons to come, and after them and after them until the end of them. And the end of them was the beginning of them…'

'The beginning!'

'Then my hand stopped its song and was still. I sat in the sun and felt in my hand, all that was God. All that was God lay in the palm of my hand!'

'In the palm of your hand!' they whispered.

'But when I folded my hand to grasp it, to hold all that was God, there was only a doll for a child to play with!'

'Only a doll!' they lamented.

'But I knew then that Hebron could never die, that Hebron would have to wake up from its slumber, from its folding of hands to sleep, would have to wake up from its long night to create the day!'

'The day!'

'And the first thing we are going to do, starting tomorrow, is to build a good road, a broad road out into the world!'

'A good road!' they vowed, 'a broad road!'

'And up and down this road we will walk carrying the work of our hands to exchange for a man who will teach us how to read, and our sons!'

'Our sons!'

Obadiah turned to Miss Gatha, and the others, suddenly remembering, turned to her too. But Miss Gatha sat with her head sunk on her chest and would not return their look. She had heard their words like distant noises, like the dust and the dead leaves tossed by the wind outside the church. She could feel their silence directed at her, their eyes on her now. They were trying to draw her into their frail new hopes, involve her in their irrelevant concerns. But Isaac had not come back. Without him, Hebron was finished, spent like the wind that sighed through the tall grass. As Obadiah walked towards her, she shrank even further into herself.

'Miss Gatha,' he said, 'as you suggested, six days out of seven this church is going to be a school!'

'A school, Miss Gatha,' they promised, pleading with her to return to them.

The wind shook the trees outside. Miss Gatha thought she heard a footstep, a heavy dragging footstep coming towards her from the far reaches of the hills. She listened and heard it again. Could it be Isaac? Could he have changed his mind at the last minute and come back? Had he returned to Hebron whilst she was away, and hidden there, only emerging now? He was always secretive as a child, always hiding things. Perhaps if she waited and did not turn her head, she might hear the footsteps again.

'And Miss Gatha, we are going to dig wells as Isaac suggested!'

'To dig wells, Miss Gatha!'

They were trying to bribe her, Miss Gatha thought, trying to offer her a new Hebron in place of her son; trying to deceive her as they had deceived Kate about Maverlyn, to persuade her that all that was left of Isaac was the memory of something he had said. But did they know what a son was, her son? All that was left of his father Moses was a ghost dragging his wooden cross at nights in the graveyard, seeking to be freed from its burden. But her son was far greater than his father, she had seen to that. He had book-learning as great as any white man, he could never disappear from the face of Hebron and leave no trace. He would come back. He was coming back, was coming. She could hear his footfalls trampling the earth. But she would have to be cunning, would pretend to listen to the others so that they could not hear the approaching footsteps, and hearing, doubt; and doubting, frighten away Isaac so that he would never come back, and all that she would have of him, strange signs scrawled by his hand on a sheet of white paper, fine as silk, and a foreign stamp to seal his distance. She looked at Obadiah. He could see the frenzy in her eyes. His voice was gentle as he spoke to her now:

'And Miss Gatha, we are going to build up Hebron strong, build it firm against the wind, going to shelter the houses in the arms of the hills. Six days we will build up Hebron, the seventh we are going to sing songs, going to rejoice in the work of our hands which is our portion under the sun!'

'Our portion under the sun!'

The door at the back of the church was opened. The wind banged the door shut. Miss Gatha did not look round. She heard the hush that fell on the congregation as the footsteps mounted the dais, dragging, burdened with some great weight. Isaac was coming across to her now. She remained still. He must not see how anxiously she had waited for his coming, must not suspect for one moment that she had ever doubted his return. He stood beside her now. She would look up and greet him, as casually as ever.

She lifted up her eyes. Kate stood behind her, her grey hair dishevelled. Her eyes gleamed as if the wind had blown bits of the moon inside them. She held a bundle against her, wrapped in an old black shawl. Its silken fringe danced before Miss Gatha's eyes. Kate stooped, placed the baby in Miss Gatha's lap, then sat on the stool beside her.

There was a noise against the roof, like that of a thrown handful of pebbles. Obadiah moved to the centre of the dais and stood listening. All the others listened with him. A gust of wind tore at the thatch, then subsided. The drops of rain fell slowly at first, one by one by one. The congregation rose to their feet. The hailstones clattered down, the rain was a rushing, roaring deluge. Obadiah gave a great cry and sprang from the dais. The others streamed out after him, laughing, weeping; and the children wide awake now, running and shouting. And the hills echoed their rejoicing.

The two old women did not move. They could hear the noise of tin pans and barrels, of calabashes being set out to catch the rain that fell on the thirsty earth, charging the land with life. And they could hear the people singing:

Hosanna, I build my house oh, ha, ha!
The sun come burn it down, ha, ha!
The wind come blow'd way, ha, ha!
The rain come wet it up, ha, ha!
My house is weak you see, ha ha!
But if I build my house and it fall down,
I can build it up right from the ground, ha ha!

They sat on in the abandoned church. The suspicion that had formed on Miss Gatha's face grew into a certainty. Isaac had raped Rose, had broken away from her and from Hebron. Her son would never come back. It was as if she had known a long time ago and had only pretended to herself. The rain beat steadily against the roof. The moon had long been blotted out. The oil in the tin lamp had burnt low and the flame was dying. A bleak darkness invaded the church. Miss Gatha shivered. She felt cold. Only in her lap was there any warmth. She put her hands under the shawl, traced the outlines of the child's body. It was perfect. Wonderingly, she turned to Kate. The sins of the fathers, then, had not been visited on the children? The fabric of her forebodings dissolved, and she wept.

Miss Gatha cradled the child against her withered breasts and rocked gently to and fro. Aunt Kate hummed a tuneless lullaby. Soon, the two old women were as soundly asleep as the child. Morning, breaking over Hebron, caught them unawares.

Afterword

By Demetrius L.Eudell

Toward Aimé Césaire's 'Humanism Made to the Measure of the World': Reading *The Hills of Hebron* in the Context of Sylvia Wynter's Later Work

> As J.F. Danielli hypothesizes, an internal reward system (I.R.S.) should be seen as functioning as the central mechanism by which human individuals are motivated to sacrifice their individual interest for that of others with whom they are co-identified – in effect for the sake of the common good. The pleasure centers and the functioning of the euphoria-inducing family of substances would 'reward' behaviors which further 'altruisitic' integration (good) and inhibit dysfunctional behaviors (evil/deilos), thus providing 'the rudiments of a physiological basis for some aspects of motivation.' However, he points out, what still remains missing to complete the hypothesis is 'any knowledge of the *social* conditioning of the I.R.S.,' that is, of how it functions 'so that *rewards are provided which relate to the necessary or desirable roles of an individual in a specific society.'* ...

As Girard implies, all literature, indeed all human narrative, functions to encode the dynamics of desire at the deep structural level of the order's symbolic template. It is, in consequence, precisely through fiction, ritual, and art that we can have access to the higher level units of our system-specific

> modes of mind and to the 'enchanted' order of discourse which must everywhere function, in the last instance, to conserve the grounding premises of its mode of inferential analogic from which its system-maintaining 'truths' are stably generated....
>
> Like the narrator of *The Invisible Man*, we as 'Minority" scholars find ourselves confronting a reality deeply enchanted by the post-atomic functioning of anachronistic true discourses inherited from an industrial order now past and gone. In order to effect a gesture parallel to that by which the ancient Egyptians went from their rule-of-thumb measuring of the post-flood marshes to the theorems of geometry, it is necessary that we now go from our present art and craft discourse [of literary criticism] to a new science of that third level of existence, human life, of whose bringing-into-being all orders of discourse, and the behavioral directive signs which they encode, are a function.
>
> Sylvia Wynter
> 'On Disenchanting Discourse:
> "Minority" Literary Criticism and Beyond'[1]

In the above cited essay, Sylvia Wynter asserts that 'all, literature, indeed all human narrative, functions to encode the dynamics of desire at the deep structural level of the order's symbolic template.' Consequently, an analysis of literary narratives can provide a particular and unique kind of knowledge, that is, knowledge of the 'system-specific modes of mind' on whose basis our present social order is instituted and reproduced. Art and religion, which function in a parallel manner to that of literature, can also reveal such knowledge. Our present 'mode of mind' or in terms that Wynter later employs, auto-poetically instituted code of symbolic *life*/symbolic *death*, as the code in adapted Fanonian terms, instituting of all forms of consciousness, is most clearly expressed in literature, because it functions within a secular, that is, post-theological understanding of our social reality.[2] Moreover, as Wynter and others, such Michel Foucault in *The Order of Things*, have noted, this specific 'mode of mind' emerged at a particular moment in history and within a particular intellectual field of meaning. This new field of meaning and being was one that was produced by the era of Liberal democratic revolutions, including the French, US, and Haitian, the latter as also a uniquely slave revolution, with the first two being fully, and the third only partially (and indeed, contradictorily so) related to the project of the Enlightenment.

As a result, during this historic moment, a new order of knowledge or *episteme* (to use Foucault's term) emerged. Such is indeed what is meant by the assertion of the 'rise of the novel' or the invention of the Classics in the nineteenth century. Correlated with this epochal intellectual shift, a new 'descriptive statement' of the human would also be put in place, one where the human would be represented, after Darwin's breakthroughs, in purely secular terms on the model of a natural organism.[3] Thus, as distinct from Western Europe's earlier ideal conceptions of being human, and in whose terms where, the ideal mode of being had been instituted/enacted in purely theological (that is, supernatural terms) during the hegemony of the Latin Christian Church, together with that of feudal medieval aristocracy, or, subsequently, in secularised humanist *political* terms during the monarchical/mercantile order (and its *reasons-of-state* imperative) from the sixteenth to the early eighteenth centuries, a new understanding of *being human* arose. As one, that is, one in whose formulation *being human* would now gradually be represented in terms of a Hobbesian state-of-nature individual who ostensibly naturally feels and autonomously wills themselves into being; therefore, as humans who can pre-exist their social institutions and founding cosmogonic narratives.[4] It was precisely this 'figure of Man', as identified by Foucault, that remained the referent subject in the age of revolution's claims of the 'natural rights of man' and within the order of figurations of the genre of fiction that had emerged *pari passu* with the rise of the industrialising bourgeoisie to ruling class status.

Thus, in spite of the fact that this new concept of *being human* had revolutionary origins, the 'figure of Man' encoding of this concept could not have been invented (and autopoetically instituted) without its Conceptual Other, this as Jacob Pandian clearly points out, if in somewhat different terms.[5] As such an Other, who did not have official recognition in the political Imaginary of then emergent nation-states, and who as such had therefore remained outside the limits of its 'universe of moral obligation' as aesthetically iconised in the system of figuration of its novels.[6] Hence, as the character Trumper in George Lamming's anti-colonial classic *In the Castle of My Skin* insightfully notes, 'the rights of Man' cannot be the same thing as the 'rights of the Negro.'[7] It has been this central dialectic to which the *œuvre* of Sylvia Wynter has consistently been directed; perhaps, with both her novel and later theoretical essays illustrating why Trumper's perceptive statement functions in a law-like manner.

Indeed, both Lamming and Wynter belong to a generation of anti-colonial writers from the Caribbean who sought to re-represent the lives and social worlds of the majority of its people, those whom Wynter identifies in *The Hills of Hebron* as being in the history books who 'would have found themselves only in the blank spaces between the lines, in the dashes, the pauses between commas, semicolons, colons' or as 'the done-to's who had made possible the deed' (*Hills*, 61; 1962 edition). Wynter's novel – as part of the anti-colonial literary canon – had therefore to disenchant the discourse of imperial history of what she more recently defines as the post-1492 ex-slave/ ex-pieza archipelago of the Caribbean and the Americas.[8]

It was precisely within such a historical context that Sylvia Wynter came into the world. Born in Cuba, where, toward the end of the sugar boom, her parents had ventured in search of work and opportunity, but with opportunities closing down, and having been unable to realise their quest, her family returned to Jamaica where she was brought up and educated; and so educated, as she has consistently stated, as a *colonial subject*. As such, as a *native* subject of the British empire, one therefore in this political aspect, co-identified with the even more excluded majority and marginalised native labour population or *damnés de la terre* population of the islands of the then British Caribbean. In other words, not primarily, in the terms of her gender, although such would remain an aspect, if at that time, as she argues, a necessarily marginally experienced one.[9] Such occurs, Wynter has noted, due to the then absolute nature of the institutionally imposed native and therefore, secondary human status that would have been primarily existentially experienced by all as colonial subjects, even if most totally so in the case of the majority of the Black and poor population of then British colonial Jamaica.

The early life of Wynter revolved around two poles that find themselves often depicted by the authors of the anti-colonial literary canon: the city and the countryside. In the case of the latter, as she recounts, Wynter usually spent holidays in the parishes of St Elizabeth and Westermoreland with both sets of grandparents, one set who grew bananas for export, but with both being essentially small, self-provisioning farmers. Like many small farmers of that time and place, the range of crops, ground provisions (in the Creole language of Jamaica) harvested (such as yams, sweet potatoes, bananas) and livestock raised were staples, and this also included the domestic production of items such as coffee, butter, and chocolate. Given the dimension of this self-provisioning, one rarely had to go to the store, and usually would only do so to purchase 'salt things'like the salted codfish that was imported from Canada; indeed, introduced as part of the initial globalisation complex of the Western world system in which the feeding of slaves, doing so as cheaply as possible, had led to such items becoming central to the Caribbean diet, not to mention to the great wealth of those who traded in these goods. With respect to the other pole, Wynter's early life was centred also around the city of Kingston. There, she attended elementary schools in one of the poorer sections of the capital city, so that while growing up, her life would be marked by a dialectic of these two poles, whereby if on the one hand, there existed a feeling of abundance and plenitude that defined the social world of self-provisioning landed farmers (however small the acreage they possessed may have been), and on the other, she would experience something of the techno-industrial form of poverty then being imposed by the post-slavery system of colonialism from 1866 onwards.

Under the colonial system of education in which Wynter was educated and socialised, no matter how 'gifted' a student from the Black population may have been, few opportunities existed for them to acquire the higher levels of formal education. Nevertheless, Wynter seemed to have had, as many others did, a series of brilliant teachers in elementary school for whom their students' success was passionately a part of their own. She was therefore well-taught in the basic subjects by the rather restricted curriculum. However, when she attended secondary school as a scholarship student, she could not take her presence there for granted, this, as she became sharply aware of the difference in both schools, with her experience of both giving her a growing understanding of the society in which she lived; one that was not only hierarchically structured and therefore sharply unequal, but was educationally designed to stably reproduce this result.

Toward the end of her secondary school education, Wynter took what was then defined in the British terms as the Higher Schools Exams, whereby on the basis of her results, she was awarded the then recently instituted Centenary Scholarship. Such was a lucky break for her, given that, as she recounts, the other island award, the Jamaica Scholarship, always went to a student from the privileged background in terms of race, colour and class. In contradistinction, the Centenary Scholarship was specifically designed to assist the students from the Black majority of the population, who had been counter-affirmatively disadvantaged by the same system of education. The name of the scholarship, Centenary, comes from the fact that it was created in 1938, in the context of the political and labour uprisings in the 1930s, doing so in order to commemorate the abolition of slavery in 1838 a century before. Wynter therefore credits this early form of what in the US has come to be known post-1960s as Affirmative Action, with allowing her to pursue university level studies, going to attend King's College, London University, just as the University of the West Indies was in the process of being established.

Wynter attended King's College, beginning with a major in English, but later changed to Spanish/Romance Languages with English as a minor. The summer after beginning her university studies, she attended summer school in Spain, where on the basis of an essay that she wrote as part of the final exam, she was granted a fellowship for one year of study at the University of Madrid. There, she spent a year studying philology under Rafael Lapesa and Dámaso Alonso, focusing on comparative philology, as well as on the Golden Age Literature defining of a then hegemonically dominant imperial Spain. At the time, Wynter did not realise that by concentrating on Spain's Golden Age, she was in fact initiating a lifelong inquiry into the origins of the modern world; indeed, it was this inquiry that was to culminate in her seminal essay '1492: A New World View', where she put forth an 'ecumenically human view' of the expansion of Western Europe, doing so in order not only to account for the cognitively emancipatory aspects of Columbus's voyages and the ones followed in his wake, but as well for the enormous price of total subjugation that would be paid by the Indigenous peoples of Africa and the Americas for the expansion of Europe into 'new worlds.'[10] After finishing her studies in Madrid, Wynter returned to London, completed a BA honours, and an MA research thesis on the Golden Age drama of Spain, concentrating on an analysis of its religio-monarchical concept of cleanliness of blood (*limpieza de sangre*), as a first form of proto-racial discourse.

Wynter spent time between finishing her degrees and the publication of *The Hills* in 1962 as a writer in London. In fact, she was one of a group of London-based Caribbean writers who sought to re-imagine the Caribbean landscape and its people outside the systemically negative terms of the hegemonic British imperial order of colonial discourse. In this context, she wrote a stage play for radio entitled 'Under the Sun' for the BBC's Third programme, which as Anthony Bogues notes in his introduction here, was rewritten for the novel. This work was followed by a translated version of Federico García Lorca's *Yerma*, which she adapted to a Jamaican setting, in order to make use of the poetic qualities of Jamaican Creole that would effectively reproduce something of the evocative power of Lorca's dramatic language.

After Jamaica achieved formal political independence from Great Britain in 1962, Wynter returned home, and after a short stint as a civil servant, began a new career as an academic, joining the faculty at the University of the West Indies in the department of Spanish literature. During this time, she continued to write, authoring the plays *Maskerade* and *Sh... It's a Wedding*, which were followed by *1865: Ballad of a Rebellion*, as a government-sponsored play intended to commemorate the Morant Bay rebellion which had been savagely repressed by Governor Eyre. She also helped to create *Jamaica Journal*, which was to become one of the premier intellectual journals of the Anglophone Caribbean. Her first essay published in the journal, 'We Must Learn to Sit Down Together and Talk About a Little Culture: Reflections on West Indian Writing and Criticism',[11] challenged what she saw as the imperialising aspects of the discipline of literary criticism, as it had been practised in Great Britain, as well as what she has come to define as the continued epistemological dependency (which in a paradoxical manner, as she argues, is directly causal of economic dependency rather than vice versa)[12] of the intellectuals and academics, herself included, of the then emerging post-colonial Third World. The essay, 'We Must First Sit Down', can therefore be seen as the intellectual precursor to the epistemological break effected by what would become her essay 'On Disenchanting Discourse', that is, as the essay where she more fully develops her argument of the need to move beyond the premises of literary criticism and toward a science of human systems, one which, because functioning beyond the limits of our present episteme, would be enabled to call into question 'the grounding premises from which the metaphysical discourses of *all* population groups, *all* human systems – including that of the West – are generated.'[13] Thus, it would be during these first years as an academic that the overall thrust of Wynter's writings would take a distinctive turn.

Wynter's thinking would also develop further as the result of interaction with the political and intellectual struggles of Blacks in the United States. The anti-Jim Crow/anti-apartheid uprisings, beginning with the 1955 Montgomery Bus Boycott and culminating in riots in the late 1960s in the aftermath of the assassination of Reverend Martin Luther King, Jr in April 1968, events that bore a direct relation to the subsequent call for Black Studies in the university system, would equally sharpen Wynter's analysis, in her own terms, of the phenomenon to which we give the folk sociological name of *race*. As a result of the institutionalisation of a Black Studies perspective in the United States, Wynter would leave Jamaica in 1974, first, to teach at the University of San Diego, in what was then a Third World Studies Programme, and then three years later to join the faculty at Stanford University in the African and Afro-American Studies Programme as well as the Department of Spanish and Portuguese, from where she would eventually retire in 1994.

Over the years of teaching and writing from the *systemically* liminal (and therefore, non-ethnic) perspective of Black Studies, Wynter had come to propose that the now still biocosmogonically chartered, and fundamentally Darwinian, belief system of *race* functions as a global and purely secular status organising principle; yet, one that can only be understood within the field of the theologically absolute Judaeo-Christian religion, out of which it arose, if as its negatively transumed antithesis. In the place of the earlier supernaturally ordained identity of being Christian that structured Latin Christian Europe in the Middle Ages, an increasingly secular concept of being human emerged, that of *Man,* in its first Renaissance, and therefore civic humanist conception, as primarily *homo politicus* or a rational citizen/subject of the State; a conception in whose now secular encoded terms, the Indigenous peoples of the Americas, together with the transported and enslaved, but also indigenous peoples, of Africa were now to be institutionalised as *Man's* irrational Conceptual Other. At the same time as, while generically classified as *indios* and *negros,* these Conceptual Others were to be empirically institutionalised, as the two forms of forced labour whose respective archipelagoes (the first that of the neo-serf Indians, the second that of outright Negro slave labour) for the commercial sugar plantations, which were to be indispensable to the putting in place of the Western world system, in its then first monarchical *cum* landed gentry mercantilist form. Such therefore means that the Clergy/Laity Line (where the former had incarnated the Redeemed Spirit and the latter embodied the post-Adamic Fallen Flesh) as the status-organising principle of the Latin Christian order of feudal medieval Europe, was now to be transformed into, in its first form, the *Man/Indian-Negro Line,* as the proto-form of what would become in *Man's* second nineteenth century Liberal humanist and specifically bourgeois form, the *Man/Native, Man/Negro* or *White/Black* status organising principle, with the Black and poor *damnés de la terre* being institutionalised within the terms of the *Colour Line* as its most extreme Other. In consequence, where before the Medieval Order had been structured on the premise of the physical non-homogeneity between the incorruptible Heavens and the corruptible Earth (fallen due to mankind's foundational transgression) because of an ontological difference of substance, now our present purely secular Western and westernised world system is organised on the basis of the premise of the ostensibly bio-evolutionarily determined differential levels of genetic non-homogeneity of the human species; levels that have then been mapped onto the phenotypic physiognomic differences between population groups. Wynter posits that the history of the modern world, in which the increasingly secular Judaeo-Christian West has primarily, because cosmo-epistemologically controlling the terms of interaction and exchange, is a history that has replaced the founding Spirit/Flesh (i.e. Redeemed/damned) line with that of our contemporary world system's analogically Naturally Selected/Dysselected Line, with the latter now serving to fulfill the same role of keeping in being our present psychic and socio-economic hierarchies, all now systemically represented as being extra-humanly determined, rather than, as they are empirically, humanly instituted.[14]

While, as Wynter more recently argued, it was to be precisely, the imperative calling in question of that principle in its then overt imperialising (because then also politically disenfranchised form) that was to be, in the wake of the 1935–1938 'native labour' uprising in Jamaica as well as elsewhere in the then British Caribbean, indispensable condition of articulation of the range of novels, including *The Hills of Hebron*, that would come to constitute the anti-colonial literary canon. Such a literary canon impelled by the attempt to destructure/restructure that 'internalised consciousness', one in which the writers, had also themselves been equally enchanted and imprisoned, as had all members of the British colonial order of the ex-slave Caribbean, including other ethnic, religious and/or phenotypic populations comprising the society, demonstrating the way in which the founding premise of the *Colour Line* cut across all divisions of race, class/education, wealth/poverty, and gender. As Elsa Goveia noted in her seminal essay 'The Social Framework', colonial Caribbean society was integrated, and therefore stabilised and reproduced itself on a foundational conception: 'that the fact Blackness is a fact of inferiority, as the fact of whiteness is fact of superiority.'[15]

Literary Knowledge and the Answer to Danielli's Question

It was therefore to be in a literary modality, that Wynter, considerably before her subsequent series of essays, was to initiate the calling in question of the systemic functioning of the premise of the Colour Line; and thereby, of the internalised order of consciousness, or socially encoded mode of mind, together with their correlated dynamic structure of desire/aversion of motivation/demotivation as it had functioned during her childhood in the then colonial order of Jamaica, a process identified both by René Girard, and more fully by Frantz Fanon.[16] Taking the novel as a form of literary knowledge therefore, can provide access to the functioning of such laws of how the post-slavery Jamaica (as a synecdoche for the post-slavery Black world) would be instituted on the basis of a specific cosmogony, one that Wynter forcefully reveals and then challenges in *The Hills.* With the expansion of the West, first into Africa in the mid-fifteenth century, and then into the Americas in the wake of Columbus's voyages, a rupture would occur *at the level of the species*, whereby a new mode of thinking would be made possible. This paradigm shift gave rise to the physical sciences, which resulted initially on the basis of Copernicus's challenge to the Ptolemaic-based Scholasticism of the feudal representation of the physical cosmos. In the nineteenth century, Darwin's breakthroughs with respect to the co-evolution of the human species, would effect the same in the biological/natural sciences. Yet, as distinct from being in a line of pure continuity with organic forms of life, or in Wynter's terms, the *biocentric* thesis (as opposed to the *theocentric* paradigm defining of the Middle Ages), Wynter posits that *being human* cannot be merely a function of purely natural processes, but rather humans exist in a relation of continuity and discontinuity with these processes, a phenomenon to which literature can give us insight.

For as Wynter has consistently argued, no human order is pre-given or naturally created; all must be narratively instituted and performatively enacted in order to exist. Thus, Hobbes's cosmo-philosophical notion of a 'state of nature' defining of human existence, conceptualised in Western terms, or more contemporarily, that of a Malthusian elaborated natural scarcity that underlies the economic imperative ostensibly determining all human behaviours, are but cosmogonic narratives, chartering of the social order, without which its auto-institution would not be possible. Indeed, it can be argued that the function of the Colour Line, in its then overly imperial form, one chartering, in bio-cosmogonic terms, of British colonialism, that had therefore functioned to institute the colonial subjects of the Caribbean as *natives*, and *secondary humans*, yet at the same time inducing them, not only to be content with, but to be happy with their inferiorised status. As she recounts, one of Wynter's most salient memories that was to drive the dynamic of the novel was 'how happy she had been during her pre-adolescent childhood to be a British subject.' Thus, for instance, every year, on Empire Day (May 24) she and the other schoolchildren would attend a ceremony where they would have their Union Jack flags, and happily sing, 'Rule Britannia, Britannia rules the waves, Britons, Britons, never shall be slaves.' At the same time, the children would be given a gilded tin box with the portraits of the British King and Queen on its cover, and which contained candy and pencils. Yet, the irony remained that while the ceremony had served to induce them to experience themselves as British, even if as native ones, that in fact, as Caribbean natives and Black Britons, their ancestors, had indeed been slaves, a historical phenomenon that did not prevent such a ritual from being strategically instituted.

Yet, such a ritual was not an arbitrary one, but rather a constituent element of the formation of a colonial society, with the system of education playing a central role, as they always do, in the enactment of the governing cosmogony. For example, as Wynter has noted, her mistake in assigning the year 1868 to the Morant Bay rebellion in the novel had occurred, as difficult as it may be to imagine in our present historical context, because nothing called Jamaican or West Indian history could have been allowed to exist as it does in the contemporary (that is, post-colonial/post-1960s) system of knowledge.[17] As a result, the anti-colonial generation had, in the wake of the 1935–1938 uprisings, taken up the task of reconceptualising the past the perspective of the 'done-to's who made the deed possible.' Yet, Wynter's novel, read in the context of her later work, not only goes beyond a project of vindication (though such is necessary), but also provides us with knowledge of the way in which the social reality under colonialism had had to be known and imagined.

It is in this overall context that the novel revolves centrally around the people that Wynter has come to define, as the 'ultimate underside of modernity' or in Fanon's terms, *les damnés de la terre*, usually translated as 'the wretched of the earth.' However, C.L.R. James has insisted that a better translation of *les damnés de la terre* would be 'the condemned of the earth' as those who belong to this category are condemned in economic terms, but also narratively, and therefore metaphysically so.[18] *The Hills*, as part of the counter poetics of the anti-colonial literary canon, was directed toward the undoing of this narratively condemned status of being placed, in the words of Helen Fein, outside the 'universe of moral obligation.' The community of New Believers, all integrated about Prophet Moses's counter-cosmogonic vision of a Black God (able to redeem them in their own physiognomic being and name and therefore from institutionalised poverty and joblessness imposed upon them) are portrayed in the novel in the context of an imagined wider universe of moral obligation, a wider humanism, one 're-enchanted' and in the words of Aimé Césaire, made to the measure of the world.[19] This itself is a constant in the anti-colonial literary canon, in which Lamming's *Castle* and Roger Mais's *Brother Man* are arguably the iconic examples.

In this respect, the novel portrays the New Believers, all of whom would at best be normally marginalised, and at worst systemically and negatively stereotyped in the figuration system of bourgeois fiction, are here instead being configured as complex self-asserted personae, this especially so in the case of the women who, it can be argued, are more aesthetically, and therefore, powerfully realised than the men, except perhaps for Prophet Moses. Thus, in this context, it is unmistakably clear that the novel is authored from the perspective of a woman.[20] At the same time, however, the portrayal of the women of Hebron does not have to be interpreted in the orthodox, and necessarily partial terms of post-colonial feminist literary criticism, but, rather, can also be understood in terms of the poetic revalorising of the entire population group, men *as well as* women together with their children. Such a revalorisation became necessary at the level of the population group, because it would be as a population that those of African hereditary descent, wholly or partially, from the post-fifteenth century/ post-Middle Passage origin in the forced slave labour archipelago of the Western world system, as instituted in its founding mercantilist phase, would become the only population together with their continent of origin Africa (and the rest of its Indigenous peoples) to be excluded, in the searing words of the historian Louis Sala-Molins, 'banished from humanity.'[21]

Consequently, while some otherwise excellent feminist literary critics have interpreted *The Hills* in complex, but nonetheless hegemonic feminist terms, it is clear that while such an interpretation does not lack validity, however well argued, this mode of analysis must necessarily fail to address the full range and complexity of the novel; above all, the recognition of what the novel, like all those of the anti-colonial literary canon, *does*, as well as *means*.[22] Indeed, in the context of the far-reaching major hypothesis put forward by the biologist J.F. Danielli as cited by Wynter, with respect to the functioning of the internal reward system, he notes that 'what still remains missing to complete the hypothesis is any knowledge of the social conditioning of the I.R.S…so that rewards are provided which related to the necessary or desirable roles of an individual in a specific society.' This hitherto unknown mechanism (one that is both bios and logos) which serves to both motivate, induce and therefore regulate human behaviours is provided by literary knowledge of all fiction (as indeed all art and religions), that is, when read outside of not only hegemonically feminist literary criticism, but of all literary criticism itself, given that, as Wynter argued in 'On Disenchanting Discourse' and more recently in an interview, within the terms of the discipline of literary criticism it cannot be seen to exist.[23]

In this context, that is, with respect to what the novel *does*, as well as *means*, in an ongoing essay, Wynter's refutation both of hegemonically feminist literary criticism as well as literary criticism itself, 'minority' or not, focuses on one of the central signifier objects of the novel, that of the apron, and by doing so, provides a direct answer to Danielli's question of the missing knowledge able to complete his major hypothesis.[24] As she argues, the apron functions in three different contextual, figurative situations: 1) Miss Gatha's relationship to Moses; 2) the death of Hugh's grandmother; and 3) Mrs. Brooks taking tea with Lady Harrington. These three figurative situations illustrate the novel's detaching of the opiate signifier rewards from the Western colonial order of discourse's normative signs of symbolic life and reattaching them to the signs of symbolic death, and therefore works against the conditioned order of consciousness instituting of the colonial social order of the Caribbean, and more generally, of the ex-slave archipelago defining of the Americas.

In the first situation, that of Miss Gatha's, a compelling persona, who reveals this dual aspect of an analysis of the novel from the insights of a primarily gender perspective versus one from the perspective of an understanding of the functioning of the system-ensemble and its auto-poetic institution. While married, Miss Gatha had subordinated her own interests and goals to those of her husband, the Prophet Moses: 'She had made a bad bargain, Miss Gatha thought – her land and property for a few pieces of clothing, for marriage to Moses and twenty bitter years; the name of Randall for that of Barton, when her maiden name had been a legitimate name, a respectable one bestowed on her by her great-grandfather, Cato Randall' (p.88). In this instance, Danielli's identification of the functioning of the mechanism that motivates individuals to sacrifice their interests for the sake of the hegemonically institutionalised and represented mode of the common good, inducing them to desire to do so by means of the semantic activation of the opiate reward attached to each such mode, can be insightfully employed to explain Miss Gatha's behaviour. As Moses's wife, Gatha should have been able to realise herself in the terms of the bourgeois governing code of symbolic life; this, especially so, given that according to this same governing code, from the standpoint of physical beauty, she as a Black woman, although propertied and with a shop, would nonetheless be represented as embodying symbolic death and therefore socialised to experience herself as Other. Moreover, it is within the same frame that Moses's devalorisation of his wife, as was the case with other New Believers, must necessarily function, as it is derived from the internalisation of the same symbolic system in which the Black population is devalorised; and therefore the Black woman must also be so in a lawlike fashion as the potential genetrix of the population group.

It is therefore precisely within the terms of her relationship with Moses that the apron would take on such powerfully symbolic dimensions. From the beginning of Prophet Moses' proposed trek from Cockpit Centre, Miss Gatha had remained suspicious of this project. Thus, when the Prophet proposed making a bonfire by destroying all 'the symbols of their past sufferings', Miss Gatha, out of a 'secret stubbornness' held onto the apron that belonged to her grandmother, as she 'had taken it up to Hebron with her as the one symbol to mark her difference from the others' (93). Here, the apron represents for Miss

Gatha, not only a symbol of an independent personal rebellion against her husband and an heirloom, but also within the terms of its bourgeois connotations (with its 'frilled edging') as a marker of difference from the majority of the New Believers, who belong to the *damnés* category of the poor and jobless. In this intellectual context, the apron comes to exemplify a non-utilitarian possession that signifies its owner's material redemption and freedom from the metaphysical threat of natural necessity/natural scarcity to which the *damnés,* as the now 'planet of the slums' ultimate Other to the now also planetarily extended and homogenised Western bourgeois (or in Wynter's terms ethno-prototype) conception of being human, *Man,* would be subordinated.

Yet, rather than interpreting Miss Gatha from the necessarily partial liberal humanist perspectives of either, on the one hand, a nationalist position, which would say her attitude toward the New Believers is one of self-hatred (or lack of self-love) or on the other, a feminist viewpoint that says her submission to Moses's interests represents an example of gender subordination and patriarchy, both can be explained in terms of the autopoetic, auto-instituting governing symbolic code defining of the social reality within which her behaviour in both instances would be logical as they would represent the ensemble of behaviours necessary for the order's reproduction in terms in which it had come to be conceptualised and actualised. The apron functions as a signifier of liberation and would therefore logically activate the opiate reward mechanism enabling her to realise herself in the positive terms of a propertied bourgeois woman rather than in the negative terms of a stigmatised and devalued Black woman.

The apron, which was worn by Hugh's grandmother, functions in a context related to, but wider than, that of Miss Gatha's. Grannie worked as cook in a guest house, while keeping the young Hugh with her in a 'broken-down' room that adjoined the kitchen. After collapsing while at work due to nagging pain, she had to be helped back to her room, where she refused to let Hugh call for the neighbourhood doctor so as to avoid having to pay for medical service with money she had saved for her grandson's future schooling, to 'give him the kind of opportunity that none of her family had ever had' (p.157). While tourists laughed and the operations of the guest house continued, Grannie died gripping Hugh's hand. Her grandson's response was instinctive and logical: 'He took off his grandmother's apron and trampled it on the floor without knowing why he did so. Then he folded her hands on her breast and placed her hymnbook between them' (p. 157).

Thus, unlike the case for Miss Gatha, the apron in this instance functions as a purely utilitarian object, one that enchained Hugh's grandmother to a new, because post-slavery, form of servitude and social subordination, the analog of the empirical chains that would have physically imprisoned her ancestors. Therefore, because unpropertied, she belongs to the category of *les damnés* and thus her apron becomes the antithesis of what it means in the case of Miss Gatha, condemnation and imprisonment as opposed to liberation. Furthermore, on two counts, Hugh's response was an instinctive challenge to the Western colonial order's normative signifier of being. On the one hand, out of a tremendous sense of dignity and respect, he does what he can as if to prepare his grandmother for church, placing her hymn book close to her heart. On the other hand, Hugh's action of trampling on the apron represents a revolt against the social ordering that had locked his grandmother in her negative and stigmatised role as a member of the category of *les damnés*. His symbolic action refuses the normative opiate punishment signifier which had served to legitimate his grandmother's total servitude (in post-slavery terms), a legitimisation internalised in the consciousness of all members of the society, which, because indispensable to the reproduction of the social order, had been necessary to its existence as such an order. He therefore repudiates her empirical place, and by trampling on the apron, he is simultaneously trampling on the order of consciousness that had proscribed the negative and subordinate role of his grandmother, and therefore in the vein of the anti-colonial literary canon, detaching the opiate signifier from normal being, and by reattaching it to the Conceptual Other, revalorises the population of *les damnés* to which his grandmother belonged.

From the perspective of mutually reinforcing modes of subordination, if under the systemic hegemony of the coding principle of the Colour Line, both Miss Gatha and Hugh's grandmother function as the antithesis to two other women, Mrs Brooks and Lady Harrington. Mrs Brooks, who on the advice of her doctor, increasingly spent time in the cooler hill climate of Mandeville, where she met Lady Harrington, the wife of a former governor. The obsequious Mrs Brooks looked forward to nothing more than tea with the haughty Lady Harrington, who not only never bothered to conceal her disdain for the natives, but who also saw everything about the society in negative terms: 'The cream too was of inferior quality. "But what else can one expect from these Jamaican cows my dear! And as for the people!"'(p. 181). Thus, the animals and the people are conflated into the same entity within the bio-evolutionary terms defining the colonial social reality.

However, here the role of the apron, while present, is only so by means of its absence. For it is not women wearing aprons who serve Mrs Brooks and Lady Harrington, but rather men in 'monkey jacket and black trousers', who serve these ladies and therefore represent it symbolically (p. 181). In this racial ordering of the society, in no way can these men be construed as being *True Men*, fully Men, or in Wynter and Foucault's terms *Man;* but rather are native men, whose feminised roles enact the ostensibly extra-human, because supposed bio-evolutionarily, determined social order. The institutionalised opiate signifier rewards would therefore be attached to Mrs Brooks and Lady Harrington, even if in differential terms, whereby the former will be slightly more inferiorised than the latter (and hence her utterly craven behavior toward her.)

On the whole therefore, what the novel, as part of the anti-colonial canon, *does* is detach the meanings'/signifiers' activating of Danielli's of opiate reward from the hierarchical relation of colonisers and the colonised and invert it, or at least call it into question by means of a revalorisation which reattaches the meanings'/signifiers' activating, at the neurophysiological level, of the opiate reward to the despised category of *les damnés de la terre.* In other words, the novel initiates and effects a transformation of consciousness, and thus, the negative meanings'/signifiers' activating of the opiate punishment dynamic would now be attached to the hegemonic colonial society, one for whom, as cited earlier, Elsa Goveia argued, the fact of Blackness had to be a fact of inferiority.[25] The consciousness therefore that would have made Wynter, as a child, delighted to be Briton or a British subject – this within the terms of Girard's/Fanon's dynamic structure of desire/aversion – would now become stigmatised and replaced by a new consciousness, one now legitimating (if perhaps only for a brief emancipatory hiatus) of the new self-conception, the new sense of creativity an agency in the wake of the 1935–1938 uprisings.

Here the role of history can also be instructive. In the scene where the Board of Governors of the Teachers Training College evaluates Isaac's essays, it becomes clear that the discourse of history serves an equally structuring role of the social order as that of the then hegemonic English literature which had been taught in schools, normally from an imperialising colonial perspective. In his essays, the 'Rise of the British Empire' and 'The Glorious Reign of Queen Victoria,' Isaac challenged the imperial cosmogony in which George William Gordon and Paul Bogle-the latter who had spearheaded the 1865 small farmers *cum* landless labourers uprisings, against the flagrant social injustices of the post-slavery era, while the former, who not actually taking part in the rebellion had lead political and religious struggles in the same vein-would have been represented as traitors , a social conditioning of the I.R.S.

that would normally have him desire to be a British colonial subject. Eric Williams brought attention to this role of history in both his classic work *Capitalism and Slavery* and in his *British Historians and the West Indies*, where he stated that his purpose in writing the book was 'principally to emancipate his compatriots whom the historical writings that his analyses sought to depreciate and to imprison for all time in the inferior status to which these writings sought to condemn them.'[26] In an interview, Wynter gives a moving and impressive account of her own Isaac-style transformation of historical consciousness,

> You must remember that, as Walcott says so beautifully, going to school we had lived in a world of the imagination whose landscape was filled with *enchanted* daffodils. For example, the first stories that I wrote were set in England, in London. I had never been to London. I am still very proud, nevertheless, about one set in Yorkshire, whose heroine was a Luddite. For some reason I had an identification with English working-class struggles. And this is where I had begun to experience a parallel sensibility to that of all subordinated groups. You see, there can be a transfer of empathy because of your ability to experience yourself in that way. Now, remember, no story is going to be set in Jamaica, because I've never been taught anything about the history of Jamaica. If I heard about the Paul Bogle 1865 rebellion, it was about these traitors against the British Empire. *And I don't think that it was just ideology. Rather, it was the conception of being a British subject.* To be a British subject, naturally you would see Bogle and Gordon as conspiring against that which made you a British subject. So, all your education was intended to constitute you as a British subject, but *I don't think it was a deliberate plot.* This was simply how the English saw themselves. And this is how they would make their native colonial subjects see themselves-derivatively. *As long as there is not a counter-voice, we too are trapped in that conception.* What happens now, after this great erupting moment, is that suddenly [you] begin to

constitute yourself as another subject.[27]

More than anything, *The Hills of Hebron* was part of that counter-voice of the anti-colonial literary canon, which sought to create a counter mode of the social conditioning of the I.R.S. in the form of Western imperialism, doing so, by disenchanting, as the scene with Isaac illustrates, the very means by which the social conditioning is carried out. By setting her early stories and subsequently the novel in Jamaica, one sees the detaching of the meanings/signifiers activating of the opiate reward, one always enacting of the, in Fanonian terms, mask of being ideally human, from the coloniser to the colonised, and therefore disenchanting an empirical reality that, however brutal, had to be made to seem just to both groups. It is in this instance that it can be seen how literary knowledge provides an answer to Danielli's question, as both the colonised and coloniser had to take for granted the institutionalised system of rewards made possible by the enchanted discourses of history and literature; indeed, as Wynter argues in 'On Disenchanting Discourse' of all knowledge itself: '...the role of Minority Discourse must go beyond this [majority discourse] to call in question the grounding premises from which the metaphysical discourses of *all* population groups, *all* human systems – including that of the West – are generated.[28] Since the initial publication of *The Hills of Hebron*, some 48 years ago, the new social conditioning of the I.R.S. has been effected in new national terms,[29] a transformation which has not resolved all the issues related to the systemic subordination of the category of *les damnés* in the Caribbean and around the world. Such is because, as Wynter argues, the global anti-colonial movement, together with the anti-apartheid Civil Rights Movement in the United States, was only a point of departure for dealing with the more fundamental issue of the epistemological order that gave rise to our present systemic hierarchies, central to which has been the inferiorised role of the category of *les damnés,* a group whose subordination and 'banishment from humanity' remains an indispensable function of the institution of our present conception of what it means to be fully human.

In this context, Wynter has put forth her 'new world view', one that moves toward a science of human perceptions and behaviours. She has asserted that all humans must necessarily know their social reality in adaptively advantageous terms, able to ensure the realisation of their specific mode or genre of being human, or in Frantz Fanon's terms, of sociogeny. Such modes of knowing, and therefore of behaving, enable the reproduction of the specific social order, which is each such genre's indispensable condition of existence. On the basis of Fanon's redefinition of the human as hybridly phylogenic (the development of type of animal or plant) and ontogenic (the development of individual organism) on the one hand, and sociogenic (nature/culture to employ Western terms) on the other, Wynter has put forward the idea of the sociogenic principle or code as the explanatory key, both to what David Chalmers has identified as the 'puzzle of consciousness' and to the laws that govern human behaviours.[30] The implication here remains that rather than the Marxian concept of modes of production being the key determinate of human behaviours, Wynter insists that it is the mode of auto-institution (or autopoetic instituted conception of symbolic life and death) that is the determinate of human behaviours.[31] The specific mode of material provisioning (or in our culture-specific terms, of economic production) is an indispensable, but only proximate, mechanism.

Her bold hypothesis insists that the human, in meta-Darwinian terms (that is, not in opposition to, but rather as a progression on), is a hybridly auto-instituting species, and therefore, a third level of existence, from the Event of our origin on the continent of Africa until today. Yet, as she further asserts, the functioning of such laws has remained hitherto beyond our conscious awareness. Nonetheless, from the liminal perspective of Fanon's 'lived experience of the Black' and of all other categories of liminality, this question can now be posed, given that all social orders auto-institute themselves on a notion of Self and Other. For it is by means of the systemic subordination of the category of the Other to that of the category incarnating of the Conceptual Self, that the latter is to be institutionalised in the value-laden terms of symbolic life, a process serving to integrate the social order in the genre-specific terms which enable it to exist as such an order.[32] Such a redefinition of *being human*, in hybridly auto-instituting terms, would make possible a 'humanism made to the measure of the world' as it would necessarily effect an epochal shift, where for the first time in the history of species, our social realities would no longer be represented as being extra-humanly determined – either by the gods of polytheism defining of humanity for millenia, by the single God of the three Abrahamic monotheisms, by the discourse of nature and natural law of the monarchical-mercantile State, or by the bio-evolutionary laws of natural selection/dyyselection of our contemporary *episteme*. We would therefore, as did Obadiah in the end of novel, while in the process of making a cradle and carving a doll for the coming child (unknowingly in the totally stigmatised Black African tradition), accepts his own agency, after stumbling upon God: 'All that was god lay in the palm of my hand (p. 312). We would therefore, in the vein of Fanon, resist any attempt to 'make man a mere mechanism.'[33]

Notes

1. Wynter, 'On Disenchanting Discourse: "Minority" Literary Criticism and Beyond', *Cultural Critique*, No. 7, *The Nature and Context of Minority Discourse II* (Autumn 1987): 218–19, 241. Emphasis in original.
2. See Frantz Fanon, *Black Skin, White Masks*, Trans. by Constance Farrington (1952; New York: Grove Press, 1967) and Wynter, 'Towards the Sociogenic Principle: Fanon,

the Puzzle of Conscious Experience, and What It is Like to Be "Black'" in *National Identities and Sociopolitical Changes in Latin America,* Mercedes F. Durán-Cogan and Antonio Gómez-Moriana, eds. (New York: Routledge 2001), 30–66.

3. See Gregory Bateson, 'Conscious Purpose versus Nature' in David Cooper (ed.) *Dialectics of Liberation* (Harmondsworth: Penguin, 1968) 34–49. (New York: Dutton, 1978).
4. Wynter developed the concept of cosmogonic narratives, as a system of representation and meaning indispensable to the instituting of all modes of being human in a recent lecture entitled, '*Human Being* as Noun, or *Being Human* as Praxis: On the Laws/Modes of Auto-Institution and Our Ultimate Crisis of Global Warming/Climate Change', Center for African American Studies 16th Annual Distinguished Lecture, April 23, 2008, Wesleyan University, Middletown, Connecticut.
5. Jacob Pandian, *Anthropology and the Western Tradition: Toward an Authentic Anthropology* (Prospect Heights, IL: Waveland Press, 1985).
6. This term, often utilised by Wynter is taken from Helen Fein's *Accounting for Genocide: National Responses and Jewish Victimization during the Holocaust* (New York: Free Press, 1979).
7. George Lamming, *In the Castle of My Skin* (1953; New York: Collier Books/MacMillan, 1970), 334.
8. As Wynter notes, *pieza,* Spanish for piece, was the unit by means of which the value of slaves were exchanged. Usually, one *pieza* was a young healthy male. An elderly person, child, or sometimes not fully abled person would be a partial *pieza,* which therefore would have to be combined with other partial *piezas* to form a whole one.
9. For Wynter's delineation of the relation between the allocation of gender roles and the governing code of symbolic life/symbolic death, see 'Beyond Miranda's Meanings: Un/silencing the Demonic Ground of Caliban's Woman' in *Out of the Kumbla: Caribbean Women and Literature,* Carole Boyce Davies and Elaine Savory Fido, eds. (Trenton, NJ:

Africa World Press, 1990), 355–72 and "'Genital Mutilation" or "Symbolic Birth?": Female Circumcision, Lost Origins, and the Aculturalism of Feminist/Western Thought', *Case Western Reserve Law Review*, Vol. 47 (Winter 1997): 501–52.

10. See '1492: A New World View' in *Race, Discourse and the Origins of the Americas: A New World View*, Vera Lawrence Hyatt and Rex Nettleford, eds. (Washington, DC: Smithsonian Institution Press, 1995), 5–57.
11. This essay was published in two parts: in *Jamaica Journal*, 2 (March 1968): 23–32, and *Jamaica Journal*, 3 (March 1969): 27–42.
12. For amplification of this argument, see Wynter's essay, 'Is "Development" a Purely Empirical Concept or Also Teleological? A Perspective from "We-the-Underdeveloped"' in *The Prospects for Recovery and Sustainable Development in Africa*, Aguibou Yansané, ed. (Westport, CT: Greenwood Press, 1996), 299–316.
13. See 'On Disenchanting Discourse', 240. Emphasis in original.
14. For the full argument put forth here, see 'Unsettling the Coloniality of Being/Power/Truth/Freedom: Towards the Human, After Man, Its Overrepresentation-An Argument', *CR: The New Centennial Review*, Volume 3, Number 3 (Fall 2003): 257–337.
15. See Elsa Goveia, 'The Social Framework', *Savacou*, No. 2 (September 1970): 7–15.
16. See René Girard, *Deceit, Desire and the Novel: Self and Other in Literary Structure* (Baltimore: Johns Hopkins University Press, 1965) and Fanon, *Black Skin, White Masks*.
17. Telephone interview with Wynter, August 2008. Wynter gave another insightful example in the interview of the way in which she adopted the hegemonic colonial interpretation of the social reality. This occurred with her use of the term *pocomania* 'little madness' which was a stigmatising representation that did not allow the dynamic set of practices and beliefs that have since come to be identified as

Kumina could not be seen in the terms of the existential African origins, which when syncretised with Judaeo-Christian forms of life, gave rise to it. This world is brilliantly rendered in the range of the work of Maureen Warner-Lewis. See for example, *Central Africa in the Caribbean: Transcending Time, Transforming Cultures* (Kingston: University of the West Indies Press, 2004).

18. See *From Du Bois to Fanon*, pamphlet published by the Pan-African Institute for Self-Reliance (East Lansing, MI, 1970).
19. For the idea of 're-enchanting humanism', see David Scott, 'The Re-Enchantment of Humanism: An Interview with Sylvia Wynter', *Small Axe*, No. 8 (September 2000): 119–207. For Césaire's statement, see his *Discourse on Colonialism*, Trans. by Joan Pinkham (New York: Monthly Review Press, 1972), 56.
20. For me a very evocative example of this occurs when, after Gee announces to Hugh that she is pregnant ('So now like you give me a baby?'), he replies: 'So what? What else God make woman for?' (p. 98). Here the sensibility of a woman's perspective is inescapably clear.
21. Louis Sala-Molins, *Dark Side of the Light: Slavery and the French Enlightenment*, Trans. *Les Misères des Lumières: Sous la raison, l'outrage…* by John Conteh-Morgan (Minneapolis: University of Minnesota Press, 2006), 6.
22. For an example of a provocative and often astute feminist reading of the novel, see Shirly Toland-Dix, '*The Hills of Hebron*: Sylvia Wynter's Disruption of the Narrative of the Nation', *Small Axe*, No. 25 (February 2008): 57–76, which makes an important point beginning with the title as to one of the seminal insights of the novel. This perspective can also be found in Natasha Barnes, 'Reluctant Matriarch: Sylvia Wynter and the Problematics of Caribbean Feminism', *Small Axe*, No. 5 (March 1999): 34–47, where she contends that Wynter 'is the figure who most embodies all the ideological contradictions in this ongoing argument between "gender" and "race"', and whose 'refusal to be labeled as a feminist' in the end 'plague our efforts to

construct a Caribbean feminist genealogy.' Going further, Alison Donnell asserts that Wynter 'denies the model of multiple and overlapping ideological demands that Caribbean feminism, in both literary and other disciplinary contexts, has sought to foreground....' See *Twentieth Century Caribbean Literatures: Critical Moments in Anglophone Literary History* (New York: Routledge, 2006), 147.

23. See 'On Disenchanting Discourse', 207–208; telephone interview, August 2008.
24. Wynter, 'Reading *The Hills of Hebron*/The Anti-Colonial Literary Canon, After Literary Criticism: Towards the Autopoetic Turn/Overturn,' unpublished manuscript.
25. Goveia, 'The Social Framework.'
26. See his *British Historians and the West Indies* (Port of Spain: P.N.M. Publishing Company Ltd., 1964), vi. See also his classic *Capitalism and Slavery* (1944; London: Andre Deutsch, 1964; reprinted Kingston: Ian Randle Publishers, 2005), where Williams's central objective remained the displacement of the humanitarian interpretation of abolition that defined British imperial historiography. Moreover, in my own work, I have attempted to develop Williams's insight, one which parallels an argument put forth by Carter G. Woodson in *The Miseducation of the Negro*, in which Woodson noted that Black students in the U.S. were demotivated, exactly in Danielli's sense of the term, by means of the 'White' and anti-Black account of history taught in the overall curriculum. I have identified this phenomenon as 'the work of history.' See my essay 'Modernity and the "Work of History"' in *After Man, Towards the Human: Critical Essays on Sylvia Wynter*, Anthony Bogues, ed. (Kingston: Ian Randle Publishers, 2005), 1–24.
27. Scott, 'The Re-Enchantment of Humanism: An Interview with Sylvia Wynter', 130–31. Emphasis added.
28. Wynter, 'On Disenchanting Discourse', 240. Emphasis in original.
29. This can be seen for Wynter most clearly in the pamphlet, *Jamaica National Heroes* (Kingston: Jamaica National Trust

Commission, 1971), and of which she is now preparing from hindsight, an autocritique.

30. See Wynter, 'Towards the Sociogenic Principle.'
31. Wynter developed this argument in the lecture cited above, 'Human Being as Noun, or Being Human as Praxis…'
32. Wynter, 'Towards the Sociogenic Principle.'
33. Fanon, *Black Skin, White Masks*, 23. The complete line is: 'I grasp my narcissism with both hands and I turn my back on the degradation of those who would make man a mere mechanism.'

CPSIA information can be obtained
at www.ICGtesting.com
Printed in the USA
LVHW012332170822
726200LV00003B/113